Also by

Finding Love in Positano

Christmas at The Highland Flower Shop

Lucy Coleman

embla books

First published in Great Britain in 2022 by

embla books

Bonnier Books UK Limited
4th Floor, Victoria House, Bloomsbury Square, London, WC1B 4DA
Owned by Bonnier Books
Sveavägen 56, Stockholm, Sweden

A CIP catalogue record for this book is available from the British Library.

eBook ISBN: 9781471411908
Print ISBN: 9781471411922
Audio ISBN: 9781471411915

This book is typeset using Atomik ePublisher

Embla Books is an imprint of Bonnier Books UK
www.bonnierbooks.co.uk
Printed and bound in Great Britain by Clays Ltd, Elcograf S.p.A.

*I have experienced many 'and just like that . . .'
moments; times when something I never expected
and could not have anticipated changed the direction
of my life for ever.*

*This is dedicated to those who resonate with that, as
Bella Reed has a few of her own in this story.*

Life is a never-ending round of surprises, isn't it?

December

Fort William, Scotland

1.

The Festive Countdown

As I unlock the door to The Highland Flower Shop a little
fizz of excitement courses through me. With Christmas only
nine days away the shoppers are going to be out in force.
Glancing at the display in the shop window I think we outdid
ourselves again this year and it's my job to keep the displays
looking perfect.

Four three-foot high white angels are suspended from
the ceiling, their golden trumpets held aloft as they hover
in an arc above an old wooden flower cart loaded with
Christmas roses. It's simple and not cluttered, allowing
our customers to gain a peek at the bounty inside. In
the depths of winter they can step into a colourful oasis,
steeped in Christmas cheer. That evocative scent from the
pine needles on the mini potted Christmas trees mingles
with the heady perfume of the hyacinths and narcissi. The
grandeur of potted orchids, brightly coloured gerberas,
the striking trumpets of the amaryllis, and the sweetly
scented freesias to name a few, are the perfect gift to
brighten someone's day. But there are also the earthier
fragrances, everything from bay leaves to the greenery we
associate with hedgerows – the bounty that nature often
gives us for free.

I hurry through to the floristry desk, just in time to hear
hammering on the back door. Swinging it open, I'm greeted
with a huge grin.

'Mornin', Bella. Another van load of holly, mistletoe and ivy. Sales must be good!'

'Hi, Angus. Thank you so much for dropping it off so early.'

'Do you want me to carry it through to the shop, or put it in the cold store? We did some major cuttin' back and the holly branches are on the large size. I didn't have time to whittle 'em down, I'm afraid.'

'Oh, that's not a problem at all – the more, the merrier. Bring it through and stack it against the back wall of Santa's Grotto. I have my safety gloves ready and waiting.'

'Good luck with that. But I did manage to pick out some of the best bits with lots of berries. See, I do listen.'

That makes me chuckle. 'I wasn't complaining, honestly,' I declare. 'I simply remarked in passing that the berries aren't so prolific this year.'

As Angus walks back to his van, he calls over his shoulder, 'Well, I can't upset my favourite florist, so I kept me eye out for the pick of the crop. You know me – remembering dates isn't my thing and if it weren't for you keepin' an eye out for me and sendin' the missus flowers for her birthday and anniversary every year, I'd be in big trouble.'

It's a small price to pay in return for Angus supplying us with as much festive greenery as we can use each December. He owns a small family farm, and he refers to his trips here as a recycling run.

I go in search of my secateurs and when I return it looks like a holly bush is walking towards me. 'Mind yersel . . .' Angus calls out. 'Bit of a monster comin' through.'

All I can see is the top of his beanie hat and the tips of his steel toe-capped boots. But oh, those berries are glorious!

'Angus, you're a real gem. We have a stack of orders to go out today and I was beginning to panic.'

He lays it down onto the floor rather gingerly. 'Right, I'll fetch in the rest.'

It doesn't take him long to fill the entire gangway between the sleigh ride and the wall. We stand side by side looking at the haul. 'Can you use it all?' he queries. 'I might have got a bit carried away with this load and I have enough for another run if you want it.'

'It won't go to waste, believe me. We're on countdown now and it's time to freshen up all the greenery in our displays before they dry out and lose that shiny lustre.'

'Well, anyone who loves Christmas knows exactly where to come to get a fix. You can't leave here without a smile on your face and a bit of joy in your heart!'

'And thanks to you, this little lot should see us through until we shut for the holidays. Oh, before I forget . . . I have a little something for you . . . well, for the missus.'

When I carry in the large, galvanised planter full of Christmas roses his face breaks out into a huge smile. 'You didn't have to do that, Bella.'

'A favour for a favour. And who doesn't love Christmas roses? They work well both indoors and out. I added a few hyacinth bulbs in between them so when you see the little shoots appearing you'll know what it is. Merry Christmas, Angus – I hope it's a good one for you and your family.'

Angus steps forward to take the planter from my arms. 'The world could do with a few more like you in it, Bella. I hope Santa brings you everything on your wish list,' he says with a cheeky grin as I give him a grateful hug.

'He's been sprinkling a bit of Christmas magic around already, Angus, so I'm happy,' I inform him. 'We've had a few technical issues, but Santa's Grotto is going to be busy today!'

As Angus steps out through the door, I can hear him chuckling away to himself and then in his baritone voice he starts singing 'The Holly and the Ivy'. He knows I'm listening and that it'll make me smile.

Anyway, now I have a lot of work to do before the others arrive. But just the fragrance from all that fresh greenery wafting around me makes me draw in a deep breath. At

Christmas time it's the smells that often bring back those evocative childhood memories. I grab a stack of tall metal bins and ease on my gloves to begin clipping. Before long I, too, am singing to myself as I work. Well – it's not exactly work when you love what you do, is it?

My best friend Holly and her five-year-old daughter Katie bustle into the shop, their eyes shining as they chatter away to each other. I'm in the middle of assembling a bouquet, so I give them a welcoming smile as they walk past the counter. By the time someone comes to relieve me for a break, they're almost at the front of the queue for Santa's Grotto.

'You two look very festive.' I grin at them. They're wearing matching knitted red bobble hats and scarves sporting tiny white snowflakes that sparkle.

Katie launches herself at me, wrapping her arms around my waist and hugging tightly. 'They were a present from Buddy the elf,' she exclaims, bubbling over with excitement.

Little does she know that I'm Buddy's personal shopper and I struggle to contain my grin. Buddy's arrival on the first of December is a highly anticipated event, one I feel privileged to be a part of.

I lean in to give Holly a hug, her eyes are full of laughter. 'Angus must have arrived bright and early. That wall is amazing, Bella.'

'It smells better than fresh air!' Katie exclaims, wrinkling up her cute little nose and sucking in a deep breath.

The heady scent of the flowers mingles enticingly with the freshness of the long trails of greenery that now hang down like a curtain on the wall behind the floristry counter. As I took the old garlands down, I did wonder whether it was a little over the top but when Angus arrived with the second load I threw caution to the wind.

'Why the frown, Katie?' I ask, following her gaze.

'The real Santa doesn't wear a fake beard,' she declares reproachfully. 'Um – does he?' Her sweet little voice wavers.

As the three of us stare in Santa's direction, it's hard to suppress a poignant 'ahh'. This time last year little details like that would have been lost on her. The curly shoulder-length, almost-white hair is real as is the beaming smile and the rotund belly, but the moustache and beard aren't exactly a great match.

Holly flashes me a mirthful look as she kneels down in front of my darling little goddaughter. I watch as the proud mum sweeps some stray hairs away from Katie's flushed cheek, her eyes full of love. 'No, super girl, of course not!' she answers firmly.

'Santa's helpers just dress up to look more like him, don't they, Mum?'

'They do. I'm sure Santa wishes he could be here in person to join in with the fun, Katie, but this is his busiest time of the year. It's his job to remain at the North Pole to make sure everything runs smoothly.'

'I see,' Katie replies in a serious tone, a little frown puckering her forehead.

Holly casts me an anxious glance, wondering what's coming next.

'Do you think Mrs Claus helps him, Mum? I mean, you're good at organising things and making lists – I hope she is, too. You know, just to make sure Santa doesn't forget anyone.'

Aww . . . my heart constricts as Holly throws her arms around Katie. 'Stop worrying, silly thing,' she half-whispers, holding her close. 'Santa has a whole team to help him, and he's never let us down, has he?'

It's heart-breaking knowing why Katie's thoughts are going in this direction. Her dad, Nick, is a lovely guy but he doesn't do himself any favours. Nick promised Katie several times over that he would be here today. Then, half an hour ago, Holly received a text:

Sorry, honey, I can't get away from work right now. Give Katie a hug from me and say I'll make it up to her. Promise! x

Doesn't he realise how important events like this are to his daughter and how excited she is in the final run-up to Christmas?

'That's true, Mum,' Katie agrees. But I watch as her lower lip begins to wobble. 'Dad's in trouble, isn't he? How is he ever going to remember *anything* now that he doesn't live with us anymore? I had to remind him twice about my birthday and that's not right, Mum.'

The irony is that Katie's innocent little comment is telling. It's only Holly who has kept things functioning properly for them as a family. The day she drew a line and said 'no more, I'm done' shocked Nick, but obviously not enough for him to man up. Several weeks on and he continues to make one bad decision after another, and the financial impact is a constant worry for Holly.

But it's not just that – every single time he disappoints Katie, Holly will take yet another small step back from him, until they are so far apart that the love she has for him will turn into apathy – or worse – resentment.

'Dad will be fine. Besides, he's not far away is he, my super girl? He'll soon get himself organised, he's just very busy at work right now.'

What else can Holly say? The reason she turned down Nick's marriage proposal shortly after they discovered she was pregnant with Katie was because she knew it was a knee-jerk reaction on his part. Nick said he was ready to settle down, but the truth is that he wasn't. And here we are, five and a half years later and he's still letting his family down. For Katie it's understandably confusing. Her dad loves them both and they love him in return, but even a child knows when it's not working.

'OK, Mum. It's just a shame for Dad to miss out. It's not quite the same without him, is it? It makes me sad, and I wish—'

Holly brushes a hand across her cheek as she stands, and I realise she needs a moment to herself.

'Hey, Katie – it's your turn next!' I interrupt, pointing to the tickets clutched tightly in her hand. Her eyes check out the flashing numbers on the small TV monitor on the wall and she grins back at me.

'At last!' Her excitement is a joy to witness.

'I think your mum is ready for a cup of coffee though,' I remark. 'Why don't you and I jump on now before I get back to work, and then you can have another ride with Mum in a little while?'

Katie's smile is replaced with a sense of hesitation. 'Are you allowed to have more than one ride, Bella?'

I give my goddaughter a wink, which makes her face light up.

'My Aunt Jane knows Santa personally and as it's her shop I think it will be just fine.' Grasping Katie's hand in mine, she giggles.

'See you in a little while, Mum!' Katie calls over her shoulder while tugging on my hand. A quick glance at Holly as she gives me a grateful, if rather watery smile, makes it hard not to heave a sigh. If two people who love each other so much and have succeeded in creating such a bright little spark like Katie can't make it work, what chance do the rest of us have?

As the afternoon continues, The Highland Flower Shop is buzzing with people.

'We made it happen, my lovely!' Dad sidles up next to me as I'm hand-tying a posy of white roses, stems of eucalyptus leaves, and sprigs of incredibly realistic ruby-red berries. 'It's been a constant stream of comings and goings. Two more ticket sales and we'll have hit the two hundred mark.'

This is the time of the year when the huge extension at the rear of the shop transforms into Santa's Grotto and the covers come off the sleigh ride. The cavernous space does add to the chill factor in our notoriously cold Highland winters, but people who work with flowers are used to dressing up appropriately for work. Thermal underwear might not be glam but it's practical. Today, though, the heating is on and the sheer volume of people milling around is enough to raise the temperature by several degrees.

The sleigh ride accommodates twelve people quite comfortably, with Santa at the helm as he recounts one of his Christmas adventures. The hand-painted, revolving canvas backdrop takes them on a magical journey to the North Pole. The sleigh, a two-seater cherry-red engine pulling five individual carriages, travels around an oval track.

'It was a close call though, wasn't it? But you saved the day, Dad.'

'With a bit of luck, it will see us through to Christmas Eve now. Pop would be proud it's lasted this long and that's down to someone's stubborn determination,' he laughs, and I join in.

'Stubborn, am I?' Aunt Jane appears at Dad's side, leaning in to give her brother an affectionate hug. 'You deserve that, considering how hard you've worked, Tom. At least we have a little over a week to fit in as many rides as we can. The extended opening hours should mean that no one misses out.'

'Cathy and I will be here every day to give a helping hand, you can count on that, and the committee are busy reorganising the helpers' rota as we speak. I'm only sorry that we lost three whole weeks to constant breakdowns.'

'Well, we have a whole year in which to get it sorted properly, so let's not worry about that now,' Aunt Jane confirms. A look of relief passes over Dad's face – like me, I suspect he was thinking this is it.

'Ye couldnae done any better, Tom,' Mrs Mac joins in.

Mrs MacTavish has worked here since the day the shop first opened; she's as much a part of the charm as the sleigh. It's hard to imagine this shop without her presence.

Aunt Jane walks over to rearrange some of the buckets of flowers to widen the walkway through to Santa's Grotto.

No doubt the lady I was serving has wandered out there to take a peep. With the Christmas music playing in the background, the laughter and squeals coupled with Santa's booming voice, it's both intriguing and jolly. Happiness is infectious. However, with a stack of orders still to be fulfilled it's not as if I don't have anything else to do and I'm in my happy zone. My fingers are busy and I'm in a festive mood.

I let my mind drift back to my early beginnings, and how this all became such an integral part of my life. My unofficial apprenticeship began at the tender age of twelve, when I spent every Saturday at The Highland Flower Shop sweeping up and making tea and coffee. Aunt Jane taught me everything I know about floristry, and it turned out I was a natural. But Mum and Dad said I needed an additional skill set – as you never know what the future will hold. I went to college and gained a diploma in business management. For the last eight years I've been working here full time and loving every minute of every day.

When Holly joined us four years ago her role included helping Mrs Mac in the office, in between serving customers in The Christmas Cave, our all-year-round festive display area on the first floor. It meant that Mrs Mac could take the odd hour off if she needed to. It works well for them both, because occasionally Holly has to leave early if her mum can't pick Katie up from school.

Even though the staff aren't family in the real sense of the word, it's what we've become and it's one of the two main reasons why our customers keep coming back.

The other reason is that when Aunt Jane moved back to Fort William after almost a decade spent managing a florist's shop in Edinburgh, luck had it that she found the perfect premises to rent. She had a vision – one that seemed almost an impossibility at the time.

We'd recently lost my granddad, George – affectionately known as Pop – from a heart attack. It was only a few months after he and Grandma Susan had made the permanent move to their pretty villa in Faro, on the Algarve. When he'd sold his shop, Pop reluctantly put the wonderful sleigh ride into storage. He and his father had lovingly built it together way back in the sixties. For two generations, his double-fronted ironmonger's store in the High Street was a local landmark. It stocked everything from paint, seeds, to homewares – but there was also a permanent Christmas display. If you wanted baubles, or silver reindeer candle holders in July – Pop could sort you out.

Starting on the first of December every year, families came from far and wide to meet Santa and take a ride in the hand-built sleigh. It took up over a third of the retail floor space, but it was Pop's pride and joy. And it brought a lot of visitors into the area.

Aunt Jane returned because the loss of a father makes you realise how important family really is and how quickly time passes. Pop's old school friend, Randall McIntyre – whose successful property investment company own a number of premises in the High Street – was very accommodating. If it weren't for him then I doubt that one of Fort William's biggest Christmas events would have continued. Being able to rent a property from someone who had fond memories of Pop, shows how well respected he was for his charitable work.

We're now into the third generation of customers for some families. The sleigh ride brings back nostalgic memories and it's still a magical experience for a generation of children used to animation and CGI. This old-school style experience has all the appeal of a trip on a steam train. Throw in a twenty-minute audience with Santa, and it makes it just that little bit special – kids and adults alike join in the fun!

The twist is that Santa doesn't hand out presents or ask children what they want for Christmas. Instead, each visitor *brings* along a gift to donate to the local charity set up to help families struggling to make ends meet. In return for their ticket, each passenger receives one of our special wooden snowflakes to hang on their Christmas tree at home. Which is why we're delighted that this year isn't a total wipeout now that they've fixed the faulty wiring.

I've never had the pleasure of meeting Randall McIntyre in person, but he's a man who has supported many charities over the years. Striking a deal with Aunt Jane to make the renting of this place affordable has allowed Pop's dream to continue in a real-life Christmas miracle fashion. And here we still are, sixteen years later, but to say things are creaking along is probably an understatement.

'I'm back.' Aunt Jane's words interrupt my daydreaming. 'Judging by the noise level coming from upstairs, your mum is no doubt rushed off her feet and might appreciate a little extra help. I know Mrs Mac is up there serving too, but Cathy is overdue a coffee break.'

'No problem – poor Mum! This little pile of delivery notes is all done and the flowers are in the cold store out back ready for when the vans return. It's wonderful to be this busy and I think on the flowers side, we're rivalling Valentine's Day.'

'A lot of people didn't expect us to pull it off this year, Bella. It's been disappointing having to turn people away because the sleigh ride keeps breaking down, but when they heard it was a *go* no one wants to miss out. It really is the season of goodwill and I'm proud of what we've achieved.' A sense of sadness sweeps over Aunt Jane's face. It's a look I've never seen before and a cold feeling stirs deep down inside of me.

'What's wrong?' I venture to ask.

'There's something I need to tell you. This will be my last Christmas running the shop, Bella. I'm cashing in my retirement fund and at some point next May I'll be moving to Faro. It's time to start handing over the reins to you.'

My jaw drops. 'Is Grandma Susan poorly?'

Aunt Jane shakes her head vigorously to reassure me. 'No. This is about Vic and me, Bella.'

Vic's fabulous villa is Aunt Jane's second home and it's

a ten-minute walk to Grandma's place. While they've been seeing each other for almost two years now, Vic understands that The Highland Flower Shop is very much Aunt Jane's baby. The plan was for her to retire on her sixtieth birthday, which is still five years away.

'Oh, I see. It's good news, then?' The positivity in my voice masks the turbulent mix of emotions running through my head.

'It is,' she replies, happily. Even so, there's an unmistakable wistfulness in her tone. 'I'll be around to give her a hand, of course, when and if my mother will allow me – she's sprightly for a seventy-four-year-old. It's all that ballroom dancing. But Vic says our lives are on hold and he doesn't want to wait any longer. He says that every day we're apart, is a day we won't get again – so it's crunch time, Bella. And my feline buddy, Art, is missing me, too – Vic says it takes Art a while to settle back into his routine after one of my visits. I hope you can understand that as much as I love this place, it's time to make the break.'

Talking about inheriting the business is one thing, the reality of it is another. Am I ready?

'I know how tough it's been on you, but—' I hesitate for a second, realising that every single day I've worked here has been leading to this, and Aunt Jane quickly jumps in.

'The business is growing steadily and while it's not a goldmine, it means the world to me to pass it down to my niece and keep it in the family. Hopefully, it will give you a living for years to come. You see, Vic is right, but it also feels a little selfish of me to walk away. However, you're more than ready to take over, Bella. You are the future of The Highland Flower Shop and you've proved that already by opening my eyes to the benefits of taking on commercial contracts. This isn't just my success, it's yours too! Now just go and rescue your mum. I'm not going to leave you in the lurch . . . we have plenty of time to ease you into your new role.'

This feels so sudden, Aunt Jane has always joked around about the day when I'm in *the driving seat*, but am I really up to the challenge of moving from being a florist and assistant manager, to the owner of a business?

September

2.

The Winds of Change Are Bracing

'What do you mean, the landlord has served notice for you to vacate the shop? I thought your aunt Jane has a special arrangement with Randall McIntyre?' My boyfriend, Adam, quizzes me as he leans in for a kiss.

He's tense and it's obvious that he has had yet another stressful day at work. As it's my turn to cook, he was expecting to arrive back to the smell of pot roast Scotch lamb meatballs bubbling away in the oven and an evening vegging out in front of the TV. Instead, I'm sitting at the kitchen table feeling stunned as I read the document that was delivered to the shop today.

'She does – or did. But Randall has retired as CEO of McIntyre Property Investments Limited. That's not the only change. His grandson recently joined the company; he's the lettings business development manager and apparently there's a problem now that The Highland Flower Shop is in my name – I'm looking into it.'

Adam places his laptop bag down on the table, then shrugs off his jacket. 'Get your aunt Jane to contact him and iron it out,' he grumbles, dismissively.

'I don't think this is something she can fix,' I reply, disappointed by his obvious lack of interest.

'You're probably panicking over nothing. You've been in charge for three months now and things like this come with the job.' Adam lets out a long sigh, brushing off my concerns. 'Anyway, I'm glad to be home. What a tough one it's been again today.'

Adam doesn't understand how serious this is, but even if I take the time to explain, it's becoming increasingly obvious that he's not prepared to listen. It's been one hurdle to jump after another since I settled into my new role at work and then Dad broke the news I've been dreading, but instinctively knew was coming. My parents are committee members for the The Highland Elves, the charitable organisation we raise funds for. One of their team of volunteers is an engineer and carries out an annual inspection on the sleigh ride. It passed last year – just, but it's over sixty years old and, as a favour, Dad asked for an overview of the work needing to be carried out prior to the next inspection.

The sleigh itself has been sanded and repainted several times over the years, but it's the mechanical side of things that are now breaking down. The one saving grace is that the beautifully hand-painted canvas backdrop, which is irreplaceable, has weathered the years well. Mostly because at the end of the Christmas season it's carefully – and lovingly – rolled up and stored in a special, ten-foot-long wooden box lined with padded felt.

It's going to be tough enough finding an affordable new retail outlet for the florist shop, let alone the amount of space needed to house The Christmas Cave and Santa's Grotto. And it's too early to get a handle on what it will cost to restore the ride itself.

It's time to dig deep, Bella, I tell myself resolutely. *Adam has problems of his own and adding your tales of woe isn't going to lighten the mood for either of you, is it?*

'You're right – my aunt might be able to do something,' I reply, trying to sound upbeat.

Adam lowers himself down onto the chair opposite me and I can see how worn out he is. He drags his hand across his eyes, giving them a rub. 'I'll head upstairs and grab a shower in a bit, but I need to sit and unwind first. Is there any chance of a glass of wine?'

If he has a headache then I'm not sure wine will help, but it might relax him a little. I can tell from his general demeanour that now is not a good time to point that out. Adam is the HR manager at an electronics factory employing over two hundred people. They recently lost a sizeable contract and are going through a round of redundancies to streamline their workforce. It's bad news, as jobs aren't exactly thick on the ground around here. Having worked through the list of people who came forward to take the voluntary redundancy package on offer, each day is now a trial for him as he calls people in to break the bad news. It's harrowing and my heart does go out to Adam.

'No problem. I'll get you that drink and then pop something in the oven. It'll take forty-five minutes at least, so there's no rush.'

It's not easy to shake off my own worries, but until I get to the bottom of what's going on there's no point at all in stressing over it. I guess it's going to be one of those evenings to indulge Adam and sit and watch one of the X-Men films. Hopefully, not one that we've seen a dozen times over, but if that's what it takes to lift his spirits, he deserves it. If he were the sort of man who could fire people without it affecting him, then he wouldn't be the man for me.

The following day, as soon as I'm settled at my desk, it's time to make the dreaded call.

'Hi, Aunt Jane, how is life in the Algarve?' My voice is bright, belying the heaviness in my heart because I'm calling her out of sheer desperation.

'Oh, Bella – it's bad timing I'm afraid. I've just arrived at our local hospital, and I need to switch off my mobile. We had a call from your grandma – she's broken her ankle and Vic and I have rushed over to find out what's going on. I'll ring you back shortly and let you know what's happening – I promise.'

The click as the line goes dead fills me with another sort of dread. They do say that bad news comes in threes. With Adam always so grouchy these days, this major upset over the lease, and now Grandma's accident, I sincerely hope this is the end of a little run of bad luck.

'I did put my head around the door, but saw you were on the phone. That was a short conversation,' Holly observes as I walk into the kitchen. It's not much bigger than a large cupboard and it's certainly not a place anyone hangs around in for long.

'Grandma Susan has broken her ankle.'

Holly looks at me, shaking her head sadly. 'Oh dear. That's the last thing you wanted to hear, isn't it?'

How on earth can I pull Aunt Jane into this dilemma now, when she has more pressing worries to deal with?

'Aunt Jane's going to call me back, but I'm not sure it's the best time to mention what's going on here.' I'm trying my best to put on a brave face. The last thing I want is for my staff to start panicking that we're going to be thrown out. Holly has known me for a long time and she can see through my bravado, but I have to remember that she's an employee. I can't really talk to her about the details and leave everyone else in the dark, at least for now.

'Jane would want to know what's happened, Bella, but I understand your reluctance. What time are you meeting up with the solicitor?'

'Two o'clock this afternoon. Maybe I'll hold off mentioning it to Aunt Jane until I see what William Taggart has to say. I'm sure there's a way around it.'

'Oh, I'm glad you're dealing with Taggart senior, he got on well with Jane. Look – there's something I need to mention. You won't like this, but the word on the street is that we're not going to be here for much longer,' Holly reveals, and my heart sinks.

'How? The notice was served less than twenty-four hours ago.'

'Oh, not from me, nor anyone else here!' Holly's cheeks begin to glow with a pink haze. 'No, Rodric heard a whisper from the shoe repairer's next door. I thought you knew that their lease is up and they're moving into the little kiosk next to the hairdresser's?'

Rodric is Mrs Mac's husband and one of our two van drivers. He retired from his job as a captain in the merchant navy nearly six years ago, shortly after their son was killed in a tragic motorbike accident. Rodric was her rock during that first year. Mrs Mac said little, but we could all see what a struggle it was for her to come to terms with her grief. As for Rodric, he drove her to and from work, but not having anything to keep himself busy during the day was hard on him. When our driver unexpectedly handed in his notice after passing his HGV test, Rodric came to our rescue and he's still here.

'The last I heard, they intended to stay,' I reply, wondering why they changed their minds.

'Well, they're definitely moving out. Apparently, a surveyor called in a few days ago to do a structural report, something about knocking through the wall into here. Rodric found out, you know how he'll chat to anyone, and he asked me to let you know.'

'I don't believe it!' I scoff. 'If that was going to happen I think I'd know about it. And why didn't Rodric tell me himself?'

Holly switches off the kettle and I watch as she pours the boiling water into the waiting mugs. 'He didn't say anything to you because he knew it was bad news and, let's face it, it's obvious that you're worried about our future here.'

I lean up against the countertop for a little extra support while I gather my wits together. What's equally concerning, is that clearly my staff are treading on eggshells around me which means I need to get this sorted as quickly as possible.

'Oh, Holly – that's so unfortunate. Can you do me a favour? Just for the time being, try to squash any chatter you hear about this? If people start kicking up a fuss on our behalf, even though it's well meant, it could scupper my negotiations before they even begin.'

'Oh, Bella, of course I will. It's been one thing after another for you, hasn't it?'

My eyes narrow, as I see a momentary look of guilt flash over her face. 'There's more. What aren't you telling me?'

She sucks in a deep breath as if gearing up to deliver even worse news.

'A man like Maverick McIntyre, well, he doesn't get a nickname like that unless it's for a reason. If they're already drawing up plans to take out the wall between us and next door then that doesn't bode well.'

'Maverick? His name is Mitchell McIntyre, according to the letter he sent me,' I inform her.

'Oh, Nick's doing some work helping him restore an old vehicle. They met a couple of weeks ago when he called into the garage to get a new set of tyres. They share an interest in high-performance cars and went for a bevvy in the pub after Nick finished work – that's how he introduced himself.'

'Really? It's a rather unusual nickname.'

'He was born and brought up in the States,' she explains, handing me a coffee and I wonder what's coming next.

'Maybe this Maverick is simply pushing his luck, thinking he can oust you and get himself a new tenant prepared to pay top whack to make him look good. Although there is a rumour doing the rounds that an agent from London is hanging around looking to buy, or rent, space here in the High Street. Have you heard of a company called Mayfair Bespoke Wallpaper Designs?'

I can't believe that this is the first I'm hearing about it. On reflection, I realise that having been so preoccupied with Adam's problems on top of my own and, no doubt walking around with a permanent frown on my face, it hasn't exactly made me approachable.

'No. But there isn't much available here in Fort William, is there? Surely, the units on the retail park would be more suitable.'

'All I've heard is that, apparently, this guy has been nosing around for the last week, or so.'

I look aghast. 'Do you think he's been in to check out our shop?'

Holly shrugs her shoulders. 'Who knows?'

This isn't just my livelihood on the line – everyone employed here is depending on me to keep the business running. And our newest recruit, Eve, has only been with us for a few months.

'What else have you heard about Maverick McIntyre?'

'Word is that he's ambitious and considering he's only been working at McIntyre Property Investments Limited for a little while, this is a huge promotion. He's out to prove himself.'

'Oh,' I mutter, disdainfully. 'I hope that he has a high regard for charitable works and tradition. Maybe if I offer to up the rent that will do the trick. We're good tenants and have a long track record, which must count for something.'

Holly is standing there with the tray in her hands looking glum. 'Can you afford to up the payment?'

It's a fair enough question. When Aunt Jane signed the lease there's no disputing that she got a good deal. After doing a little research, it was obvious that we probably only pay about seventy per cent of the current market rate. Doing a quick calculation, the answer is that it's probably doable. However, my plans to extend our delivery area and purchase a third van will have to go on hold.

The phone in my pocket buzzes and I snatch it up, giving Holly an apologetic glance as I make my way back to the office.

'Hi, Aunt Jane. How's Grandma doing?'

'She's waiting to go into surgery and she's not at all happy they can't just plaster it up. It's a bad break and she won't be able to put her full weight on her foot for anything up to six weeks. Vic and I have persuaded her to come and stay with us as soon as they're prepared to release her. If the surgery goes to plan, they're saying that could be within forty-eight hours. We can ferry her back and forth for follow-up appointments and the surgeon informed us that she'll need a course of physiotherapy.'

Oh dear – that's going to seriously cramp Grandma's style. And considering that Vic and Aunt Jane are planning an engagement party, this might put everything on hold.

'Anyway, aside from her frustrations and how annoyed she is with herself for tripping up, she's going to be fine. Just a bit grouchy for a while, I suspect, but we'll keep her spirits up. How are things at your end?'

What do I say? 'Fine. Absolutely fine.'

'And the new lady, Eve, is settling in well?'

'Yes, and she's been an absolute star. It's not quite the same as working alongside you, of course, but she fitted in right from day one. I am sorry to hear the news about poor Grandma, though – for her, and for you and Vic.'

'Oh, we'll get through it, but we're going to delay our celebrations,' Aunt Jane replies rather stoically. 'Vic has a few ideas to cheer her up in the coming weeks. He'll invite her posse over for a few afternoon teas out on the terrace. He's such a great organiser.' She's trying to make light of it, but it will be a strain.

'I'm sure you have lots to do, but thanks for letting me know and tell Grandma I'm thinking of her and sending much love.'

'She'll appreciate that. I'm about to ring your dad and let him know. He'll probably want to fly over for a visit with your mum. I suppose it's too early for you to leave them all to cope if you wanted to slope off for a few days in the sun too?'

Oh, Aunt Jane – if only you knew. 'Sadly, Adam is having

a tough time at work, and I couldn't leave him on his own. But a break will do Mum and Dad good. They'll be able to help to keep Grandma occupied.'

Aunt Jane bursts out laughing. 'Well, we're going to need all the help we can get, that's for sure!'

I glance at my watch and notice it's ten to two. 'I must go, I'm afraid – duty calls,' I say light-heartedly. 'We'll speak soon, and I'll be thinking of you. Give Grandma a big hug from me!'

'I will. Bye for now, Bella.'

After grabbing my handbag from the restroom and rushing downstairs, I head over to the counter. Eve is partially hidden behind a stunning centrepiece that she's assembling for a sixteen-seater dining table.

'That looks awesome, Eve. When Mrs Mac arrives back, tell her that I'm off to my appointment. Hopefully, it will only take about half an hour.'

'I'll be sure to pass that on and thanks, Bella, that means a lot to hear you say that.'

All I can think about as I make my way out into the pedestrianised High Street, is that I hope this meeting goes well, because everything – and I mean *everything* – depends upon it.

I love this town . . . and the High Street is the true, beating heart of the community. There are so many isolated houses dotted around the countryside and a trip to town is a real treat. It's where people come together, the tourists flock, and there's always a buzz in the air as they wander along the beautifully cobbled thoroughfare.

There's something for everyone here – from an art gallery, a bookshop, a place to buy beautiful tartan rugs, somewhere to gear-up for walkers and climbers, to the Ben Nevis pub and restaurant.

I up the pace, threading my way among the throng of visitors to a town regarded as the gateway to the west coast as it's at the end of the West Highland Way. September is a wonderful time of the year here in Fort William and there is so much on offer. With Glen Coe to the south, Ben Nevis to the east and Glenfinnan – on the Road to the Isles – to the west. With hill walking, climbing, mountain biking trails, golfing, sea views and sunsets, it's *the* place to be. And that includes The Highland Flower Shop.

Everywhere I look it's a mass of smiling faces – many instantly recognising me and not just because they live locally. And yet here I am with a frown on my face that's hard to shift. I push open the door to Taggart and Sons, Solicitors and climb the stairs to the offices, located above a beauty salon. Clutching a folder under my arm, I'm quickly shown through to Mr Taggart senior's office and I'm more nervous than I would be if I were going to the dentist.

'Gud afternoon to you, Bella. Please make yourself comfortable. Can I get you a tea, or a coffee?'

'No, I'm fine, William, thank you.'

The receptionist exits, closing the door behind her and I hand William the folder as he indicates for me to take a seat.

'This is the lease and all of the documentation you hold, I presume?'

I nod as he walks back around his desk, extracting the small bundle of documents.

'Everything Aunt Jane left is in there, including the insurance certificates. The Notice to Quit and the covering letter are at the front. It came as a complete and utter shock, as you can imagine.'

William sits back in his leather chair as he peruses the paperwork. Following a prolonged silence, he places everything down in front of him and focuses on the contract itself.

My nerves are jangling, so I glance around the room. It's impossible to tell from William's expression what he's thinking so instead I focus on the massive wall of books to my right.

'I will admit that I was a little surprised that Jane didn't involve me when this was originally drawn up. I even offered to look it over retrospectively when she was here on other business, but she said it wasn't necessary.' Is William forewarning me that this isn't good news?

'It's not what you were expecting? I've been through it but I'm not sure I fully understand all the implications,' I admit.

'Most contracts vary a little in format, but the document simply lays out the terms and conditions which bind both parties for the duration of the lease.'

'It makes for scary reading.'

'I appreciate that, Bella. Let me give you a general overview of the salient points. What you have here is a periodic tenancy agreement, which means it continues until one of the parties chooses to terminate it. Unless that occasion arises, each year it renews automatically.'

'But not this year.' I expel one huge sigh.

'We'll get to that in a moment, dinnae worry, Bella. What's important is that your aunt understands her obligations. The tenant is responsible under the terms of the fully insuring and repairing clause, not simply to have the necessary insurance policies in place, but also to maintain the property. Randall McIntyre certainly gave Jane favourable terms indeed. It was quite a deal she struck but there is no option to either sublet or reassign the lease to another party.'

Since taking over the business, I've been focusing on keeping the books balanced and watching the cash flow. Just when I was feeling like I had a good handle on things, this happens.

'Randall McIntyre knew Pop from their early childhood. Mr McIntyre realises that Santa's Grotto brings a lot of interest, visitors and trade to the town, which has an impact on rental prices. And given that he's on The Highland Elves committee himself, he knows how big a fund-raiser it has been over the years. Perhaps that's why he gave her such favourable terms, and he might continue to be lenient as we go forwards.'

William looks back at me, his eyebrows knitting together. 'Randall's philanthropic side always has a local bias – he never forgets his roots, but his business has moved on, Bella. It's a very different organisation these days. I hear that his replacement isn't a local man, but hails from Surrey, so the area is unknown to him. Even his grandson doesn't have the same connections or loyalties, mainly because he grew up in the States, and not here. There's little point in me beating about the bush. The lease isn't transferable and there is a clear breach of the conditions now that you have taken over the business. I'm afraid to say that you don't have a leg to stand on.'

'Not even if I offer to pay the going rate?'

'Sadly, that's not how it works. The lease is between Miss Jane Reed and McIntyre Property Investments Limited, so you'd be looking at a new lease agreement between you and the landlord. The fact that they haven't mentioned that option in the cover letter doesn't bode well. The Notice to Quit stipulates a three calendar month period in which to vacate the property, instead of the forty days as per the terms, which is generous. And you will need to remind Jane of her end-of-lease obligations.'

William's expression is one of regret, but it's not quite the shock he might think it is as I'd come to pretty much the same depressing conclusion myself.

'I was half hoping there would be a loophole. Perhaps you'd better spell out what exactly the obligations are before I ring her.' And after today's upset with Grandma, this is the last thing she needs.

William sighs, genuinely sorry there's nothing at all he can do. 'It's very unfortunate, Bella, but sixteen years ago Randall was the boss, and he didn't have to answer to anyone. Having stepped away, he's now one of the shareholders of a nationwide company and deals like this simply don't happen anymore. I anticipate that Jane will probably be given the option to pay the landlord a sum of money in lieu of dilapidations.'

I stare at him, no doubt looking like the proverbial rabbit caught in the headlights of an oncoming car.

'Obviously,' he continues, 'a chartered surveyor would have undertaken a survey of the property before Jane entered into the lease. On vacating, the tenant is obliged to leave the property in a good state of repair and decoration, both internally and externally. The right of occupancy will cease on the fifth of December, and I doubt that there will be enough time to have the property surveyed, agree with the landlord what remedial work is required, and have said work carried out. The usual practice in cases of breach is that the landlord will submit a claim to cover the remedial works, professional fees, and VAT.'

I swallow hard. 'That sounds expensive.'

William raises his left eyebrow and it's at this precise moment I know we're in trouble.

'It's a standard clause, however . . .' He pauses and the look he gives me makes my stomach turn over. 'I'm guessing that Jane simply assumed the lease would be allowed to continue, or I'm sure she would have paid me a visit before she left. Prepare yourself, Bella, because it will likely come as a huge shock to her.'

Or maybe Aunt Jane had so much on her mind it didn't even occur to her that it would be a problem. I mean, even I didn't think to check and that was very unprofessional of me. 'I see. Thank you for your patience in explaining this to me, William.'

I stand and we shake hands, but he lingers for a moment before letting go.

'Randall wouldn't have set up a contract like this without good reason and that was clearly to help, not hinder. Get Jane to give him a call and let him know what's going on. Legally, there's no get-out clause, but he might not be aware of this development. His grandson, Maverick, is making waves and I'm not saying that's a bad thing, but it might be of benefit to bring it to Randall's attention, Bella. In my opinion, it's worth a shot.'

As I retrace my steps to The Highland Flower Shop, I'm in shock. In three months' time the business is going to be homeless. It's tough enough coping with my change in status from being an employee to an owner, what is life going to throw at me next? And now I have a difficult phone call to make and I'm not looking forward to adding to Aunt Jane's problems.

I'm deep in thought as I stride forward, however I'm brought to an abrupt halt when I collide with someone. The impact almost knocks me off my feet as it's like walking into a wall and my bag slips from my hand. The man's reflex action is instantaneous, as he puts out his arms to grab hold of me and keep me upright. However, we both watch in horror as his phone flies up in the air.

'Are you all right?' he checks, before relaxing his grip on me and I find myself staring up into a pair of tantalisingly blue eyes.

I nod my head, temporarily winded as he scans my face intently.

'Yes, I do believe I am,' I reassure him, although I sound slightly breathless. 'I'm so sorry. I was deep in thought and oblivious to what was going on around me.'

'No, no. It was my fault entirely,' he replies rather gallantly. 'I was texting and not looking where I was going.'

He stoops to retrieve my bag and I take it from him gratefully as he grabs his phone.

'Great!' he groans as he glances down at it, immediately slipping it into his jacket pocket.

'I really am sorry. I'm happy to pay for—'

'It was an accident, it's not a problem. It's just been one of those days,' he laughs, shrugging his shoulders.

I don't recognise him and he's much too smartly dressed

to be a tourist, so he's probably here on business. Maybe he's heading in to see William.

'Same here,' I sigh.

'And you're sure you're all right? You're not in need of a strong cup of tea, or anything?' His concern is touching. I feel my cheeks colouring up as he studies my face, this time with interest.

That's quite an offer to make to a stranger who literally collided with you in the street. I'm too embarrassed to take him up on it anyway, because although the fault is probably fifty-fifty, he put my safety before his personal property.

'I'm fine – really.' For some silly reason I'm standing here like a dummy and he isn't making a move, either. 'Well, your quick reaction saved the day, so I'm extremely grateful to you. Lesson learned . . . I'd . . . um . . . best get back to work.' I turn, feeling flustered as I walk away.

'Have a nice afternoon,' he calls out and for some bizarre reason I'm half tempted to look over my shoulder and check whether he's watching me.

Get a grip, Bella, my inner voice kicks in. *He didn't bump into you on purpose to attract your attention. You literally ploughed into him and smashed the poor man's phone.* Still, it's nice to know that real gentlemen still exist.

If only Adam was that attentive, I reflect grumpily, dismissing the thought as quickly as it entered my mind. Goodness knows what he'll have to say when I tell him the bad news. That's assuming he's in the mood to listen, of course.

3.

When the Past Comes Back to Haunt You

'Hello?'

'Am I speaking to Ms Bella Reed?'

'You are – how can I help?'

If this turns out to be another of those scam phone calls telling me that my internet connection has been compromised and they need remote access to sort it out, I will scream. Yesterday was bad enough having to call Aunt Jane and tell her exactly what was happening. On three occasions I've phoned the contact number on the covering letter attached to the Notice to Quit, but I keep getting the same response – they can't talk to me directly as my name isn't on the lease. Aunt Jane was obviously shocked to hear what was going on and told me that she'd give them a call. Now, here I am on a busy Saturday morning wading through paperwork instead of serving customers because my spirits are at an all-time low and I don't want the staff to witness it.

'My name is Randall McIntyre. I was wondering whether it would be beneficial for us to meet up at your earliest convenience?'

'Oh! Mr McIntyre—'

'Please call me Randall, and I can tell by the hesitancy in your voice that you're a little taken aback by this call. I'm making contact to see if there's anything I can do to help, given the unfortunate situation you find yourself in. Do you know a little place called The Highland Retreat? It's on the road to—'

'I've heard of it. It's the spa attached to Braemor Manor, isn't it?'

'Yes. I thought it might be nice if we could have a little chat – off the record, naturally. They do a wonderful afternoon tea there.'

Aunt Jane didn't say she'd reach out to Mr McIntyre himself. What if this seemingly innocent invitation isn't in her best interests at all?

'Look, I understand your reluctance, so please do check with your aunt to put your mind at rest before we meet up. I'll book a table for Monday. Say, three o'clock? You now have my contact number and I'll see you then, unless you advise me to the contrary.'

'Oh, right, thank you.'

As the line goes dead, my fingers can't dial Aunt Jane quickly enough.

'Bella? I was about to call you.' At least her voice sounds upbeat. 'I've passed on your number to—'

'Mr McIntyre has just been in touch. He wants me to meet him for afternoon tea on Monday,' I blurt out, anxiously.

'Then you must go, because it's good of him to spring into action so quickly. Randall was unaware that I've moved to Faro, so my call came as a bit of a surprise to him. He said he'd try to find out what was going on and give you a ring to see if he could help in any way.'

There are voices in the background, and I hear her name being called. Aunt Jane pauses for a second before responding. 'I'm coming – give me two minutes!' It's followed by a gentle sigh, and she sounds tired.

'Vic's panicking because we're about to leave the hospital and someone has misplaced your grandma's medication. Anyway, Randall will explain everything – I've given him permission to tell you the whole story. You can talk openly to him, Bella – he's on our side. I'm sorry to cut and run, but your grandma is a nightmare at times and she's making a big fuss. I've unwittingly landed you with a huge problem and I feel awful about it. I'm hoping Randall can offer some advice on how best to proceed because it's . . . um . . . a bit delicate. Anyway, let me know how it goes on Monday. Speak soon!'

With that she's gone – but what does she mean by *the whole story*?

The door opens and Mrs Mac enters. Outside, I can hear the hubbub coming from The Christmas Cave. Even in September, it always astounds me how many tourists leave here with a bag full of new baubles for their Christmas trees.

'You're lookin' tired, lassie!' Mrs Mac exclaims, glancing across at me.

'Hmm . . . I am a little. I don't suppose you managed to get me an appointment with our accountant, David?'

We're almost halfway through our financial year and I need to sit down with him and look at the potential impact of a hefty increase in the rent.

'I did.' She grins at me. 'And he's comin' here. He said he'd pop in about three o'clock and he won't need to rush off.'

I could cheerfully hug Mrs Mac right now. 'Oh, you are a star – that's perfect. Eve is working flat out, and I really do need to help her catch up with the orders before we fall too far behind. But, before I head downstairs, how's Holly doing?'

'It's nae good. She's layin' down the law to Nick again, but this time she means it.' Mrs Mac's eyebrows shoot up into her fringe as she rolls her eyes.

'That sounds ominous.'

'Holly told him straight that he can't just turn up late when he has arranged to spend time with Katie and no more popping in when it suits him. She says it's disruptive for Katie and in future he must give her at least a day's notice.'

I know that neither of them is in a financial position to get solicitors involved, but if this new measure doesn't work then that has to be the next step. Holly is loath to do that because she sees it as the last resort. But how many times can Katie sit there, patiently waiting for her dad to arrive only to be disappointed? This might be the final wake-up call Nick needs to get his act together.

'Thanks for the heads-up, Mrs Mac. I'm not exactly a pillar of support for her right now, am I?'

Mrs Mac tuts. 'You've got a lot goin' on, Bella. Holly understands that. Don't you be frettin' – I'll keep a close watch on the lassie, never fear. Now you head downstairs and give Eve a hand to fulfil those orders. I'll make a brew.'

'Dinnae bother yersel, I'm on it!' We both turn around as Rodric pokes his head around the half-open door. 'One round of tea comin' up!'

Mrs Mac rewards him with a beaming smile. Suddenly, without any warning at all, my pulse begins to race and there's a pounding in my ears. I try to shake it off as I walk out into the retail area and head for the stairs. Am I having a panic attack? I draw in a deep breath – then another, and another, desperately trying to remain calm. The faces around me are a blur and I falter. Grabbing onto the handrail, I force myself to relax, releasing my shoulders and unclenching my jaw. By the time I join Eve behind the floristry counter, I'm back in control and the moment has passed.

Stress is a terrible thing and right now there doesn't seem to be an end to it, but I can't fall apart. People's livelihoods are at stake here, not just my pride. Damn you, Maverick McIntyre! If this is just about the money, then let's get down to business.

As angry as I'm feeling, ten minutes later I'm assembling an anniversary bouquet and instantly my mood lifts. As the wonderful scent of the ruby-red roses fills the air, I instinctively reach for a bunch of white gypsophila. I'm not going down without a fight, I tell myself resolutely. If Randall McIntyre is on my side, then maybe the situation can be turned around – I guess I'll find out for sure on Monday. Now, what this arrangement lacks is the soft bluey-green of eucalyptus leaves to make the vibrant colour of the roses pop. Whatever happens, we can't let our customers down.

Adam rarely works on a Saturday, but today he went in to catch up on some general admin. I wasn't expecting him to be this late. I while away the early evening thinking about what I should wear when I meet up with Mr McIntyre. Businesslike, I'm thinking, as I trawl through my wardrobe. Maybe I'll put my hair up and take a bit more care when applying my makeup. It's about creating an impression, isn't it? I mean, in smart surroundings, talking to a self-made millionaire several times over, it's time to dress to impress. I'm representing a thriving business that has a good standing in the local community. It's worth fighting to stay, and I need to look like a woman who means business.

'Bella, I'm home!' Adam calls out from the hallway. 'Sorry, I didn't realise what time it was. Have you eaten?'

I hurry downstairs and into his arms, needing to feel his comforting embrace after such a tiring day. He plants a kiss on my lips, and I'm delighted to see how relaxed he looks.

'Not yet.'

His face falls. 'Oh . . . I grabbed a burger from the deli and ate it at the office. I was starving. I assumed you wouldn't wait for me.'

'It doesn't matter. I'll settle for a sandwich. How was your day?'

'I managed to catch up on the backlog of emails and ploughed through a lot of paperwork.' He smiles down at me, and I reach out to ruffle his hair.

'Well, thank goodness for small mercies. At least one of us is keeping up.'

He looks at me, grimacing. 'Is it that bad?'

'It might be, but it's too soon to say for sure. Anyway, I'll grab something to eat and then let's chill for a bit with a drink.'

Adam makes no attempt to retrieve his laptop from his bag, which is a first. He simply dumps it in the corner beneath the coat rack.

'I'll sort the drinks while you change. Is there any reason why you're wearing your second-best trouser suit?'

'I have an appointment on Monday to talk about the lease. Will this do?' I twirl around and catch him smiling at me appreciatively.

'You wear it well. It's been a while since we dressed up and had a proper date night, hasn't it?'

Wow – what a change in him tonight. Perhaps now that the redundancies are all sorted, the pressure will ease up.

'A couple of months, I'd say.'

'Then, I'll book somewhere special for a candlelit dinner for two as soon as I get a chance. What do you think?'

'It's a yes from me!' I reply before heading upstairs.

I was hoping to bring Adam up to date with the latest developments at the shop and ask his opinion about a few things, but I don't want to spoil his good mood. I know from experience that talking about work will do just that, which is a bit of a let-down because the pressure is mounting. Oh well, I've got this – I can be both charming and a strong, entrepreneurial woman, when I need to be. This suit is going to make just the right impression if I team it with a blouse to soften it a little, instead of a cotton shirt.

As for date night . . . well, maybe it's time to glam up to

impress my man. We've both been through a few trying months and there have been long periods when Adam has been so tetchy that it's been hard to be in the same room as him. So, I'm on a high seeing him looking and sounding much more like his old self.

I smile as I slip into a pair of jeans and grab a jumper. Then, out of nowhere a cold shiver runs down my back. I don't suppose . . . I mean, Adam didn't just say he'd take me out for a meal, he said *date night*. That's special. I used to daydream about seeing him getting down onto one knee and popping the question because I knew what my answer would be. Now, the only thing I know for sure is that I'm not ready because something has changed, but I don't quite know what. The question I longed to hear now fills me with a sense of . . . panic and that's a shocking thing to admit.

It's Monday before I know it and it's been one of those days when there's hardly time to sit and draw breath. I'm a little late leaving for my meeting, but fortunately there aren't any hold-ups.

As I drive, I think about how different Adam was over the weekend, suggesting we go for a walk and it turned out to be the perfect Sunday. It's something we hadn't done in a long while and after a two-hour trek through the forest, we ended the day back home playing board games.

It's a pleasant journey and I arrive at Braemor Manor tea rooms looking reasonably calm and collected.

'Mr McIntyre, it's a real pleasure to meet you!'

Not only is he a pillar of the community in terms of the money he's reinvested and the charities he's involved with, but up close his persona is incredibly charming. His handshake is firm and welcoming as the waiter pulls out a chair for me.

'Likewise, Bella! Please, do call me Randall.'

'Are ye ready to be served, Mr McIntyre?' the waiter checks as I settle myself down.

'We are, Hamish, thank you.'

'What tea can I get you, madam?' Hamish asks, as he offers me a small menu beautifully printed on a satin finish card.

It lists them all – everything from Assam to English breakfast tea, and for the more adventurous – spiced apple chai, cedar wood and blackberry tea.

'Earl Grey would be perfect, thank you,' I reply, wondering if I should in fact have been a little more adventurous.

'Great choice, Bella. Make that a pot of Earl Grey for two, Hamish, if you please.'

'Thank you, sir.'

This is no simple tea room, it's a barn conversion in the grounds of a stunning manor house. With massive oak beams overhead, the rustic chic style is perfect. Twee most certainly wouldn't work in a vast open space like this. Even the kitchen at the far end is partially open plan. I can see a whole bank of steam ovens and at least half a dozen staff beavering away. As I glance across at the table nearest to us, the pyramid cake stand is full to brimming with a wonderful selection of tiny sandwiches, little tarts and slices of cake.

'Is it your first visit here?' Randall enquires.

'Yes. I've heard about it, of course, but I didn't realise it was housed in a barn.'

'They make everything on site and the tea-room kitchen supplies the main restaurant with bread and rolls, too. I didn't know what your preference would be, so I've ordered a little of everything.'

'That's most kind of you . . . Randall.'

Sitting here, I do feel the part. This suit was so the right thing to wear, and the pale-grey silk blouse adds a softness to the overall look. Even my handbag and shoes match. I took quite a bit of ribbing at work this morning. Our uniform consists of black trousers or leggings, with mauve-coloured T-shirts, and matching fleeces sporting the company logo, so I was quite out of place.

However, as comfortable as I'm feeling on one level, I'm not sure whether it would be impolite to get straight down to business. Should I wait for my host to raise the subject?

As if reading my mind, Randall coughs to clear his throat and glances at me with a pointed look. 'I gather that you spoke to your aunt and she reassured you that whatever you and I discuss is in confidence. Am I right?'

'Yes, and please rest assured that I fully understand that it's in both our interests to regard this as commercial in confidence,' I confirm, keen to put this on an equal footing. It's not strictly ethical given that he no longer works for the company and the lease isn't in my name.

'Ah, here we are!' Randall looks up, as Hamish and a waitress each place a cake stand down on the white linen tablecloth. Following behind is a young man carrying a tray. Hamish fusses over positioning the plates in front of us and moving the teacups around, but Randall indicates that we can sort ourselves out. It's encouraging that he's as eager to begin the conversation as I am.

'Let me pour,' I offer, lifting the teapot with one hand, as I scrunch up my linen napkin in the other to catch any dribbles.

'Thank you, Bella. Do you take milk, or lemon?' Randall enquires, as he moves the two cups into the centre of the table and places the tea strainer on top of one.

'Oh, I prefer it as it comes.'

'Ah, a woman after my own heart. It spoils the taste when adding anything to it and I can't see the point. Sugar?'

I nod. 'Please, just half a spoonful.'

His laugh is robust. 'Me too! Just enough to counteract

any bitterness, but not enough to spoil the flavour of the bergamot. And tea bags don't hit the spot, do they? It has to be tea leaves.'

I like this man. The genuine warmth in his smile as we banter immediately instils a sense of trust. He's the sort of person you instinctively know you can relax around because there's no hidden agenda – he'll always be upfront with you. I know for a fact that he's in his mid-seventies, but he looks younger than his years, even with the steely-grey hair. What tweaks my heartstrings is the thought that if Pop were still alive he'd be around the same age, and I quickly dismiss that thought before I get maudlin.

'It does, but without a wonderful spread like this to complement it perfectly, I'm afraid I often grab a tea bag for ease. I can't remember the last time I had a good old-fashioned afternoon treat like this,' I reflect.

'Well, tuck in!'

'You do know that this is a purposeful attempt on my part to get you on my side, Bella,' Randall says, finally breaking the silence after we've been eating for a while. His piercing blue eyes twinkle at me.

I daintily wipe the corners of my mouth with the napkin and sit back to study his face.

'On your side? Goodness, I'm here out of desperation and I told myself I wasn't going to admit that, so you can relax.' I give a little laugh, as something tells me honesty is the best policy with a man like Randall.

'Please, continue eating as I talk, and I'll apologise in advance for the intermittent pauses because I skipped lunch and I'm hungry. There is a little story I need to tell you before we go any further and I have Jane's blessing. It's personal and, therefore, rather delicate.'

Suddenly my appetite is waning, but I don't want him to sense my unease. Why is there *a story* attached to this? The favour he extended to Aunt Jane ceased when I took over the business and there's nothing anyone can do about that.

'I understand that this situation is of our own making, so there's really no need to explain. I'm not looking for any favours.'

He says nothing, instead he sits there with his elbows on the table, linking his hands together with his fingertips forming a triangle. It's obvious he doesn't know where to begin, which I find surprising. I wait, impatiently picking at crumbs because I'm on the edge of my seat and trying hard not to look puzzled.

'Hmm . . . this is much more difficult than I imagined it would be. No one feels comfortable exposing their deepest secrets, do they?'

'Start at the beginning,' I encourage him, with a fleeting smile, wondering where on earth this is going.

'I like to reassure myself that everyone has at least one thing they hope will remain buried in the past, but that might be wishful thinking on my part. The truth is, though, that . . . uh, this isn't something I feel ashamed about – quite the reverse. It redeemed two people who were at a crossroads in their lives when the way forward wasn't clear. But if it ever becomes common knowledge, it will hurt both Jane and those closest to me. I can't have that as another burden on my conscience.'

I'm no longer nibbling, because every single crumb I've eaten is now lying in my stomach like a huge stone as I sit in stunned silence.

'Our paths crossed very briefly, but it was enough to make us both re-evaluate our lives.'

I'm confused. He's not talking about Aunt Jane . . . is he?

'My marriage to Fiona was going through a difficult patch at the time. Our son, Douglas, had just taken up a position in the States, working for one of the world's leading aerospace corporations. It left my wife and I reeling as we'd always assumed he'd live and work in the UK. He's a gifted engineer and we're extremely proud of him but, as often happens, Fiona and I dealt with the news in different ways.

Fiona needed more of my attention, not less, as suddenly her world was turned upside down. But I wasn't in a good place at the time, either. I was struggling to accept that my dream of adding "& Son" to the company title wasn't going to come true no matter what I did. I'd built it from the ground up and it was starting to take off, but Douglas wasn't at all interested. At the time, it was a devastating blow as I'd started the company hoping to have something worthwhile to pass on to my son, but now I see that I was being unfair.'

It's obvious that Randall has my full attention and momentarily he glances away, checking that no one is within earshot.

'The stress it caused was pushing Fiona and me further apart with each passing day,' he continues. 'Then, one night, I couldn't face going home and having yet another row because I was still in the office at nine o'clock at night. She couldn't understand why I was working so hard, but what choice did I have when it was all down to me? Instead, I called into The Old Grouse Inn to grab some food in the hope that Fiona would be asleep by the time I eventually got home.'

I swallow hard. It doesn't take a genius to piece this little puzzle together and it's one of the places I'd choose as it's a quiet little pub a few miles outside of Fort William.

'Jane was sitting alone at a table, eating. I took the only other available table, which was next to hers and it wasn't long before we started chatting. Eating alone is awkward, I always find. A little later I invited her to join me for a nightcap – a wee dram of whisky. If we'd simply said goodnight and gone our separate ways . . . Desperately lonely people do desperate things, I'm afraid.'

The eye contact between us is awkward, but I'm not here to judge anyone.

'These things happen, Randall.' What else can I say? It's no one's business but his and Aunt Jane's. And she chose not to take me into her confidence about their past connection, even as she allowed me to influence the way the business was developing. Her generosity in handing over the reins to me has put her in a vulnerable position and I feel bad about that.

'Your aunt was thirty years old, and I was almost twenty years her senior. There are no excuses, Bella, because I shouldn't have let it happen. But . . .' There's a faraway look in his eyes as he casts his mind back and I find myself absent-mindedly chewing on my lower lip. 'We were two lonely people struggling to make sense of our lives. Jane had ambitions that were being stifled and we instantly recognised the one thing we had in common – a feeling of loneliness and defeat. Neither of us regretted our brief—' Randall looks around, cautiously '—liaison, but it was an impossible situation – we both knew that. When Jane told me she'd been offered a job in Edinburgh, a part of me wanted to talk her out of it, but another part of me couldn't do that to her – or my family. I had to let her go and it was the toughest decision of my entire life.'

Even if Aunt Jane was in love with Randall at the time, she isn't the sort of person to break up a marriage if there's still a chance for it to survive. She saw something in Randall, and I can see it, too. There's an underlying sensitivity in this man and that's unusual for someone who has made such a huge success of his life. Usually, that comes at a price – which is to put profit before people. But that doesn't seem to be the case for him.

Randall takes a deep breath in before expelling it. 'That's the tough bit over, Bella. Come on, let's eat and I'll explain how we're going to try to find a solution to help you out, while ensuring my grandson Maverick doesn't start asking awkward questions. Not least, the fact that I handled all contact with your aunt personally, which wasn't usual practice for me.'

Ah, now I understand! At least Randall has a legitimate

reason to help if he can. However, my head is still reeling at the thought of a liaison between Aunt Jane and Randall. The quicker I put it to the back of my mind the better, because my focus has to be on the future, not the past.

4.

A Glimmer of Hope

As Randall and I stroll around the grounds of Braemor Manor looking for a sheltered bench to sit and talk, I find myself wondering whether Aunt Jane ever really got over him. He used the word 'brief' to describe their affair, but even so, to meet up in secret wouldn't have been easy. And the fact that she didn't feel able to talk to me about this tells me that it's a painful memory. I can't recall her ever dating anyone until she met Vic. But a long-distance relationship is different. And it wasn't until Vic gave her an ultimatum that she realised taking a risk was better than being on her own forever. But it makes my heart ache to think that her one true love might be the one she left behind. The one she still can't bring herself to talk about.

'It's best to have this next part of the conversation out here so we can't be overheard. Will this do?' Randall points to an arbour set back within a twelve-foot-high privet hedge.

'It's perfect,' I remark, as I take a seat and Randall joins me. We take a moment to gaze around, watching as the breeze ripples through the treetops. Everything is still very green, but the leaves on two enormous horse chestnut trees are already beginning to turn a golden yellow, tinged with brown. Another couple of weeks and the ground beneath them will have a colourful carpet. I turn to look at Randall and he raises his eyebrows, letting out a gentle sigh.

'The problem I have, Bella, is that the company has grown

beyond my wildest expectations, and shareholders measure success by the dividends the company pays out. Having retired, I'm still a shareholder but I no longer have any authority. However, I'm frequently called upon in an advisory capacity as the new CEO settles in. But the fact that my grandson, Maverick, has recently been promoted to lettings business development manager means that the situation is, naturally, a little sensitive.'

The conflict he's feeling is very real.

'I'm proud of my grandson,' he continues, 'and the fact that he chose to move to Scotland last year tells me that he's searching for something. Something he didn't find in the US. It means an awful lot to Fiona and me that he has chosen to make his future here. As his grandparents, it will strengthen our bond and I know my son and his wife will no longer be strangers to the UK, either. It's important to me that he doesn't get wind of . . . well, something that lies buried in the past. I'd do anything for Jane because she's a wonderful woman. Kind-hearted and giving. Vic is a lucky man and she sounded really happy. I wouldn't want anything to spoil that for them.'

It's rather heart-warming now that I finally understand why Randall is taking me into his confidence. Not only does he want to protect Aunt Jane, but he too has a lot to lose.

'Pop always said that a story wasn't complete if it didn't have a happy ending.' Both Aunt Jane's and Randall's life stories are set for just that and I don't intend to let a generous gesture by my aunt tarnish anyone's happiness.

'To my dismay, I've discovered that Maverick is in talks with a new tenant for the space you currently occupy and obviously it's at the latest market price. I'm not at liberty to share commercially sensitive information, but I'm afraid that being in breach of contract puts you on the back foot. And some deals with the larger organisations encompass properties in a range of locations, but I can't really divulge any more than that. In fairness to him it's what he's paid to do – maximise profits – but it's bad news for you.'

I think back to the talk I had with William Taggart. He said as the terms had been breached, McIntyre Property Investments Limited could have given us a mere forty days to vacate.

'And I appreciate that, Randall. We've been given three months' notice, which is generous,' I acknowledge, as it would be unfair of me not to do so. 'But I was hoping our track record would be a bargaining tool. We've always paid on time; the business continues to thrive and the location is perfect for us. All I'm asking is to be given a chance to negotiate a new lease – I'm not expecting any preferential rates.' It's hard to keep the passion out of my voice.

'It's not quite as simple as that I'm afraid, Bella, but I can assure you that the lease was supposed to protect your aunt Jane.'

He looks at me questioningly, registering my surprise.

'You kept in touch all those years that Aunt Jane was in Edinburgh?'

'No. We had no contact at all. Our paths crossed very briefly at your granddad's funeral. I walked over to her, not knowing what sort of reaction I'd get but we ended up chatting for a few minutes. I shared a little story about your granddad from our school days.'

'Oh, I see.' Meeting up again for the first time in many years must have been difficult for them both, given the situation.

'Jane mentioned that she was coming back to Fort William to set up her own floristry business. I said if she hadn't already found somewhere, I had the perfect place in mind.' He chuckles to himself. 'Sorry. I'm remembering the look on Jane's face when I showed her around the shop. I knew that Santa's Highland Express had been in storage for a few months. I always felt that it was unfair on your family to bear the brunt of the costs of housing and running it. She was hesitant at first, until I pointed out the fact that part of the rent would be a legitimate tax write-off for the company, as the ride is non-profit making.'

'It was still very thoughtful of you, Randall.'

'Well, that was in the days when I ruled my own little empire. Whenever Jane and I spoke it was always about the charity, but it was my way of checking that she was doing OK. That sounds rather sad, doesn't it?'

'No,' I reply, emphatically. 'It's not wrong to care for someone, even if your lives go off in very different directions – that's fate.'

'If only Jane had let me know in advance of her decision to hand over the business to you,' he says, with regret. 'I could probably have sorted something out. There's a lot of goodwill for a company encouraging local charitable enterprises bringing business into the heart of Fort William. However, this is the situation we find ourselves in because Maverick saw an opportunity, unaware of the upset it will cause. It may already be too late for me to be able to influence what happens next. I thought it was best to be frank with you.'

'I understand, Randall.' His concern is genuine, and I believe every word he's told me. 'It's a business transaction, that's all.'

Randall nods his head in agreement, but there's a glint in his eyes as he stares back at me.

'That's as maybe, but this is different. All is not lost. Well, not yet, anyway,' he replies. 'First of all, I've reassured Jane that I'll personally cover the dilapidation costs. Your family has raised an enormous amount of money for charity. As I'm one of the committee members for The Highland Elves, if that were to become common knowledge I don't think it would look odd. Alas, what I can't come up with is a viable, long-term option for you for the future in terms of another rental.'

I can hear the regret in his voice.

'It's kind of you to give this any thought whatsoever, Randall, but as for the future, I wouldn't be much of a business owner if I can't find alternative premises.'

He shakes his head, sadly. 'I know, Bella, but I want to do something. You're no doubt aware that there is a unit at the other end of the High Street due to undergo a complete refit once the current occupiers move out. It's half the space you have now, so it's not big enough to accommodate Santa's Grotto, I'm afraid, but it's a nice spot. It'll be ready for occupation in a couple of months' time; I could apply a little subtle persuasion if it's of interest to you. You'd have to pay the going rate and the negotiations would be strictly between you and Maverick, but it would probably equate to roughly what you're paying now.'

With a deadline to vacate the shop, the alternative would be to have no presence at all in the town centre. While the commercial side of the business is growing appreciably, overnight we'd lose our regular retail customers. That's at least forty per cent of our income gone in a flash. I know the premises and, admittedly, it is one of the first shops as people head into town from the car park. However, Randall is right, it's small by comparison to what we have now. No room for Pop's sleigh ride and I'd have to shut down The Christmas Cave too. What's more, would I still be able to justify employing Holly, as well as Mrs Mac? My stomach is in knots, and even though this isn't a great solution, I don't want to appear ungrateful.

'The access to the rear of the property is good which is a bonus, as our vans are in and out all the time, so it could work,' I concede. 'At least our regular retail customers would still have easy access to us.'

Randall's face brightens. 'As two of the McIntyre Property Investments Limited board members are also linked to the charity,' he continues, 'there will be a sense of *unease* about putting the future of the sleigh ride in jeopardy. I'm wondering whether there's an empty outbuilding that could be utilised . . . I'm just brainstorming here, and I'd need to make some discreet enquiries. When all is said and done, Santa's Highland Express is a big part of the Christmas tradition here in Fort William. Your grandfather was well respected, and we all have a lot to thank him for.'

Randall's sincerity is touching, but the stark reality of the situation I find myself in is daunting. We sit staring out across the beautifully tended gardens and the grass, which has been carefully mown in neat stripes as we head into autumn.

'The truth is, Randall, that I can't risk losing any of our major contracts as I have five employees with mortgages to pay and their job security is my main priority.'

Randall shakes his head, sadly. 'I do appreciate that fact and I'll begin sowing the seed. Jane isn't one for saying a lot, but I can tell that she has taken this hard. She thought she was handing you an opportunity, not a millstone. I wish I could solve all your problems in one, Bella, but I'm afraid that's an impossibility.'

'It's very thoughtful of you to do what you can on my behalf, Randall, and thank you in advance for putting in a good word for me.'

'I'm sure you appreciate that Maverick must never find out about our meeting today, or the personal information I've shared with you. But if questions are asked about the preferential rate I extended to Jane, I'd rather it was seen as a purely philanthropic gesture, rather than one of a more personal nature. The truth, I'm afraid, lies somewhere in between. Is that acceptable to you?'

'Of course!' So, we have an understanding.

A magpie swoops towards us, settling on the hedge above our heads. Seconds later another one flies over to join it, as they exchange their raspy calls back and forth. I find myself thinking: one for sorrow, two for joy. Maybe there is a light at the end of the tunnel, assuming Randall can convince his grandson to talk to me.

'Well, I'm most grateful for your time, Randall, and for that wonderful afternoon tea.'

'It was my pleasure entirely, Bella. Talking to Jane, even though she's distressed about the situation here, I could tell that she has no regrets. She's finally found the happiness she deserves. And your grandfather, George, would be at peace knowing that your grandmother has her daughter close by. Susan is a grand lady, very determined as I remember, but as we get older it's comforting having family around us. Not least because it keeps us young!' He chuckles to himself, but he's the sort of man who will always be young at heart.

As Randall walks me back to my car, he hands me a business card.

'When it's simply an exchange of letters going back and forth, the admin team follow a set procedure and will only give Maverick an update on how things are progressing. He'll feel more of a connection if we can get him to visit the premises in person – so leave that to me. Establishing a rapport always helps, otherwise you're just a name on a piece of paper.' Randall looks at me for confirmation that I understand what he's saying.

'Right. Maybe it would help if I kick off the conversation with an apology,' I suggest, diplomatically. 'After all, I really should have read the small print in the lease, so I've not exactly made a good first impression when it comes to business acumen.'

Randall's laugh is robust. 'You've got it. He does have a heart behind that extremely professional and very polite exterior of his. Witnessing someone else's dilemma up close is a reminder that business decisions have a real impact on people's lives. And as far as I know he's never stepped inside The Highland Flower Shop. It's a real shame he doesn't have any childhood memories of taking a ride on Santa's Highland Express, but Fiona and I always fly over to the States to join the family for Christmas. We're hoping to change that this year.' He sounds wistful.

Randall grasps the hand I hold out to him. 'Anyway, you've been a blessing to your aunt Jane, Bella – the daughter she sadly never had. Now that she's handed over the business to you, I'm sure it will continue to flourish. I've come to believe that life has a way of working things out. In fact, that belief is what has kept me going and I'm glad I was stubborn enough to just keep ploughing forward.'

It's hard not to chuckle. 'I am reeling a little it's true, but knowledge is power, isn't it? Now I know what I'm dealing with, and some of the pitfalls to avoid in the future, at least I'm going forward better equipped. And a part of that is now down to you, Randall. I assume that if our paths ever cross in the future, we've never met before?'

As he releases my hand, he raises his eyebrows and nods his head in agreement.

'But this will always be a singularly pleasant couple of hours to reflect upon, spent in the company of a young woman destined to succeed. You mark my words!'

'Was yer secret meetin' productive?' Mrs Mac enquires, as I walk into the office and slump down into my chair.

'It was a fact-finding mission, that's all. I'm no expert on contract law, or lease clauses, but I'm starting to get a feel for it.'

'Can the problem be fixed?' Suddenly Mrs Mac's tone changes and I can see that she isn't just asking for herself, but on behalf of all the staff.

When an official-looking letter arrives by recorded delivery it doesn't go unnoticed and the look on my face as I opened it that day wasn't something I could hide.

'I wish it were as simple as that, but unfortunately there is no easy fix. It's time for me to look at what the options are and come up with an action plan. There's no point getting everyone together until I have a workable solution, is there?'

'We're all appreciative of what yer goin' through, Bella. Jane wouldnae have wanted to put this on you if she'd realised. If there's anythin' any of us can do, ye know you can count on us to back you up.'

As I slip off my jacket, I glance at my watch, but when I look up I'm gutted when I notice Mrs Mac sweep a hand over her cheek, swiping away a tear.

'This is a reminder that I still have a lot to learn, Mrs Mac. But I didn't spend all that time at college gaining a diploma in business studies not to make use of it. I'm just a little rusty, that's all. Aunt Jane had her vision – now it's time for me to create a new one to safeguard the future for all of us. It's time to get serious.'

Mrs Mac's face brightens. 'There you go. I knew you'd rise to the challenge. If yer needin' me to do extra hours you only have to say. I won't want payin' – I'm just glad to help out.'

Now I'm the one feeling dewy-eyed. 'It's time to think outside the box, Mrs Mac. It will take me a little while to figure out the next steps, but once I know what's happening I'll make it common knowledge. The focus must be on keeping our customers happy and not letting anyone down so—'

My mobile kicks into life and I hurry over to retrieve it from my bag, giving Mrs Mac an apologetic smile.

'Hi, Aunt Jane. How is Grandma today?'

'I'm off to make you a tea,' Mrs Mac mouths quietly.

'Fine, but she's struggling to get the hang of using the crutches. Vic just suggested she try a walking frame instead and if looks could kill – that was the one. Vic couldn't get out of here fast enough. He's going to see what other options are available. You know what she's like when she erupts and she's not one for letting people do things for her.'

'Poor Vic, and poor you. It's not the best start to kick off your early retirement, is it?'

There's an exasperated sigh, followed by a groan.

'It's bound to get better. Anyway, I've been on edge all afternoon. You're still speaking to me, Bella, which is a good sign.'

Goodness, I'm not sure how to handle this as I didn't intend to phone Aunt Jane until this evening. 'Don't be daft, it's just one of those things, and your secret is safe with me . . .' I trail off, diplomatically.

'Please don't think badly of Randall, Bella. I hope he explained – I asked him to tell you everything and to put it into context. Leasing me the shop at a preferential rate wasn't an attempt to buy my silence, I'd hate you to think he was the sort of man who would stoop to bribery. I could have loved him for ever you know, but he wasn't free, and the guilt would have ruined everything between us anyway. But this mess up on the lease was entirely down to me. Randall said he'd look into it, but I can't see what can be done.'

The office door opens and Mrs Mac walks towards me, placing a mug of tea down on the desk as I give her a thumbs up. Diplomatically, she turns and makes a hasty retreat.

'Randall said he'll sort out the dilapidation costs. I think he's going to settle the sum himself,' I inform Aunt Jane, hoping that will at least ease her mind a little. 'It's obvious the preferential rate he extended was because of The Highland Flower Shop's link to the charity, so I doubt it will raise any eyebrows.'

Aunt Jane sighs. 'It's more than I expected, Bella, and so typical of Randall. But it's your future I'm concerned about. If only I'd checked the small print in that lease, or talked to Randall about it, maybe we could have done things differently – kept the business in my name, for example.'

'We both know that wouldn't have worked. Trying to circumvent the rules is always a mistake. Besides, the business is doing well, and I'm sure I'll be able to sort something out.' The last thing I want is for her to feel she's let anyone down.

'Randall sought me out, you know – when I returned from Edinburgh. I'd hate you to think that it was the other way around because I've never felt that he *owed* me anything. What happened between us was completely unexpected and out of character for us both. It almost didn't feel real and often we'd drive miles to meet up just to spend the evening together in a little country pub talking over a meal. It was so easy being together and I think of it as my bittersweet summer. It did put a huge dent in my heart, I will be honest. But when I left Fort William almost twenty-six years ago, it was already over. I was following my dream and there was no bad feeling between us. And . . . uh . . . well, no regrets. It was simply the right thing to do and that's the truth.'

She pauses momentarily as I quietly sip my tea because what can I say? Absolutely nothing. What's the point of wondering *what if*?

'It made him happy to do something for me that would also honour his old school mate. It didn't feel wrong, Bella, and I was grateful.'

She sounds hesitant, worried I'll think less of her now that I know about their affair.

'If it helps, when Randall was telling me the story it was touching how protective he was of you and he blames himself. I'm going to meet up with his grandson, Maverick, and see what we can do.' I think it's best to leave it there for now.

'Well, that's a start, Bella. We have a track record with the company – that must count for something. You will ring me and let me know how it goes, won't you?'

'Don't worry, we'll sort something out. Mrs Mac has just brought me a cup of tea and I'm going to take five minutes to enjoy it before I head downstairs to thank Eve. I left her to finish off a big order for a fiftieth birthday party and she's been amazing.'

'Well, I'm glad that's one thing less for you to worry about.' At least Aunt Jane sounds more relaxed. If I told her our days here are numbered it would pull her down and she has enough to battle with right now. Including dealing with old memories having been raked up when she assumed they were finally buried in the past.

'If things are that bad,' Adam remarks, 'then walk away. Life's too short to put up with that level of hassle.'

He was the one who asked me how things were going and now he's angry because I tried to explain some of the problems I'm facing.

'I'm not moaning, Adam,' I reply, firmly. 'What did you

expect me to say – everything is fine when it's not? When things weren't going well for you at work I was supportive because I wanted to help you through it. And now you say something blasé like that to me when you know it isn't even an option.'

Oh no . . . now I'm adding fuel to the fire.

'You've pretty much admitted there's no easy solution. Whatever you do to get out of the fix that you find yourself in will increase the overheads. That means increasing your turnover during a period when you'll be moving premises. I think it's time you faced facts, Bella – you're fighting a losing battle.'

After months of listening to Adam's work problems and putting up with his moody behaviour, this time he's gone too far.

'Oh, so your advice is that I just give up and suddenly not just me, but everyone I employ, is out of a job?' I glare at him, and he has the audacity to shrug his shoulders and continue eating.

I quickly realise I can't sit here facing him across the dinner table because I'm likely to explode and say something I'll regret. After putting my knife and fork down on the plate in front of me with a clatter, I exit the room.

I've been there for Adam throughout his difficulties, but I'm starting to think he's not prepared to be there for me when I need a little support. I'm not simply disappointed by his reaction, it's more a case of seeing a side of him I haven't really registered before. It's as if he sees what I'm going through as my fault and there's no empathy whatsoever. When he's the one with a problem, it's never of his making. And this feels, quite frankly, like a huge slap in the face.

To calm myself I spend the next hour lazing in a scented bubble bath, my thoughts creating their own internal dialogue. Eventually, the anger and frustrations begin to dissipate. As I think back over the little upsets Adam and I have had in the past, I'm usually the one to let it go. But tonight, I was on the brink of walking out. Telling him how insensitive he's being would fall on deaf ears, and he'd probably turn it around and accuse me of taking my frustrations out on him.

Thinking back on the past makes me realise that these feelings have been hovering below the surface for a while. I'm sick and tired of making allowances for his unreasonable and self-centred behaviour.

From now on if Adam asks how things are going, I'll simply reply, 'Just fine,' and see how he reacts. It's obvious that there is no quick fix looming for me at work, and the pressure is on. I don't have the time to pander to his issues anymore, not when he has zero concern for what I'm going through.

A part of me is wary of testing him, but Adam's attitude tonight upset me. However, I need him to come to that realisation for himself and reach out to make amends. If he doesn't . . . well, I'm not sure how much longer I can go on like this. I'm a compassionate and caring person, but I'm nobody's fool and I like to think that Adam knows that.

5.

First Impressions

Randall works miracles and less than forty-eight hours later the meeting I've been dreading is about to take place. But to my horror, when Mrs Mac ushers in my visitor the look of recognition we exchange is decidedly awkward. I stand, holding out a hand and we shake, but my other hand is resting firmly on the desk for support.

'Please take a seat, Mr McIntyre. If I'd realised who you were when I . . . um . . . bumped into you the other day I would have introduced myself.'

'Same here and I apologise for the fact that I'm running a little late as my breakfast meeting overran. I hope it hasn't inconvenienced you, Miss Reed?'

Looking at him now it's hard to believe this man smiles and yet I've witnessed it with my own eyes.

'Not at all. Would you like a tea or a coffee?'

'No, I'm fine, but thank you for the offer.'

I'm glad I decided to wear my best suit rather than my uniform, as I would have felt distinctly underdressed for this meeting. He's wearing an expensively tailored navy-blue suit today and he looks every inch a professional. He's carrying a slim brown leather document case, which he places on his lap.

Keep your confidence levels up, Bella, I tell myself. *You need to get him on your side and as an astute businessman he'll expect you to be on the ball. OK, you embarrassed yourself a little in front of him the other day, but accidents happen. The key to this is gentle persuasion.* He's looking at me expectantly and I push that inner voice to the back of my mind.

'Thank you so much for agreeing to this meeting,' I continue.

There's an almost imperceptible narrowing of his eyes and it feels like a red flag – does he know something that I don't?

'Meeting?' he queries. 'I was under the impression the appointment was arranged by my office as part of a familiarisation programme. This is the first time I've had a chance to view this property and I'm grateful to you for accommodating me.'

'Oh, yes – sorry!' Now I sound like a blabbering fool and I have no idea why I'm apologising. Did Randall manage to put a spin on this so Maverick wouldn't decline the offer? It's time to move quickly on. 'I wanted to personally reassure you that we have been model tenants. Prior to the official inspection, I'm sure you can see for yourself that the property has been kept in an excellent state of repair. And please, do call me Bella.'

It's obvious that wasn't the response he was expecting, and I can see that he's not sure how to respond.

'It's most kind of you . . . um . . . Bella.' There's no hint of a Scottish accent, which isn't really a surprise but, disappointingly, he doesn't have an American drawl either. However, I can see that he's not at all comfortable being on Christian name terms, which isn't exactly a promising start. Randall laboured the point that I should make it personal.

'Before we take the tour, I would like to explain that there was no intention to wantonly breach the terms of the lease. When my aunt decided to retire and handed the business down to me, everything happened very quickly. Having gone through the lease with our solicitor, we are now both fully up to speed and can only apologise for the oversight.'

He stares back at me, his expression unreadable. It's weird, as the likeness to Randall is startling. Maverick's jaw is maybe a little squarer, and he has a cute dimple in his chin, but he's equally dashing. While his hair is jet black, it's those mesmerisingly pale-blue eyes I remember so well when his arms were wrapped around me as he kept me from falling. At the time I didn't connect it, but he has his grandfather's genes. My thoughts are in total disarray. All the salient points I've rehearsed over and over ready to impress him, are now a jumble of words inside my head. If I can't regain my focus, I'm going to come across as ill-prepared, or worse – like I don't know what I'm doing.

'He did explain that it wasn't a deliberate attempt to withhold key information from MPI, to allow you to continue to operate.'

'MPI?' My brain just isn't cooperating with me right now.

'McIntyre Property Investments Limited. I gather that my grandfather's links to a charity that the previous owner here was involved in gave rise to the generous terms negotiated at that time.' He's very polite, but he makes it all sound a little suspect. 'Regretfully, I'm not at liberty to discuss any of the details with you, given that you aren't a party to the lease in question. As there seems to be a little confusion over my visit, perhaps it would be better to postpone this walk-around. One of my team will be in touch shortly to arrange for the survey to be carried out and I can accompany our surveyor to save bothering you today.'

I stare back at him, horrified that he's dismissing me as if there's nothing to discuss. A wave of heat rises up my neck, heading straight for my cheeks. I understand his businesslike approach as he has no connection to me, my aunt, or my family – but now I'm thinking that it might have been better if Randall hadn't said anything at all.

'We did advise your offices of the change of contact details. There was no intention to deceive – only naivety on our part when it comes to understanding the full implication when I inherited the business.' A sense of irritation is beginning to affect my tone of voice and what was meant as a heartfelt explanation, sounds like a quick retort. 'As my aunt now lives in the Algarve, she asked me to express her sincere apologies for the misunderstanding.'

'Well, I do hope that the Notice to Quit has been forwarded on to her to clear up the matter.'

That was uncalled for and brusque. It's a struggle to maintain an unruffled composure as instead of sounding calm, collected and businesslike, even to my ears I'm babbling a string of excuses. How can I expect him to connect with that? But I can't give up now.

'Mr McIntyre, I've worked here as a full-time employee since the day that I left college. The Highland Flower Shop continues to be at the centre of the fund-raising efforts for a very worthwhile local charity because it's a part of our family tradition, one I intend to continue. And one that your grandfather has so generously supported in many ways over the years. This is the only lease my aunt has ever entered into and it has been a steep learning curve; however, lessons have been learned and it's a mistake that won't be repeated now that I've taken over. I hope this incident hasn't jeopardised my chances to begin negotiations with MPI in my own right.'

He raises his left eyebrow and I'm beginning to think he doesn't believe what I'm saying. 'I admire the incredible negotiation skills of someone who was so unfamiliar with commercial leases and, obviously, you will need to put your interest in writing. Right,' he says, bending his arm to glance at his watch, 'I think I've taken up enough of your time.'

Any goodwill that Randall went to some trouble to conjure up has evaporated. I sound like someone who doesn't have a clue what they're doing, and now he's implying that Aunt Jane is a manipulative woman. If she were here in person, he'd see for himself that she isn't some hard-nosed businesswoman out to get the best deal going. Squaring my shoulders, I give him an unashamedly bold smile as we make eye contact. I have nothing at all to hide so it's time to change tactics.

'It seems a pity for you to make two trips, Mr McIntyre,' I reply, humbly. 'I'm sure you're very keen to get a feel for the property and it won't take long.' While I slip on my jacket he stares back at me with a slightly confused expression on his face. Just as I'm wondering whether it's better to hand him over to Mrs Mac to do the tour in case this goes from bad to worse, he stands and glances across at me as if he's in two minds.

'It's Mitchell, but I'm known as Maverick.'

He's giving me the benefit of the doubt and that's a great start. But, without warning, I'm thrown off track because that's a genuine smile he's giving me. This man is a conundrum, but the only thing I know for sure is that I need him on my side. It's a pity he's so darned intriguing, I reflect, as his eyes sweep over me in an unexpected, and decidedly unsettling way. He's curious, but is it about me, or about Randall's connection to my family?

It's a huge relief to find Maverick McIntyre a little more relaxed and receptive on the walk around than I feared might be the case. When I eventually lead him through the connecting door at the rear of the ground floor retail area, he stands there taking it in as if he wasn't expecting such a cavernous space. That's the difference between a floor plan and having boots on the ground.

Santa's Grotto looks rather sad when it's not all lit up and I walk briskly around the sleigh, which is wearing its off-season covers, to show him the cold storage room at the rear of the building. When I glance over my shoulder, I notice that he's not keeping up with me.

'So, this is it then!' he declares, and I turn to watch him as his eyes scan the room. 'The famous ride that enchants the whole of Fort William and beyond, I'm reliably told.'

Is he being sarcastic, or am I being unnecessarily sensitive? *Suck it up, Bella*, I tell myself. *You won't grovel, but there's no point at all in alienating this man.*

'It has raised tens of thousands of pounds for the charity over the years.'

'OK . . . to humour my grandfather, and because I can't lie to him when he asks whether I did, in fact, get you to show it to me, do you mind if I take a quick look under the sheeting?'

The polite thing to do would be to give him a broad smile and peel it back to reveal it to him, but that would involve getting in a couple of extra pairs of hands. And I'm so gutted by his insinuation that both my aunt, and I, are being devious that I simply stand back.

'Go ahead,' I reply, genially.

I watch as he rolls back one edge of the padded covers and the first thing that comes into view is Rudolph. Just the sight of him sends a little thrill through me – so many memories going way back and each one of them makes me smile.

'My, that's a real Scottish reindeer if ever I saw one! What does it do?' Maverick's enquiry confuses me.

'Do?'

'You know – electronics,' he asks, and there's no sense of an undertone at all. It's a genuine question.

'He pulls Santa's sleigh . . . or to be correct, gives the impression that he does,' I reply, sounding rather hesitant. 'What were you expecting?'

'Do his eyes light up? Does he talk?' Maverick seems ever so slightly disappointed when I shake my head. 'Given that there's no animation, he's still a magnificent beast – real-looking.' Maverick seems both impressed and a little underwhelmed.

'He was made in the sixties. He's a great replica and that's the whole point – few children get to see a reindeer up close, and this is the nearest thing to that.'

'I see. Realism.' His eyebrows shoot upwards as if that's not enough.

'This isn't state-of-the-art animation, with flashing lights and robotics,' I inform him.

'And the kids accept that?'

'Yes, and the adults, too.' Why is he so surprised? Rudolph is captured in mid-flight, as he boldly pulls the carriages on their magical Christmas Eve journey around the world.

As he continues to peel back the handmade padded covers that took a whole team of volunteers with sewing machines to make in sections, he doesn't look at all impressed.

'This is . . . it?'

'No . . . there's a massive, hand-painted revolving backdrop creating an enchanting, snow-filled scene as the sleigh travels around the track. Except that it isn't working properly at the moment – the sleigh that is. It's really magical when all the lights are on and Santa is at the helm, telling one of his much-loved Christmas stories.'

Even to my ears it sounds a little lame when this room looks lack-lustre without the glittering baubles and decorations, and the background music accompanied by shrieks of laughter from young and old alike. 'Trust me,' I add, emphatically, 'it's an experience no one ever forgets – like taking a ride on a steam train.'

'Hmm. I'm not big on theme parks in general, but I just expected . . . more,' he remarks.

I stare at Rudolph, who – despite his smiley, friendly face – is probably longing to kick Maverick in the shins. I know I am.

'An authentic-looking vintage reindeer is no match for a head-nodding, fibreglass robotic version with an electronic voice? I think we'll have to agree to disagree on what conjures up the true magic of a traditional Scottish Christmas.'

That was an unnecessary and rather cutting remark to make, and I'm disappointed in myself. Maverick shrugs his shoulders and now I regret momentarily losing my temper. I wander over to give him a hand to pull the covers back over the ride. It's sad to think that he's missing the point entirely and my heart sinks in my chest. This isn't some big corporation with tons of money putting on a Christmas show, it's a bunch of volunteers pitching in to raise some money while upholding a local tradition.

'This area has great potential and there's a sizeable outbuilding beyond it.' He's thinking out loud as if he's forgotten I'm here.

'Yes. Follow me.' My hopes are being squashed with each step I take.

'It's obviously under-utilised for most of the year,' he points out, as if I'm not aware of that fact. 'We do have a smaller premises we're due to begin refitting shortly, at the far end of the High Street. It could be a bit of a cost saving for you, if you find another home for the Christmas stuff. After all, it comes but once a year.'

Is he laughing at me?

'I'm determined to keep everything under one roof and this location suits us perfectly,' I reply, adamantly.

'It does? You understand a new contract would be on very different terms?'

'I do.'

I don't even bother accompanying Maverick outside. I let him wander around the yard, the parking area, the cold store – as we refer to it, because it isn't heated – and the two smaller outbuildings by the gate where we keep flowerpots, compost and packaging materials. When he reappears, I'm still adjusting the padded covers, making the sleigh snug again.

'Well, it all seems in good order, Miss . . . I mean, Bella. Thank you for the tour, it's much appreciated.'

'It's my pleasure, Maverick. And my solicitor will be in touch shortly. I'll escort you out.'

Hopefully, I've sowed the seed that this is about a local business with added value as it has close links with the community, and that will start to germinate as he mulls it over. I'm not asking for a discount, but I want him to take my interest seriously.

The minute we step back into the shop area, both Mrs Mac

and Eve stop what they're doing and glance at each other anxiously. They were busy boxing up a batch of deliveries ready for Ivor, our other van driver, to collect. Without any forewarning, Mrs Mac steps out in front of us and Eve freezes, looking panicked.

'Mebbe it's time I put the kettle on, Bella. Are ye headin' back upstairs with Mr McIntyre?'

I stare at Mrs Mac, widening my eyes to let her know that not only is she acting very strangely indeed, but our guest is ready to leave. There's no point in prolonging our conversation now when it's obvious he thinks we're done.

'No. That's very kind of you, but I'm running late, and I've already stayed longer than I'd intended,' Maverick informs her.

But she still doesn't move an inch and her eyes are darting from side to side, nervously. Something is up, but I have no idea what and now Maverick has taken a detour, stepping between the carefully arranged islands of floral arrangements to make a quick exit.

As Eve, Mrs Mac and I stare after him, Mrs Mac leans into me.

'Ye need to stop him, Bella. There's a protest goin' on outside, lassie.'

One glance at her face and I quicken my pace, just as Maverick flings open the door. Even before he steps foot outside the chanting begins and several people start waving hand-written placards.

'Save Santa's Highland Express!'

'Shame on you – The Highland Elves rule!'

'SOS! SOS! Save our Santa!'

As Maverick turns around to look at me accusingly, I groan inwardly.

'Did you really think this little ploy of yours would work? You've had a good run for your money, Miss Reed, don't you think?'

I look at him aghast. 'This . . . protest . . . has nothing at all to do with me, please believe that.'

As I rush on ahead, waving my hands in the air to encourage the small gathering to step back, I have no choice other than to address them. I recognise a few faces and it seems that the news has reached the ears of some of our volunteers.

'Please, everyone, this isn't helping. I know you mean well . . .'

As I struggle to be heard, Maverick boldly steps forward, and a hush falls over the group. 'I'm delighted to inform you that the McIntyre family will continue to support such a worthy local charity. And you can quote me on that.'

Seconds later, he disappears, leaving me to face a flood of questions as everyone gathers around expectantly. Now I'm the bad guy in all this and just like that he has completely absolved himself of any blame. If negotiations don't continue, everyone will assume I got it wrong.

I'm seeing red and it has nothing at all to do with Christmas. An angry mist descends over me – the sort that turns a normally rational and calm woman into someone ready to battle a wild bear.

'He can't just throw you out, Bella,' someone at the back of the crowd shouts out.

'Who does he think he is?' another anonymous voice joins in. 'We're not giving in – the war has only just begun!'

With that a cheer goes up and I turn around to see Mrs Mac, Eve and Holly staring out at me from behind the glass, their faces glum. If I can't turn this situation around, it's over.

'How did it go?' Aunt Jane's voice echoes in my ear. Her tone is optimistic, but her voice wavers a little.

'We didn't have time to talk business. It was just a quick walk around as Maverick hadn't seen the inside of the shop before,' I explain.

'Oh . . . that's a pity. Well, I see you've moved on and it's not "Mr McIntyre", so that's a good sign.' She seems distant and I'm not talking about the miles between us.

'Is everything all right?'

'Yes,' she says, brightly but it doesn't ring true. 'I'm literally on my way out the door, so I won't keep you. I just wanted to let you know I've had my fingers crossed. We'll speak soon, Bella. Take care!'

It's with some trepidation that I dial Mum's number, chewing my lip as I anxiously wait for her to pick up.

'Hi, my darling, how did it go?'

Oh no . . . not Mum, too.

'It was OK. Aunt Jane just called, and something is up – do you know what's going on?'

The silence is chilling.

'Ah . . . well.' Her voice falters. 'She asked me not to say anything as she doesn't want you to worry, but Grandma had a funny turn this morning and she's back in hospital.'

A chill runs down my spine. 'What sort of a funny turn?'

'They don't know for sure what caused it, so they're running some tests. Look, this is precisely why she didn't say anything. There's no point worrying until we know exactly what's going on. Your dad and I are in constant touch, and if there's any update, I'll let you know immediately. You've got enough on your plate as it is by the sound of it, Bella.'

I tilt my head back, closing my eyes. If Mum has already heard about today's little incident that doesn't bode well. It means everyone is talking about it.

'Grandma will be OK, won't she?' I ask, tentatively.

'Your grandma has a strong constitution and I spoke to her about an hour ago. She had a good moan and said they're fussing over nothing, and it was merely a dizzy spell. However, the doctor insisted on keeping her in as a precautionary measure until they know what's going on. She's in the best possible place and, to be honest, it will give your aunt Jane and Vic a bit of breathing space.'

Mum doesn't seem unduly concerned and obviously it's the sensible thing to get Grandma checked out properly.

'Thanks for being straight with me, Mum. I'd rather know

what's happening. I could tell from Aunt Jane's voice that she was in a bit of a panic. Please tell her not to fret over the shop – it's all good and negotiations are ongoing.'

'If you need anything at all, you only have to say, Bella. Your dad and I could get the committee involved if it comes to that.'

'Oh, Mum, that's very kind of you to offer but I've got this. Please just let Grandma know that I'm thinking of her.'

'Of course, I will. I would have called you later, anyway. I just thought as you've had a bit of a day, I'd give you some breathing space.'

They do say that bad news travels fast.

'It didn't quite go as planned, but I'm not disheartened.'

'I've heard he's nothing at all like his grandfather. One of those corporate types, they're saying, who—'

'It's fine, Mum. I'm not asking for any favours. All I want is a chance to negotiate a new lease at market value, so I'm not expecting any problems.'

'Everyone is horrified at the thought of The Highland Flower Shop moving location. As you say, it's not like you're looking for a favour so I can't see how they can say no to a perfectly good tenant.'

If Mum had witnessed the debacle this morning, she'd know how fragile my chances appear to be right now.

'Don't fret – you're not in this alone and I'll let you know the minute your aunt Jane gives us an update. I'm sure the negotiations will go smoothly, Bella, you deserve a bit of good luck!'

The problem is that we don't always get what we deserve, do we? I lost round one and I can't afford to lose round two.

'If this develops into an us-and-them situation, Mum, it won't bode well for my negotiations. If you and Dad really want to help, the best thing you can do is not to add to the rumours. This is a business deal and people letting off steam isn't helpful, it's detrimental – so please, if you can, that's the message we need to get out there before things escalate and there's a backlash.'

It sounds a little defeatist, but business and emotions don't mix. If I can keep it on a strictly professional footing, I might have a better chance of pulling this off.

6.

A Shocking End to a Shocking Day

By the time I'm ready to lock up the premises everyone else has gone. Going through the figures David sent over following on from our meeting, while there will be less profit to plough back into the business, it's not a total disaster. If I can find someone to help Eve, that will free up some of my time. I can look for some new commercial clients while sorting out the premises issue. If I can sign up three new contracts – or two large hotels who offer wedding packages – we could buy that third delivery van and extend the area we cover. That should boost the profits back up again even with the increased overheads.

As I turn the key in the lock and double-check the stout handle on the back door, I hear someone calling out my name. Glancing around, I spot Nick hurrying towards me.

'Hey, Nick! Holly left hours ago. She had to do the school run as her mum was late leaving work.'

He stands there shifting from one foot to the other uneasily. 'It's actually you I came to see. I don't suppose you have time to grab a coffee?'

'Look, Nick – it's great to see you but I can't be a go-between for you and Holly.'

'No . . . that wasn't why I wanted to speak to you. I have a plan and, well, I wanted to run it past you. Just to get your gut reaction.'

Unwittingly, I let out a sigh and then I feel bad. What

harm can it do to hear what he has to say? 'Come on – one quick coffee as Adam is taking me out for a meal tonight. It's been one of those days and I meant to get away a lot earlier than this.'

As we walk across the empty parking area and turn left to make our way up to the High Street, I can sense his relief. He thought I was going to say no.

'Sorry if the timing is bad, but this won't make any sense to anyone else as no one knows Holly as well as you do. And her mum won't speak to me anymore.'

'I have to say I'm not surprised, Nick, and I don't think you are either.'

We fall into step quite naturally and it's good that he still feels comfortable around me, even though he's a little embarrassed.

'It's been quite a roller coaster for you both and now it's affecting Katie.'

As he opens the door to The Wee Nook Coffee Shop, the waft of freshly milled coffee beans makes me breathe in appreciatively. I'm more than ready for a caffeine hit.

'Hi, Alice,' I call out. As we wander past the counter, she gives me a wave.

We were at school together and this is by far the most popular coffee shop in Fort William.

'Grab a table, Bella. I'll get these,' Nick says, giving me a grateful smile.

I head towards the back corner where there is a scattering of empty tables, thinking that it's easier to talk openly if there's no chance of being overheard. Once I'm seated, I watch how he banters light-heartedly with Alice and her assistant. He's a popular guy, and it's not that he's untrustworthy, but he's . . . goodness, what's the word I'm looking for . . . inconsistent. Nick, Holly and I were in the same year group at school. All the girls fawned over him as he was on the football team. He covered what I perceived to be an innate shyness with humour, and was always joking around. Unfortunately, that meant he wasn't always taken seriously and I think it affected his self-esteem at times.

'Here you go.' He grins rather nervously as he places the coffees down on the tabletop, then slumps down onto the chair opposite me. 'I'm not here to try to get you on my side, Bella, please believe that – it's gone way too far this time. But what's so frustrating is that I know what I need to do, and I've been working towards it for a while now. It's just that even if I try to explain it to Holly, she wouldn't believe me.'

'And why do you think that is?' I ask, gently.

He stirs his coffee, staring miserably down into it. 'Because it's not the first time I've made her a promise and broken it. I get it.'

Nick looks up and I shrug my shoulders – it's a sorry fact, even if it's a big step to hear him finally acknowledge it. That's not to say that he hasn't said it before, of course, but never in front of me.

'What exactly is the plan?'

He instantly brightens. 'I'm going to sell my car to pull together the deposit on a house.'

My jaw drops. 'You're serious about this?'

'I am. Admittedly, I have a hefty loan to repay as a part of it is on finance, but I'll still make some money on it. And the reason I keep cancelling on Katie is that I'm doing as much work as I can on the side. I'll also need to replace it with a sound run-around – an MPV.'

Goodness, this is quite something. 'A family car? Good for you.'

'The thing is, one of the jobs involves me working around someone else's timetable and that means dropping everything when I get the call. And it's always at the weekend. It's not like I can plan anything in advance. It'll probably take me until Christmas to scrape together enough, but I'm determined to make this happen.'

'It's good to hear you talking so positively, Nick.'

'I know Holly is struggling to make ends meet and I'm working as many hours as I can to make sure I don't lag behind on the maintenance payments anymore. I feel bad that I can't give her any extra until I have that nest egg sorted. Something tells me if I can't do it by Christmas, it'll be too late.'

'I really hope you can pull it off, for all your sakes.'

'Anyway, sorry, Bella, I should have asked if you wanted a biscuit or something? You're already late leaving, and I've delayed you.'

'No, I'm fine thanks, but this coffee is certainly hitting the spot. Alice knows I like an extra shot and only a splash of milk.'

'I'm sorry to hear you've had a tough day. The rumours are true, then – you really are getting thrown out?'

That raises a smile – Nick doesn't hold back, and I think that's why I've always got on well with him. 'Perhaps, but time will tell. I'm not giving up that easily.'

'Why do they want you out? You're not just a shop, you're a community asset.'

'It's business, Nick. The man I'm dealing with has no sentimental connections to Fort William and I . . . uh . . . didn't handle our first meeting this morning very well. It was a lesson in how not to get someone on my side.'

'Is this Maverick McIntyre you're talking about?'

I find myself frowning as I remember the conversation I had with Holly. Oh, I think the less I say, the better.

'Yes. But, as I said, it was only the first meeting. I'm sure things will improve.'

'He's a bit of a strange one and I feel sorry for him because he doesn't really know anyone,' Nick volunteers. 'Maverick is paying me by the hour to overhaul the engine of a vehicle he's doing up. That's why I'm tied up most weekends. He's the sort of guy who is willing to roll up his sleeves, which impressed me. Fair play to the guy as he's redoing the interior himself, but he's also interested in learning more about what goes on underneath the bonnet. We have a bit of a laugh, actually . . . If he could just stop doing things like calling football *soccer*, he'd fit in a lot easier in the pub.' I can see from Nick's artful grin that he's half joking.

'*Footie* would be even better if he wants to be one of the boys,' I jest. But why on earth is he going to the pub with Nick, anyway?

'I think he struggles because of his surname. Not all of his colleagues feel comfortable around him.'

'Well, I can certainly confirm that he's extremely professional,' I observe, trying not to sound disparaging.

'Yeah, from the little he's said it sounds like his background is very different. He doesn't exactly blend in – a bit too polite for me, if you know what I mean. Anyway, I'm not about to enlighten him, as my plan is reliant upon him seeing this job I'm doing through to the end. As you say, I can't afford to mess up again.'

In a way that does make me feel a bit better, knowing that it isn't just me struggling to find a way to connect with Maverick. For 'polite' though, I'd substitute the word 'correct'. I was under instruction from Randall to make it personal, but telling the truth made me appear unprofessional and weak, and that's why things deteriorated so rapidly.

'Thanks for listening, Bella, and for not stating the obvious, like why has it taken me all this time to sort myself out. I want it to work, I really do. I look around and see my mates all getting it right as they drift away and focus on their families. I guess it's time to fight for what really matters in my life and that's Katie and Holly. I've taken a lot for granted and it's time to show them both I can be their rock.'

That's a bold statement and one I sincerely hope that Nick can live up to.

'You look amazing tonight, Bella.' Adam is gazing at me across the table as we dine at Braemor Manor for the very first time.

When he asked me where I'd like to go for a special date night, I assumed cost didn't come into it. But now we're here I'm feeling nervous. When the menu arrives and it doesn't have any prices on it, I begin to panic. Adam is keeping his cool and isn't at all fazed. I dread to think how much this truly wonderful bottle of wine is costing, or the taxi to and from the restaurant.

I keep my voice low as I lean into the space between us on what is a generously sized table. 'I knew it was exclusive, Adam, but I had no idea they didn't put the prices on things. Let's keep this to the minimum, shall we? It's still a wonderful experience.'

Coming here with Randall for high tea is one thing, he's not exactly strapped for cash. For Adam, this is coming out of his hard-earned income.

'You're worth it, Bella. You've been so supportive and I'm sorry work has overtaken my life. We've been creaking along and that isn't fair on you.'

Aww . . . he's apologising for the way in which he's literally brushed off my own concerns and troubles and that's a great start. It means a lot to me.

'I'm not that hungry, so I think I'll skip the starter and go straight to the main course, what do think?'

His smile is engaging. 'I'll be guided by you. Are you enjoying the wine?'

I pick up my glass and take a tentative first sip. 'It's wonderful!' I proclaim and Adam touches my glass with his.

'Here's to us. Now that all of our problems are behind us, we can finally get on with our lives again.'

What? I'm stunned.

'Unfortunately, The Highland Flower Shop isn't out of the woods yet,' I point out, cautiously.

Adam looks at me, seemingly surprised. 'You'll find somewhere else. It's a florist's shop for goodness' sake. New rentals come on the market all the time.'

'They don't, actually. The only thing that's available within the deadline I've been given to vacate the property is half the size of what we have now. It's not viable.'

'It's a cost saving, though. What's the minimum space you need to keep everything ticking over if you ditch the Christmas stuff?'

I freeze. *Ditch the Christmas stuff?* I gulp down the huge lump that is rising up in my throat. 'Do you mean Santa's Grotto and The Christmas Cave?'

'Yes. You earn nothing at all from the Grotto and you pass over a chunk of the profits from The Christmas Cave. Who buys Christmas baubles in spring and summer, anyway?'

I clear my throat rather awkwardly. 'Quite a few visitors, actually.'

'Take my advice, Bella. Just because your aunt Jane had a bee in her bonnet about keeping her father's obsession going, you don't have to jump on the bandwagon too. You have some lovely memories and that should be enough. It's time to drive the business forward now that you're in charge and you can't afford to let anything hold you back. Now – we're here and we might as well make the most of it. But first I'd like to make a toast.'

My heart starts beating twice as fast as I look at him through tearful eyes. He has no idea that he's upset me. As our glasses touch, I can't bear this and that inner voice pipes up, *No, not now, Adam – not when you've just stamped all over my feelings like that.*

'Goodbye to the problems of the past – here's to a bright new future! Now that the streamlining is over, my job is secure for the foreseeable future. And you're about to cut out the deadwood and see that place start turning an even bigger profit. Maybe we can look forward to having a holiday home in Faro, so we can pop over and visit your grandma and aunt, and soak up some of that sunshine to recharge our batteries.'

That's it? Our special date night is all about buying a place in the sun?

My heart sinks into my stomach. Is it relief – or anger – I'm feeling at the way he has misread what's going on between us?

'And this sort of special meal out needn't be a once-a-year highlight,' he adds. 'I have no doubt at all that in five years' time we'll be living in an executive house and dining at prestigious places like this will be a regular indulgence. Now that's worth celebrating, isn't it?'

I'm sitting here feeling foolish – Adam has no idea whatsoever about what's important to me. It's certainly not a holiday home on the Algarve, and as he's making it quite clear that he's happy with our relationship as it stands, I'm reeling. If I could wave a magic wand, I'd spirit myself away . . . anywhere but here, sitting across the table from a man who has literally just ended our relationship. And when I tell him it's over, he won't have a clue about what went wrong between us.

Booking into a hotel late at night isn't easy, even though the sign outside says it is open 24/7. After waiting in reception for almost twenty minutes, the desk clerk finally appears.

He looks at me with an ominously raised eyebrow. 'You don't have an actual reservation?' he asks, as if that was an unusual occurrence, which I'm sure it's not.

'No. I'm travelling and too tired to drive any further tonight.' It's also too late to knock on Holly's door, because I can't risk disturbing Katie. And there is no way I'm going to turn up at my parents' house and face an inquisition. My nerves are frazzled. I left Adam at the restaurant staring at me, absolutely speechless for the first time ever.

'You're leaving me? But why?'

I could have cheerfully reeled off an entire list of reasons and I realised they stemmed back almost to day one of our relationship. But I also knew that it was unfair to put the blame on him, because I'd gone along with it. Every step of the way. Making excuses for Adam when he was simply being selfish and pushing aside my own worries while I focused on him. His moods. His work problems. His demands. Tonight, I woke up and saw our relationship for what it is. Adam isn't the man for me. The problem is – what on earth do I do now?

7.

Life Lesson No. 1: You're Only as Good as the Team Supporting You

'You really do need to tell your parents that you've left Adam before word gets out,' Holly declares adamantly.

We're sitting opposite each other in her sitting room after a long day at work, our feet up on the coffee table as we sip our hot drinks.

'I know,' I sigh. 'I thought a double espresso might help before I make the call.'

'You're going to ring them?' she gasps, reproachfully.

'Would you want to handle something like this face to face with your mum?'

'I guess not. But this won't come as a complete surprise. I mean, they know how demanding Adam can be at times . . . don't they?'

A look of guilt flashes over my face. 'I let Adam make me feel that my problems don't count because they're of my own making,' I confess and am dismayed to see Holly's eyes widen.

'Are you telling me that they have no idea at all what he's put you through?' Now she sounds incredulous. 'His problems are never his fault, but yours are?'

Hearing Holly's take on it I wonder why I didn't walk out a long time ago. 'He's arrogant, Bella,' she continues. 'He's always right and everyone else is wrong.'

Even I can see that now. 'What I perceived to be his

sensitivity, wasn't that at all – he's a moaner. He didn't feel the pain those people he was firing were going through, he was simply put out that he had to go through the motions of appearing to be sympathetic. Emotional stuff drains him because the only person he really cares about, as it turns out, is himself.'

Holly frowns, giving me a sympathetic look that makes my heart sink. 'Adam does the *poor me* thing, so well, Bella. It's manipulative.'

'And, as it turns out, I wasn't the only one comforting him. Do you know what he said to me when I told him I was done and it's over between us?'

'Well, I'm betting he wasn't happy . . .' Holly's reaction is full of disdain.

'Oh, he was shocked all right. His exact words were: "It was just a one-off thing with Lynsey – I made a mistake, that's all." And I couldn't quite believe my ears.'

The sharp intake of breath from Holly almost makes her spill her cappuccino. 'What? He's been carrying on with Lynsey McGregor?'

'Yes. Sadly, that was the first I knew about it. If he hadn't said anything, I'd still be in the dark. But I've had this unsettling feeling for a while now. All those late nights stuck in the office poring over the paperwork and deciding who would go and who would stay. And now it's obvious that it was a cover-up so that the two of them could spend some illicit time together.'

'No wonder you walked out. What a horrible way to end your relationship. Unless he thought you'd be jealous and fight for him.'

She's trying to make me feel better and not like the woman whose man has been cheating on her because he thought he could get away with it.

'No, he didn't say a word until after I'd blurted out the fact that I'm no longer in love with him. He assumed I'd heard a rumour about what was going on behind my back and I was simply retaliating. He was wrong on that front. In fact, when he made his admission, I almost laughed out loud because I thought he was joking at first!'

'Geez, Bella, you're taking this remarkably well. Lynsey . . . who would have thought?'

I nod my head, angrily.

'The managing director's PA, no less. Adam has an eye on the future, and he doesn't intend to be the assistant HR manager for much longer. I doubt she'll even realise he's using her to glean information. When the opportunity presents itself, Adam will make sure he's in the right place at the right time.'

'Oh, Bella, that's . . .'

'Illuminating?'

'Appalling is the word that comes to mind. The bast—'

'No, I allowed this to happen, Holly. Fate is giving me a nudge. But do you know what – I really don't care. But when I tell Mum and Dad they won't understand, how can they?'

'Oh, Bella . . . that's awful!'

'They'll assume I'm being rash. I have until the fifth of December to find new premises for the business if I can't persuade Maverick McIntyre to offer me a new lease. The fact that I'm homeless doesn't exactly make me look like a woman who is in control of her life, does it?'

Holly bursts out laughing. 'How can you go from Miss Sensible to Miss Placed, overnight?'

Even I chuckle at that canny observation. '*Misplaced*, I like it! But it's all my fault and I know it. The thing about having an epiphany is that suddenly you see your mistakes with a clarity you haven't had before. If I can't learn from this, then I'm a fool.'

Holly frowns. 'No, you're not a fool, Bella. You're . . . compassionate. Sometimes you give too much and take too little.'

Adam lashed out at me, saying I was difficult to live with and sulky at times. I wasn't sulking, I'd just given up trying to get him to listen to me. How can you take anything if the other person isn't happy to give?

'I never thought something like this could happen to me, Holly, and that's a sobering thought. It's time to take control of my life.'

'Goodness . . . look out world, hell hath no fury like a woman determined to rule by her head and put her emotions to one side. Do you have any advice for me?'

Oh. I wasn't expecting that, and I look at her in earnest.

'Don't give up on Nick, Holly – I won't say any more than that, and I'm not suggesting whatever plans you're considering for the future should be put on hold. But he has a good heart, and that means something – believe me. When it comes to crunch time, just take that into consideration.'

Giving advice when your own world is falling apart around your ears probably doesn't count for much, but Holly is like a sister to me. Nick will always be the first love of her life – maybe the only one, who knows? He's made some big mistakes, but I've sown the seed with Holly not to rule him out completely. It's up to her if she listens.

'Let's make a pact,' I continue with gusto. 'Apparently, what you say and what you think is what you manifest going forward. I see you, Katie and me smiling, happy and having the best fun ever as we dance beneath a glittering seventies disco ball singing a golden oldie Christmas song at the top of our lungs. Goodness – it must be karaoke then, as you know I never remember the words to anything. By Christmas we're both going to turn our lives around and make our dreams come true – are you up for it?'

Holly leans forward and we chink cups.

'What harm can it do to hope for the best? Although, I think it might take a Christmas miracle, or two, to get us on the right track, don't you?'

'Hey, I'm finally free and it feels good. As far as I'm concerned, anything is possible if we work at it.'

Holly shakes her head as I sip from the mug cradled

between my hands. 'My nan always told me that "A wise person is eager to rise and ready to learn whenever they fall. But a foolish person always assumes they know best, and that's their downfall." It isn't just my life I could mess up, but Katie's too. If you ever feel I need a reality check, you will tell me, won't you?'

My eyes begin to smart. 'Oh, Holly, of course I will! And likewise, I know you'll jump in if you think I'm in danger of losing sight of what matters. Next time a man walks into my life I want you to be my voice of reason. And I promise I will listen to what you have to say.'

'You got it! And I'll try my hardest not to cut off all contact with Nick – as long as he sticks to the new arrangement. Katie comes first, Bella, because Nick has let us down so many times.'

Well, it's a lifeline, and hopefully Nick will grab it. And as for Adam, I hope he finds what he's looking for, because you don't cheat on someone you love. Did he sense that the end was coming for us? Or did he think he could simply get away with it? I guess I'll never know for sure now and, in all honesty, I no longer care.

'Bella – I can't believe what I'm hearing!' The shock reflected in Mum's voice on speakerphone fills me with unease.

'I'm sorry to break the news like this, really I am, but I wanted you to know what's going on. From tomorrow, I'll be staying with Holly for a few days while I consider my options.' It only took two nights in a hotel for me to cave in and accept Holly's offer to use the sofa bed in her sitting room.

'But . . . but . . . walking out on Adam . . . and that lovely house you share . . . I'm . . . I'm lost for—' Mum is casting around, struggling to form a sentence.

It's only natural that my parents are in shock but I'm still coming to terms with the fact that I've been living a lie. And I have no idea for how long, so I just need to make this conversation as short as possible.

'What your mother is trying to say is, um . . .' Dad continues, sounding like he too is reeling. That surprises me because I always feel he's on edge around Adam. 'The thing is, Bella, it's usually best not to act in anger – I mean, in the heat of the moment.' Now he's choosing his words carefully and I can only imagine the frantic eye contact going on between them.

Mum takes over. 'Things can get blown out of proportion, Bella. It might be a good idea to take a break, have a few days away from each other so you can both calm down and then meet up again to talk it through calmly.'

They both think this is a knee-jerk reaction on my part, but I've never been more clear-headed in my life. 'I'm done, and I couldn't be sorrier to spring this on you like this, but the warning signs have been there for quite a while. It was just easier to ignore them with everything else going on around us. I appreciate it's hard for you to understand, given that I've been keeping my feelings to myself, but it's over. In my heart I've known that for a while.'

They both begin speaking at the same time and there's a short pause until Mum's voice fills the silence.

'You're under enormous pressure at work, Bella,' she replies, softly. 'We understand that – everyone does. But Adam hasn't had it easy, either. We're here for you no matter what happens, but please don't rush into anything you might regret at a later stage.'

'Thanks, Mum – sorry to spoil your evening.'

'Is this common knowledge?' She sounds panicked. 'If anyone asks about it, what do you want us to say?'

'I'm sure word will eventually get out and when it does . . . well, the least said the better. These things happen.'

'Understood. We're here if you need a listening ear, Bella, you know where to come.'

Given that is the last thing they were expecting to hear, how else would they react? I could reel off a dozen examples of why Adam and I shouldn't be together, things

I've ignored and come to accept as normal behaviour from him. Maybe he can level the same thing back at me, I'm not saying it's all his fault. I've been making excuses for Adam's behaviour for so long now it's become second nature. Now I look back, it seems I'd become stuck in a rut, and I think the reason is that I knew our relationship was failing.

'Please don't worry about me. The truth is that I'm not in love with Adam anymore and that's something I can't change.'

'Well, it sounds like your mind is made up. We won't say a thing. Just take care.'

Sometimes the truth hurts, but strangely enough I'm not the one hurting.

I've called the entire team up to the office for an end of Friday meeting to give them an update. Everyone is looking at me expectantly and I'm having to choose my words very carefully.

'Sorry, guys – right.' I turn to face everyone, knowing that I don't really have any good news to tell them, but they deserve to know where we stand. 'The unfortunate little episode that ended up cutting short Maverick McIntyre's visit means I didn't really get a chance to press my interest in signing up a new lease on this property. The next step is to formalise that via my solicitor.'

As I gaze around it's clear there is some general unease. 'It's important that we don't add fuel to the fire by unwittingly giving out information which is commercial in confidence and may jeopardise future negotiations.'

Rodric clears his throat. 'We hear what you're sayin', Bella, but the rumours are rife. Most of them hecklin' him that day were volunteers on the Christmas rota, apparently, so word is out there.'

'Look, this isn't about pointing a finger – if it was then I'd be first in line. What this has taught me is that an emotional outburst from well-meaning supporters doesn't help our cause.'

'Well, he wasn't exactly receptive from the moment he stepped through the door,' Holly declares, vehemently. 'Maybe it let him see that the locals are prepared to have their voices heard. That isn't good news for McIntyre Property Investments Limited, is it?'

Oh dear . . . Holly might have a little axe to grind there, given what I now know about Nick's plan. If she knew why he was working all the hours he can get, she wouldn't feel quite so resentful and abandoned.

'I've heard that he has big plans, so getting someone else in here could be just the start of it,' Ivor joins in.

I hold up my hands to stop anyone else saying their piece because this is exactly what I don't want to happen.

'Like it or not, when I took over from Aunt Jane it broke the terms of the original lease. I have one aim, which is to negotiate a new contract with Maverick McIntyre. However, if he feels I'm trying to get public opinion behind me to force his arm, then all is lost. There is at least one other interested party, as I think everyone here will have heard on the grapevine. I need you all to present a united front, which is that talks are ongoing and there are no axes to grind.'

The silence is gut-wrenching. They already think all is lost. I glance at Mrs Mac, hoping she'll come to my rescue and fill the void with a few positive words. She takes the hint.

'It's nae good goin' into it thinkin' the worst. We have your back, Bella, and it's a reminder that we all need to watch what we say. The rumours will soon die down if there's nothin' to fuel them. Let's focus on the best possible outcome – that we're here to stay.'

'Thank you, Mrs Mac. It's obviously going to put a dent in the profits and I will be looking to attract a few new clients. The plan was to get a third van, but that isn't going to be possible for a while, I'm afraid. The extra work will impact us all, but rest assured that if we need additional manpower, as long as the revenue is coming in, I'll be straight on it.'

And just like that the mood changes.

'I've no problem workin' longer hours,' Rodric declares, looking across at Ivor and giving him a nod.

'I second that,' Ivor instantly responds with a big grin on his face. 'And Rodric and I have been talking about the daily delivery schedules. It's a job we could easily sort between us at the end of each working day. It'd save Mrs Mac checking with us before she prints them out each morning.'

All eyes turn in her direction – that's a brave suggestion and I wonder how Mrs Mac will react, but to everyone's surprise she merely chuckles. 'Yer our knights of the road and yer best placed to factor in the unknown – like roadworks and bottlenecks. Now we're talkin' time savin' and that bodes well for us all. And, Bella, if you need me to jump on the phone and do some canvassin', I've a few contacts in some of the bigger hotels – albeit a bit further away.'

'You get 'em signed up and we'll make sure the deliveries get there on time, eh, Ivor?' Rodric replies with a grin.

Holly glances across at Eve. 'I know I'm mainly upstairs in The Christmas Cave, but when it's quiet and Mrs Mac doesn't need me, I wondered whether . . .'

'Whether Holly could give me a hand,' Eve continues.

I stare from one to the other of them, in surprise. I had no idea Holly was interested in getting involved on the floristry side.

'Wow – you guys amaze me. Aunt Jane would be so proud if she were here today. Thank you all for your wonderful ideas and suggestions. There's no "I" in team, is there? And if we do this, we do it together. As for me, well, I'm moving into unknown waters, and I promise you that I won't back down easily. If I need to grit my teeth while turning on the charm, I will!' That raises an instant ripple of laughter. 'But I hope it won't come to that. So, while we gear up to do battle, to the outside world everything is just fine, right?'

We all raise our mugs in unison and Rodric's voice booms out, 'Here's tae us; wha's like us? Gey few, and they're a' deid.'

I love it when Rodric slips into his broader Scottish accent, and it puts a huge smile on all our faces.

'Tae us!' I confirm. The only way to ensure we get through this is to make sure I have a backup plan. Belt and braces save the day, as Pop would have said.

8.

Falling Fast and the Ground is Hurtling Towards Me

I had a missed call from Randall and when I finally get a chance to phone him back it's obvious he's in the middle of something. The sound of riotous applause in the background threatens to drown out his voice.

'Sorry,' he whispers, 'tricky moment. We'll speak shortly.'

As I'm about to put my phone down it pings and my stomach churns when I see it's a text from Adam. I've been ignoring his calls and he's getting desperate.

> This is ridiculous, Bella. I'm sorry for what I did. I didn't mean to hurt you. I can't let you go like this, and I won't give up until we've spoken face to face. If you aren't here by 8 tonight I'm coming to find you.

I intended to work late as I can get a lot done in a couple of hours when I'm here on my own without any interruptions.

> Fine. I'll be there but I can't say what time.

Seconds later it pings again but this time it's a message from Randall.

> I'm heading back from a chamber of commerce

> presentation at Claremont House. Is it possible to meet
> somewhere to catch up?

It makes sense to get together with Randall en route to see Adam as it will save me doubling back, but it means leaving now. Maybe what Randall has to say will give me a boost – I can certainly do with some good news before I face a confrontation.

> How about The Old Grouse Inn? It'll take me twenty minutes
> to get there.

Randall responds immediately.

> Perfect. See you soon.

As I dial Holly's number, I quickly gather my things together with my free hand. Slinging my bag over my shoulder, I hurry downstairs.

'Hi, Bella, I was about to call you. I had to drop Katie off at Nick's and I'm on my way home to start dinner.'

'I won't be back until late, I'm afraid. Adam wants to talk.'

'Oh, I see. Poor you – I bet you just want to slip into a hot bath with a glass of chilled wine after the day you've had. Can't you put him off?'

'No. There's no point. It's clear he still has something to say but he's wasting his breath. I have no idea how long it will take, so don't wait up. I'll creep in quietly, I promise!'

She sighs. 'Oh, Bella, this couldn't have come at a worse time, could it?'

'It's the price I'm paying for letting things slide. And I will sort out some alternative accommodation very soon, I promise.'

'Hey, friends help each other out and Katie loves having

you around. Take care and don't let him get to you, Bella.'

'I won't,' I reply, sounding a lot more blasé than I feel. But in all honesty, I'm more concerned about what Randall has to say because I need it to be constructive.

The Old Grouse Inn is a little off the beaten track, but it's one of those cosy old pubs that serves good, old-fashioned bar food and snacks. It's popular with ramblers and dog walkers, and all are made welcome. As I pull into the car park, I immediately spot Randall sitting alone at a table on the front lawn. As I get out there's a bit of a nip in the air and I grab my jacket from the back seat.

He waves and smiles at me as I approach, and I find myself troubled at the thought of admitting that I messed up the meeting with his grandson.

'Sorry, I hit traffic coming out of town,' I explain.

'It's not a problem, Bella. The waiter will be out in a bit, I told him I was waiting for someone. What would you like to drink?'

It's obvious I've come straight from work and Randall looks like he's come from a formal business meeting. He wears his suit well, but then it probably cost more than my entire wardrobe of clothes.

'A soft drink would be perfect, thank you.'

Randall looks at me intently. 'I hope you didn't mind me suggesting we meet up, but I prefer to talk in person. How did it go with Maverick?'

I'm surprised he hasn't already heard, and I find myself shifting around uneasily in my seat, as I wonder where to begin.

'What can I get you?' The waiter appears and Randall orders for us while I wrestle with my conscience.

As soon as we're alone again, Randall turns to face me.

'In short, it was a bit of a disaster, I'm afraid.'

There's no point dressing it up, because at some point he'll hear it from Maverick himself.

'It was?' He seems put out. 'I thought I did a pretty good job of discreetly bringing up the subject one evening over dinner. Fiona went overboard a little, talking about her memories of taking his father for a ride on Santa's Highland Express. But it did him good to hear it.'

Knowing that makes me feel even worse.

'For whatever reason we didn't get off to a great start and it went downhill from there. To be fair, he was in a bit of a hurry and I assumed that after I showed him around we'd head back to the office for a more relaxed chat.'

'Here you go.' The waiter is back, and he deftly places the highball glasses in front of us while balancing his tray with three other drinks on it.

'Lovely, thank you!' Randall tips his head in acknowledgement.

I'm so thirsty I could almost down it in one, but I take a quick sip before continuing.

'The thing is . . . as we were looking around the floristry section a group of people appeared and there was some chanting involved.'

'Protestors?' Randall's reaction is one of surprise.

'Yes, and it was as much a shock to me, as it was to Maverick. He was very polite, but he thought I'd arranged it. I can see why he might think that, but it's not my style.'

Randall grimaces.

'And worse, they heckled him outside. I was standing in the doorway at that point, trying to calm things down and he was kind enough to address them and say that the McIntyre family would continue to support the charity, or words to that effect. It was a total nightmare.'

Randall sits, sipping his drink and frowning. 'That explains why he's been avoiding me.'

'Apparently, word on the street is that a surveyor has been into the shoe repairer's looking at options for knocking the two retail units into one. I'm afraid it doesn't take long for rumours to spread and most of the group were volunteers on the Christmas rota, or friends of the charity. Please believe me when I say neither I, nor any of my staff, were responsible for arranging the demonstration.'

'Dear me. I've not heard anything about combining the two premises.'

We lapse into silence. It's a gorgeous September evening with signs of autumnal colour all around us as the leaves start to turn various shades from pale yellow through to burnt orange. It's very pleasant sitting here, watching the birds happily flitting around in the trees. And yet here I am, feeling like I've messed up.

'It's not your fault, Bella. With two MPI directors on the committee it's possible this might have been sparked by someone expressing a personal concern. In fact, even at this luncheon I attended today an old friend asked if the rumours were true. That's why I called you, to see if you had any news. I had no idea a surveyor had been commissioned and that needs looking into.'

I can see by his furrowed brow that this is not the way he hoped it would go.

'I did pass on Aunt Jane's apologies to Maverick and explained that it's the only lease she's ever dealt with. I said it was an oversight, but he pointed out that he was unable to discuss the lease with me, anyway.'

Randall sits back in his chair, in a reflective mood. 'It's a shame when you get off on the wrong foot like that, isn't it? It's fair to assume he's under pressure back at the office and feels like his hands are tied.'

'All I want is the chance to negotiate a new lease. I've asked my solicitor to draft a letter to that effect so that we can go over the terms. Obviously, there will be quite a step up in the rent, but I'm prepared for that and my money is as good as anyone else's. Plus, we have a track record and we're a well-established company. I did remind him of that.'

Randall's lips twitch. 'If that was a sales pitch, it was very robust. And you're right – so you're not interested in the smaller premises, even if it's possible to find something close by that might house the sleigh ride?'

I'm sleeping on my friend's sofa bed and while I sort out my personal life the last thing I need right now is for my business – or any part of it – to be homeless too.

'It wouldn't be my first choice, Randall, in all honesty, as I have plans to expand the business. I can't do that from much smaller premises.'

'Then I'll see if I can find out who Maverick is talking to while you get that letter organised. It will formally establish your interest, at the very least. As soon as I know more, I'll be in touch, hopefully on Monday.'

'Thank you, Randall. I appreciate what you're doing for me. It breaks my heart to think that after all these years I could be the one who fails to keep the sleigh ride going. But please don't risk any upset, you know . . . between you and Maverick. I'm not giving up, but I also know that nothing is guaranteed.'

He raises his glass and I follow suit. 'Here's to success, because failure is not an option.'

Amen to that!

'Can you stop doing that so we can talk?' Adam demands, angrily.

I continue packing the suitcase lying open on the bed in front of me.

'I'm listening to every word you're saying and when you run out of steam, it's my turn.'

'I'm trying to apologise and explain that it wasn't a full-blown affair with Lynsey . . . she knows a lot about what's going on in the company. A casual drink just got out of hand, that's all. I was really stressed and not thinking straight.'

I laugh, deprecatingly. 'Wow – I wish Lynsey was here because I think she'd be devastated at the way you used her. For the price of a drink not only did you get some information to further your career, but you got her to feel sorry for you – so sorry she forgot you had a significant other waiting for you at home.'

'Bella, you *are* my significant other,' he states, emphatically. 'It won't happen again I promise you!'

The case is full to bursting and I start the delicate task of squashing it down a little as I zip it up.

'I know it won't, Adam, because we're done. I told you – I don't love you anymore and that's the truth. Blame me if you like, because it's been increasingly obvious over the last few months that our relationship has become very one-sided.'

'But you can't leave me – we have a mortgage together.'

That elicits a snort from me as I stifle an explosive laugh. 'Sell it. Do whatever you need to do, but don't hang around. I have no idea how long I'm going to be able to continue paying my half.'

After heaving the suitcase off the bed, I forage around in the wardrobe to retrieve a holdall.

'Is that a threat?'

'No, it's the sad truth. Defaulting on the monthly payment isn't going to help either of us, is it?'

He recoils as if I've slapped him. This is his wake-up call, and he finally realises I'm serious.

'You aren't content with ruining a perfectly good business that your aunt built up over many years, now you're trashing our relationship too?'

As I kneel to begin selecting a variety of footwear from the bottom of the wardrobe, I glance at him over my shoulder. 'No, you *trashed* our relationship, Adam, when you had sex with Lynsey. I might not have known what was going on but I sure as hell knew that every day we were growing further and further apart. Until the day I realised there was nothing left between us worth salvaging.'

'Well, I'm not about to give this place up, so don't think you're dropping a bombshell if that's how you choose to exact your revenge!' His eyes bore into me, his jaw clenched.

'Please yourself, Adam. In which case, simply get a market valuation and pay me my half of the equity. If you'd rather I sort that out and contact the mortgage company, it's not a problem. I think I have everything I need for now. Let me know when it's convenient to come back and collect the rest of my things.'

The holdall isn't heavy, and it only takes me a minute or two to carry it down to the front door. When I return to the bedroom his back is towards me and he's staring out of the window. I groan a little as I lift the suitcase off the bed, but he doesn't move a muscle.

The moment he hears the click as I turn the latch on the front door he races downstairs.

'I was going to ask you to marry me,' he calls out, as if he can't believe what's happening.

I draw to a halt, turning to face him.

'And what a terrible mistake that would have been for us both, Adam. A piece of paper doesn't change anything, does it? When things fall apart it's best to accept it and move on. I wish you well, I really do, and let me know if you want me to sort out the house.'

You know that moment when you suddenly get a surge of energy? Well, I manage to walk down the path wheeling the suitcase in one hand and lugging the bulky holdall in the other. Standing tall, with my shoulders back – despite the fact that my muscles are complaining – I feel in control.

'Good luck sorting out the mess your life's in, Bella,' Adam calls after me. 'I'll pay you off and then sit back and watch you throw the money away just to keep the shop going. A business studies diploma doesn't turn you into an entrepreneur. You're just a glorified flower arranger!'

Better that than a cheat and a bully, I mutter to myself as I walk around to the rear of my car. He's still watching me from the doorway, the light from the hallway filtering out into the front garden. I don't feel sad, I feel relieved and that tells me I'm making the right decision.

As I drive away my mind is racing. 'You did it, Bella,' I say out loud with a sense of pride. That inner voice takes over. *Every mistake you make holds a valuable lesson if you stop to analyse it. From here on in you look to yourself to make things happen, lady, because it's down to you to make your own happy ending.*

There is no knight in shining armour waiting in the wings. Even someone as kind and generous as Randall can't perform a miracle. It's time to take control of my life by being proactive, not reactive.

9.

Time is Money

'Are you sure this is wise . . . given that everythin' is up in the air, lassie?' Mrs Mac places her hand on my arm, giving it a comforting squeeze as if it makes no sense to her at all.

'I spent all weekend mulling it over. Eve is under pressure because I'm constantly getting pulled away to sort the bigger issues. Holly is being a great help and she's happy to learn, but we need another full-time florist so I can step back and focus on the commercial pressures.'

Mrs Mac looks stunned.

'Step back? I thought spendin' so much of your time in the office was a temporary thing.'

'This is just between us for now, Mrs Mac, but I'm worth more to the business being a manager right now, than a hands-on florist. I'm going to put my energy into pulling together a backup strategy, because even though I have a plan I'm not sure everything is going to fall neatly into place.'

'But that's an extra salary to find each month on top of the rent increase. I worry about the pressure you're puttin' yourself under, Bella – we all do. All I'm sayin' is do you really think it's the best solution?'

'I do. William Taggart is going to send a formal letter to the landlords today notifying them of my interest to start negotiations. I have a few things to sort before my appointment with Brisley House Hotel – you did well to get us a foot in the door, so keep everything crossed for me. And I have the small problem of a sleigh ride that isn't fit for purpose. I need some expert advice and a rough idea of what it's going to cost to repair. I'll be gone for several hours, I'm afraid. I was wondering if you could ring the recruitment agency and see if they have any suitable candidates before I let Eve know what I'm proposing. It'll mean a promotion for her if she's happy to take the lead, but that's a conversation for another day.'

'It would save a fee if we could find someone ourselves.'

'With enough experience?' I query, thinking that's unlikely.

'Ursula might be interested. I heard on the grapevine that she's looking for a wee job as she misses the company.'

Ursula Graham, Aunt Jane's former boss and long-time friend, retired last year from the garden centre at Moldern when it changed hands. It's where, a long time ago, she taught Aunt Jane everything she knows.

'You think she'd be interested? We could be very flexible with her hours.'

'Leave it to me. She's a grand old dame and I'll see if I can sweet-talk her.'

'You're a star, Mrs Mac – what would I do without you?'

'Bella, what a lovely surprise – why didn't you let me know you were popping in? You've just missed Dad and he'll be so disappointed. Why aren't you at work?'

Mum's words come tumbling out, as I step into the hallway. I've been parked up a few doors down on the other side of the road, patiently waiting for Dad to leave. Twice a week he meets up with a group of his ex-colleagues for a pub lunch and today he left a little later than usual.

'I'm on my way back from seeing a potential new client. Sorry I missed Dad, but as he's not here perhaps we can have a little chat – just the two of us.'

Mum is already leading me into the kitchen, and I pull out one of the island stools to take a seat, as you can't visit this house at lunchtime without being fed.

'Actually, I'm glad you called in. Your dad is getting himself worked up about this problem with the lease. I did pass on your message that it's not helpful if people start taking sides, but he went off on one of his rants down at the pub, apparently. When The Highland Elves committee get together, there's obviously a lot of ill-feeling at what's happening, too.'

I watch as Mum effortlessly throws together an impromptu lunch, while voicing her concerns. Multitasking is part of her nature and that's where I get it from. Dad, on the other hand, puts his focus on one thing at a time, and at the moment, I fear, he might not be helping my cause.

'That's part of the problem, Mum.'

'Then talk to me, Bella, because I can't help you if I don't know what's really going on.'

I tell her about meeting up with Randall – carefully leaving out any reference to Aunt Jane but indicating that he's on my side. I also left out the intel Randall shared with me when he rang about an hour ago. The other company interested in the lease have a considerable budget and the location is exactly what they're after. He couldn't say more than that and he apologised for having to deliver bad news.

'Maverick McIntyre will simply go with the best offer on the table and I'm not the only interested party. He won't have a choice, it's not a family business anymore and Randall has no say in the matter.'

'Oh, right . . . we've all made a few assumptions along the line, haven't we? Your dad thinks Maverick is out to "make a few extra bucks" as he so uncharitably put it. To all intents and purposes, he's a newcomer so a lot of the tension will probably go over his head.'

Mum's take on it astounds me. She's able to stand back

and look at the facts.

'Here you go,' Mum says as she places a mini buffet on a plate in front of me. 'You look like you need a little feeding up. Dare I ask what's going on with you and Adam? Any further developments?'

'Why did I ever think he was right for me, Mum? Adam cheated on me with Lynsey McGregor! He says it was just the once, but I don't believe him.'

Mum rolls her eyes as she takes a seat opposite me. 'I had my doubts from the start, Bella, I'll be honest.'

I look at her aghast. 'Why didn't you say something?'

'Because I might have been proved wrong. And would you have listened?'

I pause for thought, as I pop a sliver of smoked salmon on a bite-sized cracker into my mouth.

'Sadly, the answer to that is a firm *no*. But the upside is,' I continue, giving her a beaming smile, 'that he's agreed to get the house valued and he'll pay me half the equity we hold in it to buy me out.'

'That's my girl. It's not how hard you fall, but how quickly you bounce back up. I could tell your mind was made up – your dad will stew over it for a while longer though.'

'That's partly why I'm here.'

'Ah . . . of course!'

Mum is no one's fool – she realises I waited until Dad left for a reason. 'I've been to see an estate agent this morning. I'm going to rent a one-bed flat over one of the shops in Fort William.'

Her face falls. 'Bella – you can always come and stay here. Your old room is just as you left it.'

'That's really kind of you, but it's more convenient if I'm in the centre of town. While I was there I also asked for a ballpark figure on what he thinks the house might achieve if it went on the market in the next couple of weeks.'

'You don't trust Adam?'

'It's not that . . . he knows I'll expect confirmation of the valuation on an official letterhead before we agree a figure.'

'Whatever happens, don't go getting an overdraft, or anything like that, my girl. Whatever you need, Bella, it's there for you – I thought your dad and I had made that clear.'

How do I broach this without causing offence?

'I appreciate that, Mum, I really do, but everything is covered.'

Mum stops, her fork halfway to her mouth. 'Oh, Bella . . . even with a big hike in the rent? It's so unfair. That's why your dad is so angry because Maverick is nothing at all like his philanthropic grandfather.'

'The McIntyre family don't own the company any longer, Mum. Maverick has a boss to answer to and it's just business. Please trust me when I say I know what I'm doing.'

'OK, I hear what you're saying.'

'Thank you for understanding that this is my fight, Mum, but it's not really a war. Now all we need to resolve is the problem of Dad, bless him! I'm thinking that he needs a distraction.'

Mum pops the fork into her mouth, her eyes lighting up as I continue.

'What if Dad had something else on which to focus his attention? I'm hopeful that my share in the equity of the house will cover the cost of getting Santa's Highland Express restored to full working order. It's something I want to do to acknowledge my small part in continuing Pop's dream. He loved kids, because he was a big kid himself all his life and that's what I remember about him. The laughter, the fun and the love!'

'Aww . . . Bella, that touches my heart!'

'Would you mind dropping a hint to Dad that it would take a huge weight off my shoulders if someone could get a firm quote for the restoration costs and a timescale? It can't be done at the shop, obviously, even if we don't end up moving.'

Mum looks at me aghast. 'Gosh . . . that's a harsh reality check.'

'Oh, that's the worst-case scenario, believe me. But if I plan for the worst, anything else is a bonus, right?'

'Spoken like a real trouper. Dad will be more than happy to throw himself into this and it will make him feel good knowing he's taking some of the pressure off you.'

There's one thing left to discuss, but I'm loath to raise it – fearful I might not get the response I'm hoping for.

'And, uh, how is Grandma doing?'

Mum shrugs her shoulders. 'She's foxing them all. The tests continue, but at least she's back home with your aunt. She has a follow-up appointment at the hospital next week.'

'Aunt Jane said it was a funny turn, but what does that mean, exactly?'

'Initially, they thought it was a heart problem, which was why they rushed her into A & E. Her breathing was laboured, and she was struggling to take in even quite a shallow breath. I think it frightened her a little, but as soon as they gave her an oxygen mask, she quickly perked up again. All the tests they've run have come back just fine, so now they're scratching their heads.'

'It's a case of wait and see what happens next?'

'I'm afraid it is, which is a little unnerving for them all. Aunt Jane and Vic are treading on eggshells, trying not to make your grandma feel like she's an invalid. Grandma Susan, as we know, isn't one for taking it easy, even though she's struggling to get around.'

Mum grimaces.

'Oh, poor Grandma. She's more of a nurse than a patient, isn't she?' I declare, feeling sorry for them all. 'I hope they get to the bottom of it really soon.'

'Me too, Bella. Me too.'

'Is Aunt Jane happy?' I ask, tentatively.

'Well, she's worried about you, but I told her straight that you have a good head on your shoulders. She'll feel better once they know for sure what's causing Grandma Susan's breathing problems. Given everything she's dealing with right now I'd say she's finally found her rock. Vic is keeping her sane and managing to inject some laughter into each day. Which is quite something given that Aunt Jane is almost as stubborn as your grandma, and your dad, for that matter. Fortunately, I'm more inclined to think before I act. Level-headed and practical, as your dad says accusingly when I refuse to get riled up over some trivial thing that I know will pass.'

'Pop certainly spent a lot of time alone in his workshop if I remember rightly and maybe it was the only place he could get some peace and quiet.'

I glance at Mum, and she bursts out laughing.

'It can't have been easy with three such stubborn personalities under one roof. Pop enjoyed tinkering, as Grandma Susan referred to it, but he loved that sleigh and he appreciated time on his own to think. Sometimes I wish your dad would retire properly and find a hobby to distract him. He gets caught up in things and put upon. Which is why he's going to love getting involved on your behalf. He's a man who needs to be needed. Who are you dealing with at the solicitors' office?'

'William. He's canny and he knows what he's doing. He did say that the little demonstration could work to our advantage. Having public opinion on our side might put off a competitor if they fear it might lead to their business being boycotted.'

'Oh, I see! All is not lost – well, yet anyway. And as for your dad and me – our lips are sealed from here forward. And I have no doubt at all he'll be on the phone to you as soon as he's made some enquiries. You might as well benefit from *mates' rates*, as he calls them, to save a few pounds.'

What I love most about my mum is that she doesn't turn a drama into a crisis. When everyone around her is panicking, she's the calm one who takes charge to get things back under control. And that's just what I intend to do.

'You are kidding? The one-bed flat above the newsagent's?'

Holly pours us both a well-earned glass of wine after Adam gave his approval for us to remove the rest of my belongings this evening. Holly and I packed out our cars and drove back to the shop to stack my boxes neatly in the corner of the general office.

Most of the contents of the house, like furniture, we bought together, but some items were gifts to each other. How do you split stuff like that? And why would I want to be reminded of Adam every time I walk past an ornament, pick up a book or use a frying pan? After much deliberation I decided there wasn't anything I wanted from our life together. Only my clothes, and the boxes up in the loft that I brought with me from my parents' house, which are full of childhood memories.

My new flat is a small, furnished short-term let. It's long enough for me to get things sorted, although I don't relish the thought of moving out so close to Christmas. But it'll do. Any non-essential items will go into storage. When the problems are all resolved I intend to have a fresh start, anyway. No baggage from the past to weigh me down or hold me back.

'It's not like I'm going to be entertaining anyone, it's just somewhere to sleep and eat for the time being. It's a three-minute walk to work, and if I don't fancy cooking for one, I'm spoilt for choice – takeaways and some excellent pub grub are on my doorstep.'

Holly heaves a sigh. 'I wish I had an extra bedroom

so you could stay here until you can find something permanent. It's such a change for you, giving up that lovely house.'

'Adam is welcome to it. Believe me, Holly, I'm glad to be out of there. He called me a glorified flower arranger and implied that I don't have the skills required to manage a business.'

Her jaw drops. 'He said *what?*'

'In fairness, I'd just called him out for cheating on me and he was angry. The next few months of my life aren't going to be easy but I'm going into it with my eyes wide open. That's half the battle won, and I'll need as few distractions as possible. I have options and I intend to investigate them all.'

'While living like a student?'

'Hey, there's a great advantage to having a cosy living/dining/kitchen room all in one. And a bedroom with a wardrobe that will only hold half of the clothes I own. No more deliberating over what I'm going to wear – it'll be a matter of what's clean and ironed.'

As she starts laughing, I put a finger to my lips to shush her in case we disturb Katie. 'At least it has a half-decent bathroom, so I'm happy. Now, tell me your news.'

She sits quietly, absent-mindedly chewing on her lip as she thinks about it.

'Nick has paid his maintenance on time for the second month in a row, which means I can put a little something away for Christmas, too. Having to pay the bank charges when I use my overdraft because the funds don't arrive in time to pay the rent, adds insult to injury. It's really good news, but he says he's working all weekend again, although he has assured me he will take Katie out somewhere on Sunday. The thing is, do I tell her now, or leave it in case he changes his mind at the last minute?'

Managing a five-year-old's expectations, when a week seems like an awfully long time away to them, is tough.

'I'd wait.'

'I was thinking the exact same thing,' she concedes.

'Not because I think Nick will let her down, I think he's trying hard to sort himself out. But kids have no real perception of time, do they? I didn't appreciate that fully until living here with you both these last few days. It's only adults who are time and date driven, isn't it?'

'I know,' Holly says, wistfully. 'I remember the days when you and I were so keen to grow up, and now we're adults I just wish I could turn back the clock. Don't you?'

Holly passes me a glass of wine and I smile at her, gratefully. 'No, surprisingly enough I don't. I've realised that everything in my life has been building up to this point. I know that sounds weird, given that my life is rather shambolic right now, but I don't have to answer to anyone. Not a teacher or a lecturer, not a parent or a boss and not a man . . . I'm a free agent.'

'Yes, well, freedom might sound all well and good but how many people can really say they are *free*?'

That's a valid point. Holly has the huge responsibility of bringing up Katie and constantly worrying about making ends meet. For me, it's ensuring the livelihoods of the people I employ are safeguarded for the future.

'Hmm . . . to me, freedom means not being around someone who has the ability to constantly make me second-guess myself.'

'Isn't that the truth!' Holly replies, warmly. 'We both had the balls to tell our men we've had enough. Nick knows his days are numbered if he continues to shrug off his responsibilities and you don't have to listen to Adam's constant whinging anymore.'

I burst out laughing. 'And what a relief that is. A fresh start is invigorating, isn't it? I feel as if anything is possible going forward now. I am finally the captain of my own ship.'

Holly raises her eyebrows. 'Now that's more like the old *you* – at last. I'm impressed.'

'Well, watch this space as I intend to get everything back on track!'

'Look out world, Bella Reed is a woman on a mission!'

Holly knows that when I put my mind to something there's no stopping me.

10.

Thank Goodness for Apps

I'm a list maker by nature. I've always been renowned for having a list for all occasions. But the main benefit of the app I'm using to keep track of my massive to-do list is that I can colour code the individual action streams. It's the perfect tool for someone like me. Being organised is the only way I'm going to get through this next phase. I might not have a lot of practical experience when it comes to being the boss, but people only doubt your abilities if you hesitate. Strength comes from that inner belief that no mistake is too big to right and moving forward is infinitely better than standing still.

Of course, my priorities aren't necessarily the same as the people I'm dealing with and I trawl through the list, pushing back some of the tasks until tomorrow. I'm awaiting a call to pick up the keys to the flat, ready to move in this evening, but I must also get this mini mountain of boxes I'm staring at into storage as quickly as possible.

Mrs Mac breezes through the office door, wearing a grin. 'I've trawled through the emails and there's still nothin' from Brisley House Hotel, but you've got one from McIntyre Property Investments Limited. I printed it out as I knew you'd want a copy for the file.'

I push back on my chair and hurry towards her, hoping it's good news. I swear Mrs Mac looks like she's holding her breath as she watches me nervously scan the rather lengthy text until I screw up my eyes and utter a jubilant, 'Yes!'

'A draft contract for our "consideration" is on the way. Oh . . .' Trying to read quickly and take in what this means isn't easy. 'There's a deadline and should it result in more than one offer, they will be reviewed "taking all factors into account". What does that mean?'

Mrs Mac shrugs her shoulders, giving a little shake of her head. 'I rather hoped that you'd get a chance to sit down and have a talk with Maverick beforehand.'

'Me, too, Mrs Mac.' Randall's suggestion to make it personal is beginning to make more sense. 'I'll give William a call.'

But William is taking part in a video meeting for the next half an hour and rather than sit around anxiously waiting for him to phone back, I continue down the list of people I need to contact.

'Nick – how are you?'

'Good, thanks, Bella. I hear you've been staying with Holly and Katie? How are my girls?'

'They're doing all right. Katie misses you.' I can't lie to him.

'I know, but I can't turn work away. You haven't said anything to Holly, have you?' he asks, tentatively.

'No, of course not!'

'I fancy that she's being a little more receptive and not quite so edgy with me. I thought perhaps she'd quizzed you and you'd put in a good word for me. If that's not the case, things could be looking up.'

Do I tell him the truth? He needs to understand how his actions affect the people he loves the most.

'Money is a big concern for her right now, Nick. She's on a tight budget and overdrafts aren't cheap but sometimes it's the only way to keep your credit score clean.'

'Oh. And that's down to me.' As he connects the dots, he's starting to see the bigger picture and I can only hope he keeps going in the right direction. 'Moving in with a mate has halved what I pay out each month and from now on I'll always send Holly the money on time. I had a lot of credit card debts to pay off and I knew it wasn't going to help matters if I ended up being taken to court. I'm free of that now.'

'That's good to hear, Nick.'

'Anyway, what's happening?'

'The reason I'm calling is that I have a stack of boxes stored at the shop that need to be moved into a self-storage facility about eight miles outside of town. Basically, I'm looking to hire a man with a small van for a couple of hours, but it has to be an evening. Do you know of anyone?'

'Hey, that's not a problem. I'll borrow the pickup from work – the boss won't mind. He owes me plenty of favours. How about tonight, six-ish?'

'That's great, Nick, thanks. See you later!'

'No probs.'

That's good of him. As I go to put my phone down it kicks into life, but it's not William's name that comes up, it's Aunt Jane.

'Hi, Bella, it's only me. Vic's popped your grandma to the doctor's surgery as she has a rash on her arm. It might be an allergic reaction to the painkillers she's on. She says I look tired and insisted I stay and put my feet up, but really she's sick and tired of me fussing over her, as she puts it.'

'Oh, not another symptom.'

'I know. And it's random – like the headaches, although her breathing is a lot better and just knowing it's not a heart problem is a huge relief. We're thinking it might be asthma now, but it's another week before she's due to see the consultant for more tests. Anyway . . . that's not why I'm calling. I heard that you and Adam have parted ways, and I was wondering how you're doing. That's not to say I'm not terribly worried about the lease thing,' she sighs, sounding anxious. 'I know it doesn't help having well-meaning people constantly questioning you. But I wanted you to know that if you need a listening ear, I'm only a phone call away.'

'That's kind of you, Aunt Jane, but I'm fine on all fronts. Breaking up with Adam was so the right thing to do. The timing is awful, but it allows me to focus on work. I'm waiting for William Taggart to call, as I had a letter this morning informing me that a draft lease is on the way.'

'That's incredible, Bella.'

'It's a positive step forward for sure.'

'You have no idea how marvellous it is to hear some good news. Honestly, it's beginning to feel that everywhere I turn there's a problem.'

'What you need is to get that engagement party back on track,' I encourage. 'It will cheer up Grandma Susan and give Vic something to plan.'

'You could be right there, Bella. We've had a couple of sedate afternoon teas to keep your grandma occupied, but she's not the sedate sort, is she?'

'No. Definitely not! You need music, dancing and cocktails. She'll soon stop taking those painkillers if she thinks you'll put her on the mocktails. It's not that I'm being unsympathetic but, as a child, I remember her telling me that the best remedy for pain is to keep your mind occupied, as then it hurts a hell of a lot less. I'm not sure whether that's entirely true, because there's pain and there's *pain*. What she needs is a good laugh and a party. And she'll no doubt be feeling rather frustrated to be the cause of delaying the celebration.'

Aunt Jane chuckles. 'Oh, Bella – I've been at a low ebb, and I think it's pulling her down too. This was supposed to be my pep talk to you, and here you are a real tonic pointing out the obvious.'

'Oh . . . I have an incoming call! Take care. Love and miss you!'

'Let me know how it goes. Sending a hug from Faro.'

Taking a deep breath, I pick up the call and am greeted by William's friendly voice.

'William, thank you for getting back to me. We've had a reply from our landlord.'

'I know, they copied me in, I've just opened it.'

'I was hoping to have a face-to-face meeting, as I'm not sure I understand what's going on.'

'Ah, well . . . I'm guessing that they're hoping for a bidding war.'

'What?'

'The clue is in the fact that there will be a deadline by which you submit what, in essence, will be considered your best and final offer.'

My eyes had skipped over that bit as I assumed that was standard practice.

'I don't want to buy the place, just rent it. Why can't I pay the going rate, given that I'm currently in occupation, even though I appreciate it will be an entirely new contract.'

'If you're up against a retailer who is prepared to pay a premium for the premises, there's a chance they'll outbid you. It's supply and demand at play here and will come down to who is prepared to pay the most.'

'Then any advantage I thought I had is wishful thinking on my part.'

There's an ominous silence.

'Can you afford to go above the current asking price per square foot?' William isn't simply asking a question, he's pointing out the obvious.

'Probably not.'

'We touched on this before when you told me about the little demonstration. The only other option is to get the whole town on your side. Make McIntyre's the bad guys in this and your competitor might be put off, fearing a backlash against them if they put in the winning bid.'

Dirty tactics? This is not the William I know.

'Isn't that a little underhand?'

'Is it, though? McIntyre's began building their empire here, in the heart of Fort William. If they've grown so big that they can forget their roots now that Randall is no longer on the board, they're just like any other company out to make the biggest profit. Charitable donations are a tax write-off, but here in Fort William, The Highland Flower Shop isn't just a business making a profit. It supports a worthwhile local charity. Me – I'm fuming. You deserve to be treated better than this, Bella – because you want to keep the tradition going, one that has benefitted every single business in the area. The more visitors we attract, the more rent they can charge, and they own a lot of prime properties. It pays to work with people, not against them.'

My jaw drops. I have never heard William as angry as he is now.

'Anyway.' He clears his throat. 'As your solicitor, I suggest we wait until we see the broad terms they are proposing and weigh that up against any information we can glean in the meantime. I'm on it, Bella.'

Goodness, he's a man on a mission.

'Well . . . thank you for your honesty. I think it's time I sat Maverick down and explained what this means to our little community.'

William's laugh is like his voice – baritone – and it rumbles down the line. 'Look out Maverick McIntyre – Bella Reed isn't going down without a fight! And I'll keep my ear to the ground, unofficially, of course.'

'Bella, my lovely, I thought it was time I gave you a little update on a brainstorming session with a few of the lads over how to get Santa's Highland Express back into working order ready for the coming season. We're at a bit of an impasse, I'm afraid as the four of us are split down the middle about the best way forward.'

As a former health and safety officer for over thirty years, Dad still offers his services as an adviser to more than a dozen small businesses, including The Highland Flower Shop. It's a minefield of legislation and obviously in our case it's crucial that the ride is fully compliant with current regulations and fit for purpose. Dad arranges the annual service and inspection, but luckily the charity's volunteers have a mixed range of skills. Many donate their professional services for free, or at a reduced rate.

'I knew it wasn't going to be a quick fix, but why can't you agree? Last year the wiring was playing up, but in the end you all managed to get your heads together and get it going again. As Pop used to say, "If it ain't broke, don't fix it."'

'OK, let me explain, because we're at a crossroads and it's unfair to give you bad news if you don't understand why. This isn't just about replacing some wiring. Your great granddad was an old-school engineer. They took a milk float and cannibalised it to pull the little carriages that make up Santa's extended sleigh. The carriages are individually linked by a metal bar with a ball joint at each end, so that it can follow the curve of the track as Santa sits at the front steering the ride.

'For ten months of the year it's not in use, then in November our little team come in to start getting it ready. We grease the joints, test the batteries, do a little sanding and repainting of the woodwork and the ride continues to deliver what it promises. But most of the key metal joints are well past their sell by date and the problem is that they're bespoke. They were handmade, so you can't simply go online and order a replacement. The cost is in the man hours involved in taking off the bits that are worn out and failing, and then getting a fabricator to make up a facsimile. We've welded what we can over the years, but there comes a point when that's no longer possible.'

'What are the options?' I swallow hard as it's even worse than I feared.

'We start dismantling it now and call in a lot of favours. It's hard to estimate how long it will take as people will be giving their time for free, but obviously there are materials and specialist skills which come at a price.'

'But you said your little group are split down the middle.'

'I hate to be the one to say this, but we did discuss the fact that if it turns out the ride doesn't have a permanent home, then is it worth the work and the cost involved?'

'Oh, Dad, is it really that bad?' It feels like it's just one stumbling block after another.

'There are companies geared up to refurbish vintage hand-built fairground rides but you can imagine the timescale involved and the cost – well, I dread to think. Alternatively, we could take the ride apart and put it back together using off-the-shelf items. We'd have to cost that out as I can't give a figure off the top of my head, but it would change the feel of the ride.'

'How, exactly?'

'You won't get the thrill of the bumps as it rumbles around – the feel that you're on an old train with that constant clickety-clack. The links between the carriages wouldn't be as flexible because the replacement joints would be much smaller. The rumble strips on the track would have to be removed to stop undue wear and tear on them. The other concern is that the bushes on the motor have been replaced so many times that it's little short of a miracle it hasn't packed up on us completely. Last year's problems reflect the fact that the unit and the wiring is sixty-plus years old and there's little point in doing all this work on the carriages, only to have the motor give up the ghost. After all, it's the heart of the ride.'

'It's crunch time then – all or nothing,' I reply, miserably. And that sort of work requires more space than the current extension in which the sleigh is housed.

'The one thing the four of us did agree upon is that the cost should be covered by the charity.'

I'm deflated enough as it is, and this feels like the final straw. It would probably mean all of the funds raised this year across the board would be used to foot the bill.

'No, that's not right, Dad. The whole point is to raise

money for a good cause and every penny of it should go to the people it's intended to help. Look, I'm the custodian now and I can tell you that Santa's Grotto and The Christmas Cave *will* have a home, you can count on it. And I have savings I can draw on until Adam hands over my share of the equity in the house, so it's all covered.'

'Everything we've worked for will be yours eventually – why not just have some cash now when you most need it?'

'No, Dad. You and Mum have got years ahead of you and I want you both to have fun, not count the pennies. I've already been handed a thriving business, so there's no need to worry about me and my future. Your dream was always to have a little place in Faro so you and Mum can get away more often now you're working part time. I'd benefit from that too,' I point out.

'All right, you know your own mind.' He's worried about me and I understand that he simply wants to help, but it's for me to sort out my own problems.

'You just make the miracle happen and draw up a programme of works, Dad, and I'll sort out the rest.'

A soft 'harrumph' echoes down the line. 'Sometimes it's just like I'm talking to your mother,' he sighs, softly. 'If anything changes, Bella, just pick up the phone as you don't have to do this on your own, you know.'

'Aww, Dad – please don't think I'm not grateful because I am, but I can fight my own battles.'

'Oh, I'm well aware of that, my lovely. Once your mind is made up there's no changing it and you've always been like that. Right, I'd best get off and break the news to the lads. See you soon.'

'Eve, please come in and take a seat.'

'Is everything all right, Bella?' she asks, dubiously, as if she's expecting bad news.

'We're making some progress, but I just wanted to thank you for filling the growing gap because I'm getting less and less time at the workbench. You've been ploughing through the orders, and I wanted to let you know that hasn't gone unnoticed.'

A little smile of satisfaction creeps over her face as she relaxes. 'We're a team and Holly has been brilliant. It's like a little production line as she preps everything for me. As I'm assembling one order, I'm calling out the list of things I need ready to move on to the next.'

'And I know Mrs Mac has been doing her best to man the till in The Christmas Cave, so Holly doesn't have to keep rushing upstairs. It's a lot of pressure for you all and I'm grateful for what you're doing, but we need an extra pair of hands.'

'Oh, Bella, we're managing, really we are. It won't be forever, will it?'

'No, but we're talking weeks, if not a couple of months and I can't let this continue. What I wondered was whether you'd be happy to take on an official supervisory role. In the short term I can get you some experienced help. A lovely lady named Ursula Graham, who is now retired but was a florist for many years.'

Eve stares back at me uneasily. 'You think I have enough experience to be in charge?'

'I do. You've more than proved yourself. You'll be able to set Ursula to work and not worry about her, but I'd also like Holly to continue to have an opportunity to jump in and help if it's quiet upstairs. Obviously, there will be a salary increase if you're happy to take on the extra responsibility. Ursula is delighted to get hands-on again and is prepared to be very flexible. It would be up to you to agree her hours so that it's mutually convenient. What I don't want is you feeling that you can't take time off because I'm not around. And, when I am, most of my time is spent in the office now.'

She looks stunned. 'Wow – I really appreciate you putting your trust in me, Bella. We all know how hard you're working, and I won't let you down, I promise.'

I'm beginning to learn that delegation is easier when you are surrounded by people who care about what they do. Eve's smile is so broad now, as she stands and walks out, that it leaves me feeling good – so I must be doing something right at last.

11.

Actions Speak Louder Than Words

After negotiating the lengthy track which has quite a few potholes, Nick drives the loaded pickup truck through the large gates leading into Mòinteach Farm.

'It's a bit further out than I thought,' I apologise. 'Or maybe it's because the access is slow going in places.'

'I had no idea they even had storage facilities here,' Nick comments as he scans around for the best place to park.

The expanse of concrete fronting a huge barn has plenty of space, but there are various animal pens off to one side and at least a dozen hulking great pieces of machinery parked up. He hesitates, until a man appears and waves, pointing in the direction from which he came. Nick turns the wheel to follow him at a snail's pace. There's a black and white collie racing around and Nick keeps a careful eye out for him.

'You do know that you could've found somewhere closer to town to store this lot.'

'Yes, but it's half the price and I can't imagine I'll need any of this stuff for at least another six months.'

'You're renting?' He sounds surprised.

'Oh ... um ... yes. The chances are that I'll be doing a bit of moving around before I commit to something permanent.' I'm keeping my fingers crossed that by then my overall financial position will be a lot clearer.

We pull up in front of a massive industrial unit. I jump out and the man walking towards me thrusts out his hand.

'Hi, I'm Paul, Paul Buchanan – we spoke earlier this morning. It's Bella, isn't it?'

'Yes, and this is my friend Nick.'

'Welcome. Let's head inside and I'll run through the blurb and show you the unit.'

Nick lingers, as the collie seems to have taken a liking to him.

'We're a family-run business and you can come and go as you please,' Paul confirms as I lengthen my stride to keep up with him. 'There's unlimited 24/7 access and if your needs change, depending on availability, we can usually sort you out at a day's notice.'

Paul places a key fob on a pad at the side of a single-entry door.

'We supply you with your own electronic fob and all of our self-storage units are at ground level as the first floor hasn't been fitted out yet. We have a NACOSS Grade 2X alarm and our CCTV records both day and night. The loading access is via the roller door just around the corner and it's opened with the same fob which operates a button on the inside. There are some trolleys there which you're free to use. But let's head into the office.'

Nick catches up, but the collie is close on his heels.

'Oot wi' ya, Rab!' Paul calls out and it works, because Rab sits patiently by the entrance as Paul closes the door behind us. 'He's a great sheep dog, but in some ways he's soft as a brush. I don't allow him in here and he knows it. My wife, Nora, spoils him – so if he's around just tell him to *get oot!*'

I laugh and Nick glances at me, a huge smile on his face. As we follow Paul into the corner office, I take a second to scan around. It's massive and yet it's all so pristine. The burgundy painted steel units are in long runs, with wide walkways between them. The only distinguishing factor to indicate the internal sizes is the positioning of the doors. Some units are literally one standard door-width, others have double doors but most of them have locks, so I assume they're in use.

'I was wondering whether this is the only type of storage facility on offer. What if someone was looking to rent a workshop, for instance.'

'Well, that's a first. Is this a vehicle you're talking about?'

'No, renovating a sleigh ride,' I reply, and Paul raises his eyebrows.

'Are you talking about Santa's Highland Express?'

I nod my head. 'Yes. It's due for a big overhaul that could take us right through to November. But there isn't enough space at the rear of The Highland Flower Shop, and it will probably be too disruptive, anyway. I'm on a budget though, so I'm not expecting anything as smart as this – just lockable, dry and with evening and weekend access. Most of the work will be done by volunteers.'

'The wife and I took both our sons every year when they were small and now they take our grandkids along,' Paul replies, nostalgically. 'Mind you, the wife and I join them whenever we can. I'm sure we can sort out a space that would do at a price to suit.'

Considering it was such a bad start to the day, things are definitely taking a turn in the right direction. Let's hope it's a trend that continues.

If ever I was tempted to try a deep-fried chocolate bar from our local chippie, it's tonight. Moving into my temporary home wasn't arduous. It didn't take long to fill the smallest wardrobe I've ever seen and arrange my toiletries on the one shelf in the bathroom. The kitchen area has everything I'm likely to need, even though it's tired and ready for an upgrade, which is why the flat is only available on a short lease. There was even a pack of tea lights the previous tenant had thoughtfully left behind.

I lined up half a dozen of them on the coffee table, because I thought it might add a little ambience to a fish and chip supper for one. The fish is great – fresh and flaky, with a crisp batter – but maybe I should have invited Nick to join me for a meal in the pub opposite. After all, he's on his own too and he must miss the chance to pop in and sit around the table to share a meal with Holly and Katie. I'm getting withdrawal symptoms and I only stayed with them for four days, but Nick's been banned from popping in unannounced for a couple of weeks now. I understood Holly's decision because it is disruptive, but it must have felt like a huge slap in the face for Nick.

Come on, Bella. You can do better than sitting here feeling sorry for yourself. You've had a great day as it turns out, so be thankful for that.

Hmm. That inner voice is bravado, as I also left three messages with MPI for Maverick McIntyre to get in touch but no one got back to me.

When I'm done eating I give Holly a call.

'Hey, you. How's it going?'

'It's quiet. Katie's sound asleep and I'm missing my best friend, so I'm comfort eating.'

'Me, too! Fish and chips, but I passed on the battered chocolate bar.'

'I had a healthy salad,' Holly retorts sounding pleased with herself, 'but I've eaten two-thirds of a bag of popcorn while I'm flicking around to find something decent to watch on TV. Have you unpacked?'

My heart constricts inside my chest. Holly is lonely. Nick is lonely. And Katie misses her dad. Loneliness, I'm discovering, gives you too much thinking time. And that can be a negative thing.

'Yes, although I only brought one suitcase and a holdall with me. Nick gave me a hand to move the rest of my stuff into storage, earlier on.'

'He did?'

'Yes, he borrowed the pickup from work. I was looking to hire a man with a van, but he offered. He didn't want to take any money, but I insisted.'

The line goes ominously quiet. 'Are you still there?' I ask, mentally berating myself for mentioning his name.

'A part of me will always love Nick, Bella, but I need someone who is prepared to put in as much effort as I do. When he does turn up, he'll bring Katie a present. That's thoughtful, right? But it never crosses his mind that I'm a working mum and since Dad died, I'm reliant on Mum to do the afternoon school run. But she has a full-time job of her own to work around and sometimes it's a problem. Or the fact that you allow me time off to take Katie for her dental appointments and to see the doctor, when it isn't always convenient. I often feel guilty when I fall asleep while reading Katie a bedtime story, because I'm exhausted from lying in bed at night worried sick about our future. I can't do this anymore. Katie deserves better. I refuse to let her grow up thinking this is normal family life – because it isn't.'

She's speaking her truth and it's painful to hear. You can't possibly understand someone else's problems unless you've walked in their shoes.

'I'm sorry, Holly, I shouldn't have said anything. I just . . .'

'We both know that Katie and I wouldn't even have a roof over our heads if you hadn't insisted on loaning me the deposit. You're not just a great friend and godmother to Katie, you're family, and your opinion matters to me. You always try to stand back and encourage me to look at the bigger picture. But you want to believe that everything will come right between me and Nick. The truth is that I need someone beside me in the moments when I'm not feeling particularly strong, or confident, and with each passing day it's getting harder and harder to imagine Nick rising to that challenge.'

I meant to help and now, unwittingly, I've made things worse. What is gutting is that she's so tired of the constant daily battle, it's eroding her belief in her own abilities. For now, what she needs is a friend to listen, and be there for her when she's struggling. If Nick ends up with a broken heart, it's his own doing and I must never forget that.

'I couldn't be any prouder of you, Holly, than I am right now. You're at a low ebb, but you'll bounce back. Whatever you decide to do, whatever you need – I'm here for you and Katie. If you want me to avoid Nick in future, then you only have to say the word.'

'You don't need to do that, Bella, but it's time to accept that even though he's trying, the fairy tale is unlikely to happen. He's not a bad man by any means, he's just unreliable. I think I've finally accepted that – it's about time, don't you think?'

It's with a sense of great sadness I have to agree because, as things stand now, she's right. Promises are easy to give, but what if they don't materialise?

'Anyway, moving on from all our dreary talk.' Holly tries to lighten the mood with her quick change of subject. 'The good news is that I'm enjoying helping Eve at work. Any news about meeting up with Maverick?'

'Eve's really grateful for the help and I am too. I rang the office and left three messages asking him to call me, but each time I was told he wasn't available. When I stressed that the matter was urgent, the receptionist finally put me through to the admin manager. He just said that the draft lease is being prepared and would be sent out in due course.' The exasperation in my tone is very evident. 'He did end the call by adding that he was glad to be of assistance.'

'That was good of him,' Holly replies, sarcastically.

'I haven't actually done anything wrong. Technically, as William pointed out to me, it's Aunt Jane who is in breach and I'm simply the new owner starting afresh.'

'Well, I saw the reaction on Maverick's face when that little protest group started heckling him. For a second there he was horrified. The look he gave you made my legs buckle – he thinks you set it up.'

'I know and that's precisely why I need to talk to him.' I can't tell Holly about the other interested party, or that William is annoyed at the tactics being employed.

'Why don't you catch him on his way into the office?'

'What hang around and ever so casually bump into him?' I laugh, assuming she's joking. Having literally bumped into him once already, I'm not sure it's such a good idea.

'No, I mean it. Better still, the man has to eat – follow him at lunchtime and see where he goes. Nick said he's a loner and there aren't many tables for one, are there?'

'Hmm, that might be a bit obvious, although an office setting didn't exactly work in my favour. I felt a little intimidated by him, if I'm being honest.'

'Maverick told Nick that he has a corporate background. I mean who would say that to a mechanic while he's working on the engine of a car? It's hardly friendly banter, is it?'

'What else did he say?'

'Well, admittedly that was a while ago as I keep any conversations with Nick to the minimum now. Maverick had only been in the UK for a few months at that point. He probably socialises with some of his work colleagues, but his grandparents live way out on the edge of Loch Awe. It must be a real disadvantage moving to a country where you're starting from scratch and don't even have old school friends you can chill with.'

Holly's right and I wonder if that's why Maverick is keen to encourage Nick to work on his vehicle at the weekends. He might not have anything better to do, so it's an excuse to hang out with someone his own age.

'I might give it a try. I need to go shopping to get a few things to brighten the flat. Everything here is so beige . . . maybe a few brightly coloured scatter cushions would help. And one of my favourite chain stores happens to be on the same retail park as McIntyre's impressive offices.'

'There you go – sorted! And I wish you the best of luck, because he's a bit of a cold one, isn't he? Not many people would react so calmly when faced with a crowd chanting, "Save our Santa" and "Shame on you."'

I groan. 'Don't remind me. The words keep coming back to haunt me.'

'Thanks for letting me sound off tonight – I needed that. You don't have to ignore Nick out of loyalty to me, but understand that he's about to seal his own fate.'

'I got it. And I'll let you know how I get on crossing paths with the mighty Maverick.'

'He's single and good-looking – turn on the charm, that'll confuse him!'

The following day I casually loiter at the retail park until I spot Maverick leaving MPI's offices. Trailing a good distance behind him, it's obvious that he's heading for the coffee shop. I hang back until there are two people standing between us in the queue. He hasn't spotted me, and I try my best to look inconspicuous while I figure out a strategy. Unfortunately, it's almost two in the afternoon, so the lunchtime rush is thinning out and I'm a little more visible than I'd hoped.

There are several free tables scattered around the ample seating area but I'm here now. I juggle the two bulky carrier bags in one hand, as I grab my purse. They aren't heavy, just awkward and I don't want to get in anyone's way.

The two women in front of me are so busy talking that they don't realise Maverick has paid and is already walking away.

'Next please!' the server calls out impatiently to them.

I watch Maverick out of the side of my eye, until he's no longer in view. The corded handles on the carrier bags are beginning to leave indents on my fingers and I stuff my purse under my arm as I transfer them into the other hand to get some relief. Stupidly, my purse slips and as it crashes to the floor the clasp flies open, scattering coins everywhere. I stare down at them, mortified.

'Next please. What can I get you?'

By now the two people in front of me are walking away, their hands full.

'Sorry,' I mutter apologetically to the young man behind the counter. 'Just a cup of coffee please – cappuccino.'

As I bend to begin scooping up the coins, a pair of highly polished brogues appear in front of me.

'I won't be a moment and I'll be out of your way,' I mutter apologetically, but the feet don't move.

'Let me take those carrier bags while you grab your coffee.' Maverick's voice makes my head tilt back as I gaze up at him, feeling hot and flustered.

'Oh . . . thanks.'

He waves a couple of paper napkins and a wooden stirrer at me. 'Do you want me to grab some for you? Sugar?'

'Please. Brown – just the one.'

Quickly scooping the pile of coins back into my purse, I jump to my feet. I can't trust my shaking hands to fiddle with coins and risk another incident, so I pull out a note. Behind me is a little old lady and I give her an acknowledging smile as she patiently waits for me to collect my change.

'We've all done it, my dearie,' she says. 'Sometimes two hands aren't enough. Mind you, having a handsome young man come to your rescue is a bit of a bonus, isn't it?' And then she gives me a wink and I start laughing as I turn to walk away.

Seriously, I couldn't have planned it to go any more smoothly than this if I'd tried. Walking over to the table where Maverick is waiting for me, I see my two carrier bags perched neatly on a long banquette seat opposite him. He's sitting on a chair with his back to me.

'Thank you so much for coming to my rescue,' I begin, as I approach him.

Maverick half turns in his seat. 'It's no problem, Bella. Please, take a seat.'

He's placed two serviettes, a packet of sugar and a stirrer on the table next to him and suddenly here I am – sitting alongside Maverick McIntyre and watching him wolf down a doughnut.

'I hope that's not lunch,' I reply, to break the ice, as I empty the sachet of sugar into my coffee.

'It is, actually. Comfort food after a long morning.' He turns to grin at me. 'I'm a believer in a hearty breakfast, then I live on coffee and the odd sugary snack until dinner.'

I glance at him, unable to hide my surprise. I'm not sure whether he's simply messing with me. He's tall, muscular and lean – I'd assumed he'd be into healthy eating.

'As someone who has only had a bowl of porridge since six this morning but four large mugs of coffee and a cup of tea, I'm not about to criticise anyone else's dietary habits.'

He wipes his mouth with a napkin and looks at me quizzically. 'I thought you might be a salad lover.'

It seems we've both been making assumptions.

'Dinner last night was fish and chips from the takeaway in town. Tonight, it's going to be Chinese. Not a salad in sight!'

'Actually, I'm rather glad to have bumped into you. I owe you an apology.'

'You do? I thought you were avoiding me – I left three messages for you for exactly the same reason.'

'Ah, right – sorry. Note to self to make sure I check my messages daily. My assistant usually flags up anything that's urgent when I'm rushed off my feet. Randall's replacement has the same disadvantage that I have, namely that he's new to the area. He's been commandeering a lot of my time as he settles in. Some things I can help with, others I can't as I, too, am only just beginning to network with the wider community. It takes time to build trust and we've made a few mistakes lately.'

Should he be telling me that?

'I'm still hungry – can I get you anything?' He jumps up before I have a chance to reply.

'Oh . . . um . . .'

'Leave it to me.'

Maverick disappears and I start sipping my coffee. The day he called to see me at the shop he'd come from a breakfast meeting, and I find myself wondering whether the reason he was in a hurry and didn't seem to be interested in listening to me, was because he was preoccupied. I stare across at him as he waits patiently in the queue and realise that I was on the defensive that day. I had already formed an opinion of him based on very little information.

Holly Jacobs, I owe you BIG time – this was the best idea ever! And it would be rude of me not to repay his kindness, wouldn't it?

When Maverick returns he's all smiles.

'Are you doing anything tomorrow night?' I ask quite casually.

'No. Why?'

'I know a perfect place to eat and wondered if you'd like to join me?'

With no hesitation at all he replies warmly, 'That would be great.'

12.

A Busy Bee Just Keeps on Going

'Randall – hi!'

'Hello, Bella. I was hoping to get back to you a little sooner, but my services have been called upon back in the office and it wasn't a request I could refuse. Anyway, I have a couple of trusted friends reaching out to see if they can at least find a temporary solution to your little problem – just in case.'

I know it's difficult for him to talk openly for fear of being overheard and I wish we could meet up, because I'd much rather say this face to face to gauge his reaction.

'That's very kind of you. And I have some information to pass to you. I've had a formal response after registering my interest in the shop and I'm awaiting a copy of the draft contract.'

'That's wonderful news!'

'As we know, someone else is interested so it's a case of waiting to see what the terms are going to be. The other thing is that I'm having dinner with Maverick tonight.'

'You are?' He sounds genuinely surprised, so either Maverick chose not to bring it up, or the two of them haven't spoken since yesterday.

'I won't bore you with the details, but he came to my rescue when I was out shopping, which was very thoughtful of him. It seemed like the right thing to do at the time, to repay his kindness. I hope it's not going to complicate matters.'

'No, not at all,' Randall responds enthusiastically. 'He'll

learn more about life here by mixing with people outside of work. Fiona and I are conscious that inviting him to our dinner parties to introduce him to our friends and long-term business acquaintances isn't always riveting for him. As a young man on his own, socialising isn't easy. He's been so focused on work and getting his house sorted, that he hasn't had much time to integrate.'

Integrate. Does Randall mean *make friends*? That's not why I'm meeting up with him.

'That's a pity. Anyway, I'm glad you called as I didn't like to text you.'

'Thank you for your discretion, Bella. A cautious approach is always wisest. I'm in a much better position now that I'm unexpectedly in and out of the office again for a brief spell. It means I might get a handle on what's going on behind the scenes. Anyway, enjoy your dinner!'

I did wonder whether my offer could be misinterpreted, but Randall didn't seem at all disconcerted by it – in fact, he seemed pleased. However, it's not something I can share with anyone else – including Holly, in case she lets anything slip. I've chosen a quiet location for my rendezvous with Maverick, which happens to be one of my favourite places to eat.

'I just spoke to your dad and I told him I'd give you a quick call, Bella,' Aunt Jane explains. 'We're putting the party on hold as this rash your grandma has is driving her mad. As if a broken ankle wasn't enough to slow her down, it's the final straw and she's losing her temper – big time!'

'I'm sorry to hear that, Aunt Jane. Other than that, Grandma is her usual self?'

'More energy than she knows what to do with, Bella, which is part of the problem,' Aunt Jane admits. 'She spent the morning sitting out by the pool and bemoaning the fact that the medication she's on stops her from enjoying one of her favourite cocktails.'

'If Grandma is complaining then I take that as a good sign. I'd be more concerned if she weren't – if you know what I mean.'

'I do . . . Vic knows a few people who are into alternative remedies – maybe we should consider that. I'll talk to him about it. Anyway, how are things at your end?'

'Busy. We're taking on more staff and Dad is preparing a detailed breakdown of the restoration work on Santa's Highland Express.'

'Oh my, that's brilliant news, Bella! They say everything happens for a reason and I needed to be here to see your grandma through this. I know that I left everything in good hands, and I really do believe that this time next year we'll all be counting our blessings.'

'One thing I wanted to say, Aunt Jane, is that Dad is worried sick about Grandma. And I know Mum isn't happy that he's taking on way too many commitments considering that he's supposed to be semi-retired. They don't get over to Faro as often as they'd like and right now I'm adding to their worries, even though I'm doing just fine. But Dad is conflicted. They're more likely to fly over if they have a little encouragement. You and Vic could really do with a break, and it wouldn't hurt to let him know that.'

'It would really perk her up and he's always been her favourite,' Aunt Jane reflects.

'Has he?' We both know Dad was always the least demanding one, as Aunt Jane and Grandma often butt heads.

'But your dad won't easily step away from his responsibilities in Fort William, Bella.'

'Once the plan for overhauling Santa's Highland Express has been set up, he can step back. It's time he learned to say *no* more often, don't you think?'

'Yes, it is,' she concedes. 'And it would give us all a boost to see him and your mum.'

'Then can I count on you to help make it happen, Aunt Jane, and you can trust me to keep on top of everything here?'

'Sometimes life needs a nudge, doesn't it? Let's make things happen, Bella. I'll call your dad back. Then we can all put our heads together and figure out how we're going to get your grandma fighting fit again. But if you want anything – anything at all – just let me know. A lot of people owe me favours and it would only take a phone call.'

'Just having Randall on my side is enough, Aunt Jane. He has a lot of contacts and he's very discreet.'

As she starts speaking, the words catch in her throat. 'I know . . . and I'm glad you can appreciate how tough it was for me at a time in my life when my feelings were conflicted. But some things aren't meant to be, and Vic is a wonderful man who has had a lot of heartache in his life. We'll have a good life together, here in Faro.'

'Then the sooner we get the problems out of the way, the sooner you can get back to arranging the engagement party and making those wedding plans!'

'Actually, Vic and I decided it would be nice to hold off having the party until the spring, when you fly over. Your mum and dad said they'll liaise with you over possible dates. I miss your company, Bella, and our long walks among the gorse and the heather. The leaves will be turning now in the Highlands, and the wind will carry that earthy smell which was always a signal that winter is coming. Christmas will be very different for me this year, but you can send me lots of lovely photos when the time comes. Goodness, now I'm feeling a little homesick,' she laughs. 'Anyway, it's lovely to hear your voice and you take care. Everyone sends their love.'

As the line disconnects, I realise that I really do need to press forward now with a sense of urgency. That backup plan might not turn out to be in vain if we're in a bidding war for a new lease. The person with the deepest pockets will win. And I also need to sort out a lockable workshop for the volunteers to begin stripping down Santa's Highland Express.

Going in search of Mrs Mac, I find her downstairs at the floristry desk, introducing Ursula to Eve. As soon as she spots me, Ursula homes in to throw her arms around me.

'It's been a while, Bella, hasn't it? How is your grandma Susan and is your aunt Jane doing well? Are they driving each other mad yet?'

The onslaught of questions puts a huge grin on my face as she releases me.

'Yes, it has, and Grandma's a little under the weather, but they're trying to get her sorted out. So, yes they are driving each other mad as Aunt Jane is constantly fussing over her and you know what Grandma's like.'

Ursula grimaces. 'Oh dear, that's not good to hear. But this is all looking wonderful, so business must be brisk.'

'Thank you and it is, but that's down to Eve and Holly, as I'm getting bogged down in paperwork and plans to expand the area we cover. An extra pair of hands will make all the difference.'

'It's a real pleasure, Bella. Sorry I can only work five hours a day, but Monty pines when I'm not there. My neighbour will look after him, but she does the afternoon school run for her daughter and I have to be back by three o'clock.'

'Ah, how old is Monty now?' I remember seeing him once when Ursula called round to see Mum. He's one of the softest, cuddliest dogs I've ever met but then golden retrievers usually have a good nature.

'He's eleven now. Monty likes his naps, bless him, but he really enjoys his walks, and my neighbour is always happy to help me out.'

'Well, whatever you can do is much appreciated. I'll leave Eve to settle you in and grab Mrs Mac if you don't mind. See you later!'

Eve looks happy and Mrs Mac gives me a beaming smile as we head back upstairs.

'I think they'll get on very well together,' Mrs Mac half-whispers, as we walk past Holly, who is ringing up a basket full of baubles and a box of crackers. It always makes me smile that no matter what time of the year it is, people's eyes light up when they see Christmas decorations. I recall Adam rudely throwing out there that I ditch *the Christmas stuff*. The business is as successful as it is because the shop is full of feel-good vibes, but he couldn't understand the attraction. It's rather sad, now I come to think of it.

'Right, what did you need me for?' Mrs Mac asks. We step into the office, and she shuts the door behind us.

'I'm heading out as I have a few people to see, but if any urgent emails arrive can you give me a call?'

'Of course. You seem a wee bit more positive today, or is it wishful thinkin' on my part?'

As I shovel a few items into my handbag, I stop what I'm doing and look directly at her. 'We all know the outcome we want, but I can't take anything for granted, Mrs Mac.'

She sucks in a deep breath and expels it slowly. 'Then you're a canny lass, because I'd be worried sick if you were bankin' on gettin' Maverick on your side.'

'Oh,' I reply, brightly, 'I haven't ruled out that option either.'

'Bella!' I turn to see Nick hurrying towards me, as he wipes his hands on a rag. My heart instantly sinks.

'What are you doing in my neck of the woods?' He beams, lengthening his stride to catch up with me.

'Oh, I'm looking at one of the units.'

'I didn't know there were any self-storage units around here. I suppose you'll soon have half the contents of a house to store as well. Breaking up is a real nightmare, isn't it?'

'Yes . . .' I glance at my watch, relieved by his assumption. If word gets out I'm looking at commercial and not retail premises for the business, I can't even begin to imagine the panic that would ensue among the staff. 'I ought to get on as I'm running late.'

'Actually, I'm glad I caught you, I was going to give you a call.'

I can't let Nick use me as a sounding board any longer, not after my last conversation with Holly, so crossing paths is unfortunate to say the least. My stomach constricts as I wonder what's coming next.

'It's a bit awkward raising this, but I'd feel bad if I didn't. You know you were looking at workshop space for the sleigh? Well, I know it's mostly volunteers who will be working on it, but I have this mate and he's really strapped for cash.' Nick looks at me in earnest.

'The budget is very tight I'm afraid and—'

'He's got two young kids and his firm have just cut all overtime,' he adds. 'He's a mechanic, but on the side he strips down old cars and refurbs stuff. If you need another pair of hands . . . he's useful and if he knew it was for charity, he'd take whatever you could afford to pay him. He'd be grateful for any work you could put his way, that's all. I haven't said anything, obviously, but I can text you his number if you like.'

You know that look someone gives you and you realise it's going to be impossible to say no? Well, Nick is doing just that.

'I can't promise anything but let me have that number and I'll see what I can do.'

Nick flashes me a grateful smile and then, as I turn to go, he suddenly steps in front of me.

'You've been a good friend, Bella, when I haven't always deserved it. I know a fair bit about Maverick by now. I don't know if this will help, but it might. Two things. Firstly, his father is tough on him and he's disappointed that Randall enticed him back here. On the other hand, Maverick is out to prove it was the right thing to do. Secondly, Maverick is mad keen on golf. I'm not sure what you can do with that, but I thought I'd mention it. I'll dig out that number and the guy's name is Greg.'

As I walk away from Nick, I can see that it means something to him to help a friend. I'll talk to Greg and see if I can use him in some way. Now I'm off to vet an industrial unit on the edge of the business park, because it might be the only answer if I end up having to split the business into two.

13.

Mixing Business and Pleasure Could be a Big Mistake

'Sorry I'm late, I took a wrong turning. This is a great place, but it's not easy to find.' Maverick hesitates as I stand to greet him – do we shake hands?

It's an awkward moment, but I'm determined to put him at ease. After all, this isn't a business meeting, so I simply indicate for him to take a seat opposite me at our rustic table for two.

'I'm ravenous,' I exclaim, as he sits down.

'Thank goodness. I'm hoping for something hearty and filling.'

'You'll get that here all right. I know the chef and if you're prepared to take pot luck, he'll cook us up a feast. Assuming you aren't vegan, vegetarian or a pescatarian, in which case his assistant will create something bursting with flavours from . . . um . . . rice, or tofu or . . . if you have food aller—'

'Stop right there. Are you nervous?'

I look at him, aghast. 'No, of course not.' Oh . . . that sounded defensive.

'I like meat and fish. The truth is that I'll eat pretty much anything. Tofu isn't my favourite I'll admit, but some of the vegetarian options I've tried are excellent. But I'm in the Highlands and I appreciate the quality of the produce here.'

'Have you tried haggis, neeps and tatties?' I enquire, my lips twitching.

'Yes – more than once! And I can heartily recommend the whisky gravy too.'

One of the waiters approaches and we settle on two glasses of red wine. I wish now I'd booked a taxi, but it's quite a way out of town and I can't let down my guard.

'I watched a lot of videos about Scotland before I decided to come here. It's strange when it's where my father was born. My mother's family were originally from Ireland but they moved to Seattle when she was a teenager.'

'Goodness, that's quite a mix of accents to influence you,' I remark, and he laughs.

'Not really, although my mother can slip into quite a brogue when she has a mind to, but my father never had a broad Scottish accent. Believe it or not, I had a diction and elocution technique coach.'

'You did?'

'At school I took the lead part in various plays. I even played the bard himself – William Shakespeare. But the highlight for me was playing Abraham Lincoln – I received a standing ovation for my rendition of the Gettysburg address. My proudest moment was when I spoke the line "all men are created equal" because I believe that's true.'

'I'm impressed. Do you think you missed your calling?'

He shakes his head dismissively. 'Acting isn't a profession that would have impressed my parents, but I had a lot of fun and some of my peers gave it a shot. One of them ended up getting a part in a sitcom that ran for five seasons, but the others ended up in regular jobs.'

And just like that, the conversation is easy and relaxed. Out of the corner of my eye, I spot someone walking purposefully in our direction.

'Hi, Bella! It's great to see you – how're you doing now that you're the boss lady?'

I jump up to give Finn a hug and Maverick rises up out of his chair.

'I'm doing good, Finn, really good. This is my friend,

Maverick McIntyre. Maverick, Finn McGrath is the owner of The Hunter Gatherer Inn.'

They shake hands.

'This is quite a place you have here, Finn. The location is amazing.'

'Well—' Finn throws his head back, laughing '—it's amazing for me, but we get a lot of customers booking online who struggle to find us.'

'Me, too,' Maverick admits. 'But when you get here it's pretty impressive. Are you from Scotland originally?'

Finn indicates for us to settle ourselves back down, as he pulls up a chair.

'Ah – the name – I'm half Scottish and half Irish, but I lived in London for a long time before I returned home.'

'Finn was a bit of a legend at school,' I explain. 'He'd left by the time I started at secondary school, but our Health and Food Technology teacher still talked about him.'

'As I failed at pretty much every other subject, she was determined not to give up on me and thank goodness for that,' Finn retorts.

'I think I was one of your first customers when you took over the inn, if I remember correctly.'

Finn winks at me, sporting a broad smile. 'You were – and the first one through the door if my memory serves me right. So, you guys are here to eat and I have some cracking good lobsters. And a selection of slow-matured, lean but well-marbled Highland beef steaks with a succulent flavour. Quality beasts, who've had the benefits of a happy life roaming free and that makes all the difference.'

'Sounds good to me,' Maverick responds, obviously impressed. 'A friend of my father's owns a cattle ranch in Tenino, Washington and we often visited during the summer holidays. It's only just over an hour outside of Seattle. I was taught from a young age to treat the animals with respect.'

That's something I wasn't expecting to hear.

'Oh, what I'd give to see that for myself,' Finn declares, easing himself upright. 'We support local, organic farmers and I can guarantee you some of the best ingredients that Scotland has to offer. But I also spent a little time in Italy so I hope you can handle carbs,' Finn throws over his shoulder. 'Two creamy lemon pasta starters with lobster coming up.'

'Maybe we should save this red wine for the main course,' Maverick leans in, as he raises his glass. 'In the meantime, thank you for inviting me here, but as you did the hard work finding the right place, I insist on paying.'

There is no way I'm going to let Maverick foot the bill. Our glasses chink and as our eyes meet it would be easy to fool myself into thinking I'm on a date.

'Oh, no – really, you were in the right place at the right time in the café yesterday, and it was gracious of you to come to my rescue. Again.'

He bursts out laughing. 'Yes, I can see a pattern forming here, but it was nothing – merely my good deed for the day,' he jests. 'But at least I kept my phone well out of the way.'

Maverick attracts the eye of one of the waiters. 'Can we get a large bottle of water, please? Bella, do you prefer still or sparkling?'

'Still for me, thanks.'

We're still bantering back and forth when the guy returns with two glasses and a jug of water with a slice of lemon and some ice cubes in it. Maverick pours and I don't know why I felt so nervous earlier on.

'My grandfather tells me that he went to the same school as your granddad,' Maverick remarks.

'Yes. I can't really remember Pop sharing any stories about his time at school, which is a shame.'

'That's a pity. I bet they were a handful. Granddad told me he behaved himself most of the time but he said all the lads used to lark about occasionally.'

'Pop was such a character, and he was a man with a big heart when it came to kids. It's why he started fund-raising.'

'And that's the reason you're so intent on keeping the tradition alive now you've taken over the business.'

This is my chance to ram it home, but instead of grabbing the moment I point in the direction of the kitchen. Our waiter is approaching with a large tray.

'Lobster tails poached in white wine and thyme, with a little linguine and a lemon-infused butter sauce.'

In true Finn style, the plate is picture perfect. The portions are small, the colours vibrant and the smell wafting up makes my stomach rumble.

'This is so deserving of a glass of chilled Californian Chenin Blanc,' Maverick comments as he stares down at the plate in front of him. 'I should have picked you up, so that at least one of us could have had the full experience.'

And what do I say?

'Maybe next time.' Nooo!

Maverick smiles at my answer, before saying, 'Excellent, it's a date then.'

This was supposed to be my chance to get him on my side, not get him to ask me out on a real date. *Bella, have you lost your mind?*

You know when you awaken with a start and instantly find yourself groaning when you engage your brain? That's me this morning as fragments of last night's conversation with Maverick replay in my head.

Did I really agree to have lunch with him on Sunday at the golf club? Thankfully, he said we didn't have to actually play, which is excellent news as my skills are certainly not up to that.

Scanning my emails as I munch on a bowl of cereal, there's a reply from Paul Buchanan. He says he can empty out one of the brick outbuildings at the farm, which has been used as a workshop in the past but not for a long time. It will take him a few days to get it sorted, but it has a workbench along one wall. It's a third of the price of anything else I can find so it's a no-brainer.

It's good news and I jump up to grab my phone and call Dad.

'I've found a temporary home to house the sleigh ride and it won't break the bank! It's up at Mòinteach Farm and has unrestricted access and plenty of parking.'

'That's great timing, Bella, as we had a long session last night working on the Gantt chart and have now broken the work down into phases and tasks. Obviously, the start and end dates for each step in the process are only a rough estimate. But it will allow us to start approaching people with the necessary skills and see where the gaps are. We already have half a dozen volunteers willing to begin taking it apart ready for transportation.'

Nothing makes Dad happier than feeling he's achieving something, and this is quite a step forward.

'That's music to my ears! Oh – and I'll forward you the number of a guy named Greg. He's a mechanic by trade and he also overhauls old car parts apparently. He can't work for free, but he knows it's for charity and that the budget is tight. He's just grateful for any work we can put his way.'

'Let me have it and I'll give him a call to find out what he can do. I'm glad you rang, as your mum thinks we need to fly over to the Algarve to give my sister a bit of a break. That's why I wanted to press ahead and get the programme of works mapped out as it'll be Cliff I'll be leaving in charge.'

Cliff and Isla Derwent have always been great friends of my parents, not least because of their involvement with The Highland Elves committee.

'I'm so glad to hear that, Dad. Everything will be fine here, you know that.'

'But you've got such a lot going on, Bella and—'

'No *ands*, *ifs* or *buts*, Dad. It's the right thing to do and, in truth, I'll feel happier once Mum reports back. No offence to Aunt Jane, but nursing isn't her thing, whereas Mum at least saw me through childhood asthma, a broken arm, a bad case of chickenpox, and she remains calm and doesn't fuss, which is comforting. Maybe that's what Grandma needs right now.'

'You're right and I know everything is going to be fine. Seeing us will put a big smile on your grandma's face.'

'And let her know that as soon as I can I'll fly over to see her in person. Tell her I'm working on it.'

I'm scrolling down my inbox as I'm talking, and I stop – letting out a loud gasp.

'What is it?' Dad asks, sounding concerned.

'We've just got ourselves a new client – Brisley House Hotel, no less!'

At last, something positive to grab on to and raise everyone's spirits.

The last two days have flown by and so much has happened. We had a little celebration at the shop after work on Friday evening to toast our new contract. But I also wanted to acknowledge Ivor and Rodric, for the way they're now organising the delivery schedules. Not only does it save time, but it has also trimmed our fuel costs. And it's allowed Mrs Mac to spend a little time each day phoning around to try to get me appointments with some potential new clients.

I can press ahead more confidently knowing that the events coordinator at Brisley House Hotel is already chasing Mrs Mac for the inserts to go into the detailed wedding folders. And it won't be long before our catalogue is sent out to wedding planners to begin firming up their orders for the spring.

As I blow-dry my hair, my head is whirling with everything that's happening. When my phone lights up, it's Holly and I immediately switch off the drier.

'Happy Sunday. How are you two doing?'

'Good, except that Katie isn't here, I'm home alone.'

I pause and then realise what that means. 'Oh, my goodness, Nick actually turned up?'

'He did. He's taking Katie to have lunch with his parents and then he's taking her to the cinema.'

And then the penny drops. Maverick is taking me to lunch, so Nick won't be working on his car. Maverick *is* doing it for the company then, as much as the thrill of restoring an old classic.

'That's wonderful news, Holly. I bet Katie was overjoyed.'

'Her face was a picture and it made me feel tearful. He hasn't been in touch for at least ten days, and I was convinced he'd forget. What are you doing today?'

Oh no – she's lonely and hoping we can get together.

'This is just between us, but I'm having lunch with Maverick.'

'You are?'

I wince. Naturally, she's shocked because I only told her about the incident at the coffee shop and chose to omit that I'd invited him to dinner at The Hunter Gatherer Inn. That wasn't a date, I was just repaying his kindness. However, today could be seen as something a little different and I'd rather keep that quiet.

'It's no big deal, just a way for him to find out more about our community. I think he's getting a little pressure to resolve this issue with the lease quickly and he can't understand why some of the directors at MPI are discussing it behind his back.'

'MPI?'

'McIntyre Property Investments Limited.'

'Ah . . . at least that's easier to say,' she laughs. 'And it's good to hear that you have his ear.'

'Naturally, it would be unprofessional of me to put pressure on Maverick or try to state my case. All I can do is to be myself and hope it at least reassures him that there's no reason to rule me out as a tenant. The timing is perfect as business is booming and it's the boost my confidence needs. I felt he wasn't really taking me seriously at our first formal meeting, and I didn't make the best impression as I was nervous.'

'But today . . . it's not business, it's social?' I'm uncomfortable hearing that sudden rise in Holly's tone.

'Sort of.'

'But he's buying *you* lunch?'

'Oh, I didn't realise it was that late and I'm only halfway through drying my hair. I'm thrilled that Katie is going to have a good time today and I'm sorry I can't be there for you. I'd much rather have a girls' day but . . . uh, duty calls.'

Duty, is it? that little voice in my head mocks. *Then why did you drive all the way to the storage unit at the farm to dig out something to wear?*

'Go – get ready and be utterly charming. If he's going to rob me of your company at least make sure it's worth your while.'

'I'll do my best!'

The Mountain View Golf Club has a great clubhouse and wonderful views towards Ben Nevis. It's seven miles north of Fort William and while Pop wasn't a member, he was a regular guest as he knew a lot of people who were.

After a rainy start to the day, a strong easterly breeze is sending the clouds on their way. I decide to put my hair up in a clip, teasing out a few strands to soften it. I don't want to look like I've spent a lot of time getting ready, even though my makeup is flawless and took over half an hour to get right. Wearing a pale-blue long-sleeved jumper and silver-grey leggings, I'm feeling good.

As soon as I draw to a halt in the car park, I spot Maverick talking to two guys and there's a peal of raucous laughter. Considering that Nick said that Maverick didn't really know anyone they all seem very matey from a distance.

The moment he spots me walking towards him he excuses himself and greets me with a warm smile.

'Perfect timing,' he states. He's wearing a dark-tan jacket with a white open-necked shirt and a pair of navy twill trousers. It's a good look for him.

'Have you been here before?' he asks as we walk over to the main entrance.

'Yes, on a number of occasions as a child, with Pop. I've never been in the clubhouse though.'

'Oh . . . well, they do an amazing Sunday lunch, and it reminds me of home. My dad would often take over the kitchen when I was back from college for a visit and whip up a traditional British Sunday roast.'

'That's nice and I bet your mother appreciated it too,' I muse. 'My mum taught me how to cook but it was just the basics.'

'Oh, my mother rarely cooks. It's been tough on her over the years, as they do a lot of entertaining but it's mostly business-related. She oversees the caterers and is the perfect host, making sure everything runs smoothly and my dad relies heavily upon her.'

Why am I not surprised?

'It sounds like they work as a team.'

He nods. 'Yeah, I suppose you can say that. But it's a tireless round of dinners and functions, and his work dictates their lifestyle. When he does power down as he refers to it, he's not really sure what to do with himself. It's like he doesn't know how to relax, and our family holidays were sometimes a bit of a washout.'

'You think life is a little more relaxed here in Scotland?' As soon as I register his reaction, I realise I've said something out of place and that wasn't my intention.

'Not really. It's more about family politics.'

There's no sense of conviction in his tone and I'm left wondering what's really going on.

'Having inherited my aunt's business I guess I'm lucky, as her dream also happens to be mine. It helps when my life isn't panning out quite the way I thought it would.'

Oh no! Honesty is *not* the best policy here and I've just filled an awkward silence with an admission I can't take back.

'It isn't?' Maverick questions, as he swings open the door, inviting me to go ahead of him.

'No one knows for sure what opportunities tomorrow will bring. I thought I had another five years until my aunt handed over the reins to me and, suddenly, here I am!' I laugh, light-heartedly.

A waiter strides forward with a cordial greeting to escort us to our table and I'm grateful because it draws a halt to our conversation. As soon as we're seated, while we're waiting for our drinks to arrive I have no intention of giving Maverick a chance of picking up where we left off and I dive straight in.

'Moving to the UK was a huge step for you. You must feel proud to be working for the company your granddad started.'

Maverick looks at me, furrowing his brow. 'The truth is that I feel I'm five years too late. If MPI was still a private company then my being here could have made a real difference. What matters to my grandparents now is that we're making up for lost time.'

I wasn't expecting such an honest answer. 'You feel that was a missed opportunity?'

'Like your aunt, Granddad didn't build his business solely to make money. It made him happy when I accepted the job, and despite what some people might think, he had nothing at all to do with my promotion.'

As the waiter brings our drinks, Maverick settles back in his seat and I watch as his eyes glance over me with interest.

'Here's to what promises to be a great lunch in good company.'

Our eyes meet and his smile is gentle and warm.

'It's an invitation I couldn't refuse,' I reply, grinning back at him. 'I don't know anyone else who's a member.'

He laughs. 'So that's the only reason you said yes?'

'No. I think you and I have a few things in common, don't you?'

Maverick takes a moment to think about it, his eyes not straying from my face. 'I guess we do. We're both trying to live up to family expectations, which isn't always easy, or practical.'

'For me it promises to be a bit of a struggle, but what does that mean for you?'

Two waiters appear and as they lay our plates in front of us the smell of a traditional Sunday lunch with all the trimmings makes my stomach begin to rumble. Maverick passes me a small pot of horseradish sauce, as he continues.

'Granddad will think of something, anything to keep me here.' His expression is one of amusement.

'Oh, I'd assumed he was expecting you to work your way to the top.'

'It means more to him that I settle here for good. If I told him tomorrow that I'd found another job somewhere else, I doubt it would bother him. The company is his past, not his future.'

I sit and watch as Maverick tucks in.

'And you're a part of the new plan?'

Maverick's eyes light up and I turn my attention to the melt-in-your mouth beef, while I wait for him to respond.

'I wouldn't mind betting that's his intention. I'm sure he'll enlighten me when he's ready. He's not the sort of man to simply sit back and enjoy the fruits of his labour, is he? For him it's about the legacy he leaves behind and I'm rather curious to see what happens next.'

Discovering that Maverick regards his job as simply that, puts a whole new spin on the situation for me. 'That's a wonderful way to look at it, Maverick.'

'I've managed to surprise you . . . and not in a bad way.'

I put down my knife and fork, glancing at him guiltily. 'I'm sorry if our first meeting was a little awkward. It makes me cringe to think back on it.'

'Me too. Let's agree to put that behind us, shall we? How's your lunch?'

'Perfect.' Great food and . . . wonderful company, I couldn't ask for anything more.

'I sort of hoped you'd give me a call to let me know how it

went with Maverick,' Holly admonishes, playfully. 'Anyway, I thought you'd like to hear that Katie had a great time with Nick, and when he dropped her back he gave me a box of chocolates.'

'He did?' Chocolates? Hmm . . . he could do better than that, but it's a start.

'I know – too little, too late, but there you go. Anyway, come on – was it fun?'

'The food was good, and I got to find out a little about Maverick's life back in the States.'

'And you told him what exactly about you? The fact that you're suddenly single again and free as a bird?'

I chuckle. 'No. I sort of touched on the fact that finding a new home for the sleigh ride once it's all in working order again would be a major headache.'

'And how did he react to that?'

'He didn't really get to respond because by then we'd finished our meal and when we went outside for a stroll we bumped into some colleagues of his.'

'What a shame, still he got to know a little about you, which is a good thing. And you sound quite upbeat to me, so I'm guessing you felt more at ease. Did he mention the protestors?'

'No, thank goodness. When we parted company, he did apologise for the delay in getting the draft lease sent out and said his office would be in touch this week to arrange for the surveyor's inspection.'

'That's good news, I assume?'

I let out a long, slow breath. 'I hope so.'

Holly knows that I can't discuss the details. But with Randall footing the bill for the dilapidation costs once the report is in, it will be a huge relief for Aunt Jane.

'Did you make plans to see Maverick again?' Holly interrupts my reverie.

'No,' I reply, as if that would be weird. Although, as we were saying goodbye Maverick had commented on how stunning the scenery is and asked if I enjoyed hiking. The answer was an enthusiastic yes, and I found myself holding my breath for a moment, thinking he was going to suggest getting together again. Unfortunately, someone Maverick knew called out to him and when he turned back to face me the moment had passed. He changed the subject and I was gutted.

'What else did you talk about?' Holly presses.

'He wanted to find out more about The Highland Elves and who exactly from his company were on the committee.'

'Oh – he was pressing you for information!' Holly blurts out, sounding disappointed.

'I told you it was more of a social invitation, as he's genuinely interested in finding out what makes the community tick. We also talked about my family's role in the charity and how it all began.'

On reflection, his questions were rather pointed, and he now has a much better understanding of who is closely linked to whom, and therefore likely to be on my side. Did I unwittingly fall into a trap after he softened me up by talking about his grandparents?

'I forgot to mention that Nick asked if Katie could sleep over at his parents' house sometime soon. I guess they've finally accepted that we're not getting back together. I thought it was nice of them to reach out. Katie does miss them, so I suggested that his mum give me a call and we can arrange something.'

'It must be quite an adjustment for them not seeing her so often,' I reflect.

'I know, but it's not my fault. I'd rather Katie goes to stay in the school holidays as that's when I really do need the help. Besides, Mum has Katie on the Saturdays I work and Sunday we like to do something special together. I'm sure they'll understand. Right, I need to iron Katie's school uniform for the morning. You might not feel today was a big success, but the fact that Maverick is even mildly interested in getting to understand how the community here works is something.'

'It can't be easy for him when his grandfather is such a pillar of the community, and he doesn't really know much about the history of the company that bears his own surname. Sleep well, Holly, and I'll see you at work tomorrow.'

As I lie in bed unable to sleep, the more I think about that parting conversation with Maverick, the more convinced I am that he intended to ask me out again. Perhaps it dawned on him that from a professional point of view it might not look good. Or was he nervous, thinking I might say no?

Even though my backup plan covers the worst-case scenario, it won't work unless I can get Maverick on my side. But now I, too, am feeling conflicted. My heart is beginning to influence my head and that doesn't bode well for clear thinking – even though that thought makes my pulse race. And, selfishly, that's why I found myself walking away disappointed, not knowing when our paths will cross again.

14.

And Just Like That Everything Falls Apart

'Morning, Mum. Is everything all right? I've just arrived at work. How was your weekend?'

I nestle the phone beneath my chin, as I use my free hand to wave to Eve and Ursula. They're busy going through the order slips while they await this morning's delivery from the wholesalers.

'Good. I just wanted to let you know that I've managed to book a flight. Dad and I are setting off in the early hours of Wednesday morning and we'll be gone for two weeks.'

'That's great news, Mum. Have you told Aunt Jane?'

'I'm about to give her a call. I don't know what you said to your dad the other day, but suddenly he agrees it's the right thing to do. And I'm glad, because it's been a while since he saw his mum and I'd hate her to think that now Jane's out there we're going to be strangers.'

'Oh, Mum! You and Dad have always been back and forth on a regular basis, but she understands how busy you've both been recently. Hopefully, things will quieten down again and you'll be able to fit in a lot more trips. Where are you staying?'

'Your grandma wants us to take her back home and stay with her for the duration of our visit. Do you think that's the right thing to do? You don't think your aunt Jane and Vic will feel we're taking over?'

When I push open the door to the office, Mrs Mac is busy processing orders and gives me a brief glance and a nod on the way past.

'I think they'll be grateful for the break,' I tell Mum, firmly.

'Good. Right, I'll make that call and get the ball rolling. Goodness, I didn't expect to be packing our bags quite so soon but there you go! And it's all good with you?'

I can tell from her tentative tone that the question covers a whole myriad of concerns and it's hard not to laugh. 'Everything is fine, Mum. Really it is.'

'Then if you're happy, we're happy. Take care, Bella.'

Dumping everything down on the desk, I turn to look at Mrs Mac.

'No Holly?'

'Katie got upset goin' into school this mornin' and had a bit of a meltdown, by the sound of it. Holly parked around the corner and waited until the school secretary rang to confirm the teacher had managed to settle the wee girl down. Holly sounded tearful herself when we spoke. She's on her way in now, the poor lassie.'

'Oh, what a pity when Katie was doing so well.' I can't help but wonder if it was seeing Nick yesterday that has brought this on. It's such a shame.

My phone pings, and it's a text from Adam. My heart sinks in my chest. I wonder what he wants.

I need to see you to talk about money.

My eyes widen in surprise.

OK. I'm free this evening.

I knew this was coming but why hit me with it at nine o'clock on a Monday morning? Unless he just wants to spoil my day by reminding me that I'm paying both a mortgage and rent.

I'm working from home today. Can't you call in this morning?

Oh, so he snaps his fingers and I'm supposed to jump?

Sorry. I'm rushed off my feet. It will be after seven at the earliest.

I wait for a few seconds and when he doesn't respond I put the phone down and switch on the PC. He's having to consider his response. The next sound I hear is another ping.

No. Lynsey will be here and it's not fair on her.

Not fair on *her*?

Are you telling me that she's living in our house?

Another pause.

That's none of your business. Do you want to talk figures, or not?

Now I'm angry.

I'll text you William Taggart's contact details. I think it's best you go through him in future.

'You absolute git!'

Mrs Mac looks up, shocked. 'What's wrong?'

'It's only Adam being Adam. But, not for much longer, as it seems his new girlfriend is putting her foot down and that's good news for me!'

Mrs Mac shakes her head, not really understanding what's going on, but if he was hoping I'd drop everything to get this sorted, I've just deflated his ego. However, he's succeeded in putting a smile on my face as in one way it is good news. I'd better give William a quick call to warn him what's coming. A little cash injection into my savings account will give me the safety net I need and, if I'm lucky, it won't all be gobbled up by the restoration work on the sleigh.

Before I can get a chance to make that call, Mrs Mac's phone rings.

'Thanks for the warning, I'll let Bella know.'

'What is it?'

'Holly just walked in without sayin' a word and she's cryin'. Eve thought you should know. Do you want me to check on her?'

'No, she'll be in the cloakroom I expect – I'll go.'

As I make a hasty exit, I notice that there are two customers wandering around The Christmas Cave. I pop my head back around the door to alert Mrs Mac, who immediately follows behind me.

I thought perhaps Holly would be splashing some water on her face, but she's not at the handbasin and I can hear gentle sobbing coming from the toilet cubicle.

'It's me, Holly. Mrs Mac told me what happened. Blow your nose and let's go make you a cup of coffee.'

I find myself pulling a face – how do I know what to say in a situation like this? I can only try to imagine how tough it must be to hand over your child when they're breaking their heart. Especially given the situation Holly is in.

'I'll . . . just . . . give me a second.'

There's a loud moaning sound that chills me to the core, then some sniffling and then the sound of the bolt sliding back with some force behind it.

'It's Nick's fault.' Holly's words greet me, her eyes are blazing. 'Consistency and routine is important to a child, it's what gives them a sense of security. He strolled in yesterday looking so pleased with himself for turning up. And look at the mess he left me with this morning. Katie seemed fine, but as I went to say goodbye to her, she just clung to me for dear life. It was like her first day at school all over again.'

Walking up to Holly, I throw my arms around her and hug tightly. 'I'm so sorry. You don't deserve this, really you don't.'

When I let go, she draws back, dabbing her eyes with a mass of damp tissues before throwing them in the bin.

'Come on,' I encourage her, as she steps over to look at herself in the mirror. Her face is red and blotchy, and she grimaces at her reflection.

I grab some paper towels while she scoops cold water over her eyes and lets out an exasperated moaning sound.

'Here, dry your face and you'll feel better with a hot drink inside of you.'

'It's separation anxiety – I know that. Lots of kids go through it and it isn't just at the start, but often in year two and sometimes year three. But Katie loves school and being with her friends. She's unsettled after yesterday because it's been weeks since Nick last took her out for the day. Is this my fault?'

I stare at her aghast. 'Why on earth would you think that this is your fault?'

'I stopped him calling in without advance notice because I thought it was too disruptive for Katie. He'd call in on his way home from work and obviously she wanted him to eat with us. But because she was always a little on edge, half expecting him and then disappointed when he didn't arrive – which was probably five nights out of seven, I drew the line. Was I wrong to do that?'

It's hard hearing Holly doubting the decision she made in good faith, only wanting to do the right thing for her daughter.

'You need to talk to a professional, someone who understands what you're going through and can give you some professional advice. You can't blame yourself for this and it might just be a hiccup. You need someone to turn to who understands the trauma both you and Katie are going through.'

'The thought of that makes me feel like a failure – surely

I should know what's best for my own child.' She sounds defeated.

'You do, but it's like grief – everyone's experience is different. No one has died, but the reality is that you've lost a partner and Katie has lost a live-in dad. You know that I'm your greatest supporter because you are a super mum to the most awesome girl. But there comes a point when reaching out to someone for help is the right thing to do.'

'And we've just hit it. Let's grab that coffee and I'll make a call. Then I'll get straight to work.'

When I eventually get back to my desk there's a message to call William urgently and he picks up immediately.

'Good morning, Bella, do you have time to pop in to see me? I have an appointment in half an hour, but I really need to speak with you straightaway and I'd rather not do that over the phone.'

'Oh, William – I was about to call you anyway. I'll pop in – give me five minutes.'

Adam must be in a hurry if he jumped straight online to get William's phone number.

'Mrs Mac, I'm going to see William, but I won't be long.'

'OK. The printers have just sent through the proofs of the new price lists and our weddin' brochures. I'll print them off and do a read-through in case I can spot any errors. Maybe I'll get Eve to have a look too and then you can cast your eyes over them when you get back. We need to approve them by three, if you want them to be ready tomorrow.'

'Sounds good to me. Right, I must dash.'

I know it's not ideal to be working on my phone while walking, but there are a few things I can quickly strike off my to-do list. It's the mental lift I need this morning, as so far it's all been firefighting when I desperately need to be tying up loose ends and pushing forward.

After switching off my phone, I slip it into my shoulder bag and run my fingers through my hair before I push open the door and climb the stairs to Taggart and Sons.

'Morning, Bella.' William greets me as he turns away from the reception desk. 'Come straight in. No interruptions for the next twenty minutes,' he calls over his shoulder as he escorts me to his office.

For some bizarre reason a slight chill travels down my spine. It's reminiscent of the walk of shame when I was called to the head teacher's office once and given detention for getting into an argument in the playground.

As I take a seat, William shuts the door and walks around to the other side of his desk. His face is grim.

'If my ex-partner, Adam Hamilton, has already been in touch I can only apologise for the fact that I wasn't able to forewarn you. We recently split up, and I was going to call you first thing to ask if you could help sort out the issue of the shared equity we have, in the house we purchased together. It's just been one of those days when nothing has gone as planned, I'm afraid.'

William stares back at me, frowning. 'No, that's not why I called you here, but it's something I can most definitely help with. McIntyre Property Investments Limited have emailed over the draft lease.'

His frown deepens even further, and I clear my throat, nervously.

'It's bad news, then?'

'There are a couple of surprises, but I'm sure you've had some back and forth so it's possible that I'm lagging behind a little in where things stand.'

'Surprises? None that I've been informed about, other than the fact there's another interested party and the lease is going to be awarded based on the bids submitted.'

'Ah. Right. Putting that to one side, there are two major issues that I feel will be of concern to you. The first is that the ground floor of the shop next door will be incorporated into the premises, thereby increasing the overall size. Which leads me on to the other pressing matter, which is that the new lease doesn't begin until the first of February.'

I can't believe what I'm hearing.

'Sorry, William, I need to let that sink in. I wasn't expecting it, although I'd heard rumours about changes to the shoe repairers next door. Even if I was looking for more space, which I'm not – and I put in a successful bid – I'm still forced to vacate by the fifth of December? What do they expect me to do for the best part of two months?' My head is spinning.

'Take a deep breath, Bella. Would you like a glass of water?'

He's worried I'm going to freak out, and I think he might be right. It's hard to calm myself when this has obviously been the plan all along.

'No. It's just a shock, that's all. Sorry, William, please continue.'

'The terms of the new lease are full build out to a standard retail specification throughout, with an additional eight hundred square feet at ground floor level. It doesn't include the flat over the top of the adjacent property and the access to that will be moved to the rear, which is stated in the letter. At present, as you know, it's through a separate front door at street level with a staircase up to the first floor. That will be ripped out and subsumed to enlarge the additional ground floor retail space.'

I'm stunned. 'They're gutting the whole property and enlarging it?'

'Yes. They're maximising the rental opportunity. This isn't personal, Bella, but I know that's how it feels given your family's history. I'm afraid there isn't anything we can do to fight this – you do understand that?'

'Even though it's obvious that this is being done to accommodate the other party?'

William sighs. 'Even if that is true, we can't prove it. If Randall was still in charge the outcome would probably have been the same in this financial climate.'

I nod my head, feeling numb. We've loved that building and treated it as if it were our own. And it's going to be ripped apart, extended, redecorated and turned into a blank box ready for the next tenant. We don't stand a chance. This is it then – the end.

'It's going to devastate Aunt Jane because we've played into their hands, haven't we?'

'This is off the record, Bella, but it would have been difficult for them to oust her without a breach of contract. It simply gave them the opportunity to bring forward plans earmarked for the future. If the rumours are true, there's a London-based firm looking for a prime location in the High Street. They'll no doubt pay a premium and a big one.'

Hmm. Holly said the same thing; an agent for Mayfair Bespoke Wallpaper Designs, apparently. I'd bet a tenner that he had a coffee at The Wee Nook Coffee Shop. It's not always careless chatter, using a café table as a mobile office tends to attract attention.

'Of course – another five years and my aunt would have retired anyway, and they probably assumed she'd sell the business. Handing it over to me is what's caused the problem, isn't it?'

He's obviously uncomfortable talking off the record, but I can feel the empathy.

'Yes, because the people who are rooting for you aren't thinking with their heads, but with their hearts. The man in charge of McIntyre Property Investments Limited doesn't want bad publicity, or to get on the wrong side of public opinion. Neither does Maverick. However, for a modest investment it will certainly pay off for them in terms of future income from the property.'

He's choosing his words carefully while making it clear there is nothing to be done.

'I'll have no choice now but to bow out. And Maverick McIntyre didn't have the backbone to tell me to my face what was going on.'

William recoils, looking very uneasy. 'That's not the way to look at it, Bella – trust me. If there was anything at all that we could legally address, I'd be on the case. Anger is counterproductive. Don't waste your time, use it to move forward because you have a deadline and a lot of decisions to make rather quickly. All I need from you today is confirmation of how you want me to respond.'

Closing my eyes for a moment to try to clear my mind doesn't really help. Am I being unfair to Maverick? After all, he doesn't call the shots or really understand the situation I'm in.

'Look – this is a shock and there's no rush,' William adds, reassuringly. 'The deadline to submit a formal bid is in ten days' time. You don't have to pull out today, you know.'

Is that a devious little twinkle in William's eye?

'You're right. I'd like to take a little time to think it through.' Why should we make it quick and easy for them?

William gives me a warm smile and even though mine is lukewarm as we shake hands, I know that it gives him some pleasure to know that we will continue to be a thorn in MPI's side for a while longer.

'It's funny, William, but something told me this was a battle I wasn't going to win and I'm not completely unprepared. But that shop means so much to me.'

'And to so many people for miles around, Bella.'

'It won't shut us down, William, but nothing will be quite the same again, will it?'

15.

It's One Dilemma After Another

There is no one I can talk to about what I discovered this morning. Holly is fragile, Mum is frantically packing suitcases and Dad is making lists as he hands over control of the programme for the restoration work on the sleigh to Cliff. If I confide in Mrs Mac she wouldn't say a word to anyone, but Rodric will take one look at her face and know something is very wrong.

The four people I know I can trust to have my best interests at heart all have problems of their own to contend with. Adding my woes to theirs would be unfair of me and so, for the first time ever, I'm entirely on my own.

I'm feeling so disconnected from reality that when I offer to help downstairs and Eve tells me quite confidently that they have everything under control, I'm disappointed. Which is silly, as I know they have all the resources they need. Even Mrs Mac has asked me twice in the last couple of hours whether I'm feeling OK. She thinks I'm stewing over Adam's texts, but I really don't give a damn about that. I know it will be worth every penny to let William take charge of the negotiations, as Adam won't be able to mess him about. The fact that Lynsey is now firmly in the picture, means it's in all our interests to get the finances sorted out quickly. And what a relief that is for me.

I force myself to focus and I realise that I'm just trying to put off the inevitable. I've done my research and I know what the options are. None of them are perfect, but the industrial unit I viewed on the edge of the retail park isn't going to hang around for long. Once I've made a firm commitment there is no going back, but it will only solve a part of my problem.

I'm not sure how Maverick will take it when William breaks the news that I'm withdrawing my interest for the new lease. And, in my naivety, I made such a fuss about it. But worse than that, I rejected out of hand the offer from Maverick to consider the premises undergoing renovation at the other end of the High Street. Unless something else comes on the market, that might prove to have been a costly and foolish move.

By three o'clock, my head is pounding, and when I instinctively glance up I didn't even realise Mrs Mac was standing in front of me looking fretful.

'Bella, ye need to pack it in for the day, lassie. You've one of yer bad heads brewin' and the colour has drained from yer face.'

If I slump any further forward, I'll end up sprawled out over the desk. I sit up, my shoulders sagging.

'The good news is that in five minutes ye could be laid out on yer bed with a cold flannel easin' that head. Come on, I'll put these papers into the file while ye grab that bag of yours.'

I'm too wiped out to argue because Mrs Mac is right.

'Sorry. Maybe ask Eve to lock up, as you were here early this morning?' I suggest.

'Don't you go worryin' about that – just get yourself home and sleep off that bad head of yours. You'll be back to yer old self in the mornin', for sure.'

As soon as I'm out in the fresh air the pressure eases a little. The High Street is full of tourists and locals alike, people sitting on benches taking the weight off their feet while they enjoy a takeaway coffee or munch on a snack from one of the eateries.

It's a huge relief when I unlock the door to the flat and step inside. I simply dump everything down on the floor and head into the bathroom. Grabbing the first thing to hand, which is a bath towel, I hold it under the cold tap and squeeze it lightly. Kicking off my shoes I make my way over to the sofa and flop down, putting up my legs and groaning out loud. Then I cover my forehead with the blissfully cool towel and sink into a deep sleep.

As an annoying sound seeps into my consciousness, I wonder if it's a bee and I'm in danger of getting stung. But it's dark and I can't see a thing. Then I realise there's a towel over my head. The buzzing noise continues as I yank it off and look around for the offending sound.

No, not a bee – it's my phone and it's on vibrate. I roll over gently, relieved that the pain over my left eyebrow has gone. I ease myself up onto my feet and reach out to grab my bag, not really concerned that the phone's stopped buzzing. I didn't even realise I'd turned off the volume and then I remember it was in case Adam called.

There are two missed calls, and they are both from Randall. He must think I'm very rude ignoring him.

'Randall, sorry . . . it's been a bit hectic.' It isn't until I glance across at the clock that I realise it's just after seven in the evening.

'I heard from an unofficial source that draft leases have been sent out in regard to the premises you occupy. I'm assuming you were one of the two interested parties?'

'Yes, but I probably won't be putting forward a bid, I'm afraid.'

'Oh, Bella. I feared that might be the case. Have you decided what you're going to do?'

'Discussions are ongoing as I'm considering a couple of different options. None of them are perfect, so it's a case of weighing up the pros and cons.'

'Ah, I understand.' I can hear the disappointment in his

voice. 'It'll be a sad day for many people, including me, to see another company move in. I wish I could have done more.'

'Randall, please don't blame yourself. It's not the end, it's the start of a new chapter, that's all.' Sadly, it's not just Randall I'm trying to convince here, but also myself as I say goodbye.

Grabbing a bottle of water from the fridge, I call Holly.

'Bella, are you feeling a little better? I was tempted to give you a call but I didn't want to risk waking you.'

'I'm just a bit dehydrated, that's all. Bless Mrs Mac, she was right to make me head for home.'

There's a rustling sound and Holly lowers her voice. 'Katie's almost asleep, hang on a second.' More rustling. 'I'm in the kitchen so I can't disturb her.'

'How was she when you picked her up from school?'

'Katie told me that she had this sudden pain in her heart when I kissed her goodbye and that's why she cried. Can you imagine that?' Holly's voice falters.

Oh, my goodness. Now we're both feeling choked up. 'Oh, bless her!'

'I thought about what you said, but it just sent me into a bit of a panic. I'm in this online group for single parents. There's a lady I've been chatting to offline over the past couple of weeks and I messaged her. She's almost at the end of getting her, and her two sons' lives, back on track. We're going to meet up for coffee one lunchtime next week to talk openly. She's had help herself, some useful, some not. But it's a starting point, for me – at least.'

'That's wonderful, Holly. Only someone going through the same thing can really understand what's helpful and what isn't.'

'It means a lot to me that you understand that, Bella. Now go drink some water and have some hot buttered toast. It'll settle your stomach. Sleep well, and tomorrow can't possibly be any worse than today, can it?'

On the way into work my stomach is rumbling. My taste buds are always weird the day after a migraine, and I couldn't even finish my coffee this morning. I ended up throwing the toast in the bin as it tasted bland, and I figure what I need is something sugary – comfort food. The best shortbread in Fort William is three doors down and I make a beeline for The Wee Nook Coffee Shop.

'Morning, Alice.'

'Hi, Bella. Are you settling in all right?'

'I am! I'd forgotten how easy it is to keep things tidy when you live on your own,' I remark, and she laughs.

'It means you did the right thing although it did come as a bit of a surprise when I heard the news. Coffee?'

'No, thanks, but can I have eight slices of shortbread please – actually, make that nine, I'm sure I can eat two.'

Alice lifts the tray out of the glass-fronted display cabinet and carefully layers the generously sized slabs into a bag. 'I figure you deserve it with what you have going on. How are things going over in Faro – is your grandma back on her feet?'

'Not yet, she's had a few problems. Mum and Dad are flying over to lend a hand.'

'Well, ask them to pass on my best wishes for a speedy recovery and tell Jane she's sorely missed. I often forget she's in a sunnier place and I half expect her to pop in for a macchiato to kick-start her day. She was a part of my morning routine. I could set the clock by her.'

'It takes a while to get used to big changes, doesn't it?' I reply, sombrely. Aunt Jane leaving was the tip of the iceberg, there are a lot more changes to come.

'Yes, but life doesn't stand still, does it? Is there anything else I can get you?'

'No, that's perfect, thanks. I think I'm going to be really popular at work today.'

I pay and exit, gingerly holding the bag as flat as I can

on the palm of one hand. Not that anyone would refuse to take one if they don't arrive in one piece, I smile to myself.

'Bella.'

I wasn't even aware there was anyone behind me and when I turn my head Lynsey McGregor is standing two paces away, staring at me.

'What do you want, Lynsey?'

'I'm not here to make trouble, Bella, I promise.'

'Really? You were obviously hanging around waiting for me to open up.'

Instinctively, I start walking again, diving into the pocket of my padded jacket to pull out the bunch of keys. I'm three strides away from the shop door and she can't follow me inside.

'I . . . um . . . wanted to thank you.'

'For what?' I call over my shoulder as I insert the key in the lock.

'For letting him go.'

The bag of shortbread slips, listing to one side, and I clutch it to my body as I half turn to look at her.

'He couldn't accept it, you see – he couldn't admit to himself that your feelings for him had changed. It made him want to cling on even tighter, even though he was turning to me more and more. At first it was just a drink after work, and we'd sit and talk about life in general. Then he started to open up and he told me he was losing you and he didn't know what to do about it.'

'And you comforted him – fine, I get it, Lynsey, and I wish you both well because I've moved on.'

It sounds harsh, but it's true.

'Adam can't bring himself to say sorry, you see – not to you. He's angry with himself, because even though he knew it was over long before you walked out, he feels he wasn't good enough and that eats away at him.'

Leaning my back against the door jamb for support, we're face to face. I can see by the way she's clasping and unclasping her hands, how nervous she is – in fact, the shoulder strap of her bag suddenly slips down to her elbow making her jump.

'Sorry, I'm so sorry, but I thought you ought to know. He's lost without you because a part of him can't quite accept what's happened and that's why I moved in with him. I love Adam and I really do believe that when he's not such a mess, his heart will tell him why I was the one he turned to.'

My emotions are churning, or maybe it's my stomach still complaining. I don't feel upset or angry, I feel a sense of annoyance. Both Adam and I were complicit in this. I pushed aside my truth, by letting one day follow another because I wasn't ready to face the upheaval.

'We all made mistakes, Lynsey, but it's time to leave the past behind.'

'He won't cheat you. The house has already been valued and there's money to pay you what you're due.'

Lynsey has my admiration, because I'm guessing she's using her savings and is prepared to sign on the dotted line to make the house their new home together. I have no idea what reaction she was expecting, as her face isn't giving much away. My gut instincts are telling me that her motive is genuine, but she also wanted to look me in the eye and hear me say it was over. And now she knows that's the truth.

'Using a solicitor wasn't because I was expecting there to be any arguments, but because I thought it would make everyone's life easier. I don't begrudge anyone their happiness – and that includes Adam and you.'

She doesn't take her eyes off me as I turn the key in the lock and step inside. As I go to close the door, she continues to stare at me and I pause, wondering whether I should invite her inside but we're done talking. Then she nods her head several times, as if in relief, and I watch as she walks away.

I continue to clutch the paper bag tightly to my chest as I walk on wobbly legs over to the floristry desk and lay it down flat. Then I open it up and grab a broken piece of shortbread. It doesn't take long for the effects of the sugar to kick in and my stomach settles. Some endings are explosive, some are like a damp squib. This one was somewhere in between because it happened over a long period of time and I'm happy with a lacklustre finale. Now, let's get these safely upstairs and if I eat all the broken bits and pop them on a plate, no one will be any the wiser.

As I slip off my coat, the landline rings and I hurry into the office to pick it up.

'Good morning, you're through to The Highland Flower Shop, how can I help?'

'Oh, I was expecting Mrs Mac. Hi, Bella, it's Ursula. I have a little problem with Monty this morning.'

'He's not well?'

'No, nothing like that. My neighbour can only look after him when her husband is working from home, and he's been called into the office today. She's allergic to dog hair, so she can't come into the house but she's fine with the dog walking. I was hoping I could get the lady opposite to call in to check on him, top up his food, and do the handover for his walk, but she was literally on the way out and won't be back until mid-afternoon. I'm really sorry about this as I know Eve was counting on me being there today. It's going to be a busy one.'

'Why don't you bring him in with you? It's just one day and you can put his bed and bowls in Santa's Grotto. It's not the end of the world if he wanders through into the shop, is it?'

'Oh, Bella – that's so thoughtful! He sleeps for long spells and he's a good lad, so I'm sure he won't be a problem.'

'There you go, then. And you can break off whenever you like to take him for a walk. In fact, if Rodric's around you probably won't even get a look in.'

If all problems were as easy as that to fix, life would be blissful!

Several hours after Mum and Dad arrived in Faro on Wednesday, Grandma Susan was on the phone. She was back home and excited about sleeping in her own bed again. Talking to her, it was hard to believe there's anything wrong and Mum texted me yesterday to say they'd all slept well. Even Dad was pleasantly surprised at how perky Grandma looks. As I'm out most of the morning I said I'd call them later. In the meantime, no news is good news, although I will be glad to get an update.

As I arrive for a second viewing of the industrial unit on the edge of the retail park on a rainy Friday morning, it's crunch time.

Accepting the fact that no one – not even Randall – can save the day is sobering and this is one of the biggest business decisions I'll ever make. And, strangely enough, it was Lynsey who spurred me into action. Having lived the last year of my life pretending everything in my personal life was just fine when it wasn't, I don't intend to make the same mistakes at work. Putting the blame on Maverick or MPI is using them as a scapegoat. It will be my fault entirely if I don't make some quick decisions and get things moving.

'If you want a bit of time to wander around on your own,' the agent offers, 'I have some papers to drop in to one of the other units and they'll no doubt offer me a coffee. Say . . . half an hour?'

'That would be a great help, thank you.' The agent is being very patient with me as it's my second visit, so he knows I'm not a time-waster.

The large open space is characterless, and as I trail around it takes a lot of imagination to consider how best to kit it out. There's a door and a window to one side, which leads into a small reception. It's a third of the size of our current office and it will only take one desk and some of our filing cabinets.

I step through a side door that takes me into the long run right through to the back of the unit. To my right is the space accessed by an up-and-over roller door, which will easily accommodate both vans nose to tail.

When the agent returns, I've finished taking photos, which will help me when I sit down to work on the floor plan.

'I think I'm done,' I inform him. 'If I email you my solicitor's details as soon as I get back to the office, can you send the paperwork over to him to look at?'

That provokes a big smile. 'Of course, no problem at all.'

'Great, and I'll give you a call early next week.'

As we shake hands, in my head the deal is done. The vision isn't quite there and I have no idea how the team will take the news. But I probably have a week at least to get my act together before I reveal the new look for the business. Everything is about to change and there is no going back.

This is progress, but why do I feel so defeated as I walk back to my car? And then I spot Nick. In a couple of months' time the chances are that I'll be bumping into him six days a week.

Please don't mention Holly, or Katie – I can't face it this morning.

'Hey, Bella. Back again already? You sure are busy at the moment. I've got news of my own – I just found a buyer for my car!' Nick beams at me and I stare back at him in amazement.

'You have?'

'A friend of Maverick's, so I know the guy can come up with the money.'

'That's wonderful news, Nick, I'm thrilled for you.'

I never thought I'd see the day Nick would stand in front of me looking happy, knowing the car he's spent two years working on is going to another home.

'It turns out there was an even bigger profit in it than I first thought. I'll still be doing work on the side, but that's extra cash now and it's like a huge weight has been taken off my shoulders. Anyway, I literally just got the call and when I spotted you I . . . well, you know more than most how much this means to me.'

What can I say, knowing that it's probably too late after Katie's meltdown on Monday? He's completely unaware of that by the look of it, and my heart sinks.

'I do. Anyway, I must dash as all this running around means the work on my desk is piling up.'

To my surprise, he steps forward to give me a hug.

'Exciting times all round, Bella!' he exclaims and what I see in his expression is relief, a man who was drowning and has suddenly been thrown a lifeline. The old me would have seen this as a leap forward but the new me is a realist. Expect nothing and you'll never be disappointed; hope for the best but accept that there are no guarantees and be prepared to keep tweaking the plan.

It seems that Nick is finally taking responsibility for his actions. There's even a spring in his step as he heads back to the garage. The moment I slip into the driver's seat I make no attempt to turn on the ignition, instead I dial William Taggart's number. It's time to get the ball rolling.

'Hi, William, it's Bella. I've just had a second look at a commercial unit on the north side of the retail park. I've asked them to send the paperwork over to you and maybe we can get together sometime next week when you've had a chance to go through it?'

'That's good news indeed. I'll make sure I attend to it as soon as it arrives. How are you doing?'

He's a very astute man and caring. 'I'm doing good, William, thank you. Have a lovely weekend!'

'You too, Bella. You too.' I switch off my phone and pop it into my bag. Having just made a truly mega decision, I'm going to need a little quiet time to let it sink in.

As soon as I get back to the office, I check my voicemail in case Mum or Dad called and note that there are three messages. Worryingly, the first two are blank but the third one stops me in my tracks.

'Bella, it's Maverick. Um . . . sorry, I tried you a couple of times but I, um, guess you're tied up. When you get a moment can you give me a call? Thanks. Bye.'

Glancing at the number I'm guessing it's his personal

mobile, as I have the office number listed under the company name. Moments later, the sound of his voice instantly puts a smile on my face.

'Bella! Sorry about the garbled message. I realised afterwards that it might worry you but it's not business related.'

That grabs my attention. 'Oh, I see. I've been meaning to get in touch anyway to thank you for the wonderful lunch last Sunday, but this week has been crazily busy. It was fun to sit and talk.' *Fun?* I wince, thinking that didn't sound very convincing.

'I'm glad to hear it as . . . uh . . . you mentioned that you enjoy hiking and while I'm more of a rambler, I was wondering whether you have a favourite trail? If you're free tomorrow, I thought it might be . . . *fun* . . . to spend a few hours communing with nature.' There's a muffled laugh. Is he flirting with me?

Tempted to blurt out an enthusiastic *yes* without thinking, I relax my shoulders and take a few moments. 'Tomorrow . . . hmm . . . why not? It's a great way to unwind.' *Cool response, Bella*, that inner voice fills my head.

'Fantastic! I'll pick you up around elevenish?'

'Perfect. I'll bring a picnic lunch on the condition that you carry it,' I declare, injecting a little humour of my own.

'Fair enough.'

'I'll see you tomorrow then.'

Sauntering along to the kitchen wearing the biggest grin ever, I'm about to make a round of teas and coffees before I get back to work when my phone starts ringing and it makes me jump.

'Hi, Mum!'

'I had to give you a call, Bella, to tell you the good news. Grandma is sitting in the garden with three of her friends having tea. She's the life and soul of the party and she's even managing to keep an eye on Dad and give him instructions. He's weeding the borders and deadheading the plants. He's in his element and I haven't seen him this relaxed in a long time.'

'That's incredible, Mum. How's Grandma's ankle?'

'She has this walking aid, like a metal stick with feet on it but she can't get the hang of it because it's rather cumbersome. As soon as her tea party is finished, we're taking her to a shop where she can try a few different options.'

'Fingers crossed it will make all the difference.'

'I know,' Mum whispers, positively. 'Vic admitted to us yesterday that at times she's hardly been able to get around without someone walking alongside to support her. We're thinking now that she had a reaction to the anaesthetic, as she hasn't had a single episode since we've been here.'

'I can hear the relief in your voice.'

'Jane and Vic looked frazzled when we arrived, Bella. It's been tougher on them than either Dad or I had realised. Vic's taken your aunt off for an overnight stay at a hotel a couple of hours' drive from here, which will do them the world of good.'

'I can't tell you how happy I am to hear that Grandma is on the mend.'

'Dad was more worried than he let on but we both knew that, didn't we? He's finally able to relax. We've borrowed a wheelchair as tomorrow we've been invited to lunch by a friend of hers. Apparently, this lady owns a charming little villa about a five-minute drive away.'

'Ah, that's lovely.'

'I thought so too, until Vic mentioned the property will be going on the market sometime next year,' Mum laughs.

'Grandma can't help herself, can she?'

'Your grandma is good at sowing the seed and your wish of having access to a holiday home in Faro might not be out of reach. But your dad doesn't make impulsive decisions, so this is a clever strategy.'

'I hope there's room in the garden for a pool. Just to cool off when it's really hot,' I tease her.

Mum bursts out laughing. 'Don't you start . . . and promise me you'll take a little time for yourself this weekend. You deserve it.'

'Hand on heart, I'm planning to do just that!' Although I think it's best that I don't mention Maverick's name.

16.

The Turning Point

I spend the entire afternoon furtively trying to fathom out how to make the industrial unit accommodate our needs. Every time Mrs Mac approaches my desk, even though she can't see my screen, I get flustered. I can't share this with anyone until I have the loose ends all tied up and one big component is still up in the air. Going live with only half a plan is likely to undermine my team's confidence in me, and rightly so. Just figuring out the logistics of splitting the business – and the team – into two has required my full attention. I'm conscious that it's going to be a massive upheaval for us all.

The truth is that I made a huge mistake rejecting Maverick's offer to look at the empty property at the other end of the High Street. One that I hope is reversible, because if it isn't it puts everything else in jeopardy.

'You look like ye need this, lassie,' Mrs Mac comments as she places a mug of tea down in front of me. 'Don't ye go overdoin' it, Bella. Stress is nae good for anyone.'

'I know, Mrs Mac, and thank you.'

'I'm about to send out that mailshot. Holly said she'll stuff the envelopes for me once you approve the cover letter. You'll no doubt wanna make a few changes, but I did ma best.'

'You always do and you have no idea how grateful I am.'

'It's tough goin' but ye'll get there.'

'Yes, I didn't realise how different it would be sitting in this desk,' I reply, candidly.

'You think I'm sittin' over there, oblivious to the fact you're steppin' up for us all? And it's takin' a toll on you, Bella, that's obvious.'

'Do you think you can manage without me tomorrow?'

Mrs Mac looks me straight in the eye. 'We've more than enough people in to cope. Only Holly is off tomorrow. It's high time you grabbed a little downtime, lassie. All work and no play . . . as the sayin' goes.'

Hmm . . . but I wonder what her reaction would be if she knew I was going to be hanging out with Maverick? He's not exactly Mr Popular around here right now.

'So, this is Aonach Mòr – the eighth highest mountain in Britain.' Maverick looks impressed as I climb out of the passenger seat of his VW camper van. It wasn't quite the mode of transport I was expecting, I will be honest, as Nick's speciality is performance cars.

'It is and it's even better the higher up you go. The van is rather nice,' I remark.

'It belonged to my father and was stored in a garage at my grandparents' previous property. When they moved house, they asked him what he wanted to do with it and he didn't want to let it go. When I first arrived, and Granddad showed it to me, I made a call and my father seemed pleased that I was interested in bringing the old girl back to life. A specialist company stripped it back to the bare shell and re-sprayed it for me. It's been a challenge but it's such an icon I couldn't let her rust away.'

That sort of work doesn't come cheap, but then I should imagine money isn't really a problem for Maverick.

'I can't believe you haven't already taken a ride on the mountain gondola when it's virtually on your doorstep. Have you done any sightseeing at all?' I question.

He shrugs his shoulders. 'A little. I spend a lot of time at the weekends working on the interior of the van, while a friend of mine has been rebuilding the engine and teaching me a thing or two, along the way. At long last she's running like a dream.'

'It's been quite a project by the sound of it but I am a little surprised. I can't quite see you as a camper van type of guy.'

He shakes his head. 'I'm not, well, I wasn't but she's growing on me. It's my attempt to put a smile on my father's face when he flies over for his first visit. When it's complete, I'll be sending him a video.'

'That's a thoughtful gesture.'

As they say, never judge a book by its cover. Maverick's company vehicle is a BMW 3 series, so I was expecting his old classic to be a saloon car.

'There are still a few integral components to fit inside, but it shouldn't take more than a couple of weekends to finish it off.'

'Thank goodness for that.'

Maverick frowns. 'It'll look awesome once I've installed the handmade kitchen unit I've commissioned. I'm pleased with the standard considering I'm not a pro and I've done most of the inside work myself.'

'Oh, I wasn't implying that it doesn't already look fabulous, because it does, and it is a classic . . .' Do I tell him? I suppose if the work is almost finished it won't really make any difference. 'Nick usually sees his daughter on Sundays, and it has caused a few problems.'

We walk as we talk, slipping on our backpacks as we head over to the ticket office.

'You know Nick? I didn't realise he had a daughter.'

'Yes, I'm her godmother. His ex, Holly, works at the shop.'

'Does this mean I'm in someone's bad books?'

I shake my head. 'No, he's been glad of the work.'

'Well, I've been grateful for his expertise and the company, but now I feel bad. I wish he'd said something. We could have worked on it in the evenings.'

We hurry over to join the small queue and I insist on

paying for the tickets as Maverick so kindly drove us. As we go through to the base station, Maverick's face is a picture.

'Wow – this is quite something.'

'Don't hang around. It doesn't stop, it's on a continuous loop.' With only four people in front of us, they all clamber into one gondola and seconds later we're given the nod to board the next one. No one follows behind us, so we have it all to ourselves.

'It's a real shame about the cloud cover. How long does it take to get to the top?'

'About fifteen minutes. It doesn't go right to the top – just 2,132 feet up the north face. It's popular with experienced mountain bikers who enjoy the thrills of the various routes back down. Climbers use it as a short cut to some of the challenging winter climbs. Originally it was built to take skiers up to the slopes.'

Within seconds, the steep climb takes us high above the tops of the thick forest of trees and looking down on them always gives me a thrill. It's a little breezy but the forecast says it'll warm up as the day goes on.

'What types of trees are here?'

'Scots pine, birch, alder and Sitka spruce,' I reply. 'Also, rowan – known as mountain ash. They're easier to spot as they're tough little trees that love a remote, windswept habitat. Pop told me that they keep evil spirits away, so they're often found next to abandoned crofts.'

Maverick is delighted when we catch a glimpse of two bikers to our right, as they descend what looks from here to be a perilously steep route. It twists and turns and then is swallowed up in a cluster of dense firs.

'It looks like madness to me but given that they come here in their droves it must be the thrill of a lifetime. Two cars in front of us you'll notice a bike strapped on the back of the gondola,' I point out.

'Ah, right. So, what's up there?' Maverick asks, straining his neck but all we can see looking directly ahead are the pylons and the steel cables supporting the long line of gondolas ahead of us. Then the mountainside disappears into a thick band of grey rolling cloud obscuring the peaks beyond.

'Believe it or not, aside from the station at the top, the Snowgoose Restaurant and Bar is a real bonus. Beyond that, there are several manageable walks to choose from. I thought we'd head for Sgurr Finnisg-aig. It's a forty-minute trek there and back and not arduous, but enough of an ascent to make casual hillwalkers feel they've achieved something.' I grin at him.

With that I stare down at his feet and a pair of almost new hiking boots. He did say he was more of a rambler. But at least he has a good-quality insulated walker's jacket with a hood. It's going to be nippy up there, but the bonus is that as the autumnal chill starts to bite the leaves are now changing colour and there's a raft of different hues from orange to gold, to brighten a somewhat grey-looking day.

'First one to the top then,' he jokes.

The gauntlet has been thrown down. But I've done it many times before, so we'll see.

Either side of us, the landscape opens out as we leave the trees behind. The steep, grassy slopes and low-level shrubs steer my gaze across to the mountain ranges behind us. I draw Maverick's attention to the distant view, and he turns in his seat. A landscape of greenery interspersed with lochs and rivers is incredibly calming, even with the constant rattling of metal against the cables – not only from our car, but other gondolas as we watch them descend.

My least favourite part of the ride is as the gondola approaches the station as there's a jolt, but seconds later we exit the building and stop to put on our backpacks.

'The restaurant will be full at this time of the day; if we don't hang around for too long, by the time they've finished lunch we'll be on our way back.' He looks a little crestfallen. 'Are you hungry now?'

'Rather foolishly I skipped breakfast.'

'Big mistake; you can't walk on an empty stomach. Let's find somewhere a little sheltered to sit and eat our picnic before we set off then.'

'Sorry, I wasn't thinking. After you.' Maverick indicates for me to take the lead.

'There's a little knoll over there, it's next to a tiny stream. I didn't have time to pop to the supermarket I'm afraid, so it was a case of raiding the fridge. This is the last thing I was expecting to do today.'

'I caught you off guard, didn't I?' He grins at me.

'No, it was a . . . pleasant surprise. Right, it's a bit rocky here but there's a dip the other side of the knoll and we'll be out of this annoying wind.'

It keeps catching the wisps of hair tucked into the hood of my jacket and face-on it can take your breath away at times, but Maverick doesn't seem bothered.

I pull out a folded waterproof mat and lay it down as Maverick retrieves the two lunch boxes that I gave him to carry. I settle myself on the mat, leaning over to dip my hands into the tiny babbling stream alongside us. The icy cold makes my fingers tingle. Maverick leans forward to do the same and I laugh as he recoils the moment his fingers touch the water.

'That's way colder than I was expecting. Although there's snow on the top of Ben Nevis all year round I'm told. What exactly are we looking out over?' Maverick asks, as he starts eating.

'The Great Glen, the hills of Knoydart; Loch Eil and Loch Linnhe stand out the most. And if you look behind us, we've overshadowed by the Càrn Mòr Dearg, and Ben Nevis, if you can spot glimpses of the mountain between the rolling clouds. We could get lucky, and they might clear a little to give us a better view by the time we make our descent.'

It's pleasant sitting here in the hollow, eating and feeling at one with nature. The air tastes and smells different at this elevation. The water running off the mountains is so clear as it trickles downstream that it sparkles.

'Take care whenever you step off the path,' I warn Maverick. 'There are patches of seriously boggy ground the higher we go and some rather big boulders. It's not too bad here, but the tufts of wild grasses, gorse and purple heather can hide some tricky patches of uneven rocks. It's easy to turn an ankle if you don't watch where you're putting your feet.'

'I appreciate the advice.'

'And I appreciate the company,' I admit, as we briefly glance at each other. 'It's been quite a while since I managed to get up here. I'm saving my dessert for when we get to the viewing point.'

'I think I will, too. Thanks for bothering to do this. Sandwiches always taste better when someone else makes them for you,' he remarks, as I pass him a bottle of water.

We pack everything up and I take a moment to gather my hair into a ponytail, pulling up my hood and securing it with the toggle before we pick our way back to the main path. The trail starts off with well-compacted dirt and gravel. There's a straggly line of people walking in both directions, which is promising. At popular times of the day it can end up being a bit of a stop/start journey, particularly on the narrower, tricky parts of the trail.

'Look, there's a mountain hare!' I point out.

Maverick smiles at me. 'I take it this is one of your favourite walks?'

'Yes. My ex and I came here often. I love it in all winds and weathers.'

'What's the dream now that everything in your life has suddenly changed?'

I expel a puff of air, my lips vibrating slightly as I shake my head. 'I'm taking it one day at a time, I suppose.'

'It doesn't look like that to me. Quite frankly, I don't think you're giving yourself enough credit given that you are also driving forward a business in the midst of some major changes.'

'Thanks. However, the reality is I'm learning that some mistakes can be costly, but defeat doesn't sit well with me.'

Maverick lapses into silence. I don't want him to feel awkward about the dilemma I find myself in because it's not his fault. I wouldn't have accepted his invitation if I didn't think he would be good company, which he is, but I can't pretend I don't have a lot of problems at the moment. I can't expect him to be honest with me if I'm not prepared to do the same.

We walk past a brook running parallel with the path. A young mum and her little boy are standing on two large flat stones in the middle of it. The child is throwing small pebbles into the water, loving the fact that he's splashing his mum.

Both Maverick and I smile at them as we continue on.

'It must be a comfort to have some family around you, but I bet you miss your friends,' I remark, in an attempt to change the subject.

'Yes. I don't think people realise what a huge adjustment it is to turn your back on everything and everyone you know. Learning how to fit in isn't easy at times, which is one of the reasons why I joined the golf club. I play an OK game, but it's as much about connecting with people outside of the office, as it is working on my handicap.'

'You're finding it hard going?' I turn my head to glance at him and our eyes meet.

'A bit like you, all I can do is take it one day at a time. Getting to know the locals might make my working life a little easier. Even if it just stops me unwittingly putting my foot in it. I seem to be doing a lot of that lately,' he confesses.

I give him a genuinely sympathetic look. 'I'm sure it'll get easier as time goes on.'

'Well, it can't get any worse, can it?' He flashes me a cheeky grin.

With that, Maverick pulls a beanie hat from the side pocket of his backpack. I watch as he eases it over his head. It suits him. He's a good-looking man, striking and not just because he's six foot something . . . two, maybe even three. He exudes energy, something I find strangely compelling.

We're getting a little out of breath as the terrain becomes more rugged. Stepping off the path to drink some water, we let a small group of people pass.

'I spend at least one weekend a month at my grandparents' place and the odd overnight stay mid-week. But Granddad is caught up making plans now he's retired. It's costly to run an estate like that properly unless they turn it back into what it was several years ago, a hotel. Grandma sees that as a daunting prospect at their age, but she's a realist. I'm sure they'll figure it out.'

'Are you ready for the climb?' I ask and he nods his head.

Steps have been fashioned out of large boulders packed in with smaller stones, gravel and earth. It's single file now to accommodate the people walking back down. If you're on the trail, you need to keep your eye on your next footing as a fall could do some serious damage. Maverick's stride is longer than mine, so he doesn't have the same problem I have. I can't always step from boulder to boulder in one go. It's a case of taking it slowly and when you need a breather, finding somewhere suitable to step aside and enjoy the view.

'You go in front,' Maverick indicates. 'I'll be right behind you.'

This next section takes a while and I try to process everything that Maverick has chosen to share with me. One thing I do know for sure now is that it isn't just to get me on his side.

'How much further is it?' Maverick calls out as I side-step onto a relatively flat boulder to let a man and a young girl pass.

'When we get to the brow it flattens out and we'll be a stone's throw away from a show-stopping view.'

'Thank goodness. I don't think mountain climbing is my thing,' he mumbles as he comes to stand nearby, but it's too exposed to hang around for long and I set off on the last leg of the journey.

'You won't regret it, I promise,' I shout over my shoulder, hoping the wind doesn't obliterate my words. But we're tackling the steepest section now and it's impossible to talk. I just keep going at a steady pace so I don't have to stop now and again to let my legs recover.

When my feet finally land on a reasonably flat surface once again, the breathlessness and the aching calf muscles are forgotten. I stand aside, waiting for Maverick to catch up. I didn't realise he'd fallen quite so far behind, but he's very gentlemanly and naturally gives way. As there are more people descending than climbing, he could be a while. The moment he spots me his face lights up with a beaming smile.

'You weren't joking when you said that this trail makes casual hillwalkers feel they've achieved something. It's the nearest I'll ever get to climbing a mountain.'

I laugh, genially. 'But wait until you see the view. I promise you won't be disappointed.'

There are at least twenty other people wandering around the rocky plateau. A young couple hold hands, leaning into each other as they take in the breath-taking, panoramic view that extends out for miles and miles. At the summit there are two stone mounts, one is flat-topped and has an encapsulated map showing the distance of some of the most notable landmarks.

'There you go,' I point out with a giggle, 'you've climbed 2,175 feet. Not bad for a beginner.'

We're both drawn to the edge, beyond which the land slopes away gently in places but steeply in others. After a while Maverick turns to glance at me. I can see that he's captivated – the view still has that same effect on me even after all these years. The sky overhead is finally beginning to clear in patches and suddenly the sun peaks through. Rolling shadows glide swiftly over the low-lying ground as the wind pushes the clouds along. Here and there, the sun's rays light up a tiny area and it's mesmerising. Like someone has switched on a spotlight, which fades as quickly as it appears. Beyond the hills, the mountains give a dark backdrop that seems impossibly far away. It's such a vast scene that even the sizeable forests and glens are merely tiny features. Acres of flat grassland bounded by hedges are just blocks of muted colour.

'You're right – it's well worth the effort to make it up here.' But Maverick is still studying my face.

'What's wrong?'

'Nothing. You just look really happy.'

I glance away, embarrassed. 'Come on, let's find a sheltered hollow in the hillside to sit for a while before we retrace our steps.'

It isn't long before we're sitting side by side wolfing down the remainder of the picnic lunch and I feel strangely at peace. Our business relationship is starting to slip into a sort of friendship. We share a lot of the same problems, which is a strange bond to link two people, but there's something soothing about knowing that he understands the issues and difficulties I've been facing. I can't help comparing today's climb to the last time I was here with Adam. He was so grumpy that day, we hardly spoke. It ruined our walk. Even the little pleasures in life that we tried so desperately to grab onto seemed to push us further apart. Subconsciously, both Adam and I knew that.

Maverick is little more than a stranger, but he's good company and I enjoy chatting with him. He grabs the empty containers and pops them into his backpack. I watch him arch his back as he scans the horizon, and a warm feeling engulfs me. He's asked me out twice now within the space of a week.

He offers his hand to help me to my feet.

'This was the perfect place to come, Bella, thank you.' Even though I'm standing he makes no attempt to let go of my hand. I gaze up at him and our eyes lock as he moves closer to me. 'I had no idea what I was missing . . .' He trails off, looking a little flustered before he finally lets go. My heart is pounding in my chest, as for one second there I thought he was going to lean in and kiss me.

October

17.

Living the Dream

The last week has felt like a virtual roller coaster ride. Have I doubted some of the decisions I've made? Yes. Not least because I really need to talk to Maverick about business, but after our wonderful day out together last weekend, I'm having trouble compartmentalising my personal life and my work persona. And then, out of the blue, Randall invites me to a weekend party at his home which is situated next to Loch Awe. It's a gathering for The Highland Elves committee and their patrons, to work up some ideas for the festive season fund-raisers. The likelihood of Maverick not being there is slim. The upside is that at least I won't feel guilty grabbing this chance to plead my case to him, because I need a presence in Fort William.

As I'm checking my overnight bag, there's a ping, and glancing at my phone, I see that it's a text from Randall. The nerves are starting to kick in and my heart misses a beat – I'm a couple of hours away from being transported into someone else's world. It's a far cry from what I'm used to, but he said that as my parents are in Faro, my presence would create a bit of a buzz.

> Good morning, Bella. Cliff and Isla are going to drop by to pick you up around ten o'clock. Isla will text you when they're in the car park off the High Street. See you later.

I half wondered whether he'd ask Maverick to pick me up. I've not spoken to him since he dropped me off after our trek and I'm nervous about seeing him face to face again. I can't imagine Randall would hold a party without his grandson being there.

> Perfect. Thank you for arranging this, Randall, as I'm not sure I could have found you. ☺

His reply is very gracious.

> Everyone gets lost the first time – believe me!

At least the car ride will be relaxing, as having seen Cliff with a few drams inside of him dancing the Highland fling at numerous New Year's Eve parties over the years, I know he and Isla are on my side. If I dig myself into a hole at any point, one or the other of them will jump in and come to my rescue. Fate must be looking out for me, because too many coincidences are happening right now.

The first half-hour of the journey is all about how Mum and Dad are doing in Faro and then Isla brings me up to date with her family news. They have two sons and a daughter, and six grandchildren. Then Cliff mentions the topic we've been avoiding.

'We were sorry to hear that you and Adam have split up, Bella. Sad times, for sure!'

'Um . . . yes, indeed. It . . . sometimes things don't quite pan out as you expect but the worst is now behind us and we're both moving on.'

Isla pokes Cliff in his ribs with her elbow, unaware that it's within my line of vision.

'Sometimes it's for the best,' she adds.

It also means it's probably common knowledge that Lynsey McGregor has moved in with Adam. I've nothing to hide and if there are rumours going around, I can't see the harm in putting my version out there.

'I'm glad Adam has found someone else to share his life with.' It's easy for me to accept that now, having owned the fact that I probably fell out of love with him a long time ago.

'And how about you, Bella? How are you doing?' Cliff asks. He'll know from talking to Dad a little about the problems with the lease, even though no one knows the whole story.

'I'm trying to take Aunt Jane's vision forward and if ever I needed to be completely focused on one thing only, it's now. The timing of the split turns out to be rather ironic, when you think about it.'

Isla turns her head to look at me. 'I always say to Cliff, that relationships get stale if you dinnae treat each day as if it's the first one of the rest of your life. I've seen too many couples live the lie and fall foul of it. I hope things soon settle down for you, Bella. It's been a tough time.'

'It has,' I reply, not wishing to gloss over it. 'But it's made me realise what's important to me.'

'That's good to hear. Many folk live their lives as if it's a dream and then look back with regret on the years they wasted going through the motions. Your mum and dad are proud of you, Bella. If you need any arms twisting, just let Cliff know, as he's owed a few favours here and there. Aren't you, luv?'

'I am, but I think Bella isn't going to let anyone mess her about, Isla.' He glances briefly at his wife as he pulls the car to a halt and indicates left. 'We're just on the turn-off now. It gets narrow in places and the road seems to go on forever, but if you've not been this way before you'll enjoy the scenery.'

Cliff is right, it does go on and on. Here and there I spot the odd signpost with the name of a property and a track that disappears into the forest. There are some hotels, and the colourful signs are easier to spot. Who wouldn't want to come and stay for a break away from the constant hassle and endless noise that we have learned to regard as normal? Here it's quiet. Nature rules. And if the roads get icy, or there's driving snow, as Pop would have said, 'ye hasten o'er to the fire and throw on another log' because you might just be stuck indoors for a wee while.

'I'm so grateful to you both for giving me a lift. I'm sure by now I would have been completely lost.'

Cliff laughs. 'You drive until you're sure you've missed it and then suddenly you see the sign for "Lachlan" peeking out from the hedges on the left-hand side of the road. After that there's a track down through the woods and suddenly you feel like you've arrived in the quietest place on earth – a haven.'

Well, he's right but I didn't expect the winding, country lane laden with vibrant autumnal colour to suddenly lead us into a large turning circle in front of a stunning country residence. My first impression as we draw up in front of the property is that this is heaven on earth.

As Cliff rolls the car slowly around the sweeping curve to park to one side of the glass-fronted entrance, I realise Maverick wasn't joking when he said it was a former hotel. As the engine dies, we fling open the car doors with one thing on our minds – the loch.

And there it is . . . a stone's throw away from where we're standing. As I zip up my padded jacket, the gentle grassy slope in front of us leads down to a flat expanse where four braziers sit in a row. Each is set on a circular patio and surrounded by four sturdy seats made from recycled barrels. Beyond that, it's a short walk to the rocky edge where the waters of Loch Awe lap gently back and forth. A sense of total peace and serenity descends upon me as I gaze out over the glinting water.

Framed by a myriad of trees either side, standing on the flinty-grey chippings, bordered with sweeping curves of manicured grass, the bank on the far side makes for another postcard-worthy view. The land beyond rises gently, a wondrous landscape of trees and grassy slopes, with low-lying shrubbery carving patterns to draw the eye. The pale-blue sky is obscured by billowing white clouds that look like vast islands as they dwarf the scene and it's a view no one could ever tire of, even though there's a bitter chill in the air.

The property itself is a curious, uneven U-shape, with one extended arm housing a row of beautiful arched windows. The central section of the U, which connects what looks like the original house to the long rectangular building with the amazing arches, is some sort of glass configuration. It might even be an orangery. In the middle is the entrance, which is rather like a hotel reception. The house is even bigger up close than it appeared on the satellite images.

'Welcome, welcome!' Randall's voice makes me reluctantly tear my eyes away from the amazing vista in front of me as he walks towards us, grinning from ear to ear.

'It still has the exact same effect on me, Bella,' he calls out. Randall stops to shake hands with Cliff and leans in to give Isla a hug, before joining me. 'It takes my breath away and every day I notice something new. Anyway, let's get you all inside. How was the journey, Cliff?'

'There was only one real hold-up due to roadworks, and the usual congestion in a couple of spots, but not bad at all. Are we the first to arrive?'

'Yes. Fiona and I thought it would be nice if we had a quiet lunch together. The others will be arriving late afternoon. Let's grab the bags and show you up to your rooms so you can get settled in time for lunch at one o'clock.'

'We moved here five years ago. All the rooms are named after birds, and this is "The Lintie", that's the linnet. You have the corner suite on the first floor in the original house. It sits alongside the loch,' Fiona informs me as she inserts the key into the lock.

It was Randall's suggestion that Fiona show me to my

room, as he headed off in the opposite direction with Isla and Cliff.

'Here you go – it's one of my favourite rooms because it has a dual aspect.'

As I step inside, wheeling my case behind me, a seating area on the far side of the room is bathed in sunshine. Two comfortable armchairs, placed either side of a small table, look out onto the full length of the water.

'This is stunning, Fiona!' I exclaim, as I manoeuvre my suitcase next to an impressive free-standing rosewood wardrobe. Two of the doors are mirrored and the central section is made up of four drawers, above which are two smaller doors. With a cornice at the top and a plinth at the bottom, this magnificent piece of furniture fills the wall space between the internal doors.

'I'm so glad you like it,' Fiona replies as I walk over to the window. With the pale-coffee-coloured carpet, muted colours on the walls and the unusual angles of the ceiling given it's a corner room, it's utterly charming.

'The view of the loch is unbelievable,' I mutter, almost to myself as my eyes take in the breath-taking view.

'It's calming gazing out onto a body of water like that. Randall loved the property and the setting, but he said it was too big. He's right of course, but I won him over.'

I turn back around to look at the king-size bed with its chunky rosewood headboard, inset with decorative metalwork. The crisp white linen and deep red scatter cushions make it look comfortable and inviting. Fiona has walked around to the other side to draw back the heavy floral drapes in a rich burgundy, reds and muted browns.

'Quick, come and look at this,' she beckons. 'It's a white-tailed eagle. He's canny that one and looking for his lunch.'

I hurry to join her and catch sight of the magnificent bird effortlessly gliding on a steep descent before he swoops, plucking a fish in his claws, and then speeds off towards a clump of trees nestled on the bank on the far side of the loch. 'Oh my!' I exclaim, as Fiona lifts the sash window, but reluctantly closes it rather quickly when the strong breeze puts a distinct chill in the air.

'Keep an eye out for him. He'll be back tomorrow no doubt, and you might get a closer glimpse. What I love about this room is that you can sit up in bed and see the loch as it heads off into the distance and turn your head to the left to glimpse it from another perspective entirely. I only put special guests in here.'

When I turn to look at her, her eyes sparkle as her lips twitch with repressed laughter.

I don't quite know how to respond. 'Oh . . . that's really kind of you.'

'It's my pleasure, Bella. Your grandfather was a wonderful man and Randall and I have fond memories of riding on Santa's Highland Express with our son, Douglas. The Highland Elves Charity is dear to our hearts, and it's benefited so many families over the years. It's a pity your parents are missing the first of this year's gatherings, but it's wonderful having you here. Anyway, get yourself settled in, m'dear. The bathroom is through there.' She points towards the door on the other side of the wardrobe. 'Lunch is in the atrium in about an hour's time. Do you have any special dietary requirements?'

'No, I'll eat anything. Um . . . can I check whether the drinks' party tonight is formal?' I enquire, tentatively.

'People like to dress up a little, but we don't do formal black tie here – Randall and I like our gatherings to feel more homely. We rarely stand on ceremony, although he does have a little surprise in store for later.' She grins back at me. 'I'll see you in a wee while and if there's anything at all you need, just let me know.'

As Fiona closes the door behind her, I collapse down onto the bed, stretching out and staring up at the ceiling. The gusty breeze filtering through the treetops outside casts dancing shadows of light and dark above me as the leaves gently sway, the ground beneath them a growing carpet of colour. My mind is whirling. Would Fiona have welcomed me so warmly, or be content to mix socially at charity events with my parents if she knew Randall's secret? I feel as if I'm here under false pretences when that's not really the case; the past has nothing at all to do with me. I'm only interested in the future, but that doesn't help that teeny little stab of guilt at being complicit in a lie. I don't subscribe to the idiom, 'what you don't know, can't hurt you' when it comes to secrets, however in this case it's really none of my business.

Heaving a dejected sigh, I ease myself up and grab the suitcase to lay it on the folding rack next to a rosewood desk, the sort that has a series of intriguing little drawers. It makes you want to open them in the hope of discovering some little treasure from the past. Like a love note, or maybe a dried flower – from a romantic stroll one summer, long ago. Smiling to myself indulgently, I grab my toiletries bag and walk past a matching console table that has a small coffee machine, a rack of pods and a courtesy tray. This is every bit like a hotel and yet the room feels welcoming because of the attention to detail and the beautiful, hand-picked pieces of furniture. As Fiona said, 'homely'.

When I open the door into the bathroom I stop in amazement. The proportions are such that even with a full-sized bath with a shower over it, a vanity unit along one wall with an inset sink and the toilet opposite it, there's a large empty space in the middle. What draws my eye yet again is the sash window and aside from the view out over the loch, in the foreground there's a great view of the grassy bank and the metal braziers. Who wouldn't want to spend their evenings outside under a starlit sky as night descends, when there's hardly any light pollution here?

I'm conscious that Mum is anxiously awaiting a call. She was a little surprised when I told her Randall had invited me but said that everything Randall does is for a reason. I go in search of my phone, and she picks up almost immediately.

'Bella, my darling, I've been thinking about you. Are you at Lachlan?'

'I am and it's incredible, Mum, it really is.'

'Fiona is a great host, but I suppose that's a given when you're married to someone like Randall. Their previous home was a large manor house set in a couple of acres and I vividly remember the very first charity event we attended there. They had a huge firework display – it was amazing. They always put a lot of thought into making their guests feel at ease.'

'I also love that the rooms are named after birds.'

'I know! Oh, to have a house that has enough bedrooms to name them! But then you also need the help to keep everything running and that doesn't come cheap.'

'I haven't had time to explore yet, but the views draw you straight to the windows to stand and stare out. I should be unpacking but I wanted to let you know I arrived safely. Oh, and Cliff and Isla send their regards.'

'Ah, that's nice! And you have no need to worry about anything, Bella. Hold your head high, my dear. Our family might not be wealthy, but we're honest hard-working folk and that means a lot.'

If only Mum knew the real reason I'm feeling anxious, she'd probably be disappointed in me. It's not just a sense of awkwardness around Fiona, but I'm not relishing the thought of admitting to Randall that I messed up. When I turned down the other premises Maverick offered me, it was my ego talking. As things stand now it's the only thing that can save the business and I can only keep my fingers crossed that it's not too late. I'm hoping Randall might know the answer to that and if it's good news then I guess I'll be keeping my fingers crossed Maverick will be joining the party.

'I know. And having Cliff and Isla here really helps when

I think about tonight, as I have no idea who else has been invited.'

'Well, it's usually people who are willing to put their hands in their pockets and the committee members, of course, so dismiss those nerves of yours. You're among friends, Bella.'

'I will. And how is Grandma today?'

'Wonderful. She's using her new walking stick and there's no stopping her. We're about to set off to Vic's house and she's upstairs fussing with her hair. Anyway, enjoy yourself and everyone sends their love.'

A quick brush of my hair, a light flash of a lip wand and I grab my fleece before wandering downstairs. The long narrow corridor runs the full length of the part of the property that sits facing down the loch. At the end, a right-hand turn out onto a galleried landing leads me back to the grand staircase. It descends into what was obviously once the hotel reception area. There's a wonderful old stone fireplace with two wingback chairs and the hint of smokiness in the air tells me it's still in use.

There's no one about and I decide to explore. A set of glass-paned doors lead into a sizeable sitting room with another fireplace, but this time it's contemporary white marble. The ambience of the room is elegant country chic, with several comfortable-looking sofas and tartan scatter cushions. On the mantelpiece three leaping cast iron stags are reflected in the mirror behind it – the powerful animals looking majestic.

To the left-hand side of the fireplace is a single glass-paned door, and peeking through, I see it's a billiard room. I notice that there's a TV set on the wall and a card table in one corner.

'There you are!' Isla's voice makes me turn and I walk over to her.

'Just trying to get my bearings,' I explain, and she nods her head in agreement.

'Yes, it takes a wee while. I think Randall and Cliff are in the bar – shall we join them?'

'Of course.'

'What room are you in?' Isla asks, as we walk back through. She leads us past the staircase and into the charming, limestone-tiled annex that links to what I should imagine is the long arm of the U-shape. This central section between the two buildings is set around a pretty courtyard.

'The Lintie.'

'Oh, I love that room! We're in The Woodlark, it's in the second of the two original buildings. It was a coach house and stables back in the day and the rooms above it look out across the loch.'

'I went online and had a look at an aerial map. I could see the two stone buildings but couldn't quite work out the interconnecting bit.'

Isla draws to a halt. We linger in front of the glazed panels to our right, looking out onto the courtyard.

'It's a pretty little seating area, isn't it? It's wonderful at night with the fairy lights glowing as you look up at the stars. Originally this was an open walkway, and the square garden was bounded by low stone walls, pillars and arches like a traditional quad. The atrium dining room and lounge is the room you glimpse on the far side of the courtyard and it's an addition. The access is via the bar, up here on our right. Randall and Fiona kept the garden in the middle open to the air but turning this into a covered corridor really made the two buildings feel like one.' We begin walking again.

I stop to take it all in. I'd assumed the room beyond was a large conservatory, but I can now see that isn't the case. 'It's been cleverly done,' I reflect, as Isla places her hand on my arm.

'Come and take a wee look at this,' she says, 'it's the pièce de résistance in my humble opinion.'

We turn left as we approach a flight of stairs with a half-turn in them.

'Our room is up there on the first floor,' Isla points out, as she opens a pair of double doors.

'Now this is what I call a party space, don't you agree?'

When we pulled into the turning circle in front of the property, the long line of arched glass windows reaching almost floor to ceiling dominated the whitewashed stone buildings. Now we're standing inside and looking out onto the turning circle, edged with its manicured lawns, through unobscured windows. Each one frames the view perfectly and is tantalisingly different.

It's actually two rooms knocked into one but with dividing doors that fold back. As we wander along and stop in front of one of the archways, I notice it's a pair of French doors which open out but the others are fixed panels of glass.

'This was the hotel's breakfast and dining room. Glorious, isn't it? As you can see, there's still a table and chairs in front of each arch as they do use it occasionally, but mainly for parties and big celebrations. Randall and Fiona love Christmas and New Year – and they always have a house full.'

'I was under the impression they flew out to be with their son and his family in the States at Christmas?'

'Oh, they do. But they celebrate Christmas here before they go and it's a great gathering of friends and neighbours.'

Aww . . . it can't be quite the same. I try to visualise this room when it was a hotel with a long serving counter and a dresser with condiments – perhaps even a wine rack. Now the carpet is inset with a wooden dance floor, but the natural stone wall interspersed with glimpses of the loch and the gardens commands our attention.

As we retrace our steps, Randall appears. 'Cliff sent me off to look for you, Isla. I didn't know you were giving Bella the tour.'

'I was in danger of getting lost.' I give him an apologetic smile.

'Oh, you'll soon get your head around it. Come on through to the bar – it's my pride and joy,' he jokes.

'What man doesn't want a bar?' Isla chuckles.

'So, where's the kitchen?' I enquire.

Randall points to the far corner and a swing door I hadn't even noticed.

'It runs the entire length of this room. Don't let Fiona know that I told you her secret, but we have a chef who lives locally. Unless it's a toasted cheese sandwich – which is my wife's speciality – or a reheated croissant, it's Bernie who's in charge of that department.'

'It's wonderful to have someone who lives on the doorstep,' I remark.

'Bernie ran a successful French restaurant in Oxford for many years. Shortly after he moved to Loch Awe we invited him and his wife over for drinks and he took one look at the kitchen and rolled up his sleeves. He cooked us the best meal we'd had in a long time. The rest is history.'

'That's a lovely story,' I reply, impressed.

'Twice a year we hold a gourmet evening here in aid of The Highland Elves charity. Some of Bernie's old contacts come along and they're a generous bunch.' Randall winks at me as we cross the corridor. He holds open the door to the bar for Isla and me to pass through. 'Fiona loves to entertain and she's in her element when we have a large group here. I'll make sure you get an invite to the next one. I'm sure our guests will all be fascinated to hear all about the restoration work on Santa's Highland Express.'

As Isla follows me through the door, we glance at each other. Fiona wants to fill their wonderful home with family and friends, but for now, sadly the emphasis is on friends and neighbours, it seems.

Randall appears alongside me and I hang back as he leans into me. 'It's going to be a great party tonight,' he informs me, his eyes sparkling. 'And I have a plan to get us all on the same page. It just might help!'

Oh no . . . I think the less said the better right now but it's not for me to point that out.

18.

Luck Is on My Side

Lunch is wonderful. We enjoy an aperitif sitting on the sort of sofas that almost swallow you up as you sink down into them and, to my relief, the conversation flows with ease.

When we take our seats around the enormous dining table in the centre of the room, we only manage to take up one end, which makes it easier to chat and the ambience is so relaxed I feel quite at ease despite my apprehensions.

All the ingredients for the meal are either grown on site or sourced locally and chef Bernie is a master at visual presentation. We begin with pigeon breast, cavolo nero and butternut squash. The main course is Scottish salmon with celeriac, caviar and samphire. To finish, he serves a trio of apples with meringue. Usually, I can only manage to eat two courses, but the portions are modest and it's all about the infusion of flavours, not the quantity. Oh, how I wish I had my phone on me and could sneak a few photos, but that wouldn't be appropriate.

The subject turns to holidays. Cliff and Isla have recently returned from a trip to Greece with one of their sons and his family. They regale us with stories about their youngest granddaughter who is three, and I note a wistful look in Fiona's eyes.

To have all this, I reflect as I gaze around me, and yet for Fiona it's a bitter-sweet achievement. I sense that her longing to be surrounded by family gnaws away at her. It will never truly feel like home while her son and his wife live so far away. Maverick is now a part of their lives and that is obviously a huge comfort to both her and Randall, but their joy is incomplete.

'The sun has finally put in an appearance and it's warming up, so shall we take coffee outside?' Randall suggests, and we all nod in agreement. 'Right. Let's say ten minutes and there will be flasks of hot tea and coffee down by the fire pits.'

We disperse and just as I'm pulling on the padded jacket I left on the hanging rail inside the front entrance, Randall calls out to me.

'I hope you brought some walking boots with you,' he chuckles as he sidles up next to me. 'Tomorrow after breakfast we're planning a tour of the area.'

'Yes, I did, and it sounds like fun.'

'The sense of peaceful tranquillity is restorative,' Randall says, a rare frown wrinkling his brow.

'Restorative?' I query as he holds open the door for me.

'Oh, well . . . you know what I mean. It's nice to get away from the hustle and bustle.'

As we step off the gravelled area and descend the gentle slope of the grassy bank, Randall hurries forward to help Cliff carry an extra barrel seat across to the first brazier. They're all piled up with logs ready to light this evening and I'm rather excited at the prospect of seeing the loch as twilight descends.

'As lovely as it is inside, this view is forever captivating, Fiona,' Isla comments, as we watch the men finish moving the seats around the circular paving stones.

'Did you know that Randall's original intention was to build us a stone cottage back up near the ridge behind the two log cabins and reopen the hotel?'

'Really?' Isla exclaims.

'In my defence,' Randall chimes in, 'it's one of the many options now that I'm retired. My wonderful wife fell in love with Lachlan, even though it's impractical to keep it solely as a home in the longer term.'

There's a little amused eye contact going on between Fiona and Randall.

'Let's just say that Randall's plan is undergoing a few revisions,' she muses, and he shakes his head at her.

'Yes, m'dear, and I don't think you're finished yet.'

'It's simply a case of striking the right balance, my darling. This is too beautiful a location to keep to ourselves, but I also want us to be able to enjoy some peaceful quality time with the people I care about. I have faith that you'll come up with a solution to keep me happy!' she declares and it's hard to keep a straight face.

The sound of a car's tyres scrunching on the gravel, makes us all turn our heads, and when the driver's door opens, Maverick steps out. As he walks towards us, his face brightens the moment our eyes make contact. When he joins us, he doesn't seem at all surprised to see me here.

'Sorry I'm late. What did I miss?'

'We were just talking about hotel wars.'

Maverick's face lights up. 'Brave man – Grandma doesn't look at all concerned though, so I guess you still haven't convinced her.'

'Well,' Randall replies, 'if you spent more time here at least I'd have an ally – your grandmother is a tough negotiator, and she knows my weak spots.'

Maverick walks up to give Fiona an affectionate kiss on the cheek. 'Just admit you've met your match, Granddad,' Maverick states, winking at Fiona and her face immediately lights up.

What surprises me is a sense of closeness between the three of them that I wasn't expecting. Whenever Randall and I have talked he's indicated a sense of treading on eggshells around his grandson. I assumed, because Maverick is so black and white when it comes to business, that was the nature of their wider relationship. Obviously, I was mistaken, as that isn't the case at all.

'You're forgiven for being late as you've arrived in time

for coffee, but you missed a superb meal,' Fiona addresses Maverick and he gives her a rueful, if apologetic, smile. 'Right, let's take a seat, because here come Travis and Glenda right on cue.'

Maverick walks off to grab one of the barrel chairs and effortlessly lifts it above his head. After a bit of rejigging he sets it down directly opposite me. I acknowledge his smile as his eyes meet mine for a few tantalisingly brief seconds before the refreshments arrive.

Cliff was telling me over lunch that Travis and Glenda live in one of the log cabins behind the main house. They seem to do a bit of everything, as Glenda served lunch and Travis parked Cliff's car around the back. But Fiona mentioned that Travis also runs the estate. I assume that Glenda is the housekeeper.

Glenda opens a low folding table, sets it down next to Fiona and Travis then lowers the tray of Thermos flasks onto it.

'Is there anything else you need, Fiona?' he checks.

'No, thank you, Travis. How is it going in the kitchen? We can always call in our extra help a little earlier than planned if Bernie is feeling the pressure.'

'Bernie – pressure? He's in his element and he has everything under control. If you need anything, give me a call as I'm going to start setting up the atrium for this evening. I'll be back and forth to the storeroom. Great timing, Maverick,' Travis acknowledges with a tilt of his head.

Maverick gives him a wry smile. 'I know how far I can push it. Any later I'd be in trouble.'

Fiona gives Maverick an indulgent smile. 'Oh, I do love it when there's that party atmosphere in the air,' she admits, as Isla helps her to pour the drinks.

'How many people are coming tonight?' I enquire, gingerly.

'About forty, maybe a few more. It's going to be a full house overnight, too.'

'There's my case in point,' Randall interrupts, waggling his finger at Fiona. 'Look at that smile on her face! My wife loves to be busy and surrounded by people. It's what makes her happy and the house loves it, too.'

There ensues a long conversation about various options, including running gourmet weekends and special events which would be less demanding. Fiona sits back looking amused, as Randall and Maverick spark off each other with ideas. It's rather heart-warming to witness.

After a while the group disperses. Isla returns to the room to call her daughter and Cliff and Fiona stroll down to the edge of the loch. I pick up the tray to carry it back up to the house.

'Here, let me take that, Bella,' Randall insists.

'No, I've got it.' Maverick steps forward.

'Fine. In that case, I'm off to check on the chickens.' Randall strides off in the opposite direction, looking rather smug.

As Maverick takes the tray from my hands, he gives me a brief smile.

'Um . . . thank you. I'll, uh, bring in the table.' He waits while I collapse it before setting off.

I don't know whether I should say something to him now that William has formally withdrawn my interest in the lease, but before I can think of a way to ease that into the conversation, Maverick asks me a question.

'What do you think of Loch Awe?'

'It should be called Loch Awesome,' I jest, and he laughs.

'My mother would love it here,' he replies, somewhat wistfully.

'She's never visited?'

'No. I'm afraid not. But I'm working on it. My father isn't one for long jaunts away from home as he's a workaholic. He finds holidays tedious.'

'So, they've never visited Scotland together – even before Randall and Fiona moved here?'

As I hold open the entrance door for Maverick to go through, he gives me a wry look. 'It's a long story.'

'I'm a good listener,' I reply, lowering my voice as we walk along the light-filled corridor and on into the breakfast-come-party-room.

On entering the kitchen it's a beehive of activity.

'Oh, bless you!' Glenda calls out, as she stands in front of a run of gas burners, stirring a large pot. 'Dump it over by the sink and I'll sort it out in a bit.'

'How's it going, Bernie?' Maverick enquires as the chef continues chopping while glancing in our direction.

'It's going just fine, Maverick. Tonight is another of your granddad's tactics so we need to pull this off with style.'

'Grandma won't cave in if she doesn't think it's the right thing to do,' Maverick points out. 'Grandma isn't easily swayed as she has her eye on the future.'

'I know. But she's in her element entertaining and she's a lady who needs to keep busy.'

The look they exchange is poignant and I wonder what's really going on. It's like the proverbial elephant in the room – something no one talks about, but there's no denying it's there.

'Can I just say that lunch was the best meal I've ever eaten, Bernie. Thank you!'

He stops what he's doing to look at me. 'That's kind of you to say so, Bella. My father knew old George well, as way back we lived a few miles from Fort William. As a child that sleigh ride was the highlight of my Christmas. It's wonderful that you've all managed to keep it running.'

As Maverick takes the folded table from my hands and places it on a rack, I'm stunned that Bernie even knows who I am. But what can I say?

'It's dear to my heart,' I reply, and he tips his head in acknowledgement.

'We'll leave you to it, shout if you need anything – I can fetch and carry.' Maverick grins at Bernie.

'Oh, I'll draft you in if we're struggling, don't you worry. See you later!'

As we walk back out into the corridor, Maverick turns to me. 'Do you fancy a walk? We have plenty of time to get ready for tonight.'

'Great.'

He looks down at my feet.

'You'll need something a little sturdier than those!'

'Give me a minute to pop up to my room and I'll meet you outside.'

Once I'm out of view I race up the stairs two at a time.

'That's better.' Maverick remarks, looking down at my feet.

'You're not averse to getting them a little wet and dirty, are you? I thought we'd walk along the shoreline but it's not easy underfoot.'

'No, that's perfectly fine – I'd enjoy that.'

It isn't long until I realise there's no sand – mainly large pebbles interspersed with uneven boulders, and when Maverick extends his hand, I'm glad to take it. I'm relieved at how natural it feels to have his hand envelop mine.

'It's hard going, but the rocks help to stop the soil erosion,' he explains. I did wonder, as it does look like these were dumped here on purpose. 'Shall we sit for a while – there's a sheltered spot over there beneath the pine trees.'

'It looks lovely,' I reply, slipping down the zip on my jacket a little as it's definitely getter warmer.

Maverick follows suit. 'I thought it was just me getting hot and bothered because I'm out of shape. I rarely get to the gym these days,' he says. 'It's taken my legs a week to recover from our hike.'

The look we exchange is one of amusement.

When we finally settle ourselves down, it's a beautiful spot.

'Oh, there's a boat!' I exclaim.

'Most of the locals have fishing permits, although Travis mentioned it's the last day of the season. It's mostly brown trout, perch and pike, I believe. There's a bit of a problem with rainbow trout escaping from a couple of fish farms next to the lake.'

'That's a problem?'

'Yes. It's frowned upon, but Granddad is the expert and it's partly what drew them to Loch Awe. Grandma is determined to get his mind off business and onto relaxation.'

'You don't fish?'

'Occasionally. Granddad would love me to spend more time here, but my working day is a long and tiring one. At weekends I spend time on the VW but once that project is done he's confident that he'll succeed in getting me hooked. Figuratively speaking, of course.'

'You don't sound too unhappy about that.'

'I'm not, I love it here. But golf is the sport I choose to relax, although my handicap is mediocre.'

'Does that matter?'

Maverick bursts out laughing. 'It does to the other golfers. It's yet another thing in life that's supposed to be fun but ends up becoming competitive. Me – I just enjoy whacking a ball around and it's a way of getting to know people.'

I'm pretty sure he's understating his skill at the game. But it's nice to hear that he isn't a corporate robot going through the motions because it's clever to boast about having a good handicap. He must feel lonely at times, and maybe even a little homesick.

'Aside from hiking, do you have any other hobbies, Bella?' Maverick enquires.

'I garden . . . except that for the next few months while I'm living in the flat I don't even have a window box. After that, well, your guess is as good as mine where I'll end up.'

Maverick's jaw drops. 'That sounds daunting!'

'It's life.'

Maverick kicks the end of his boot against a flat rock, flipping it over. 'Starting over again isn't easy.'

That comment came from the heart.

'It's better than living with someone who is cheating on you. Fortunately, I have the support of family and friends, especially Holly – who is always there for me, so I know I'm extremely lucky. However, the business is taking up a lot of my time, and rightly so as our links with the community and the charity are so strong.' There's a point to laying my soul bare. I want Maverick to understand how important the business is to me.

'I'm sorry to hear that, Bella.'

I don't want his pity, but I do need his help.

'Sorting out my personal life is not important, but keeping The Highland Flower Shop going *is*, Maverick. You don't owe me any anything, but I need to ask you to give me a second chance, one you might think I don't deserve.'

He expels a deep breath, which isn't a good sign. 'I will admit that when I saw the letter from your solicitor withdrawing your interest I was rather puzzled.'

'I simply can't make the figures or the timeframe work, I'm afraid.'

'Oh, I see.' His reaction is at least one of genuine surprise rather than annoyance, as I'd feared. 'I'm afraid that from a developer's point of view the property is well overdue for an upgrade. We can only carry out that level of renovation work when there's a change of tenancy, which was the case.'

I get that now, but there is no way I could cease trading for almost two months. Judging by the look on his face that fact is only just sinking in.

I hurry to reassure him. 'I fully understand MPI's situation, Maverick, but for me there isn't a simple solution I'm afraid.'

'That's a great pity, Bella, and something I hadn't quite cottoned on to.' He gives me a sobering look.

I'm not trying to make Maverick feel guilty to get him on my side, but it's important that he takes my request seriously. I need him to put his trust in me that I'm not just messing him about for the second time.

'We've built up a solid customer base and a lot of goodwill

over the last sixteen years. People who don't jump online to order a bouquet because they like to call in and choose the flowers that they're sending to their loved ones. We've flourished while others have fallen by the wayside and a part of that is because of my family's history. People are loyal and that still counts for something – but only if we're visible.'

'It just goes from bad to worse, doesn't it?' The look on Maverick's face is grave.

'This isn't general knowledge at the moment, but I'm going to split the business into two. I'm taking an industrial unit on the edge of the retail park. I'll run the commercial side of the business from there, but if I don't have a retail presence in Fort William then forty per cent of our income could disappear overnight.'

Maverick is clearly taken aback by my honesty.

'I assume you're talking about the small shop at the far end of the High Street? I will admit that I only put it forward because Granddad had a word with me the day before my visit, suggesting it would benefit MPI if we could relocate you. When you said the unit was too small, I passed the file over to our admin manager. Off the top of my head, I think there have been a couple of viewings on it, but without getting an update I have no idea where it's at with regard to potential negotiations. The work is due to be completed mid-November, I think.'

I thought Maverick might be dismissive but that's not the case at all.

'It would be a lifeline for me.' My words seem to echo around us, as I stare out across the loch.

'Goodness, Bella – I feel really bad about this. That's a logistical nightmare you have on your hands and what about the sleigh ride?'

This is tough. 'It's being moved to an old workshop on a farm for a complete overhaul. If I can keep both income streams going, then I hope to be able to afford to find it a new home in time for Christmas.' I wish I felt as confident about that as I sound.

When our eyes meet, what I see isn't a derisory putdown, but empathy. 'Geez, that's quite a task you've set yourself. Managing three properties is quite an undertaking.'

I let out a deep breath. 'I know. Thankfully, business is booming but everything is on the line here, and nothing is guaranteed until I get a retail outlet pinned down.'

Maverick picks up a round pebble and absent-mindedly throws it into the loch.

Considering how small it is, a cascade of little droplets of water rain down on us, making me recoil and Maverick looks at me apologetically. 'Oops, sorry about that!'

We lapse into silence for a few moments.

'I know what it's like when you're trying to do the impossible because it's expected of you,' he continues.

My eyes widen in surprise. 'You do?'

'Yep. My boss has his eyes focused firmly on the bottom line and profits, and Granddad still lives in a world where you do favours for old friends. The two don't mix when you step away from business, I'm afraid. New CEO, new friends.'

And here I am, asking him to do the exact same thing for me when I've rejected the help that he has kindly offered me so far. 'One thing I can say for sure is that being an employee is a lot less hassle than being the boss and I'm beginning to wonder whether I'm up to the task. It's galling, as I'm not a quitter.'

'But something tells you that if you can just get your ducks in a row, Bella, you still have a shot.'

That makes me smile. 'I like a challenge. Or maybe I'm just too stubborn to know when I'm beaten.'

'That's not a bad thing. I don't give in easily either. Look, if a contract hasn't already been signed, the premises are still available. If that turns out to be the case, you'd have to get things moving straightaway.'

'That's more than I deserve. Thank you, Maverick.'

'Don't thank me yet – although I'd hate to be the bringer of bad news the second time around. Besides, I can't help feeling some of this is partly my fault.'

'Why?'

'When you showed me around the shop I wasn't in the best of moods. After my breakfast meeting, two of the directors waylaid me saying I should tread carefully. They hoped I knew what I was letting myself in for in advance of meeting up with you. I didn't understand why everyone was so worried about a backlash. I got the message the moment I stepped out of the door and saw the placards.' He grins at me, artfully.

'Please believe me when I say that I was genuinely horrified.'

'You should be proud of the fact that people turned out to fight your cause. I felt like a villain as I walked away. If I didn't fit in before, any leeway I was being given as a newcomer went up in flames that day. In fairness, I didn't fully comprehend how difficult your situation was at the time. Or how our plans to refurbish and enlarge the premises wouldn't suit your interests. You were just a name on a lease.'

'Villains aren't supposed to have regrets,' I point out and we end up laughing as Maverick extends his hand to pull me to my feet. He might be the villain of my little tale, but I'm beginning to see another side of him and it's not at all what I expected. And in a twist of fate, I guess I've caused him just as much stress without even realising it. This time we stand looking at each other, unable to disguise the little buzz that's going on between us.

'It's funny,' Maverick states, his eyes travelling over my face with abject interest, 'I thought it was going to be just another of my grandparents' party weekends. But with you here things are definitely looking up.'

I shake my head at him, laughing. 'I think I've been

invited for a reason and I'm pretty sure it wasn't to keep you company. I'm simply filling in for my parents.'

'Well, I'll make sure doing the rounds doesn't monopolise all your time, as that wouldn't be fair on you.'

The look Maverick gives me sends a rush of adrenaline coursing through my body and I know I'm beaming from ear to ear.

'Come on.' He tilts his head in the direction we came from. 'Let's take a walk up through the woods. After all the stress I've caused you, communing with nature is the perfect antidote. And I'll get onto that little matter first thing on Monday morning, I promise.'

There's a glimmer of hope and it's enough to make my spirits soar – the villain might just turn out to be a hero after all.

19.

A Favour For a Favour

'Don't you look lovely!' Isla exclaims, as I join her and Cliff in the atrium. The room is packed, and I was grateful to make a beeline for the first two faces I instantly recognise.

'The colour isn't too much? It's my party dress,' I half whisper, as Isla leans in to give me a hug.

'It's perfect.'

Scanning around I don't feel out of place. In a long-sleeved knee-length, figure-hugging dress in a fabulous raspberry colour, it was a daring choice for me. Wearing full makeup and having spent over half an hour painstakingly applying nail varnish, I'm glad I made the effort. I feel good.

'And I love your dress, Isla, it's very chic.' She's wearing a silky, halter-neck dress that falls to just below the knee with a matching cropped jacket, and the silvery-grey is a good colour for her.

'Oh, it's just something I threw into the suitcase,' she laughs.

Cliff rolls his eyes. 'We won't mention the dozen shops we walked around before you found it, will we?'

'No, my luv, we won't!' Isla states, emphatically. 'Who knows what to wear at these things. But I think we'll do, don't you, Bella?'

Glancing around, I think she's right. 'If Mum were here, she'd say we've nailed it.'

'I'd best fetch you both a drink,' Cliff says, as he leaves us to natter.

'How was your wee walk with Maverick?' Isla asks, pointedly. 'Is there any news about the lease?'

'I'm in the process of considering the options,' I hedge.

'You won't be staying?' Isla's face drops.

'It's not a simple decision, Isla, and right now I'm trying to figure out the best way forward.'

'Is there anything we can do to help, Bella?'

I shake my head, leaning in closer and lowering my voice. 'It was unrealistic to think that we could go on forever based on the goodwill extended to us by Randall.'

Isla looks stunned.

'Don't worry,' I reassure her. 'There are other options, but it involves change. This is just between us, so please don't breathe a word to Cliff. Placards and petitions won't change a thing. It's time to take things forward in a new way – whatever that turns out to be.'

As Cliff returns with a triumphant smile on his face and three drinks balanced in his hands, Isla looks in need of fortification. There is no magic wand, and she realises I have no choice but to make the best of a bad situation. Which isn't exactly what she was expecting to hear. I like to think that Maverick won't get grilled by the other committee members tonight as that would be unprofessional, but rumours are rife and there are others here who might ask out of pure curiosity, not realising it's a sensitive topic.

Fortyish guests turn out to be more like sixty-something in number and it's a great evening. The buffet table is constantly being restocked and a team of four servers mingle with what Bernie calls his 'specials'. The skewered Scottish prawns drizzled with whisky cream are my favourite – although eating them involves napkins strategically placed. Succulent and juicy – they're a taste explosion.

I lose track of Isla and Cliff part-way through the evening, but I've been chatting with so many different people that any sense of nervousness is now long gone. Randall and

Fiona keep a close eye on me, appearing from nowhere to introduce me to someone new so that I'm able to circulate. A number of folk simply want to say how thrilled they are that Aunt Jane didn't sell the business and congratulate me on taking over. Quite a few of them have a story of their own to tell me from the past. Not just about Pop either, but my parents too. Mum and Dad have been on the charity's committee for as long as I can remember.

Shortly after ten o'clock, Travis appears and ushers us into the party room. There's a buzz of excited chatter as it's obvious something is about to happen. I scan around as not everyone is here but the sound of bagpipes is a clue.

When the glorious piper enters, we all start clapping. Behind him, in a matching kilt, is the bearer of the McIntyre coat of arms attached to a pole, with gold tassels hanging down each side of it. Next in line, which puts a huge smile on my face, are Randall and Maverick wearing what I assume is the McIntyre tartan. A mighty roar goes up as they parade into the room, the music and the spectacle enthralling us all.

Everyone loves a ceilidh and Maverick heads straight towards me, holding out his hand.

'May I have the pleasure of the first dance, Bella?' he asks formally.

'Aye, that you can!' I respond, in my best Scottish accent. I wasn't born in the Highlands, but I've lived here for most of my life. I like to think I've acquired a hint of that warm timbre.

'It's only the second time I've worn traditional dress and it takes a bit of getting used to.' He lowers his voice as he comes closer. 'It's also heavy, but it's worth it to see Grandma's face.' Maverick does look extremely proud wearing his family's tartan, which features green, gold and yellow on a black background.

'What does *per ardua* mean at the top of the crest?' I enquire, as Maverick and I saunter over to the dance floor. It stands in pride of place behind the music console.

'"Through difficulties", so I guess I was born to be a fighter.' Maverick turns to smile at me. The way he's holding himself demonstrates a real sense of pride. I wonder how long Randall has waited for this chance to have himself and his grandson piped through the door? When I glance across at Randall, deep in conversation with Fiona and looking a little flushed, I'm guessing it's been a lifelong dream.

As the strains of 'Scotland the Brave' fill the air, Maverick reaches out to grasp my hand and lead me over to the dance floor. The Gay Gordons is great fun and one of my favourites. He stands to my left, placing his arm around my shoulder as I put up my right hand. Then he reaches across in front of me to take my left hand in his and off we go. Three steps forward and turn, then three steps back and stop. It's all going well until it's time for him to twirl me under his right arm and it sends me off-kilter when he starts to spin me the wrong way. We sort of collide, he panics and ends up stepping on my foot. I laugh, trying to get him back on track again, but I'm not the best of teachers and we're out of step with everyone else. Maverick almost trips himself up, so we edge ourselves off the dance floor just as Isla comes hurrying towards us.

'Can I have a wee dance with Maverick, Bella?' I can tell by the look on her face that she can see things aren't going smoothly.

'I'm still trying to get the hang of it,' Maverick warns her.

'Och, that's no problem. We'll soon sort you out.'

I give her a grateful smile as she whispers in my ear that the McPhersons are eager to talk to me. They own the biggest hotel on the loch. It's further down on the opposite bank and they offer packages to family parties celebrating birthdays and anniversaries. Then she gives me a meaningful look. While it is with some reluctance that I pull myself away from Maverick, I'm leaving him in good hands. However, I take a moment to stand back and watch them rejoin the group.

Moments later, Maverick and Isla have linked arms and she's swinging him around, making a perfect changeover when the caller shouts the instruction. With his military-looking black tunic decorated with gold braid and buttons, his kilt swinging like fury and his white socks, garters and black shoes, he does make a handsome sight indeed. And he's having fun.

At one o'clock, the two executive minibuses return to collect the people heading back to Fort William and the surrounding area. Shortly afterwards, a third vehicle arrives to drop local people back home. That leaves a group of twenty-two in total staying overnight.

'Can I have everyone's attention,' Randall calls out. 'The braziers are lit and hot drinks will be served in ten minutes' time. Wrap up and we'll convene our meeting under that glorious starry sky!'

There's a loud murmur of approval as people head off in different directions. Making my way up to The Lintie, I'm halfway along the narrow corridor when Maverick calls out to me.

'Bella, we didn't get a chance to talk all evening. You've been in demand.'

Turning on my heels, I wait for him to catch up.

'I'm next door to you, in The Woodlark. I can't believe Grandma put you in my favourite room.'

I try to repress a little grin. 'Sorry about that. If I'd known, I'd have suggested we swap.'

'Oh, no, we couldn't do that. Grandma always has a meticulously laid out plan. It'll take me a few minutes to get out of this, but I'll hang around so we can walk back down together.'

'Great. I won't be long.'

So, Fiona had a cunning plan after all. Ever so coolly, I slip off the wrist strap of my clutch bag and moments later I'm closing the bedroom door behind me. Then I collapse back against it. I couldn't have dreamed of finding myself here like this, spending time in the McIntyre home. Let alone sleeping in the room next to Maverick.

It's time to wrap up warmly, and after donning a pair of jeans and my favourite pale-blue fluffy jumper, all it takes is a touch of lip gloss before I slip on some sturdy shoes.

I grab my coat, and as I open the door and turn to put the key in the lock, I hear Maverick coming out of his room.

'You were quick,' he says. I turn to look at him and he's literally staring at me, taking in every little detail.

'What's wrong?'

'Nothing. Nothing at all. You look cosy.'

I glance at his charcoal, crew-neck jumper as he shrugs on a thick woollen coat. 'You do, too.' And not just cosy. He's handsome all right and it makes my stomach flutter.

There's an awkward pause and for some reason he seems nervous. 'That autumnal breeze coming off the loch can be quite chilly at night and first thing in the morning,' he continues. 'You . . . um, looked like you were having a good time mingling this evening.'

'Yes. It was fun. People were most welcoming and I now know a few things about what Pop got up to as a young lad.'

'I'm sure it was all good. I get the same – old friends of my grandparents want to tell me about my father's childhood. I'm learning things about him that he'd never tell me himself.'

'I guess we all have moments that either get forgotten, or we simply choose not to share,' I agree, as we head down the staircase.

He starts laughing. 'When I told my father I was coming to live in Scotland, his reaction was "why?" because he saw it as a whim. I should be one hundred per cent focused on my career and this was a sideways move, at best.'

Maverick holds the exterior door open for me.

'Presumably you had a good reason for coming in the first place though?'

'Yes. Family is important to me.'

What a lovely thing to say. 'It takes time to settle in but it will get easier.'

'I know and it was the right thing to do. Granddad has been a different man ever since he nearly lost Grandma. Moving here is a good example – they could so easily have found a smaller, more manageable property next to the loch, but she fell in love with the place. Now they have difficult decisions to make and that's the price you pay.'

As we step out into the night air, the smell of woodsmoke drifts across to greet us but I'm oblivious to it.

'I had no idea – poor Fiona!' I gasp, incredulously.

'Oh, she's fine now. But it was touch and go at the time. She walked away from a car accident with a few scrapes and considered herself lucky – we were told she was fine. The next day she collapsed and was rushed into hospital with a blood clot on her lung.'

'I can't imagine how scary something like that must be. Randall must have been beside himself with worry.'

'It turned both of their lives upside down because she had further complications. Grandma was a partner in a solicitors' practice at the time and having to give it up was hard on her. She's not the sort of person who likes to sit around, and a few months later, they moved here in preparation for Granddad's retirement.'

'You're still worried about her?'

'No.' He shakes his head as we slow our pace, not wanting to be within earshot of the noisy group gathered around the braziers. 'But it made me realise that they aren't getting any younger and I don't want to regret . . . well, I've always wondered what it would be like to live over here.'

'You're not doubting your decision, are you?'

'Not at all. There's never a dull moment being around my grandparents. They're two firecrackers, as my dad would say. I was in real estate back home and the job here is fine, but I'm not sure it's what I want longer term. My father is aware of that, and he finds it concerning.'

'But from what you were saying you think Randall – I mean, your grandparents – have plans for your future here?'

Maverick turns to stare across at the happy group laughing and bantering, oblivious to the fact that we're watching them.

'I'm hoping that over time MPI will come to mean less and less to Granddad. And once he and Grandma decide what they want to do with this place, they'll be way too busy to waste time looking back. He's already seeing the changes with a recent restructuring of the company and before too long that will help him to let go. I see it as a good thing. But they can't manage this place alone, so who knows? And with that, I think I've bored you enough with my life history . . . Come on. I hope the coffee is still hot as I'm beginning to flag.'

'Right, everyone, gather around,' Cliff calls out, beckoning to us. 'It's time to tackle our agenda before people start disappearing. Let's welcome Bella as a guest to one of our official fund-raising meetings. Everyone here is either on the charity's committee, or a patron, Bella. Thank you for joining in.'

There's a round of whoops and hand-clapping as a huge smile forms on my face. I wonder whether some of them will even remember any of this in the morning. At least out here the noise isn't bothering anyone.

'I'll hand over to Randall, in his capacity as our events coordinator.'

There are a few ad hoc whistles – this is a noisy bunch.

'Aside from another of Bernie's gourmet dinner parties here at the end of November, we're looking for some fresh ideas in the run-up to the big push at Christmas. It's time to brainstorm.' Randall raises his voice to quieten the background chatter.

'We should approach the local council to allow us to increase the size of the Christmas fayre this year,' someone pipes up.

'I agree,' Fiona joins in. 'We turned a lot of potential stallholders away last year. Have there been any developments regarding a possible pop-up skating rink?'

'We're still looking into that,' Cliff confirms. 'It's the same old problem – parking is the big issue unless we set up somewhere on the outskirts of town. Maybe on one of the playing fields if we can get permission. We should have some news on that ready for our next meeting.'

There are a lot of nodding heads.

'Any other ideas?' Randall calls out, encouragingly.

'How about an evening event actually in the High Street. Stalls with local produce – cheeses, meats, vegetables and wines perhaps? But selling tickets so that people can get to try say, half a dozen different items of their choice?' I throw out there.

'I like that idea! Did you make a note of that, Isla?' Randall asks the official secretary.

'Yes – I hope I'll be able to read my writing when I type this list up. Firelight isn't the best when taking notes.' There's a little ripple of laughter.

'Anyone else?' Randall continues.

'Let's get the bagpipes in and have a bit of a ceilidh, one evening in the square. If it's held in the week leading up to Christmas, we can organise a couple of stalls to sell mulled wine and soft drinks – it should attract a bit of a crowd.'

'How about a dance competition?' Isla suggests. 'That would go down really well. I'm sure if we approached the dance clubs and schools within a thirty-mile radius we'd find a few who would love to take part.'

People start chattering among themselves and Randall raises his hand.

'That's a great start and if you can think of anything else just drop me an email. Same time, same place for our next meeting, Cliff?'

Cliff has been the chairman ever since I entered my teen years. Dad says between him and Isla they keep everyone on their toes.

'Yep – the room above the pub in the High Street. But can

I just take this opportunity to thank you and Fiona for yet another dazzling get-together to thank our wonderful, and generous, patrons. I think everyone will agree we've had a cracking time. There's just one item left to cover I believe, Randall?'

'Ah, yes . . .' He reaches out to clasp Fiona's hand in his. 'Sadly, it's time for me to think about stepping back a little. As you can imagine, running this place is a bit of a full-time job. In the short term, to save on some of the travelling back and forth to meetings, I may be joining you by video call. However, I am actively looking for someone to step up and take over the role as the events coordinator. Fiona and I will, of course, continue to be patrons and hold many fund-raising initiatives here at Lachlan. But it's time to find someone with a little more vigour and a few less years on the old clock.'

No one says anything and it's obvious this is an unexpected turn of events.

'On that note,' he continues, his voice more upbeat, 'I declare the meeting officially closed. If anyone would like to join me in the bar for a proper nightcap—' Randall raises his mug, giving a wink '—I have a rather fine malt whisky set aside especially for tonight.'

There's a buzz of chatter, as people walk over to Randall, expressing their thanks not just for this get-together, but for the work he's put in over the years.

Maverick leans into me, his voice low.

'Well, judging by the reaction I don't think anyone was expecting that. Do you fancy a drink inside?'

I shake my head. 'Not really. It's a little heavy for me this late . . . I mean, this early in the morning,' I laugh.

'How about I get us another coffee – a hot one this time?'

'You must have read my mind.'

'Great. You take a seat around the brazier and keep warm, while I pop back inside.'

I make my way over to one of the barrel chairs and am surprised when Fiona hurries over to me.

'That was a great idea about an outdoor wine and food tasting party,' she enthuses.

'When you say it like that, it sounds like a street party.' I grin back at her.

'It's a novel idea and I think we should give it a try. I also like the thought of a dance-off – it always amazes me what ideas people come up with when they've had a drink or two. I don't know about you, but I'm exhausted and the last thing I want is a wee dram at this hour of the morning. By the way, breakfast will be between nine and ten tomorrow. I mean . . . later this morning . . . I think we're all going to appreciate a bit of a lie-in given the late finish.'

The final stragglers are now making their way back inside, but Randall is already out of sight, no doubt standing proudly behind the bar tending to his guests.

'It's been a very enjoyable evening, Fiona. I can't guarantee I'll remember every single person's name in the morning, but it's been lovely to meet so many of the committee members.'

'We have a little summer do for the volunteers but it's usually a picnic in the afternoon, as that means they can bring their families with them. We also have a treasure hunt for the kids – it's hilarious. They end up shinning up trees and doing all sorts of things, so we all need to have eyes in the back of our heads. Anyway, I'm keeping you and it is a little nippy.'

'Oh, I'm going to draw up a chair closer to the fire. Maverick is getting us another coffee.'

'Ah, I see. Well, I'll wish you goodnight and, uh, sleep well. I'm so glad you could make it, Bella. Your presence made a real difference. It was lovely to see people sharing their memories with you and it took a bit of pressure off Maverick – you know, with what's happening.' She raises her eyes to the heavens.

'It's unfortunate, but once things are sorted out it'll all be forgotten.'

'I can understand the ill feeling, Randall and I are upset

too. Your family has attracted a lot of goodwill for the work you've all done over the years. I wish there was a quick and easy solution.' Her voice is regretful.

'I know, but you and Randall did your bit, too. Pop left an impression on everyone he met. As soon as Christmas Day was over, he was counting down to the next one,' I reflect with a hint of poignancy. 'Christmas will always be a magical time for my family because of that.'

'Grandma, would you like a hot drink?' Maverick calls out as he walks towards us. We both look up.

'No, m'dear – thank you, I'm off to bed. And, Bella, I'll leave you in Maverick's capable hands. Sleep well both. See you in the morning.'

She leans in to kiss Maverick's cheek and then steps forward to give me a hug. As she pulls away, she glances upwards. 'Oh, just look at that sky. I keep telling Randall that we must get a telescope,' she mutters to herself as she walks back up to the house.

Maverick and I exchange a warm-hearted smile, as he passes me a steaming hot mug of coffee.

'Grandma feels this is where she's meant to be, and nothing makes her happier than sharing it with other people. Here, let me pull two of the barrels a little closer and I'll throw on another log. Just be wary in case it starts spitting.'

This feels very surreal. Me, Maverick and a sky full of stars as we look out over the velvety dark-blue waters of Loch Awe. The darkness surrounding us is comforting, broken only by the light from the fires – some of which are now merely glowing red embers – and the solar lights dotted around the garden.

'Can I ask your opinion about something?' Maverick indicates for me to take a seat.

I put down my mug to hold up my hands and warm them. 'Fire away,' I reply and then begin laughing as it wasn't meant to be a pun, I'm just feeling the cold.

'When Granddad made his announcement he looked directly at me. He wasn't hinting . . . was he?'

I glance at Maverick, tilting my head to one side – is he serious? Now I understand what Randall meant when he said he had a plan to get everyone on the same page.

'He was I'm afraid and it was blatantly obvious. Fiona and Cliff immediately looked in your direction too.'

'Damn it. That means I'm in deep trouble.'

'Why? He'll ease you into it and you'll soon get to know everyone. If you really want to fit in, this is your chance.'

He looks dumbstruck. 'I'm sure there are better candidates than me.'

'None with the name McIntyre and that opens doors.'

Maverick sips his coffee, staring into the flames.

'Company politics I can hack, community protocols are another thing entirely when I'm in the dark and have no one who appreciates the bind I'm in.'

'That's not a problem. You were kind enough earlier on to offer to help me out and in return I can be there for you. Any problems you have related to the charity I'm just a phone call away. If I don't know the answer, I can discreetly make enquiries and get back to you.'

Maverick turns his head to stare at me, narrowing his eyes.

'That's a generous offer, Bella, but I can't guarantee anything until I know whether those premises are still on the market,' he explains candidly.

'And I'm not expecting you to, but if they are I'll be on it without delay. I'm not asking for preferential treatment, but if they're available I'm anxious to get the deal done quickly. I don't have a problem with that, do you?'

He deliberates for a moment. 'Hopefully, it's not too late and we can act quickly. I'm not just saying that because I need someone on my side, Bella. I really do want things to turn out well for you.'

As I stare back at Maverick my heart is beating so fast I'm feeling a little dizzy and this has nothing at all to do with what we're talking about.

'I know,' I say, slightly breathlessly and Maverick's face breaks out into a beaming smile. I'm not sure the connection Maverick and I are making is quite the one that Randall had in mind as he leans in to kiss me softly on the lips. Suddenly, my head is spinning. I close my eyes, savouring the moment, and my heart rate soars. I think he's a little surprised when my arms instinctively curl around his neck and I pull him even closer. When it comes to a first kiss it's everything I thought it would be and so much more – I feel giddy with anticipation for what's to come.

Well, I've learned a valuable lesson. If you really want something in life you don't sit back and wait for it to come to you. No, you must reach out and grab it. Which is precisely what I'm doing.

20.

What Have I Done?

Turning up at work at one thirty in the afternoon on a Monday feels wrong, but I ease my conscience by telling myself that this morning has already been extremely productive. As I walk towards the floristry desk, Eve and Ursula are deep in conversation.

'Morning, ladies! Did you have a relaxing Sunday?' I enquire and they both nod their heads, but I can see something is up.

'I hope it's all right,' Ursula queries, 'but I had to bring Monty in with me again, Bella. My neighbour was so apologetic, but her asthma is bad today. Her other half isn't around so she can't risk going into the house to feed him.'

'Oh, Ursula, I'm sorry to hear she's unwell, but please don't worry. Monty is a sweetie, and we can't manage without your help.'

'That's really kind of you, Bella. How was your weekend? I hope you managed to switch off and enjoy yourself.'

'I did and it was brilliant, thank you.'

My phone starts to ring, and I give them both an apologetic smile as I raise it to my ear.

'Mum – how is life in Faro?' I quickly walk over to the staircase, taking the steps two at a time.

'Good, but after spending the day at Vic's place, Grandma Susan's rash is driving her crazy.'

Grabbing onto the banister rail, I half turn to look back at Ursula and Eve.

'Mum, could it be a pet allergy?'

'Hmm . . . but Vic has always had cats, so I don't think that's the problem.'

'Cats? Art has a new friend?'

I continue making my way upstairs, waving to Holly as I hurry over to the office.

'Yes. Vic took on his neighbour's cat about a month ago. The old lady had to move back to live with family in the UK. Art was fine with it, as they often laze around in the sun together. Sheba is very pretty, a big ball of white fur – oh!' Mum gasps. 'You might be onto something there. It's worth investigating as Art is short-haired. Anyway, how are you this morning after your wonderful weekend at Lachlan?'

'Great – I had a lovely time. And by the end of the day I hope to have some good news to share with the team.'

'Oh, Bella, that's wonderful! I'll call you later so you can update me and, in the meantime, I think it might be worth a quick trip to the doctor's with your grandma. Love you!'

As I dump everything down on my desk, Mrs Mac comes bustling in behind me.

'It's not bad news, is it?' she gives me a dubious look.

My eyes light up. 'No. We might have sussed out the root of the problem.'

'I'm glad to hear that, lassie. At least yer mum and dad are there to help sort yer grandma out. I hope they get to the bottom of it soon because she'll be feelin' fed up, of that I have no doubt.'

'Mrs Mac, I'm only around for about half an hour and then I probably won't be back again until four thirty. Could you put a sign on the door saying that we'll be closing half an hour early today and make sure everyone is here?'

Her expression is pinched. 'More trouble?'

'No. This time it should be good news, but I can't elaborate on that until I've signed on the dotted line.'

Her eyebrows shoot up and she crosses her fingers, holding them up, and I do the same. 'It's not quite what everyone is expecting but the next couple of hours could seal our future.'

'When I said you'd have to work fast, Bella, you certainly took that on board,' Maverick sounds impressed. 'Like I said, the other party are still in two minds because there's a slightly larger premises due to come on the market sometime in the next couple of months. They're not in a hurry as it's a new start-up.'

I'd heard that Highland Herbal Supplies might shut its doors and, putting two and two together, it's not hard to realise that's the premises he's referring to. Wallace has been selling online for quite a while, now. His son and daughter-in-law who set up and run the website for him, have proved that he doesn't need to keep the shop as well. It makes sense for him to give it up.

'That's good news for me, then.'

Maverick stops to give me an encouraging smile. 'It was a bit of a relief for me too, I will admit. I don't think I could have stomached seeing a look of disappointment on your face.'

It matters to me that he finally understands that this never was about taking advantage of Randall's generosity.

I'm excited when Maverick unlocks the front door. As I follow him inside, it hits me that this is going to be The Highland Flower Shop's new home. I can feel the hairs on my arms standing up as goosebumps make me shiver ever so slightly. It's another bright October day but it's colder in here than it is outside – cold and empty. It's all freshly painted, with new flooring and a new ceiling but it feels soulless. The space is mostly open plan with a downstairs cloakroom at the rear next to a small kitchen, on the other side of which is a good-size room that could be split to form a small office and a storage room.

'What are your thoughts?' Maverick asks, eager to hear what I have to say.

'It's a nice little property. It's a pity the upstairs isn't available.'

Maverick purses his lips. 'Yes, I realise that would have made all the difference for you. But the flat was let out on a long-term lease. I hear they're good tenants, you probably know them.'

'I do and that's not a deal-breaker, it just would have been useful. There's room for a couple of vans out the back and that stone-built workshop will come in handy.'

Maverick is on edge, but for me reality is beginning to kick in because I know my staff are going to be in shock when I reveal the plan. 'William has already been through the contract you kindly had your office send over first thing this morning. I have an appointment with him a bit later to go through it in detail and sign. He'll get someone to drop the agreement back to MPI by five o'clock. I really appreciate you dropping everything for me, to help make this happen.' I extend my hand and we seal the deal.

'It's the least I can do, Bella. I know this isn't the solution you wanted, but I really hope you can make it work. I'm delighted for you.'

'And I meant it when I said that I'm only a phone call away as you take over Randall's role for the charity.' It's hard to keep a straight face, as he hasn't let go of my hand and doesn't realise it. I gently pull away.

'Oh, sorry . . . my head was elsewhere for a second there. It was great to sit and chat, looking out onto the loch and enjoying one of Bernie's hearty Scottish brunches yesterday, wasn't it?'

'It was. And thanks for dashing out to do the viewing yourself this morning. You didn't need to, you know.'

'Maybe not, but I wanted to do it, Bella. The new lease on the other property was always going to maximise the shop's true potential,' he confirms. 'It wasn't an intentional plan to put it beyond your reach – I don't operate like that. It was strictly business and standard practice when it comes to managing a portfolio. Unfortunately, when two parties want the same property it will always go to the highest bidder.'

Maverick's sincerity is touching and now I feel bad. I didn't know anything about him when this all kicked off and I was suspicious of his motives. I questioned his integrity and that was unfair given the situation.

'I'm sure this is going to look lovely once we have everything set up. One quick question – I'm going to need some refitting done at this and my other unit. It's not a huge job, but if you have any contact numbers that you'd be happy to pass on, I'd really appreciate it.'

'Consider it done the moment I get back to the office.'

We trace our way back to the front door to say goodbye and I leave him to lock up. It's an awkward parting, so I just say a cheery 'have a good week' and off I walk. I decide to take the long way round to the rear of The Highland Flower Shop, in the hope that no one I know has spotted me. As I walk, I give Mrs Mac a call.

'Are you free for about an hour?'

'Of course.'

'Give me ten minutes and I'll be sitting in my car in the yard. We need to go for a little ride together.'

Mrs Mac's face is expressionless as I open the door into the tiny office to the side of the huge up-and-over roller door.

'Welcome to our new commercial base.'

I was obviously expecting her to be surprised, but the stunned silence is eerie. I keep walking and lead her out through the internal door into the cavernous open space.

'But there's . . . there's nuthin' here, Bella. It's like a garage repair shop.'

I need Mrs Mac on-board if I'm going to convince everyone else that my vision will work.

'If we use the small office at the front as a general reception, I've drawn up some plans to section off some of this space. The two vans will fit nose to tail and come to about here.' I march across the floor and spread my arms wide. 'Imagine a stud wall with a door in the middle. During the day when the vans are out, delivery drivers can unload under cover if it's wet.'

Mrs Mac is staring around as if she thinks I've lost my mind.

'Walk with me,' I encourage. 'I know this isn't what we're used to but it's our new way of working. When I get back, I have a meeting with William to sign the lease on that empty property at the other end of the High Street.'

Mrs Mac's eyes widen in surprise, as if she can't quite take it in. 'You're splittin' the team up?'

'It's the only way.'

'But the new premises isn't big enough to accommodate The Christmas Cave as well. And where will Santa's Highland Express go? You can't set it up in here – this is . . . soulless.'

The pained look on her face tears at my heart.

'It's the best I can do, Mrs Mac. We'll run the commercial side of the business from here and keep our local customers and walk-ins happy with our new premises in Fort William. We'll need to sit down with Ivor and Rodric to work out whether our bulk deliveries come here and then one of them does a daily run into Fort William first thing each morning. My focus had to be on what we could afford.'

Mrs Mac steps forward to throw her arms around me. 'You did yer best, lassie, and no one couldnae have expected more.' Her hug is all the reassurance I need.

'I'm not giving up on finding a home for Santa's Grotto and The Christmas Cave, Mrs Mac. It's just that for now what matters is keeping the business running to guarantee we have a future. If we continue to expand our clientele, then I'll be able to look for a permanent place to house them.'

'I know the sleigh ride will be up at Mòinteach Farm for a while, but what about all the Christmas stock?'

'We'll be packing it up and putting that into storage

alongside the sleigh in the workshop for now. It was the cheapest option. I'm devastated we don't have room to put it all on display at the new shop, but we're in the business of selling flowers and I can't lose sight of that.'

'But you've no permanent solution in mind as we speak?'

'No, but that's just between us, Mrs Mac. Something will turn up, I'm sure of it.'

Mrs Mac lets out an ominous sigh, but she pushes back her shoulders and gives me a fixed gaze. 'I'm sure you're right, Bella.' She points a hand at the back wall. 'We'll need to separate off a storage area with lots of rackin' and a proper office. I know you've been drawing up a plan, so the sooner we get on with it, the better. You'll be wantin' two staff to run the shop in the High Street. And they'll both need to be flexible.'

'I'm thinking Eve and Holly would manage the shop well together. We'll also require two florists here, of course'

'Presumably, I'll be running the office and you'll be back 'n' forth between the unit and the shop?'

'Yes. Once everything is sorted, I can split my time between my desk and the workbench whenever anyone is on holiday. Hopefully, I'll be more hands on, than off as it's the part of the job I really enjoy.'

'Then we should buy a little kennel for Monty, as Ursula is goin' to want to be a part of this. She told me that bein' retired isn't all it's made out to be. I thought she was mad, but do you know what? Boredom eats away at you, Bella. If Monty is happy, Ursula won't be goin' anywhere other than here. So that leaves us one short. There are plenty of folk out there lookin' for jobs, so let's show everyone that we're here to stay.'

My eyes fill with tears. 'Oh, Mrs Mac, you have no idea how hearing you say that has lifted my spirits. Even Mum and Dad aren't aware of what I'm doing. I feared I hadn't got it right, but what else could I do? I don't intend to let Pop down – I'll figure something out.'

'If anyone can do it, it's you, Bella. Let's get back and I'll nip over to the café and buy a Dundee cake. Coffee and a sugar rush is the perfect way to get everyone on-board. We go in with huge smiles on our faces and a positive outlook on what's tae come.'

Mrs Mac is ready to roll up her sleeves to get stuck in and if she can see my vision then, with a bit of encouragement, so will the others.

The other downside to all this is that we have just under two months to get everything packed up and organise the mother of all moves. But before that we have several hurdles to jump that will require my full attention. If we can't get both premises fitted out quickly, that's going to cause problems.

'Right,' I state, firmly. 'Let's head back. I'll pop in to see William and then set up a spreadsheet to draw up an action plan and prioritise the next steps.'

Mrs Mac shakes her head, looking bemused. 'If anyone is up for a challenge, Bella, it's you. But rest assured that we're all here to do whatever we can to back ye up.'

'Oh, Bella, you'll never guess what! You were right – Sheba's fur is causing your grandma's problems.' Mum's voice is slightly breathless and it's obvious she's walking. 'Dad and I are just on our way to fetch the car so we can drive your grandma home from the clinic. They've prescribed antihistamines. Vic has found someone who is happy to rehome Sheba, which is great news.'

Mum sounds delighted and I bet it's a huge relief all round.

'Things will soon be back to normal then,' I reflect.

'Yes, thank goodness! Now that your grandma is settled into her own home again, we've all decided that it's best she doesn't move back into the villa as she's doing so well. We're going to find someone to go in for a few hours every day to clean through until her cast comes off in about ten days' time. When she visits Vic and your aunt Jane, as long as your grandma remains outside in the fresh air, the consultant says she should be fine until Sheba moves out.'

'That's wonderful news, Mum. It really is.'

It seems today has been a bit of a landmark for us all and that bodes well, doesn't it?

November

21.

The Old and the New

November the first kicks off with the coldest night so far, dipping below freezing and continuing the cold snap. It doesn't deter the shoppers thankfully, but we can't really crank up the heating too much being a florist's shop.

'I'm just popping over to the café to grab some cakes to cheer everyone up,' I inform Mrs Mac. It's not much fun ferrying between the cold store and the shop when the wind is cutting, and it makes your face sting. 'See you in a bit.'

Having shrugged on my padded coat, I can't find my hat. It's such a short distance I figure I'll brave it. It turns out to be a big mistake as the wind whips my hair into a frenzy. I end up looking like a scarecrow as I head into The Wee Nook Coffee Shop to join the queue. I'm still trying to straighten out the mess I'm in when a familiar voice says, 'This is a bonus, I didn't think I'd see you until this evening. You look a bit windswept there, Bella. It's not the best day to pop across the road for a break, is it?'

I half turn to see Maverick looking highly amused but desperately trying to keep a straight face.

'No, it isn't, but I'm here to buy cakes for the team,' I retort, grimacing as I struggle to pull my hair back and gather it into a ponytail. 'There's a scrunchy in my right-hand pocket – would you mind fishing it out for me?'

Maverick's eyes sparkle, happy to have an excuse to get up close and personal. 'Of course, here you go.'

It only takes a few seconds to secure my hair and he tilts his head to stare at me approvingly. 'That's better. You'll stop and have a coffee with me though, won't you?' he pleads, shamelessly.

'I wasn't going to stay . . .' I reply, knowing I shouldn't but I'm wavering.

'Well, that didn't sound like an outright *no*, so I'll get the coffees while you grab a table.'

How can I refuse when he gives me one of his special smiles? As I saunter off, Alice catches my eye and I give her a wave. In return, she looks quite pointedly in Maverick's direction and then back at me, giving a thumbs up. I shake my head at her, chuckling to myself.

I text Mrs Mac to tell her I've been delayed, and slipping off my coat, I sit back to relax. When Maverick walks towards me carrying a tray there's a spring in his step and he looks dashing with the collar of his woollen overcoat upturned.

'What's wrong – you're staring at me. Don't say my hair is all over the place too.'

'Hardly, although the top is a little ruffled. What are you doing in town today?'

I take his coat from him and place it on the bench seat beside me as he takes the seat opposite.

'You aren't my only client, you know. Just the most demanding one,' he informs me, as he places the cups and saucers on the table.

In fairness to him, this last couple of weeks it has felt like that. 'I know . . .' I try hard not to look at him adoringly, as the way he's gazing at me melts my heart. 'I do appreciate all the help you've given me, Maverick. Especially over at the commercial unit.'

'Did you get them to make the changes I suggested on our little tour at the weekend?'

'I did and it's all in hand.'

'Great. That's another dinner you owe me then.'

We're doing the thing that couples do when they're sitting

around a table and instinctively lean into each other. I start laughing.

'What's funny?'

'Us . . . people are going to know that we're seeing each other just from our body language.' I cast around, but the only person looking in our direction is Alice, who is highly amused, but she's also discreet.

'I don't really care. Do you? We'd have a much wider choice of restaurants and pubs on the nights you don't come to my place, if you didn't keep insisting on us being *careful* not to be seen.'

I pucker up my face. 'I know.' My voice is apologetic. 'But it's just easier for now.'

'Easier? I keep telling myself it isn't because you think your family and friends will be horrified to discover we're dating.'

That admission makes me feel awful and I reach out to touch his hand. 'Point taken, but I need a little bit longer to drop a few hints and say some nice things about you.'

He looks pleased. 'I know Holly isn't my biggest fan and with a little over three weeks to the move, your entire team probably hate me—'

'No, they don't! Hate is way too strong a word, but trust me to find a way to include you, especially when it comes to being around my parents. I'll think of something, and in the meantime, I'll start sowing the seed.'

'Then I can finally breathe a sigh of relief.' Maverick looks at me in all seriousness. 'I want to be seen with you, show you off. They'll all wonder how I got someone as beautiful and intelligent as you to go out with me, being the bad guy that I am.'

We start laughing and heads turn our way. The truth is that I too can't wait for it to become common knowledge but there are a few little hurdles to jump first. Still, I'll be leaving the café with more than just a big box of cakes and I'm happy. This is a conversation that we've both been skirting around and just like that it's no longer an issue. The excitement I'm feeling is on a par with rolling all my past Christmases into one! And some. It's not going to be easy to pretend something wonderful hasn't happened when I get back to the office, that's for sure. Mrs Mac will certainly know that something is afoot.

The days fly by and it's Friday the twenty-third of November, the relaunch at our new home in the High Street. As if that isn't thrilling enough, tonight the Christmas lights in Fort William will be switched on and The Christmas Cave has a pitch at the fair. My parents and a couple of volunteers are erecting a small shed which they have affectionately named 'The Chalet' and will be selling some of our Christmas stock in aid of the charity.

I'm sitting here in what Eve and Holly have named the tearoom, grabbing a short break. Pulling out a second chair, I put up my aching feet and grab my phone.

'Mrs Mac, I'm sorry to trouble you as I know you're busy organising the packing up of The Christmas Cave, but I've just sent you an email. I've designed a small handout and I wondered if you could spare someone to print off fifty of them on some of the heavier paper? They need to be guillotined, as there are four on each A4 sheet.'

'Handouts?'

'If one more person pops in to ask where the sleigh is and why can't they buy a Christmas bauble, I'm going to lose my voice.'

'Oh – I see. We should have thought of that. I'll be after gettin' someone on that straightaway. It won't take long. Aside from that little oversight, how's it goin'?'

'Everyone loves the new premises, and I couldn't be happier. Holly spent the first hour walking up and down the High Street with a tray of bite-sized cupcakes with our redesigned logo on top. The Highland Flower Shop's new location is catching people's attention and we're getting a steady stream of customers old and new through the door. But Eve, Holly and I are struggling to cope, because everyone is coming in to look around and it's one question after another. I thought handing out a leaflet would save us repeating ourselves over, and over again.' If even a whisper gets out that there's still no sign of a permanent home for Santa's Grotto and The Christmas Cave, I won't just lose face, people will start pointing the finger at Maverick again. The official line is that there will be a pop-up Santa's Grotto this year along with a Christmas stall, but December is almost here and that's now looking like an impossibility.

'I feel bad not being able to nip across the road and help pack up today.'

'It's going well here, so don't ye go worryin' about us, lassie. And I'll get someone to sort that printin' now. It won't take long.'

'You are a gem, Mrs Mac, thank you.'

It seems that many of our regular customers have come to see for themselves what's happening. Eve and Ursula had this amazing idea of making some eye-catching hand-tied posies. They're back at the unit, while the rest of the crew is at the old shop. Few people stepping inside are leaving empty handed, which is amazing. Customers old and new are doing their bit to support us and it's really appreciated. And yes, there are still some disconcerted rumblings, but Eve, Ursula and I are giving out nothing but positive vibes about how happy we are to be here in our fabulous new premises.

There's a tap on the door and it opens slowly. My heart stops for a second because so many well-wishers want to speak to me in person and that's very kind, but my throat is raspy from all the talking. Even though I'm on my second mug of coffee, it's only just easing. But it's Maverick's head that looms up and I beckon him inside.

'Are you in hiding?'

I roll my eyes. 'Sort of. Come on in and shut the door. I've been on my feet since six this morning and Eve and Ursula insisted that I take a break. Here, have a cupcake – they're

253

really good.' I slide the plate across the table as I indicate for Maverick to take a seat.

'Do you fancy a coffee?'

'No, sadly it's a flying visit. I . . . uh . . . received this report and I don't quite know what to do with it. Am I supposed to plan something – like organise a special fund-raiser? And who puts a figure to how much it's going to cost? Cliff sent it to me after the last meeting, and I didn't want to appear as if I don't have a grasp on what's happening.'

Maverick passes me an envelope as he takes a seat opposite. While he's waiting for me to comment, he picks up a cupcake, peels off the tiny paper case and pops it into his mouth whole.

'Mmm,' he mumbles. 'Nice! Loving the new logo, by the way.'

'Thanks. Oh – this is just for information, that's all. It's the report I commissioned on Santa's Highland Express.'

'I didn't realise and I panicked a little.'

'The costs have been covered so you can just file it away,' I reply. 'These are yummy, aren't they?'

Having just eaten three of them, I think that's my entire day's sugar allocation in one go.

'Why doesn't the charity foot the bill?'

'Technically, from now on I, on behalf of my family that is, own the sleigh ride.'

'But all the proceeds go to The Highland Elves Charity, don't they?'

'Yes – the operative word being "charity". People give their money in good faith and I'm not going to take it from them under false pretences.'

'But that's not fair on you.'

'It's not a problem. That's why it's been up at Mòinteach Farm undergoing some serious restoration work. I'd assumed Randall or Cliff would have taken you up there to have a look. It's almost finished actually, and you'll get a copy of the annual inspection report when that's carried out. We're not expecting any problems, other than it still doesn't have a home.'

Maverick looks a little disconcerted. 'I've more questions than I have answers right now – paperwork is coming at me from all angles, and no one realises I don't know what I'm doing. Granddad has locked himself away in his study costing out various options to present to Grandma for the future of Lachlan.'

'Seriously, there isn't much you can mess up as everything is approved by the committee before it goes ahead. But if you want, we can go over the final programme of events for December before you issue it. I'm happy to answer questions as best I can even if it's simply to direct you to the right person.'

'I'd appreciate that. I panicked when I read this as I had no idea what a major job it was. Why didn't you tell me?'

As our relationship has continued to blossom, I made a conscious decision to keep my work and my private life separate.

'There are a lot of volunteers who are helping out for free and I have two contractors dealing with the specialist stuff. It's all sorted and they're on schedule.'

'You're frowning, Bella,' Maverick reflects as he stares at me.

'The budget is tight, but it's going to be worth every penny we spend.' And William has confirmed that the funds I'm due from Adam should be in my account next week.

But money isn't the problem. It's obvious now that finding a permanent home for the sleigh ride this year is little more than wishful thinking. I've been talking to the local authority and the chamber of commerce, but even with a concerted effort from Randall and other members of the committee, nothing suitable has materialised. The new location must be easily accessible, with plenty of parking and reasonably central. We usually start up the ride on the first of December and it operates during shop opening hours with a rota of volunteers. I haven't rejected the offer of a large hay barn at Mòinteach Farm, but it throws up so many issues there's not enough time left to resolve them. The reality is that only a miracle will see the sleigh ride in operation this season and I'm too gutted to talk about it.

'I can relax a little, then,' Maverick says, sounding relieved. 'Things seem to be going well here. How's it looking over at the commercial unit today?'

'The fitters are still working through the snagging list – there are a couple of issues with some of the racking and the odd sticking door, but it's fully staffed and we're keeping up with the orders. The office is in a bit of a shambles because Mrs Mac is busy supervising the packing up of The Christmas Cave. Once that's done maybe we can get back to some semblance of normality.'

'It's a huge task emptying the old shop. Do you have enough help?' Maverick sounds a little disappointed that I've kept him out of the loop.

'My parents are there and a few of the charity's volunteers pop in and out as and when they can. If the vans have a lull in deliveries, they've been dropping by to pick up a load. We should get everything all wrapped up tomorrow morning as I've organised an early start. The cleaning company will be in at lunchtime.'

'You've done well to achieve what you have in such a tight timescale, Bella. Anyway, you look like you need a hug.' He stands and walks around the table, wrapping his arms around me the instant I jump up out of my seat.

'I'm here for you, Bella, whenever you need anything,' he whispers into my ear. 'I don't want you pretending everything is fine when it isn't.'

'I know. And if I needed anything, I'd say.'

'Are we still on for tonight?'

'Yes. Why, have you changed your mind?' I'm teasing him because I can see he hasn't.

He pauses, and just as he's about to say something there's a sharp rap on the door and we spring apart.

It opens and Dad peers in. 'Hi, Maverick, you're the last person I was expecting to see. How are you?'

'Good, thanks, Tom, and you? I'm just on my way out. Thanks for your help, Bella.'

And with that he's gone.

'Here you go,' Dad says as he passes me a stack of neatly cut, A6-sized sheets of paper. 'Did you invite him, or did he pop in to wish you luck?'

'Thanks, Dad, appreciated. And no, I didn't. Maverick popped in on charity business. How's it going over there?'

Dad grimaces. 'It's taking a lot longer than we thought to pack up all those delicate Christmas trimmings. Mrs Mac's standards are high so I'm leaving them all to it. I'm in charge of taping up the boxes and stacking them, ready to load up the vans. Some of the boxes will be put to one side ready for The Chalet at tonight's fair.' He looks directly at me, questioningly. 'Maverick's not causing you any problems, is he?'

'Not at all – everything is fine.'

'To tell you the truth, I didn't think Maverick had what it takes to pull a programme together. He was ominously quiet at his first committee meeting, and I thought he didn't want to be there. But after seeing the way he's been getting more hands-on, I'm impressed by the energy he's bringing to the table. He moved quite a few of the ideas for the winter fund-raisers forward, which made November a bumper month.'

'I'm glad to hear that. It must be a relief for Randall.'

'I suspect it is. Cliff mentioned that Fiona is coming around to the idea of running an events business from Lachlan so they're going to be busy.'

Dad and Mum have only really mentioned the McIntyres in passing, even though they brush shoulders at meetings and at some of the events.

'Can I just ask . . . and this is going to sound weird as I know you respect Randall, but you've never really regarded him as a friend, have you?'

Dad's face freezes and his demeanour instantly changes.

'He's an entrepreneur, a businessman through and through, Bella, and you must never forget that. It's easy to be philanthropic when it's in your best interests and it's a tax write-off to boot. Now, I'd best get back or Mrs Mac will come looking for me. And Eve and Ursula could do with another pair of hands, as there's a queue forming. Well done, my lovely – your mum and I are proud of what you've pulled off today.'

Does Dad think Randall used Aunt Jane, knowing full well the more visitors we draw to Fort William, the more likely it is to attract bigger names to the High Street? It's not like Dad to be so scathing. It suited my aunt as well as Randall.

'Dad, before you go can I say one thing?'

'It's obvious you're itching to get whatever it is off your chest. Now's the time to say it.'

'I don't hold any grudges. Business is business, and if I can't stand on my own two feet then I don't deserve to be in charge. I don't want to owe anyone anything. Do you?'

He pauses, narrowing his eyes. 'You've got a valid point there, Bella. I guess I just felt aggrieved for what you're going through. And you're right – Randall's done his bit and I guess Maverick is only doing his job.'

'I'm glad we see eye to eye on this, Dad. I don't want any bad feeling.'

He bows his head and when he looks up I can see he's taken my words on-board.

'And there won't be any. Not from here on in.'

Seconds later, he's gone and I spring into action, grabbing the pile of handouts. I have no idea whether he and Randall had a falling out at some point in the past over something to do with the charity. Or perhaps Dad was a tad disappointed Randall didn't ask him to take over as events coordinator. I guess I'll never know for sure, but Dad will hopefully move on. The one thing that the conversation made clear to me is that he doesn't know about what happened between Aunt

Jane and Randall. That's one complication I no longer need to be concerned about.

'Holly, come in! I'm just getting ready for tonight's festivities.'

'I can't stay long myself as I'm on my way home to change. I thought it might be appropriate to drop in and toast today's hugely successful launch. Here you go!' She hands me a bottle of Prosecco and then follows me upstairs.

'Ah, this is so thoughtful of you. Who's looking after Katie?'

'She's with Nick's parents.'

'She is? I thought they were just doing the school runs for you today.'

'After they dropped her off this morning Nick's mum rang to ask if Katie could stay overnight. Apparently, Katie thought that was the plan all along and was getting all excited about it. I didn't have the heart to say no, so I went straight from work to drop some clothes in for her. We're going to meet up a little later for the turning on of the Christmas lights and they said Nick will be there too.'

'Ah, that's nice if you can all enjoy it together.'

I head straight for the kitchen to grab two glasses while Holly drops her bag down on the floor and collapses onto the sofa.

'I heard the packing went well over at the old shop today. Although I'm sure Mrs Mac kept them all on their toes,' Holly chatters away as I grab some glasses.

'She rang me earlier on and mentioned that two of the volunteers took in some home-made cakes, which was a nice gesture.'

'Well, Ivor said the pizzas you ordered at lunchtime went down well too.'

'It was the least I could do. I was hoping to pop in and thank everyone, but we were rushed off our feet all day, weren't we?'

'It was crazy, but in a good way,' Holly admits. 'But it's all down to you, Bella.'

Stripping off the foil and popping the plastic stopper, the Prosecco immediately starts to fizz and I quickly direct the stream of bubbles.

Carrying the glasses across to sit next to Holly, she takes one and we pause; she looks at me expectantly.

'To new beginnings and old friends!' I declare as we chink.

The bubbles are refreshing, and I could do with a bit of sparkle because today was a very mixed bag of emotions for me.

'I can't believe we had people queuing,' Holly chuckles. 'Which is good, so why do you look jaded tonight? Is it just because you've been working flat out and it's beginning to catch up with you?'

'You're probably right. There are times when I dip . . . I feel like the wind has been knocked out of me and I wonder whether I have the strength to get back up.'

'But you always do, Bella. And you've gotten us this far – the end is in sight.'

'I'll be happier when everything settles down and the new routine is running smoothly.' There are so many loose ends to tie up, and I hate not having all the solutions lined up and ready to go. 'Anyway, how are things with you? I'm really sorry we haven't had time to sit and talk for ages now.'

'I know . . . I feel bad about that, too. But I'm going through a bit of a difficult patch right now.'

My pulse quickens – I hadn't even noticed, so what sort of friend does that make me? 'Is this about Katie?'

'No. She's settled down rather nicely because she's seeing more of her dad.'

'She is?' I hate the way my voice goes up at the end, as if that was the last thing I was expecting – even though it's true.

'Yes. I'm as surprised as you are, and it's partly why I took the offer from his parents when they reached out. Initially, I said they could have Katie overnight during the school holidays, but we got chatting and they said that they wanted to help. They weren't thinking about Nick, but about what I needed. You know that my mum does what she can and while she loves the company, without Dad she has the house and her job to juggle. Nick's mum doesn't work, so it's easier for her.'

Reading between the lines, I jump in. 'And they miss seeing Katie.'

'Yes. It's tough on them, too. But I don't want to be seen as the single mum who can't cope.'

'No one looks at you and thinks that Holly!' I reply, adamantly.

'Nick's changing, Bella, and I don't quite know how to handle it.'

'Is it for the better?'

'It would seem so . . . but I'm wary.'

'Caution is sensible Holly, but you never know – this Christmas could be full of surprises—'

'—or the worst one ever and I'll be drowning my sorrows. Oh, my goodness – this is like déjà vu. Didn't I say something similar this time last year?'

We look at each other in the way that only best friends can, recognising the pain, the disappointment and . . . the hope that never dies.

'Well,' I tell Holly firmly, 'if it looks like Christmas is going to be a bit of a let-down then you, me and Katie will head off somewhere nice together. We'll rent a cottage, turn off our phones and bake gingerbread men. We'll sit out at night drinking hot chocolate with those tiny marshmallows heaped on top and turn our backs on the world.'

'Oh, Bella, if only . . .'

'No, Holly – I'm serious.'

My best friend for ever looks at me dubiously and then we both start laughing.

'Oh, why not? You and I have been through the proverbial mill this year. I think the people we care about will cut us some slack, don't you?'

'Christmas Eve through to New Year's Day. What do you think?'

Holly frowns. 'But that means putting down a deposit, which we could end up losing. How late can we leave it to decide?'

'Oh, you're hedging your bets and thinking I should do the same. Leave it to me. Wouldn't it be wonderful to get away to recharge our batteries and come back in the new year with renewed energy?'

Holly's eyes widen. 'You're serious, aren't you?'

'I am. If things don't turn out as I hope, then doing something completely different is the only way I'm going to survive the holidays.'

Holly knows exactly what I'm referring to; she understands how important it is for me to keep Pop's dream alive and I've failed. It's going to be the first Christmas since Santa's Grotto began that the sleigh ride hasn't been in operation.

'Nick is promising me all sorts of things but I'm not taking it too seriously,' she confides. 'I want to believe he can make it all happen, but history tells me that it's unlikely. I'm in, Bella. There comes a point at which we have to suck it up and move on.'

'I'll keep an eye out for something rather special. But nothing – *nothing* – would make me happier than to end up staying there alone.'

'Ah . . . and if it's me and Katie on our own, then we'll still be smiling. And I'll start saving now, because if that's where we end up, I want it to be an amazing break. As loath as I am to say this, I've been wondering whether Katie and I should think about moving away. Mum says she'll come with us if that's what we decide to do. Both of my aunts live in Glencoe, so I'd never have to worry about finding a babysitter.'

I knew there was something major going on with Holly, but this is a real shock. The thought of not being an almost daily part of her and Katie's life is hard to imagine and I'm devastated. But I also want them to be happy.

'You must do whatever's best for you both, Holly. But it's a tough decision to make.'

'I know and one I've been wrestling with for a while now. If Nick doesn't make good on his promises then I'll have no choice. A fresh start is the only way. Imagine trying to date someone else knowing there's always a chance I'll bump into Nick?'

'I understand. But no matter where you end up, I'm there for you both always.'

And with that the battle lines are drawn, and do you know what? It's a relief – as if we've given ourselves permission to fail and then move on if that's how things turn out. But it would be with much sadness in our hearts.

22.

The Night Sky Is Glowing!

Shortly after Holly heads home to change, my phone pings and it's a text from Maverick.

> Sorry, I'm running late. I'm about ten minutes away. I'll meet you outside the flat!

Tonight is a biggie for me, as although the High Street will be crowded, the likelihood of not bumping into at least a few people I know is slim. Glancing out of the window, I see it's packed already and the buzz of chatter is like a constant low-level hum. I look in the mirror to adjust my red Santa hat and wind a thick scarf around my neck. What I see reflected back at me is a smiley face and an excited glint in my eyes. Maybe it's time to let people cotton on to the fact that Maverick and I enjoy spending time together. Why not?

After grabbing my gloves and making my way downstairs, when I step outside it's a sea of smiling faces. A few acquaintances wave as they walk by but it's mostly customers and shop owners with their families. My eyes scan the steady stream of people to my right but there's no sign of Maverick yet. Suddenly my phone starts buzzing and I yank it out of my pocket.

'There's nowhere to park and I'm just driving around in circles,' Maverick moans, sounding fed up.

'Head for the rear of the new shop and I'll go and unlock the gate.'

'I rather hoped you say that. See you shortly.'

A quick dash back inside to get the key and as I quicken my pace I can't help acknowledging the irony of Maverick being responsible for I don't know how many properties in this street and he can't find a place to park.

The minute he sees me he toots his horn, winding down his window. 'That'll teach me to think ahead in future. Who do these cars belong to?'

'That's Holly's and that one is my parents' car. The vans are parked up at the rear of the old shop tonight. If I'd known, I would have given you a key. They'll both be able to get out if you park right up against the fence.'

Suddenly, there's a blast of music as the speaker system down in the square is turned on. I wait impatiently while Maverick makes the tricky manoeuvre and then sprints towards me, looking shamefaced.

'Sorry.' He throws his arms around me, pulling me close. I look up at him unable to hide my contentment as his lips meet mine. It's like someone is letting off fireworks, but the explosions are all inside my head.

He pulls away reluctantly, grasping my hand in his and tugging. 'Come on, I don't want to miss the big turning on ceremony.'

But the speeches have already begun and even increasing our pace I doubt we'll make it down to the other end of the street in time.

'You're fine with this tonight, are you?' he checks. 'You know, being seen with me and holding hands. I thought your dad was a little frosty this morning when he caught us together.'

'Dad said some pretty nice things about you, actually. He's impressed by the hard work you've put in for the charity. There will be a few surprised faces I'm sure, but people are beginning to see you in a different light.'

Maverick's face lights up. 'That's a good start.'

In the background the chairman of the local chamber of commerce begins the big countdown and Maverick and I draw to a halt. There are few people around us as everyone is pressing forward but we have the best view, with almost the entire length of the Fort William shopping centre in front of us.

'Three . . . two . . . one!'

The yelling, clapping and sound of children blowing brightly coloured cardboard whistles drifts towards us as a tunnel of Christmas lights sparkle overhead. Strings of lights go from one side of the thoroughfare to the other, turning the pedestrianised street into a festive corridor. Gazing up, the outline of a snowman, with his arms outstretched standing next to a group of Christmas trees, welcomes us. Beyond that there's a cascade of shooting stars suspended in the air and further down two bells, surrounded by green holly leaves and bright red berries glow against the dark blue of the night sky.

'It's pretty, isn't it?' I sigh, turning to face Maverick.

'This time last year I knew the lights were being turned on but I gave it a miss, knowing I'd get to see them on one of my visits. But you're right and it's rather special being here in person to witness it.'

'If I'd known you then I would have dragged you along,' I chide him. He looks a little cold and I find myself reaching forward to turn up his collar. 'Come on, let's saunter down to grab a hot drink. But rather than standing around for a while if you aren't in a rush to get home, how do you fancy a slight detour?'

'I'm up for pretty much anything.' He flashes me a wicked smile.

'Really? Hmm . . . right. That's good to know! Let's head for the stalls.'

The crowd is enormous and it takes a while as there's a queue for the hot Christmas punch. I stand back, sheltering in a doorway while Maverick patiently waits his turn.

'Bella! Bella!' Katie comes rushing towards me, a half-eaten star cookie in one hand. I kneel down to give her a hug, looking over her shoulder as Nick and Holly walk towards me. They walk separately but they're chatting and laughing, there's no sign of his parents.

'Hi, guys!' I call out, but Katie isn't done with me and proceeds to tell me that she's in the school nativity play.

'And what part are you playing?' I ask, loving the general air of excitement I see on that beautiful little face of hers.

'I'm one of the three wise men and I get to wear a crown,' she enthuses. 'Did you know they brought gifts? We've got to make a box and cover it in gold, haven't we, Mum?'

'We do and soon.' Holly looks lovingly at her daughter and as I glance at Nick I see a hint of regret flash over his face. These are the precious family moments he's missing and tonight is a good reminder of that.

Maverick appears, looking a little awkward and not just because he has a steaming cup in each hand. I stand, reaching out to take one from him.

'I went for the non-alcoholic one but they both smell the same,' he apologises, as Holly and Nick exchange a look of surprise.

'Maverick, this is Holly and my daughter Katie,' Nick states proudly.

'It's good to meet you both. That's quite a cookie you have there, Katie.'

She looks back at Maverick, shyly. 'You can get one over there.' She points with her free hand. 'They're really good.'

'We were looking for Grandma and Grandpa,' Holly reminds Katie. 'It's nice to see you taking part in the celebrations, Maverick. And I'll see you tomorrow, Bella. Bright and early!'

'Maverick has also offered to lend a hand,' I reply, as she leans in to give me a hug. When Holly steps back her face is a picture of confusion.

'Oh, that's . . . kind. Right, well . . . enjoy the rest of your evening!'

Once they're out of earshot, Maverick looks at me, frowning.

'You said you were up for anything.'

'Yes, but won't it look odd my being there?' he questions.

'You didn't throw me out, the decision was mine to walk away and you kindly found me the perfect alternative. I think it's time we put an end to the grumblings, don't you? Now – this is definitely the punch with alcohol in it so you're safe to drive and I'll direct you.'

We saunter back to the car, stopping to admire the beautifully lit-up chalet sporting The Highland Flower Shop logo. It's surrounded by customers, and I'm delighted to see that Dad and Cliff have also hung decorations on long strings over the exterior. I wave to Mum and Isla when they spot us through the window and Maverick starts laughing when they stick their hands through to acknowledge us.

'Where's the glass? No wonder they're all wearing thick coats.'

'Maybe they ran out of time,' I giggle. 'But they've done a wonderful job, as usually the shop stays open. Still, where there's a will there's a way, as Pop would have said.'

It does look lovely and maybe instead of looking back I should be celebrating what could be the start of a new, festive tradition. But tonight everything around me is sparkling and I'm feeling happy and optimistic.

Having collected one of the spare keys from Paul up at the farmhouse, I'm struggling to get it to turn in the lock.

'Do you want me to have a go?' Maverick offers but I persevere, and it finally shifts.

Stepping into the dark and gloomy interior, I run my hand along the wall. The switch is further inside than I remembered and when I flick it on everything is covered up with tarpaulins, even the long workbench. Down at the far end, the boxes they've been ferrying here from the shop are all sealed in plastic and standing on wooden pallets to keep them off the floor.

Maverick makes his way around the hidden mound in the middle of the floor. 'What a find this place is. A restoration job on this scale requires plenty of room to spread out and they certainly have that here.'

Together, we carefully lift the edge of the cover, but it's held down in places with weights restricting our access. Even so, it sends a little thrill through me to see how near the renovations are to completion. The carriage we're looking at has had a basecoat of paint and is awaiting the final detail, the mechanism between it and the rear of Santa's carriage looks reassuringly robust.

'They're doing a great job. It's good to see it with my own eyes.' Actually, it's a relief, because it gives me hope.

We carefully cover it back up and Maverick makes his way over to the workbench. I sidle over next to him.

'That's a fork pin joint, it connects the carriages together,' he explains.

It's easy enough to figure out that the pin with the single eye slots into the space between the two eyes on the fork and there's a long metal piece which holds the three eyes together.

'Seeing an original one lying next to a shiny new replica, the old one certainly took a bit of a battering over time,' I point out. Having read the report word for word, most of the technical stuff went over my head but now I can see for myself I can understand Dad's concerns.

'Everything wears out eventually when there's a repetitive action involved,' Maverick acknowledges. 'Still, once everything has been replaced it will be like new.'

It's reassuring to hear that as I have no experience at all of mechanical things. I'm sure he'd say if he thought the replacement looked too flimsy, but to me it appears they're replacing it like for like. The irony is that we have a working ride and nowhere to put it.

Maverick pulls a face, glancing over at the boxes. 'That's a lot of stock standing around not earning you, or the charity, a penny.'

'It's sad, too. I'm going to miss walking past the baubles every day of my working life. People buy Christmas trimmings all year round and sales were always quite steady, although they peaked between September and December obviously. When people realise that twenty per cent of the profit goes to the charity they tend to dig a little deeper into their pockets and over the year it all adds up.'

'You've nothing to feel guilty about, you know. Don't take this the wrong way, but even your aunt couldn't have kept it all going without being subsidised.'

I look him straight in the eye. 'But I do . . . feel guilty.' And with that my eyes begin to fill with tears. I'm so embarrassed that I instinctively turn my back on him. Without warning, I feel Maverick's hands on my shoulders as he gently turns me around to face him. His eyes are full of empathy as he looks down at me.

'Listen to me, Bella. You're trying to do the impossible and you know it.'

'Yes, but I simply want to keep things running . . . like normal.'

'My granddad is reaching out to every contact he has within a reasonable radius of Fort William. They're all aware of the need for a permanent solution, as packing this lot up every year and having to transport it back and forth isn't practical. It's time to face facts – it's probably not going to happen this year, but you're not in this alone. You have no idea how much goodwill there is for what you're doing, Bella. People would be horrified to know this is tearing you apart.'

It's a struggle to stop my bottom lip from wavering. Maverick throws his arms around me and suddenly the only sound I can hear is the blood pounding in my ears as my heartbeat is racing.

'I know and I am grateful,' I mumble. 'But it's hard to accept defeat.'

'You're special, Bella, and you don't even know it.' Maverick's voice is low as he whispers into my hair. My pulse is racing and suddenly I don't feel so alone and vulnerable. I feel protected.

'No, I'm just stubborn and,' I sigh, tearfully, 'you know what they say about pride – it comes before a fall.'

His hands slide down my arms, his eyes unblinking as I lean into him for comfort. 'That's defeatist talk and it's not your style, is it? You're getting cold. It's been a weird day, to say the least. And you must be hungry because I know I am. What you need is a hearty meal. In my fridge waiting to be cooked, I have two Aberdeen Angus fillet steaks. What do you say?'

'You're right and we do have something to celebrate, although I'll no doubt have to face a tirade of questions tomorrow,' I groan.

He beams at me. 'Yes, but I'm worth it, aren't I?'

Maverick's hands catch mine and we linger for a few seconds as we take a moment to let it all sink in.

He reaches out to gently cup my cheek in his hand. 'You should be standing here proud of what you've achieved, Bella. So, cheer up as I'm about to impress you with my cooking skills.'

I hand Maverick the key to lock up and he releases me with some reluctance. There's a sensitive side to him that most people have yet to discover, but as they get to know him better they'll see for themselves that he has a genuinely good heart.

'You've gone very quiet,' Maverick comments as we walk back to the car.

'Just wondering whether there was anything I could have done differently.'

'I'm not sure many people would have had the same level of determination and resilience to tackle what you've had to deal with these past months, Bella.' Maverick unlocks the passenger door, holding it open while I slide onto the seat.

In the few moments it takes him to walk around to the other side and sit behind the wheel, I ponder whether I should ask him the question that's been on my mind all evening.

When the engine kicks into life, I decide to go for it. 'Do you get homesick for the US?'

I study Maverick's side profile, the curve of his cheek and the light stubble on his chin. 'You're curious about the life I walked away from and that's only natural. I was in an on/off relationship for a few years, but we finished just before I left for the UK. It was probably one of the things that prompted me to come, if I'm honest. Although the main reason is that I want to grab as many memories with my grandparents as I can. My maternal grandparents have always been in my life, and we get on fine . . .' He hesitates and I sit quietly, allowing him to gather his thoughts. 'It's like parents always say they don't have a favourite kid when they actually do. I guess I have favourite grandparents. I promised myself a while back that I wouldn't be one of those people who end up regretting the things they didn't do.'

It's a brave thing to admit and I admire that.

'I have some amazing memories of Pop. We spent a lot of time together in the summer holidays every year. My grandma would be indoors baking or making lunch and Pop and I would be in the greenhouse tying up tomato plants, or in the garden weeding his vegetable patch. In between, we'd spend time on his putting mat trying to get a hole in one.'

'It's things like that you remember forever, isn't it?' Maverick understands and I try to hide my surprise at his words.

The car rocks back and forth as the ruts in the track get a little tricky to negotiate. Maverick focuses on avoiding a couple of potholes badly in need of filling in. We lapse into silence for a few minutes as I don't want to disturb his concentration. Once we're back on the main road, he glances at me for the briefest of moments.

'Me and my ex . . . we chat on the phone occasionally,

but Louise would never leave her family behind. It takes a special sort of person to handle that sort of upheaval.'

'And you're one of them?'

'Having family here makes it's a lot easier for me. She'd have no one.'

'Except for you.'

'Yes. As it turns out, I wasn't enough. We'd known each other for a very long time, and I guess it was comfortable but in hindsight our relationship wasn't really going anywhere. The way I look at it is if you really want something to work you'll find a way and we didn't.'

He doesn't sound at all regretful, but then he could level the exact same comment at me. I get that, as it can sound like you're making excuses if you try to sugar-coat the truth.

'It's awkward when people ask how I'm doing,' I admit. 'They expect me to be devastated that my relationship ended so abruptly. The reality is that it was a massive relief, only the timing was awful. I can't say it's fun renting a tired and cramped little flat, but it's been a boon being able to walk to work. Obviously, now I have to drive to the unit, but it's not that far.'

'Have you decided what you'll do when it's time to move out?'

I don't like to say that it depends on how much is left once I settle up the final invoices for overhauling the sleigh ride.

'I have a couple of options open to me. It's not high on my list of priorities right now.'

He laughs, but it's coming from a place of understanding and sympathy. 'I can see why, given how busy you've been. There's plenty of room at my place, you know.'

It's a throwaway comment but it catches me off guard, and I don't quite know what to say. He's joking, surely? But before I can dwell over it, the conversation goes off in another direction.

'I do admire a woman who isn't fazed by a challenge.

But I will admit, Bella Reed, somehow I think you're going to get through this and come out the other side a winner.'

All I can do is smile graciously back at him, while inside I want to tell him that I do hope so . . . because right now I'm thinking it's fifty–fifty and I don't like those odds.

23.

Moving On

'You and Maverick looked very cosy together last night.' Holly stops pouring hot water into the coffee mugs and glances at me questioningly. 'After everything he's put you through this past couple of months, Maverick is the last person I expected to see you with.'

She looks at me accusingly. It's understandable, as this is the day we move out the last of our things from the old shop. I'll be returning the keys to MPI in just a couple of days' time.

'He's not the enemy, Holly, and if Maverick hadn't acted quickly we probably wouldn't be here in this beautifully refurbished property.'

'Yes, well . . . it's funny how he can make things happen when it suits him. I expect he was on a bit of a guilt trip,' Holly says with a tinge of sarcasm, as she passes me a mug.

'No, it was thoughtful of him. Anyway, you know full well there was no way we could vacate the old shop while they upgraded the property, even if I could have afforded it.'

'It was perfectly fine as it was,' she says with real conviction. 'The old central heating never let us down once, did it? And how long does it take to give it a lick of paint?'

'Now you're being unfair. Once Maverick realised what a tough position I was in he was horrified. As I've come to know him better, my respect for him both as a professional and as a man who cares about people has grown.'

Holly chews her lip, realising that she's sounding off. 'Oh, sorry, I didn't realise he had a heart . . . that makes all the difference.'

'Sarcasm doesn't suit you, Holly.'

She shakes her head, dismissively.

'If you ask me, he's just desperate for company. There are still a lot of people angry about what happened. Anyway, what's his house like – grand, is it? I expect they pay him well for pushing old tenants out so they can up the rent.'

Without realising it, Maverick has indirectly caused a lot of stress for Holly in terms of both her personal and her work life. If venting helps, then so be it.

'It needs a little TLC inside. But he's on his own and like everyone else he has to work to pay the mortgage.'

'Maverick can't afford to get in an interior designer to sort it out for him? His family have money – why don't they come to his rescue?'

I can't help but raise an eyebrow at Holly's scathing remark.

'Money isn't always the answer, Holly. Maverick has a demanding job, he's still working on the VW van and he's back and forth to Loch Awe to spend time with his grandparents.'

'Nick has been helping him restore a Volkswagen camper van? Maverick must be paying him well then, because I assumed it was a high value performance car,' she laughs disparagingly. 'And why are you making excuses for him, anyway?' Holly gives me a withering look.

'I'm not. It's the truth.'

A little smile starts to play around the edges of her mouth.

'Oh, my goodness – you really have fallen for Mr Corporate Guy in his expensively tailored suits. You're more the welly boots and wandering along the seashore picking up driftwood type. Or hiking up a mountain, not caring if your mascara is running down your face.'

She knows me so well, but she's way off about Maverick.

'Now you're being mean, Holly.'

She can see I'm not happy with the way this conversation is going.

'Maybe I am, but getting him on your side is one thing, Bella, dating him is another thing entirely. No wonder you've been downplaying it.' She makes it sound like I'm a traitor.

'He's just a guy doing his job. Outside of work he's different.'

'Oh, so you're ready to start seeing someone again and the person you pick is Maverick McIntyre? He's upset a lot of people, you know. People who won't understand the attraction.'

'He's taken on the role as events coordinator for The Highland Elves now that Randall is stepping back. Maverick is trying to do his bit, so please do me a favour and give him a break. Please, for my sake?' It's an appeal I know she won't refuse.

'Look – I'm sorry. Ignore me. I'm not in the best of moods this morning. I don't want to see you get hurt, that's all,' Holly replies, miserably. 'I just think it's too soon for you to rush into anything.'

'I'm taking it one day at a time, a bit like everything else right now. We're all going to be a little on edge today, Holly, that's understandable. But I'm relying on the team to make sure it's business as usual while I wrap things up across the road.'

Holly gives me a weak smile. 'It just seems wrong not being there with you. I hope it goes well, Bella, and you know we'll all be thinking of you.'

We finish drinking our coffee in silence and when I check my watch I'm conscious that it's time for me to head over and unlock before family, friends and volunteers start arriving. A loud tap on the back door makes Holly jump up as Rodric, in a hurry to offload today's delivery, disturbs us.

'Let's hope today is a good one,' Holly says, as she gives me a quick hug before unlocking the front door.

'That's the spirit,' I agree with enthusiasm. 'And stop worrying about me.'

For the next hour, a constant stream of people filter in to help clear what Mrs Mac and the team didn't manage to pack up yesterday. It's a busy Saturday back at the unit and at the new shop, so today it's down to me to direct operations. It's touching to see so many familiar faces, people who are giving their time for free and are happy to do so.

Dad and Maverick are hard at work taking apart the old floristry counter, which is going to be repurposed and turned into shelving for Ivor's garage.

As lunchtime approaches we're almost done, and the shop is now little more than a shell. 'How are you holding up, Bella?' Mum half-whispers, linking her arm into mine and giving it a squeeze.

'Emotional,' I admit.

'I know, but it's time to thank everyone for their help and send them on their way. Are you up to giving a little speech, or should I get your dad to say something?'

'I'll do it.'

As we look at each other, she nods her head, then waves to Dad who does a wolf whistle to gain everyone's attention.

'Now that we're nearly done, Bella would like to take this opportunity to say a few words.'

Everyone stops what they're doing to look at me expectantly.

I clear my throat, knowing that I must be upbeat and positive, even though deep down inside that's not how I'm feeling today.

'First of all, I would like to say a huge thank you to everyone who has joined in to help over the last few days. To my wonderful team who are hard at work as Saturday is our busiest day, my amazing family and awesome friends – you have all touched my heart.' I pause, as suddenly no one is smiling and that's not good. 'If Aunt Jane were here today, she'd be overwhelmed by the way people have so kindly come to our aid and the well-wishers we've had popping in to check out our new premises.

'Thanks, too, go to McIntyre Property Investments Limited for their charitable support both past, present and future. And to Maverick for getting hands-on this morning. As The Highland Flower Shop brightens the other end of the High Street, plans are afoot to find a new home for Santa's Grotto and The Christmas Cave. After a complete overhaul of the sleigh ride, we're hoping an age-old tradition will continue for many years to come.'

There's a tremendous round of applause, and the smiles are back. People press closer, wanting to shake the hands of myself, Dad and Mum. But I'm numb inside. Saying you're going to do something is one thing, actually making it happen when it will be little short of a miracle is another.

By noon, everyone is gone, and I hand the keys over to the team of professionals who have come in to do the final clean through.

'If you can pop them through the door next to the newsagent's shop when you've finished, that would be great.'

'No problem at all. And good luck, Bella.'

'Thanks. It's a bit of a landmark day.'

And with that I walk out for the very last time. The sky is overcast rather like my mood and I head straight for the flat, ignoring the bustle of Christmas shoppers around me.

'Hi, Aunt Jane. It's all done, and the cleaners are in.'

'I've had the phone next to me all morning, Bella. I've been a bag of nerves. How are you doing?'

'I'm fine, just a little overwhelmed. It wasn't quite as bad as I feared. All our supporters popped in to say farewell to the old place, some stopping to lend a hand taking stuff out to the skip. That'll be collected this afternoon.'

A gentle sigh travels down the line. 'If I'd sold off The Highland Flower Shop, we both know that it's inextricably linked with Pop's legacy and the charity. Take that away and all you have is a shop selling flowers. You can't sell, or pass on, goodwill that comes from a family's long-term connections with the community, can you? That wouldn't have been fair on the new purchaser, but it wasn't supposed to be a millstone around your neck, Bella.'

'That's not the case at all. If you could have seen the support we had, not just at the old shop but at the launch of the new premises yesterday, you would have been smiling from ear to ear.' I lie back on the sofa, putting my feet up on the coffee table.

'That's all I wanted to hear. You're surrounded by people who care about you as much as you care about them, that's what counts.'

'How are things at your end?'

'We're off to spend the afternoon with friends. Grandma and Vic send their love and thanks, Bella. I can finally relax.'

As we disconnect I have a feeling Dad has probably spoken to her, as there was no mention at all of Christmas. I didn't have the heart to bring up the subject either.

Today Maverick and I are going out for Sunday lunch as a treat to thank him for helping out yesterday. He rolled up his sleeves and got stuck in alongside everyone else and I felt it broke the ice. Particularly with Mum and Dad.

After lunch, I promised him that I'd glance through the final programme of events kicking off on the first of December and leading up to Hogmanay. When my phone rings my heart skips a beat; it's not Maverick calling to cancel, but Grandma, which is a wonderful surprise.

'Bella, sweetie. I've been sitting here thinking of you. I was just talking to your mum and dad. You've certainly had a lot to deal with but you're a battler.'

'Thanks, Grandma. It's onwards and upwards now.'

'You are taking time out for yourself, aren't you?' Grandma Susan asks, pointedly.

'Yes, of course I am. Anyway, how's that ankle doing?'

'Oh, I'm almost ready to run a marathon,' she chuckles.

'The reason I'm calling is that I'm going to send you some money, so I need your account details.'

'Why are you sending me money? I'm doing fine.'

'I didn't say you weren't. But now that you're *on your own*—' Grandma lowers her voice as if it's a sensitive subject '—a little boost to your nest egg might come in useful.'

Oh dear. This means that she's been quizzing Mum about the flat I'm living in.

'Grandma, that's really very kind of you but it's not necessary. Why don't you treat yourself to a new kitchen, or something?'

A loud tut echoes down the line. 'I like things just the way they are, and you know me, I can't abide dust and mess. No, I want you to have something substantial you can use as a deposit on a house, and I won't take no for an answer.'

I haven't the heart to tell her that no mortgage company would take me on right now. I've had some major bills to foot to get the shop and the unit kitted out, and while business is getting busier by the day, my overheads have increased significantly. A few months down the road hopefully the profits will reflect the hard work, but it's too soon.

'Renting is easier for me, Grandma. Buying something requires a lot more time and effort, because I'll want to decorate throughout. No, renting is perfect for now.'

'But it doesn't sound like much fun, Bella.'

I really need to divert her attention.

'I nearly forgot! We have a new employee, although he isn't on the payroll but he's in the doghouse already – quite literally. While Ursula is here working full-time her golden retriever, Monty, has his own abode in the corner of the work area. Everyone takes it in turns to take him for a walk and he really brightens our day.'

'Ah, bless! Animals are such wonderful companions. Funnily enough, just the other day I was talking to Vic about getting a puppy.'

Memories of what Grandma went through with Sheba, make me feel uncomfortable.

'Do you think that's . . . wise?'

'Oh,' she replies, instantly, 'I'm not allergic to animals in general, Bella. Only long-haired ones who moult everywhere. I'm rather fond of both Sheba and Art. They often kept me company when all I could do was sit in the garden at the villa and read. It was terribly boring at times. You know me, I like to be independent, and you take after me, Bella. I've come to learn that just occasionally a little help goes a long way. Anyway, I'll leave you to it as I'm about to join some friends for Sunday brunch. Love you, sweetie, and I do hope you can get out to visit me before too long – I miss you. I know it isn't easy, but everyone deserves a little holiday to recharge their batteries, don't they?'

'And I miss you too, Grandma. In the spring, I promise.'

'Let me know when you've booked your flight,' she instructs me, and I can imagine the look on her face. It's not a request, it's an ultimatum. 'Then I'll know I can start getting excited!'

The moment I put down the phone to finish doing my hair it sparks into life again. This time it is Maverick. I had a weird feeling he was going to call.

'I hope you're not phoning to cancel on me.'

'No, of course not! There's a change of plan though. I don't suppose you fancy having lunch at Lachlan. It'll be just you and me, literally. Granddad and Grandma have been away for a few days and they were due home this morning. They've been delayed and won't get back until later this afternoon. Travis and Glenda are on holiday for a week and a load of building materials scheduled for delivery yesterday are now arriving this afternoon. It's not a straightforward drop and Randall can't get hold of his groundsman. I couldn't really say no.'

'It's fine. I'm almost ready.'

'Perfect, because I'm in the car park ready and waiting.'

My face breaks into a huge, beaming smile. There are times when it's rather nice to be taken for granted, I reflect.

'Bring some walking boots just in case we get time to have a wander.'

'I'm on it. Give me ten minutes tops. See you shortly.'

It's a good job that we left promptly because less than twenty minutes after we arrive at Lachlan, there's a loud rumble and a honking horn. We grab our coats, pull on our boots and head outside. The builder's lorry has four huge bags of chippings and a stack of chunky lengths of wood, the sort two people would struggle to lift off. It has a crane on the back, so this should be a relatively quick and easy drop.

We loiter while the driver grabs some paperwork from his dashboard and then jumps down from the cab.

'Mr McIntyre? Sorry about letting you down yesterday. We ended up having to get the vehicle towed back to the yard. Still, it's a nice bit of overtime, so I'm not complaining. This is a view and a half, isn't it?'

Maverick holds out his hand and they shake. 'It's not a problem and yes, Loch Awe is stunning.'

'Here's your paperwork. Now there's something about special instructions, but it doesn't say what they are.' The driver scratches his head.

'Not to worry. We'll show you exactly where it needs to go. You're driving around the back. There's a bit of a slope but it's not too bad. There are two drop-off points.'

'Great. I'll fire her up and you go on ahead.'

We take a short cut across the turning circle and walk through the alleyway that leads into the rear car park. Overhead is one of the bedrooms above the old coach house.

'It looks like Randall is gearing up to tackle some serious work,' I remark.

'The plan is to trial letting out the two log cabins as holiday accommodation. They're far enough away from the house to be quite separate. It's like a retreat hidden from view. The idea is to use the railway sleepers as a low retaining wall and infill an area in front of each of them with chippings. The grass is rather sparse there because of the trees.'

'I thought Travis and Glenda lived in one of them?'

'Oh, they did, but they've moved into the stone cottage the other side of the chicken run. It's had a lot of work done to it and it's a lovely place now.'

As we walk towards the cabins, looking around I can't even see the main house from here and with the separate access road it's very private. The forest setting is enchanting.

I stand out of the way as Maverick waits for the lorry to appear and he waves him over. The driver winds down his window, waiting for his instructions.

'Two bags on this side and four of the sleepers. The other half of the delivery needs to go on the far side of the other cabin over there. You'll see the front door when you drive round.'

Thirty minutes later the last bag of chippings is off-loaded, and Maverick discreetly hands the driver a tip. The man gives me a wave as he drives off. He thinks we live here, and I find that rather amusing.

'Perfect timing! Now, let's head back inside and see what's in the fridge.'

'Would it be too nosey of me to ask if we could take a peek inside one of the cabins first?'

'No, of course not. I'll pop back inside and grab a key.'

I watch Maverick as he hurries away, deep in thought, and I wonder what he's thinking. His stride is purposeful and confident, just like him. I like the fact that he's always so polite and yet he's not prepared to bend the truth to make something more palatable. He also has a conscience – he's proved that to me already and it means a lot.

The land behind the main buildings inclines sharply and the view of the loch is different yet again from this vantage point. The forest floor is strewn with leaves that crunch wonderfully underfoot – it all adds to the charm. Out on the loch a small boat with two people in it slowly makes its way towards a private jetty on the bank opposite. What a wonderful way to spend a Sunday.

When Maverick returns, the moment our eyes meet his smile just keeps on growing.

'What?' I ask as he steps closer.

'You look so relaxed and content standing there.'

'I feel it. It's so re-energising being out here in the fresh air. No traffic, no people – well, aside from the charming little boat over there and you, of course. No wonder Fiona is hesitant about turning this back into a hotel.'

Maverick steps onto the small wooden porch in front of the first of the log cabins, key in hand. 'And yet she loves people and entertaining. I'm sure Granddad will come up with the right plan of action. Letting out the cabins as a trial is a great idea.'

He beckons me inside and it's charmingly rustic, but this certainly isn't roughing it by any means. The cabin is on a split level. In the cosy sitting room there's a large wood burning stove in one corner and two wooden-framed three-seater sofas. The cushions are laid on top in sealed plastic bags.

'The stove is eco-friendly,' Maverick explains, 'and it's pretty efficient. It keeps the cabin warm all night in winter if it's stoked up just before retiring for the night.'

'You've slept in here?'

'I have.'

He leads me over to one of two internal doors. The first is a shower room and toilet, the second is a small – but adequate – kitchen.

'Oh, I wasn't expecting it to be self-contained. That's perfect. How many does the cabin sleep?'

'Four, the bedroom is up here. The other cabin is slightly bigger.'

The wooden staircase leads up to the second level and it's obviously custom made to accommodate the differing levels.

'It's an extension to the original build,' Maverick explains. There is only the one room, but it's plenty big enough to house a king-size, as well as bunk, beds. Glancing out of one of the windows to the side, I'm looking down onto the loch and I can get a clearer view of the jetty opposite. Having moored up, I watch as the couple follow a winding path leading to a cottage half hidden by well-established trees. It looks idyllic.

'The other cabin has a similar layout, but it has two bedrooms. This is perfect for a young family, don't you think?' Maverick sidles up next to me. 'Or a couple looking for a romantic getaway.'

'Is that an invitation?' I look at him, narrowing my eyes.

'If it were, would you say yes?'

I start laughing. 'On your grandparents' property . . . um, I think not.'

'Oh,' he brightens. 'It's not a blanket *no* then?'

Maybe it isn't but for now I'm going to keep him guessing. 'It's hard to think when my stomach is growling.'

'I'd better remedy that and quickly,' he replies warmly. Then suddenly his lips are on mine and he has his answer. It's just a case of picking the right place and the right time.

24.

Surprise!

Sitting here opposite Maverick and looking out onto the loch and the wintery landscape beyond, I want to pinch myself. Not least because earlier on when we kissed something in me changed and I'm ready to throw caution to the wind.

I liken it to that feeling you get as a kid on Christmas Eve. All that tingly excitement and expectation you're trying to contain. Inside you're buzzing on the one hand, but terrified on the other that you'll spoil everything, firm in the belief that Santa won't come until you're asleep. Maverick is watching me intently.

'Having stayed here when it was full of people does this feel a little strange, just the two of us?'

'A tad. When are they due back? We really do need to look at that paperwork,' I remind him.

'Oh, I'd forgotten about that for a moment. I've been a little distracted.' His eyes twinkle at me, teasingly. 'Sometime this afternoon, but they didn't say when exactly.'

'We'd better eat up and get on with it then.'

'Can I just say that I'd much rather we wrap up and go for a walk. There are so many things I want to say to you and it's easier to do that here for whatever reason.' His words are touching, the look in his eyes sincere.

'I think we're both done eating, don't you?' Maverick nods his head, his expression brightening. 'I'll clear the table and wash up the few dishes while you go set up the table so we can get this task out of the way. After that, I'm all yours!'

Maverick expels a slow, deep breath. The nervous anticipation between us is tangible – I don't think either of us thought we'd get to this point. My heart is pounding and it's not easy to act as if my emotions aren't all over the place.

'Give me five minutes and we'll make this super quick,' he blurts out, making me laugh. 'I just don't want to look foolish if there are any inadvertent slip-ups in the programme. Your expert eyes should spot anything out of place immediately.'

As I clear the plates, he strides off but then stops in the doorway to call out, 'Did I mention how lovely you're looking today?' Then his face falls and he looks flustered. 'Not that you don't, um, always look good. But that blue jumper suits you.'

And then he's gone. My hands are shaking slightly as I gingerly carry the dishes into the kitchen, backing myself through the swing door. A sensation of unfettered joy is bubbling up inside me and it's hard to focus on doing something so mundane as washing up.

Standing at the sink and allowing my thoughts to wander, the question is how am I going to act calm and collected when Randall and Fiona walk through the door? *Take a few deep breaths, Bella*, that inner voice of mine tells me. *Don't get ahead of yourself.*

When Maverick returns and I join him, we sit together leafing through the various sheets of paper. But the atmosphere between us is different now. He keeps losing track of what he's saying and that makes me giggle. And I'm not really a giggler.

'I don't know why you were so worried,' I sum up, after going through everything in detail. 'They usually schedule the Christmas carolling sessions to coincide with the Christmas markets, so that's worth checking. Aside from that everything looks fine to me. And I like the new layout you've used for the programme.'

What is deflating to see is the note at the beginning that the location and availability of rides on Santa's Highland Express during the month of December are to be confirmed. The reality of that statement hits home.

'I'm rather relieved to hear you say that. I wasn't sure if I should have stuck with the old format as I don't want to upset anyone.'

'No. You've put your mark on it and that's a good thing.'

'You have no idea how relieved I am to hear you say that.'

'You did well, you should be proud of yourself.'

The scrunch of car tyres on gravel makes us turn our heads to look out onto the turning circle.

'They're earlier than you thought,' I remark, a little disappointed to see them back so soon. I'm nervous about how they will react when they see that Maverick has invited me here.

'Yes, I'd rather hoped we'd have a bit more time alone to talk. As I think we should . . . that's not Granddad's car – what the—' Maverick jumps to his feet almost toppling his chair in the process. 'I have no idea what's going on, but that's my mother getting out of the rear door and she isn't alone. What on earth is she doing in Scotland?' He glances at me nervously and I nod my head, indicating for him to go.

Scrambling to pull the papers into a neat pile as Maverick disappears, I'm not sure what to do next. I can't stand here watching them as I'm in full view, so I start walking towards the door. But I can't resist casually glancing out of the windows as I pass each of them. There are two women, and Maverick embraces them both as the driver carries their luggage inside.

I can't pretend I'm not here, so I slowly make my way along the corridor giving them as much time as I can without it looking like I'm loitering.

'This place is utterly charming and the photos didn't do it justice, don't you agree, Louise?' The older woman's eyes are drawn to the courtyard and the atrium beyond.

The young woman replies, 'It's gorgeous, Olivia – really gorgeous!' But her eyes are on Maverick, not the view.

Louise is beautiful, a head-turner. Maverick said it was over between them, so why is she here – unless she's changed her mind.

'Well, this is a real surprise – I had no idea you were coming. Everything is all right, isn't it?' Maverick queries but his mother shakes off his concerns as she wraps her arms around him, a tender expression on her face.

'Am I not allowed to miss my son and pop over to surprise him? I thought you'd be thrilled to see me. You've been on at me for years to make the trip.'

'I'm delighted, of course I am. Welcome to bonnie Scotland. Bella, come and meet my mother and my . . .'

He pauses, awkwardly.

'. . . Louise.'

Hastening forward, I offer my hand and Olivia shakes it. I can see she's curious to know who I am and why I'm here, but she simply says, 'Lovely to meet you, Bella.'

Louise's handshake is delicate, and I wasn't expecting that. She winces a little and I let go really quickly. Oh dear – this is a nightmare. As if it's not bad enough, the sound of another car pulling up heralds the arrival of Randall and Fiona. They bustle in through the door excitedly.

'Olivia . . . and Louise! My, this is unexpected. Where's Douglas? Did we get the day wrong? We thought you were staying in Edinburgh tonight.' Fiona looks crestfallen, but quickly recovers her composure. She was obviously expecting her son and, instead, Maverick's ex turns up. Fiona embraces Olivia while Randall gives Louise the briefest of hugs. Maverick is standing there wondering what's going on.

Ooh . . . this isn't just awkward to witness, but my emotions are in free fall.

'Douglas sends his sincerest apologies,' Olivia replies, sounding a little disappointed herself. 'As usual, it's because of work. One of the company's new planes was forced to make an emergency landing on its maiden flight and Douglas ended up having to drop everything and fly off to Los Angeles. Louise kindly stepped in at very short notice, as you know how I hate travelling alone. Instead of getting a taxi to the hotel—'

'It was my suggestion,' Louise interrupts, glancing in Maverick's direction. 'We slept on the plane and in the car. Coming straight here means we've gained an extra afternoon and evening to spend together.'

As they chatter away, my heart feels like it's being ripped apart. I'm wishing I was somewhere else – anywhere, other than here. Whether Fiona senses that, I don't know, but she immediately turns her attention to me.

'Bella! It's so good of you to come to our rescue.' Fiona hurries over and to my utmost surprise she kisses me on the cheek as if we're old friends.

All eyes are on me and even Maverick looks a little bewildered.

'We've been going through the Christmas programme,' I reply, feeling the need to explain my presence. But Fiona isn't showing any sign of surprise to see me here, as if it's perfectly natural to find me and Maverick spending the day together.

'Randall, I told you that you were probably putting Maverick out and he'd have plans on a Sunday. You really should have put that delivery off,' Fiona berates him.

'Is it inconvenient descending on you a day early?' Olivia pipes up. 'The jet lag was nowhere near as bad as I'd been warned and we were so eager to get here I didn't stop to think we might be putting you out.'

'It's no trouble at all. It's simply wonderful to see you both,' Fiona replies, shaking off her obvious disappointment that Douglas isn't with them. 'Our housekeeper and general manager are away on holiday, so Maverick and Bella kindly came to our rescue today to house-sit.'

The words trip off her tongue as if it's a common occurrence.

'Randall and I have been doing some research and stayed overnight at a wonderful place that hosts weddings,' Fiona enthuses. 'Just before we left, they insisted on taking us to see some friends who have set up a glamping business in the grounds of their hunting lodge. It was amazing and well worth the detour.'

The look of satisfaction on Randall's face tells me that it was probably something he'd planned in advance. What is it with this family and surprises?

'We can talk about that later, darling,' Randall interjects. 'Let's get everyone settled.'

I assume Randall will escort his guests upstairs, but instead he walks in my direction to give me a friendly hug. 'It's really good to see you, Bella,' he says, warmly.

Louise doesn't look impressed, until the attention is turned back onto her and Olivia. Maverick offers to carry the expensive, and beautifully matching luggage, which is going to take at least two trips. Everyone disappears leaving me all alone and if I'd driven myself here I'd say a quick goodbye and be out the door. Instead, I hurry back to the kitchen and put the kettle on.

Gazing at the impressive coffee machine I wonder how complicated it is to work. There's a light on behind the panel so it is switched on and I grab a mug. Popping it under the spout I press the button for an espresso. Seconds later there's about an inch of coffee in the bottom. Well, if the only way I can make myself useful is to make the teas and coffees, then I can give it my best go. I'm under the impression that Americans prefer coffee to tea, but Fiona enjoys a cup of Earl Grey. It'll keep me occupied setting up a tray ready for when they come back downstairs. At least I'm not standing around looking as foolish as I feel.

Know your place, Bella, that inner voice rebukes me. *I warned you not to get ahead of yourself.*

'Maverick wasn't happy you wouldn't let him drive you home, Bella,' Randall comments, as he indicates to turn right onto the main road and head towards Fort William.

'I know, but he hasn't seen his mother for almost a year. Or Louise, for that matter. It wouldn't be fair of me to pull him away. Besides, we sorted everything that needed doing, so it's all good.' *Keep it simple, Bella*, I tell myself firmly. This is no one's fault but mine for getting carried away.

'But we've spoilt your plans, so the least I can do is to drive you home. Strictly between you and me, I'm not a fan of Louise, so I'm happy to leave them all to it. They're staying for a week anyway and I doubt they'll miss me for a couple of hours. It's a real blow that Douglas had to change his plans last minute, but that's the nature of his job. Naturally, if I'd known our visitors were going to arrive a day early, I would have postponed the *surprise* trip to the glamping site. Fiona was blown away, though, and I think we've finally found our first major project to kick off the new business.' He's grinning to himself and obviously Fiona's reaction was even better than he anticipated. 'I'm pleased for you both, Randall.'

'Lachlan leaves a lasting impression on everyone, but Fiona's dream is for it to become a family concern.'

'It is?' Maverick had hinted that Randall was making plans.

'Olivia wants Douglas to do something less demanding and that's what this little trip was all about. If Olivia falls in love with Scotland and Lachlan, by the time she heads back here with Douglas for the Christmas holidays she might have won him over. This could be just the little project to catch their interest and, hopefully, kick-start the next phase of their lives. It's an exciting time for us all.'

I'm pretty sure Maverick will need to be sitting down when he hears the real reason behind the visit, but I have no doubt that he'll be delighted.

'Little isn't quite the word I'd use to describe the potential to develop Lachlan,' I muse.

'Precisely, and Fiona and I aren't getting any younger. It's a topic we've discussed with Douglas, and he knows that we're looking to the future.'

It's also clear that Randall will do anything, anything at all to make his wife happy and that's touching.

'It sounds like this could be the perfect solution for everyone.' I keep my voice upbeat, but it's a real struggle. I know Randall is simply grateful to have a listening ear and as we've shared confidences before he feels comfortable chattering away.

'Of course, by nature I want to run with it, but Fiona restrains me and rightly so. This isn't about us, but about our son and his wife.'

'It'll be wonderful for Maverick too, having his parents close by,' I respond without thinking. Why don't I just shut up, Randall is bound to change the subject, but I can't help myself.

'Yes, it will and with a bit of luck he'll be a big part of it,' Randall declares, chuckling to himself. 'And I haven't given up on building that wonderful cottage for Fiona, up on the ridge. It's a pretty spot and we wander up there often.'

'I imagine the views are totally unobstructed.'

'Yes, it looks out over the tops of the trees and it's a one-hundred-and-eighty-degree vista.'

It's touching that family has always been everything to Fiona and Randall and now they're hoping that Lachlan is the key to bringing them all together again. From the snippets I've heard, and observed, Olivia is clearly tired of taking second place to Douglas's career. But what if inviting Louise to step in for him has an added twist with a purpose? Is Olivia hoping that Maverick will realise how much he's missing his ex? And what if Louise is captivated by the thought of living in Scotland? Maverick loved her once, could he fall in love with her all over again? It's time to change the subject before I burst into tears and end up making myself look like an absolute idiot. Taking a deep breath, the first thing that pops into my head is Holly and Christmas.

'Randall, will you be offering the cabins as holiday lets this winter?'

'We're in the process of setting up a website and we'll be listing the two cabins once we've defined the outside seating areas. It might not kick off until early spring. Why?'

'I'm looking to rent somewhere quiet and secluded for a friend and myself from the twenty-fourth of December through until the first of January.'

Randall keeps his eyes firmly fixed on the road ahead. 'That's easily doable. It won't take long to get things sorted and there's a special rate for friends.' He sounds pleased. 'Send me an email confirming the dates and we'll put it in the diary.' This time he turns to glance at me for a moment before focusing once more on the road ahead. 'I apologise if our timing today was unfortunate. Is everything OK?'

I tried my best to put on a big smile and appear lively, but it was tough and Maverick, too, was struggling. In hindsight, the timing was spot on because it probably saved a lot of heartache all round. Well, almost.

'Yes, everything is fine. Maverick did well, putting the Christmas programme together this year and it's packed full of events – you can rest easy.'

'So, we're all on the same page?' He's grinning to himself now. 'And, um, things are going well?'

Everything Randall does is for a purpose, but this time his intervention has wider implications about which he has no idea at all. 'The dissenting voices are growing quieter by the day.'

'I meant are things good with *you*, Bella? It's frustrating not to have found a permanent site for Santa's Grotto. I'm still keeping an eye out.'

'That's very gracious of you, Randall. I've ruled out the

hay barn at Mòinteach Farm because of the access, but Paul has offered to talk to some of the other farmers to see if he can find something more suitable. As long as there's a decent access road, and enough parking, it'll do for this year. But we need to get it organised quickly.'

Randal sighs. 'It'll certainly be a test run to see how people take to an out-of-town location. It might be the answer going forward, although it's not what any of us envisaged. It hasn't been for the lack of trying, I can assure you.'

'I know, and my family and I appreciate it. So many people have dropped by the shop to support us and the first question they ask is when will The Christmas Cave be up and running. It hasn't really sunk in yet that it might end up being a stall at one of the events in the High Street.'

'Ten out of ten for hanging in there, Bella. If there's anything I can usefully do, then please don't hesitate to give me a call, will you?'

'Of course.'

It's obvious Randall regrets the fact that there isn't a one-fit solution, but I wonder what he'd think if he knew that today my hopes have been dashed in a very different way. And I hate to admit that is an even bigger disappointment to me right now than accepting what is a very personal defeat. But in my heart I know that Pop will understand that I did my best.

25.

Hiding Myself Away

Today is a major turning point as our newest recruit, Stuart, arrives to work alongside Ursula. The team taking us forward is now complete and there's a definite buzz in the air this morning. But I can hardly get up the strength to move from my desk. By lunchtime, Mrs Mac takes one look at me and shakes her head.

'You're foolin' no one, lassie. You're as white as a sheet and you aren't doin' any good here, so you might as well go home and climb into bed. Can you drive?'

'I can drive. I look worse than I feel,' I croak.

'I doubt that, Bella, my poor wee girl. Come on, I'll carry your bag to the car. Let's get you on your way.'

'A good night's sleep and I'll be fine,' I insist. But my throat is on fire, and I can hardly swallow. I haven't got time to be ill, so I'm hoping it's a twenty-four-hour thing. Unless it's psychological. My self-esteem reached an all-time low yesterday on the way back from Lachlan. I made coffee for everyone, and it wasn't even my house. I felt like a waitress, even though Fiona and Randall were trying to make me feel at home. Maverick was reeling – I couldn't be sure whether that was just from the shock of seeing his mum, or the fact that Louise was with her. Maverick and I didn't get a chance to talk privately before I left and in hindsight I think that was a good thing. What could he say given the situation?

As I ease myself behind the wheel, Mrs Mac walks around

to put my bag on the passenger seat. She leans in to say goodbye and gives a little grimace.

'I know exhaustion when I see it and that's why yer comin' down with somethin'. Rest, lassie – that's what ye need now. Take care of you.'

I've been staying with Mum and Dad for the last two days. I quickly realised that driving was a silly idea given the state I was in and their house was closer. When Mum opened the door she took one look at me and marshalled me straight upstairs into my old bedroom. All I've done is sleep, drink copious mugs of honey, lemon and ginger tea and ignored the constant string of pings from my phone.

There's a light tap on the door and Mum peers in to check on me.

'Are you still contemplating getting up for a bit today?'

I said that I would two hours ago and yet here I am, lying here thinking.

Mum opens the curtains further to let more light in and then comes to sit next to me on the bed. 'What's wrong, Bella? It's not just a bad throat, is it?'

My eyes begin to fill up.

'Oh, my darling.' Mum throws her arms around my shoulders and I rest my head against her. 'Everything is going to be just fine. You'll soon be back on form again, and Dad says you're not to worry as he's going up to look at that barn at Hazelmere. He said the ride could be up and running in a week and there are plenty of people to help.'

My phone pings, then pings again in quick succession.

'Someone needs to talk to you. Don't they know you're poorly?' Mum remarks, sounding annoyed.

'Oh, it's usually spam. I should turn off my notifications,' I reply, dismissively.

It's probably Maverick again. He wants to talk, but I just can't face him right now.

'Something is worrying you, Bella. I can tell.'

If it was only one thing maybe I wouldn't be struggling, but it's several things.

'Holly had a bit of a rant the other day. I know it wasn't really directed at me, it's this whole thing with Nick because it's coming to a head. It's going to be awful going into the holidays if it doesn't pan out for them, so I've arranged for the three of us to stay in a log cabin between Christmas and New Year.'

'You're definitely not coming to Faro, then?' I can see the sadness reflected in Mum's eyes.

'No, and I am sorry. But I'm really concerned about Holly, and I can't think of any other way of lifting her spirits. Besides, I've promised Grandma I'll take a whole week off in the spring to spend some time with her.'

'You're a loyal friend, Bella, and I understand you wanting to be there for Holly and Katie. Maybe next year we'll all be able to get together. In the meantime, I'm off to the farm shop and when I get back, I'm going to make a big pot of chicken soup,' Mum declares with a knowing smile.

'Now if anything can get me eating again, it'll be that. And while you're gone I'll have a leisurely soak in the bath.'

The bathroom is luxurious – who doesn't love a slipper bath? Lying back surrounded by bubbles, everything here is light, bright and fresh. I didn't realise how much I missed having a permanent home and that, too, is starting to pull me down. It must be the same for Holly.

I never wash my hair while I'm in the bath, but today I'm so physically tired that I don't have the energy to do it separately. I'm not sure bubble bath acts in quite the same way as shampoo, but it's all I have within hand's reach. My muscles are certainly aching a little less today and when I tentatively ease myself out of the bath, my legs aren't too bad. However, after wrapping a towel around myself and putting my hair up in a clip, I suddenly feel light-headed. As I sit on the bathroom floor, little rivulets of water run down my neck. Several minutes pass and when the doorbell rings, I groan to myself.

Come on, Bella, I tell myself, firmly. Throwing off the towel, I pull on my dressing gown and grab the hand towel to wrap it around my hair.

'Coming!' I call out. Grabbing on tightly to the handrail, I make my way downstairs on slightly wobbly legs.

Turning the key and opening the door a couple of inches, I look out expecting to see a man with a parcel, or Dad back earlier than expected having forgotten his key. But it's Maverick.

'Goodness, you look . . . I mean, sorry. I went to the flat and when you didn't answer I was worried. I rang and spoke to your dad and he said you were staying here. I, um . . . wanted to give you these.' He holds up a large bouquet of flowers as I watch him through the three-inch gap.

The biting chill coming in makes me shiver and I have no choice but to walk away from the door and let him step inside.

'Thank you, that's very kind but you really shouldn't have gone to the trouble.'

Maverick shuts the door behind him and there's an awkward silence as I take the flowers from him. It's obvious they're from The Highland Flower Shop. He could simply have had them delivered.

'I wouldn't have come if I'd realised how unwell you are. I thought you were simply avoiding me because I could understand why. I wanted to explain . . .'

A flush of heat flashes over me as I'm about to suggest we do this another time because I'm not feeling so good. However, I start to buckle at the knees and Maverick steps forward, tossing the flowers to the floor and catching me in his arms. My vision is blurry, and I can feel the colour has drained from my face as he takes my weight and steers me into the sitting room. I collapse down onto the sofa, my head back and my eyes closed.

'You need a cup of tea,' he mutters, and I make no attempt

to answer him. My head is still spinning as waves of nausea wash over me and I close my eyes . . . just for a second.

Suddenly, I come to with a jolt, conscious that the towel on my hair is leaving a damp patch on the sofa. As I ease my eyes open, Maverick is seated in the armchair opposite.

'How long was I asleep?' I ask, horrified to think he's probably been watching me the entire time.

'Not long enough for the tea to get cold. Here, this will perk you up.'

I ease myself upright, dragging the towel off my hair and it falls down around me in straggles, but at least it's no longer dripping. Taking the mug from Maverick, he grabs the soggy towel and disappears back into the kitchen with it.

When he reappears he looks at me sheepishly. 'I shouldn't have come. It was wrong of me not to believe you when you said you weren't up to visitors. Why are you here on your own?'

'Mum popped out to the farm shop. She'll be back any minute.'

Nestling the mug in my hands, I take a sip and it's just the right temperature. Warm enough to be soothing for my throat without inflaming the rawness.

'Thanks for the tea,' I croak, hoping it will do the trick.

He grins at me. 'My mother swears by chicken soup.'

'Mine, too – that's why she's at the farm shop.' I give him a weak smile, but it hurts to sit here looking at him.

'I can't apologise enough for what happened and how awful it must have been for you when Mum and Louise turned up like that. I had no idea they were coming, believe me. It seems that I've been left out of the loop on quite a few things.' Maverick sounds genuinely sorry.

'Please, you don't have to explain anything. It was a little uncomfortable, but I understand. Louise misses you and she's hardly going to fly over on her own, is she?'

Maverick's brow wrinkles. 'You think that . . . no – you have it all wrong, Bella. Louise didn't come to rekindle our relationship. She came because my mother needed a travelling companion. They did some sightseeing, but it was more about getting a feel for what it would be like to live over here.'

My head must still be fuzzy because I'm not sure that makes any sense – is he talking about his mother, or Louise? Louise is surely only interested in Scotland because of Maverick.

That frown of his is getting deeper by the second and then there's the sound of a key in the lock and Mum calling out, 'I'm back!'

Maverick's shoulders sag. I can see how desperate he is to talk and now we can't.

'Oh, Maverick, this is a nice surprise. Did you bring these with you?' She holds up the bouquet and a few broken petals fall to the floor. He nods his head. 'Well, I'll just go and put them in some water. Aren't they lovely, Bella!'

Mum turns and bustles out into the hallway, flowers in one hand and a carrier bag in the other as if it's perfectly natural to return home to find a bouquet lying on the floor. I wonder what she's thinking as she calls out, 'I'll make a fresh pot of tea – do you take sugar, Maverick?'

Maverick mouths at me, 'Should I go?'

'It won't take a minute.'

He sinks back into the chair as we look at each other nervously.

'No sugar for me, thank you, Cathy,' Maverick calls out and then turns to me. 'I don't want Louise,' he whispers, his eyes searching mine. 'I want to be with you. Do you think you'll be well enough to go to lunch at Lachlan on Sunday? I feel that my grandparents should be the first to know as it was Granddad who put us in touch.' Maverick grins at me and just like that the man who succeeded in stealing my heart has turned my world upside down for the second time around.

December

26.

A Miracle Maker is a Keeper

It's Monday the third of December and I'm finally ready to return to work. Even the sun has put in an appearance this morning, melting the little flurry of snow we had yesterday. I know it's going to be the start of a brilliant week and it was so the right thing to take a few days to recharge my batteries.

It seems that everything has run without a hitch, thanks to Mrs Mac's leadership and the team all pulling together. I can tell from the smiles, though, that everyone is pleased to see me.

Monty, bless him, followed me into the office and is now sprawled out on the floor next to my chair. The big chew I brought him isn't really the incentive, I tell myself, and it's great to be back.

'I dealt with what post I could, Bella. I know there's a wee pile there, but you dinnae need to plough through it all today. The emails are up to date and you've seen all the important ones.'

'How's Stuart settling in? I'll have a chat with him later, of course.' It's the one thing Mrs Mac didn't mention when we spoke.

'Like he's always been around. And he has a wicked sense of humour,' she declares with a grin.

'That's so good to hear, Mrs Mac. Eve tells me business is brisk in the High Street and I'll be going over to give her and Holly a hand a bit later. And now the Christmas programme is in full swing, too.'

It really kicks off after the lights are turned on in the High Street and I'm looking forward to a spell of doing what I enjoy most – making holly wreaths, garlands and putting together baskets of winter flowers.

'And don't you go frettin' over Santa's Grotto. A year out will make everyone appreciate it even more.'

'I'm delighted to tell you that, apparently, it's all in hand.'

Mrs Mac's eyes light up. 'It is? And how on earth did ye manage that from yer sick bed?'

'I didn't. Dad and Maverick have been sorting it out while Cliff oversaw the task of getting the sleigh moved to its new home.'

'Come on then, tell me more . . .'

'Your guess is as good as mine. I was rather hoping that you would have heard something on the grapevine.'

'Not a single peep.'

'That's a shame. But I'm getting a sneak preview later this afternoon before it officially opens next Monday,' I confirm. 'Two weeks of rides will still raise a lot of money and it's going to be open from ten in the morning through to eight o'clock at night.'

'Well, we've a lot to be thankful for and seeing you back at your desk looking so well is one of them! Right, Rodric's just pulled up and I need to give him an updated delivery sheet. It's all go!'

As Mrs Mac exits, I'm surprised to see Holly appear.

'You're looking a little better than you did at your mum's,' she says, stepping inside and shutting the door behind her.

'Thanks, I feel it. I'm hoping to pop over to the shop in the High Street later this morning. Problems?'

'No. We've had a rush order and we're out of lilies. Both vans are busy, so I drove over to collect them.'

'Well, you're looking very cheerful today. How's Katie? Is she enjoying her new dance class?'

'She's loving it and it's really helping to build her confidence. She was so nervous at first, but they all do the same routine and now she's acting like a right little diva doing all the moves!'

It's wonderful to see Holly looking carefree – there's definitely something different about her.

'We need to catch up properly, very soon.'

'I know. There's a lot going on.' Holly's voice takes on a serious tone.

'What have I missed? I assume this is personal?'

'My home life is never short on drama.' She rolls her eyes. 'At least things are settling down nicely at work now.'

Something major is going on and judging by the look on her face it's not all bad news, but this is hardly the time and the place to start questioning her.

I have important news too. After a long chat with my parents yesterday morning, Maverick and I headed off to Lachlan for lunch. Breaking the news to Randall and Fiona that Maverick and I are officially a couple was nerve-wracking. Holly is the next person I want to tell before word gets out, but I need to choose the right moment. Even so, I find myself catching my lip between my teeth to avoid breaking out into a humongous smile. Depending on what she has going on, me brimming over with joy might not be appropriate right now.

'How do you fancy you, me and Katie going out for a meal next Monday evening?'

Her face falls. 'Aww . . . I can't do Monday evening. Katie is staying over at Mum's.'

'She is?' That's unusual, given that her mum starts work early. Monday is an odd night for Holly to have plans – unless she's seeing someone!

'Yes, um . . . Mum said she'd like a bit of company. We'll get our heads together and arrange something, Bella – I promise.'

'It's fine if you're not ready to tell me, I won't be offended.' I pull a face.

Holly shakes her head at me. 'A few things are still up in the air, but you'll be the first to know. You always are! Right, I need to grab those flowers and get back to the shop. See you later.'

As I focus on catching up with the paperwork, it's hard because there are so many disparate thoughts whirling around inside my head. Holly's situation, obviously, and then there's Maverick. He's so excited about our future together, but when Mrs Mac returns well over an hour later, there's one thing on my mind.

'Sorry about that, Bella. I had to sort the flowers for Holly and now we're runnin' low. I've amended our order from the wholesalers for tomorrow. Say, twenty minutes for cake and coffee in the warehouse?'

'Perfect, Mrs Mac, thank you. Can I ask you a quick question?'

'Fire away. If I ken the answer, I'll tell ye.'

'Please, take a seat. Did Aunt Jane ever talk about Randall McIntyre, I mean . . . in general?'

'Is this to do with you seein' more of young Maverick?' Mrs Mac enquires, narrowing her eyes as she peers at me.

'Yes.'

'When yer Aunt Jane returned to Fort William, Randall did everythin' he could to help her out.' The look she gives me is to the point. 'He's a man with good intentions and a charitable heart, if that's what yer askin' me.'

Mrs Mac's reply is curt and I realise that she probably found out about the affair soon after it began. Having worked alongside my aunt from the first day the shop opened, why am I not surprised? Everyone needs a shoulder to cry on and I'm guessing Mrs Mac was that shoulder.

'I didn't want to misread the situation, that's all.'

'If yer worried about Fiona McIntyre—' Mrs Mac lowers her voice '—I wouldnae lose sleep over it, Bella. I doubt Fiona would have let Randall help yer aunt if she'd got wind of it, now would she? Anyway, it's all in the past and it's best left alone.' She goes to leave the room, then turns back around to look at me. 'You've no colour in yer cheeks, lassie, and we can't have you fainting on us – I'll be cutting you an extra-large piece of cake!'

As Mrs Mac disappears through the door, my phone rings and it's Mum.

'Well? How was your lunch at Lachlan yesterday?' Mum asks, anxiously.

'It was incredible. Randall and Fiona were so kind. When Maverick announced our news they were absolutely delighted. Randall said, "It's about time you two got your act together!" and he went off to get a bottle of champagne. Fiona rose up out of her chair to hurry around the table and give us both a congratulatory hug.'

'I told you it would be fine. You're perfect, Bella, in every way and Maverick's heart is in the right place.'

'Oh, Mum! I still can't believe this isn't just a dream.' I can feel my cheeks glowing from the happiness rising up inside of me. 'It took a while for him to grow on me, but now he has I know he's a keeper.' Mum bursts out laughing. 'Anyway, I must go as I have a lot to get done before Maverick picks me up later this afternoon.'

'Oh, I forgot that he's taking you to see the new home for Santa's Grotto for the first time. I'm keeping everything crossed for you, my darling. If it's not quite what you expected, try not to let it show . . . will you? Your dad said that Maverick has pulled off the impossible, but he's nervous until it has your seal of approval.'

'I'm not completely heartless,' I declare. 'I'll give you a quick call this evening to let you know how it goes.' There's an ominous groan just before the line disconnects. What does Mum know that I don't? I wonder.

I'm sitting in a car park with a blindfold on while Maverick makes sure everything is ready for the big reveal. I have no idea where we are, but I heard the crunch of gravel as we approached and he turned the car around, which means there's a car park and it's not in the middle of a field. The passenger door opens and a blast of cold air makes me shiver.

'Are you good to go?' Maverick checks, sounding a tad nervous.

'I most certainly am!'

He hooks his hand under my arm. 'Right, up you come.'

I ease myself out, zipping up my coat, as he slams the door and locks the car. He holds my left hand and wraps his other arm around my waist. Matching his stride with mine, we set off. I can hear the low rumble of voices in the distance, but I can't hear any cars. Or animals, for that matter – so hopefully we're not on a farm. Putting my complete trust in Maverick that he won't forget to tell me if the ground is uneven, we keep going and it takes a few minutes. At one point we step onto what feels like a brick pathway with a couple of twists and turns, then we cross a patch of frozen turf before drawing to a halt.

'Are you ready?' he checks, letting go of me and I feel his hands fumbling with the blindfold.

'Yes.'

'One . . . two . . . three.'

My eyes try to take it all in at once but I'm not sure what I'm supposed to be focusing on. We're in a garden centre – oh, I know where we are, we're only a couple of miles from Fort William. There are some greenhouses and we're standing in the lovely walled garden where they display the specimen plants and trees. I've been here numerous times with Mum.

'You're looking in the wrong direction.' Maverick points to the top of a structure just beyond the greenhouses, but it's barely visible. 'Come and take a look.'

I follow him as we step back onto a small pathway which leads us around to the far corner and there it is – a magnificent dome. My hands instinctively fly up to my face. It has a semi-opaque covering, and you can just about glimpse the framework but not quite see what's inside. I'm completely overwhelmed.

'It's huge!' I gasp, as I gaze at the structure. 'It wasn't here when I last came with Mum to buy some rose bushes.'

'That's because it's new. It belongs to The Highland Elves charity.'

My jaw drops. 'How much did it cost?'

'They wanted thirty-five thousand pounds – it's an ex-display model. But when I told them what it was for, they gave us a discount.'

As much as I really wanted the perfect home for Santa's Grotto, I'm horrified that the committee approved this sort of expenditure. It's crazy.

'You don't like it?' Maverick falters.

'No . . . it's wonderful but that kind of money is—'

'I said the charity *own it*, not that they paid for it. MPI very generously donated twenty thousand pounds towards the cost and Granddad made up the shortfall.'

'Randall has more than done his bit over the years, Maverick. And why would MPI make such a generous donation anyway?'

Maverick gives me a knowing smile. 'Granddad pointed out to the board that the locals were disgruntled about losing Santa's Highland Express. He said it was a pity if the new tenants, Mayfair Bespoke Wallpaper Designs, found themselves being boycotted.'

'He didn't! But that's not strictly true, is it?'

'I'm not so sure. I think you seriously underestimate the level of support that's behind you, Bella, and the new CEO wasn't prepared to take the risk. Anyway, for MPI it's a tax write-off, for the sleigh ride it's a permanent home. I'll run through the details of the deal your dad and I negotiated with The Woodside Garden Centre so you can see for yourself how accommodating they've been. They're really excited about the opportunity and the extra trade I hope it will bring in for them. But for now, I want you to let it all sink in because it's a big change.'

If Dad is in on this too, then so is Mum and that's why she was nervous when we spoke earlier.

Up close it reminds me of an igloo. There's a covered entrance tunnel and Maverick steps up to undo the central zip in the arched plastic panel indicating for me to go inside. I was expecting it to be chilly in here, but it isn't at all – it's a comfortable temperature. And in the centre I recognise the shape of the mound and the lovingly handmade covers.

'And here it is. That unit over there is the heater and air conditioning. That's why I disappeared to turn it on so you can see how quickly the space heats up.'

'Is it all right to come in?' a mystery voice calls out.

'Please do. Bella, I'd like to introduce you to Quinn and Yvonne Montgomery, the owners of The Woodside Garden Centre.'

We shake hands and they can tell by the beam on my face how happy I am. 'This is a dream come true for me.'

If I can't have everything under one roof, at least this is a fitting home for the sleigh ride. It's not your traditional garden centre, it's more of a market garden that sells both plants and produce, with greenhouses the public can wander around. Being privately owned, the sales office is simply a large garden shed but the grounds are extensive and attached to a fabulous manor house.

'We're proud to welcome you here, Bella. Who hasn't taken a ride on Santa's Highland Express over the years, and we're thrilled to be a part of keeping the tradition alive. A lot of folk weren't too happy to see you move, but wait until they check out the sleigh's new home.' Yvonne leans in to give me a hug. 'We inherited the house from my grandfather. He knew George back in the day and this is a proud moment for us.'

'Ah, here it comes! We don't often celebrate, but we had to mark the occasion.' Quinn hurries forward to take a bottle from the young man walking towards us.

Yvonne produces a silver bucket, hidden beneath one of

the covers. She unwraps the green and white check cloth nestled inside it and hands us both a glass as Quinn pops the cork. It flies high in the air but luckily doesn't hit anything.

'What's the height in the centre?' I ask, trying to work it out.

'It's ten metres high and twenty metres in diameter,' Maverick informs us.

Yvonne is busy trying to catch the overflowing bubbly that erupts from the bottle with the remaining two glasses. Once the flow has calmed down, Quinn begins pouring.

'I think Bella should propose the toast,' Yvonne suggests as they all turn to look at me.

'Oh my – now I'm flustered . . .' I tail off and Maverick kindly comes to my rescue.

'Here's to the past, the present and the future – and to all the people along the way who have helped Bella and her family to keep her pop's dream alive. It's going to be a very special Christmas indeed!'

As we chink glasses, I know that even if I had been able to string some words together I couldn't have put it any better.

'Can we have a wee look at the sleigh now it's fully assembled?' Yvonne asks.

'Of course.' Maverick hands me his glass and immediately walks over to begin peeling back the covers. Quinn hurries over to give him a hand.

My heart is beating so fast in my chest as I gaze around. To my delight there's plenty of room to put up the backdrop. To one side is enough space to erect a large display of baubles and Christmas trimmings – it couldn't be more perfect than this! I can just imagine an elf standing at the entrance checking in the next group of people about to take their turn on the ride. Santa's Grotto and The Christmas Cave have been transformed into The Christmas Dome. It's bright and yet cosy.

As Santa's sleigh is revealed it gleams with its fresh coat of cherry-red paint and gold highlights. I notice that the sleigh bells are back. Over the years some had fallen off and we kept them in a box. Eventually Dad took them all down intending, one day, to reattach them. It was never the same without them to my mind and now it's complete.

'Come on,' Maverick beckons. 'All aboard, ladies. It's not up and running until the electrician tests the connection tomorrow, but that doesn't stop you being the first to officially take a seat.'

Quinn is laughing, but I notice that he's already easing himself into the second carriage. Yvonne and I head straight to the front. I slide across, allowing her to sit behind the wheel.

'Oh my, this does bring back a lot of memories,' she exclaims, her voice tinged with excitement.

I run my hands lightly over the dashboard, marvelling at the attention to detail. Every inch of it has been lovingly restored to its former glory.

'I think someone should ring the bell,' Maverick comments, as he stands back to take a photo on his phone.

I indicate for Yvonne to do the honours and she's loving it. 'Oh, I can't wait for the rides to begin, Bella. This corner of the garden was always a bit of a dumping ground, wasn't it, Quinn? We've been saying for a long time that it needed attending to, but we didn't really need the extra space or have the money to develop it. And now it's filled with something that will bring joy to so many people.'

Pop's beloved sleigh ride will go on for many years to come and what better setting than in a beautiful walled garden? With espalier trees covering the aged stones, and row upon row of bushes and shrubs, even in winter it's a wonderful place to visit.

'Right, let's get this covered up as I expect there'll be a bit of a queue at the tills,' Quinn reminds Yvonne. 'Word is already filtering out and people are coming to have a nose around outside in advance of going live.'

'We'll wrap it back up, you two need to attend to your customers,' I reply. 'And thank you so much for the champagne. It isn't really a celebration without a few bubbles, is it?' I add.

Quinn and Yvonne leave us to put the sleigh to bed and then Maverick turns off the heating unit. As the blast of hot air subsides, we take a moment to wrap our arms around each other and savour the moment.

'You're not disappointed?' Maverick draws me into his arms, planting a kiss on the end of my nose.

'Disappointed? I'm ecstatic. It's like a giant snow globe! And at probably the prettiest garden centre for miles around. I believe that Quinn and Yvonne are the second generation of their family to run it and you can tell it's not part of a chain. It's quirky because they're quirky. I mean, there's no café or shop, it's all about the plants and yet they put out a little paddling pool for the kids in the summer and bowls of water for dogs. It couldn't be more perfect, but how will the arrangement work?'

'The Highland Elves will continue to run a rota of volunteers each Christmas as per usual. You own the ride, the charity owns the dome, which is only fair. As for baubles and decorations . . . the garden centre would benefit from having an all-year-round shop. If you're happy to donate the stock and allow Quinn and Yvonne to take it over, we can come to an amicable arrangement to offset that against keeping the dome and the sleigh ride here permanently. It would be a great start for them to build upon. At the moment they display a few jars of home-made jams and chutneys at the tills in the shed, but that wouldn't fill many shelves. With an all-year-round Christmas display, this could make all the difference to them and expand their customer base. And they're happy to continue to donate twenty per cent of the profit on the sale of the trimmings to the charity.'

He's right. It's time for me to step back and this is the perfect solution because it will help yet another locally based family business to keep on thriving. Pop would be overjoyed.

'You nailed it, Maverick, and that's one of the many

reasons why I love you.' I plant a kiss firmly on his lips to seal the deal and it takes him by surprise, but his eyes light up as I release my hold on him.

'Oh, so it's not because you think I'm tall, dark and handsome, or clever, or an astute businessman?' He pulls a face.

'No. It's because you're kind and thoughtful. You notice the little things that matter, and you do stuff simply to please other people, even when it's not really your thing. Like getting involved with the charity.'

'You mean my attempt at redeeming myself because everyone blames me for turning your life upside down?'

And he keeps on doing precisely that . . . even causing me to revisit some of my long-held beliefs. I have a sudden flashback of the other night, lying in bed wrapped in Maverick's arms and feeling not just a sense of utter contentment, but also peace. I finally understand what the word 'soulmate' really means. It's not just about physical desire, it's a meaningful connection on all levels. We're in tune with each other and I'd trust him with my life. Which is odd, given that there are so many things I still don't know about him and vice versa. But did that hold us back? No. Instinct alone was enough to dispel that natural moment of hesitation before you give yourself to someone for the first time. He understood that having been hurt before, this time I had to be one hundred per cent sure. And now there's no turning back, because true love is addictive.

I'm grinning and Maverick pulls me even closer. Savouring the moment, after a minute or two I push my head back and stare up into his eyes. 'Well, I'm sure they don't really blame *you*, let's just say that what happened has upset a few people, but I think you've done more than enough to win them round.'

'No, I think *you* won them round when I made you fall in love with me. Your dad has been really good to me, and he has played a big part in making this happen. I knew that he alone would know what your reaction would be to my crazy, last-minute idea. And he was right. He knows his daughter.' Maverick lets out a sigh of satisfaction.

'I showed Cliff the photograph of the dome online and he was concerned about whether you'd be happy with the new arrangement. He said I should go with the barn idea, and we'd get the sleigh ride out of storage every year. I had to go with my gut feeling that he was wrong. When I made the decision, there were a few rumblings among the committee members but your dad, he immediately sprang into action. And just like that, together we made it happen. I think he twisted a few arms,' Maverick jests.

I know there's an element of truth to that statement because my mum was nervous about my reaction. Perhaps she had her doubts too, but this isn't about pleasing me – it's about the common good.

We both start laughing. In my head I'm already hearing the soft jingle of bells as the ride starts up and the distant sound of Christmas music that will be playing in the background. Closing my eyes, I can imagine it full of people browsing and awaiting their turn to take a ride.

'And this is precisely why I fell in love with you, Bella Reed. Because you made me see that dreams can come true. Courage, determination and hard work turn an ordinary person into a miracle worker. You've more than earned your turn to be happy and my job is to make sure it stays that way!'

27.

No Turning Back

After Maverick collected my things this morning to take them back to his place, I'm here alone at the flat doing a quick clean through ready to hand the keys back tomorrow. Outside, I can hear the Christmas carollers, braving the weather on the penultimate weekend before the big day. So much has changed over the last few months that my life is now unrecognisable. But I don't have any regrets at all, even the time I've spent living here. Ironically, deciding what happens next was easier than I thought it was going to be.

My phone lights up and I hold it to my ear, surprised to hear Holly's voice.

'I thought you might appreciate some company. I'm outside the flat now.'

Hurrying over to peer out of the window, she waves up at me and I edge it open to call out, 'I'm on my way down!'

It's sleeting and she looks cold. When I swing open the front door she bustles in – a bucket loaded with cleaning materials in one hand. In the other is a small cardboard cake box from The Wee Nook Coffee Shop, which she thrusts at me. 'This is courtesy of Alice,' she explains. 'She popped it into the shop yesterday. It's a leaving present.'

I let her squeeze past and then shut the door. 'I hope it's shortbread,' I call out as she mounts the stairs two at a time.

'Oh, it is!'

'Why didn't you tell me you were coming over? Where's Katie?'

Holly dumps the bucket down next to the kitchen sink. 'She's staying overnight with Nick, at his parents' house.'

'Oh. That's nice.'

'I thought you might appreciate another pair of hands given that your mum and dad are having fun in the Algarve. I bet you wish you'd gone now, with this snow.'

'It's only a dusting, although they're forecasting more to come.'

'And I know a little girl who is overjoyed about that as she's looking forward to building a snowman.' Holly grins contentedly. 'How did it go moving your stuff out this morning?'

'It didn't take long. It was mostly clothes, which went straight to Maverick's house.'

'What are you going to do with all the things you still have at the self-storage facility?'

I pop on the kettle as Holly opens the wall unit to grab two plates for the shortbread.

'Nothing, at the moment.'

'Isn't that a little inconvenient at this time of the year? Your party clothes are in the container, aren't they?'

Focusing on spooning coffee into the mugs I studiously ignore eye contact.

'It's all on racks, so it's easy enough to grab what I need.' Holly lets out an 'Ah!'

'What does that mean?'

'You've moved in with him but you're treading on eggshells?'

I let out a huff. 'I don't want Maverick to feel like I'm invading his space.'

'But you're fully committed?' Holly leans her back against the countertop, bending her head to catch my eye. 'It's obvious you are, so why the hesitancy?'

I pause for a moment because she has a point. 'It's not that, I'm just being diplomatic. If I didn't have to move out,

I'd probably have stayed here a while longer. But we both agree it's the right thing to do although, naturally, it's going to take a little getting used to. I mean, he's always had the house to himself.'

'Look, a lot has happened in a short space of time, Bella. A little caution is understandable, but don't let it hold you back. He wouldn't have suggested it if he wasn't ready and it's obvious that you don't have any qualms about it.' She flashes me one of her no-nonsense stares.

'Falling in love is wonderful and every day I wake up I can't believe how lucky I am, but we're still getting to know each other. This is the next step and it's a big one.'

'Aww . . . I'm so happy for you, Bella, but you need to relax and go with the flow. Come on, let's sit down for a bit. We have plenty of time to make this place sparkle.'

'I doubt that anything could make this place sparkle, so a quick clean will do. I think the kitchen is being ripped out next week anyway,' I remark. This has great potential to be turned into a lovely home for someone launching out on their own for the first time.

We settle ourselves down and it doesn't take us long to devour Alice's thoughtful gift.

'Katie absolutely loved her ride on Santa's Highland Express yesterday. Nick took her while I was working. He sent me some photos on his phone. They were bowled over by the dome – wish I'd been there, too.'

'Ah, maybe you'll find time to take her again yourself. It's pretty amazing.'

'How are you feeling about the new set-up? Obviously we all miss the good old days, chatting to people as they queued and seeing the excitement as Santa greeted the children.'

'I know, but it was the right solution all round. What's the word on the street?' I ask, tentatively.

'We're still getting people popping in to ask about the sleigh ride. You were right bringing in those white skeleton trees – even though Eve and I had our doubts as there isn't much to them. But it works. It's a clever bit of marketing and it adds to the ambience of the shop. Customers love it and it's almost put a halt to the endless questions of where's the sleigh and where did the Christmas display go? We just point and they're enchanted. Eve's going to ask you if we can keep them up permanently.'

That's unexpected. 'Goodness – I hadn't even thought of that. I stole the idea from Braemor Manor after Maverick took me to tea there. They had the same trees in the barn. I like the sparse look and the stark white is a lovely silhouette. They trimmed them with silver snowflakes. I could imagine some of our wonderful baubles and decorations on display and, yes, that's a brilliant idea. They look wonderful in between the floral displays and it's different.'

'Great, but wait until Eve asks you herself before saying anything, won't you? It was her idea.'

The people who make the wooden snowflakes handed out each year to anyone taking a trip on Santa's Highland Express, designed a special star for the top of each of the six, five-foot-tall trees. Sprayed silver, each star shows a picture of the sleigh ride and details of the new location. On the other side is a photograph of Pop sitting in the sleigh. The branches are hung with small silver stags' heads for now, but if the trees are staying I guess we will be selling a few decorations after all!

I let out a contented sigh. 'Now – are you going to tell me why you're really here? It'll only take an hour to spruce this place up and you know that.'

Holly finishes off her shortbread, making me wait. It's obvious that she has something important to say and she's not sure how I'm going to react. I sit back, cradling the coffee mug in my hands. We've always been in and out of each other's lives on almost a daily basis and if this is it, she's heading off to start again somewhere else, I'll be gutted.

'You know when I told you that I was ready to give Nick one last chance? Well, you aren't the only one whose life has been turned upside down recently. We're house hunting together.'

'Oh, Holly, that's brilliant news!' I exclaim. There were bridges to mend and old wounds that needed healing, but to hear that they're ready now as a family to put down roots fills my heart with joy.

'Something in him has changed, Bella. He started turning up promptly and involving his parents whenever he had Katie. He's finally acting more like a dad than a single guy, and that's when I started to have faith in him again. But it's not just that . . . we missed each other. It was like something was missing from my life and it's taken this last year and a bit of craziness to fully appreciate that fact.'

'You're not doing this just for Katie, then?'

'No. I told Nick straight that we needed to start from scratch. He had to make me fall in love with him all over again.'

'How?'

'We began going out on dates, just the two of us.'

'You kept that very quiet,' I muse.

'There was no guarantee Nick and I could turn things around. There was one rule. I said I'd draw a line under the past, but if he put one foot wrong then we were over forever.' A warm feeling wraps itself around me as I study her face. 'I didn't think he could do it, Bella, but he did. We told Katie yesterday.'

'You're that confident?'

'I am. He loved that car of his, but selling it shows that we're the centre of his world. We've decided that he won't move into the flat with us, instead we're going to wait until we find a house to turn into our home. Then we'll finally get married. Just a very small gathering of close friends and family. But Katie really wants to be a bridesmaid, so we're going to dress up just to please her. I'd love you to be my maid of honour, not least because you have way more dress sense than I have. My mum would have me buy some frothy thing, but I know with you there that common sense will reign. I don't want to end up looking like a cupcake.'

'Of course, it will be my pleasure! I would have been miffed if you'd chosen anyone else.'

'You never gave up on Nick and he really appreciates that. He admits that he deserved what he got, but that it taught him what's important in life. For whatever reason, you happened to cross his path one day and it was something you said that made him stop and think. He said it changed everything.'

I smile to myself. 'I can't think what, but if that's the case then it must have been fate because I didn't have an agenda.'

'No, because you've always been a true friend to me and a wonderful godmother to Katie. I know that you wouldn't cut Nick any slack for messing up, but you didn't write him off either. The other thing I wanted to ask . . .' She hesitates.

'Come on – what is it?'

'You know the log cabin? Obviously, you're not coming now that you're with Maverick—' she flashes me a suggestive look '—so would it be all right if Nick joined me and Katie?'

It's the subject we've both been avoiding talking about and I feel bad about that. I didn't like to pull out and spoil the surprise I announced at Katie's birthday party. But Maverick was disappointed that I'd be staying so close to Lachlan, but not with him. He understood that I couldn't let down a childhood friend and my gorgeous goddaughter, and we left it at that.

'Oh – yes, naturally you three should be together. And I can't wait for you to see it. Katie is going to feel like she's living in a gingerbread house,' I laugh.

'Thank you, Bella. I know it was supposed to be a girls' thing, but I couldn't pull you away from your first Christmas with Maverick. Even if Nick wasn't joining us.'

And that's what friends do for each other. We stand and hug.

'What a way to mark stepping into the next phase of our lives, Holly. It's true that no one knows what's around the corner.'

'This time last year if someone had given us a glimpse into the future, we'd have said *no way*. But here we are, another year older and another year wiser. It's been tough at times, but we got through it and it's only when you stand to lose everything that you realise what's worth fighting for.'

'I couldn't agree more, Holly.'

'How did it go this afternoon? I felt bad not being there to lend a hand, but it took Granddad and me a couple of hours tramping around to find the perfect tree to please Grandma. As if she doesn't have enough trees inside the house, but it does look good in the courtyard,' Maverick admits.

'It didn't take that long if I ignore the hour I spent chatting to Holly,' I confess.

'Holly turned up – ah, that was kind of her.'

'Yes, it was. And we were able to sit down and catch up properly for the first time in ages.'

'And she's doing all right?'

'She is, but there's been a slight change of plan over the Christmas and New Year period.'

Maverick's face falls. 'You're heading off to Faro with your parents. I understand. I'm sure your aunt and your grandma miss you.'

'No, nothing like that. I'm flying over in the spring, and I was kind of hoping that you'd come with me to attend Aunt Jane and Vic's engagement party. Anyway, I digress . . . Nick is joining Holly and Katie for their stay in the log cabin.'

Maverick's grin is ear to ear. 'Really? You're not fooling with me?'

'I'm not. They're getting married sometime after Christmas and I'm going to be a maid of honour, whatever that entails. I'll have to look it up online.'

'That's brilliant news all round! Nick's a good guy. He had a few friends who weren't the best influence. You know, single guys yet to . . .'

'. . . understand what settling down really means? You said *had*?'

'I don't like to break a confidence, let's just say he woke up and realised there was more to life, a whole lot more.' Maverick raises his eyebrows and I get the message. 'Does that mean that you're free to join the family for Christmas and new year at Lachlan?'

Staying in one of the log cabins is one thing, joining Maverick's family for the entire festive period is another; especially since his parents are flying in on the twenty-second of December. The intention was for us all to have a special dinner together so that he could introduce me to his father, but this is a daunting prospect.

'Do you think it's a little too soon? I mean, I'm little more than a stranger to your parents . . .' I groan and he flashes his eyes at me. 'I hardly left your mother with the best impression, thinking I was the hired help.'

Maverick bursts out laughing. 'That's all in your head, Bella. She could see you were there with me, and Louise saw that too. My mother did say she owed both you, and me, an apology. In hindsight, she felt it was a faux pas to ask Louise to be her companion on the trip.'

'Really – you're not just saying that to make me feel better?'

'I wouldn't do that to you,' Maverick says, reaching out to sweep the hair away from my neck and plant a gentle kiss on it. 'My mother was impressed, actually.' He starts chuckling away to himself. 'She thought you were at home there and assumed we were already sleeping together.'

'She did?' I gulp.

'Think about it. You disappeared into the kitchen as if that was normal and what was even funnier, is that my grandparents played along.'

'They did rather, didn't they?'

'When you were out of earshot, they trotted out the story about your family connections and the good work you've all done over the years. My mother was touched by the way you were struggling to overcome the challenges. In fact, she was the one who came up with the idea of a dome.'

'She was?'

'Yes. My father's company hired something similar for a big presentation at the factory when they launched their latest twin jet aeroplane. It's a project he's been working on for years and now it's come to fruition he has some big decisions to make. But it made me jump online as I liked the idea of a dome.'

And all the while I was in the kitchen, feeling like the outcast and wishing the Christmas fairy could sprinkle a little magic dust and spirit me away.

'So, I didn't make a total fool of myself?'

Maverick snuggles up close to me, throwing his arms around my shoulders as I sink into him. It feels like the sofa is going to swallow us up, it's so cosy here tonight.

'Are you kidding me? Why didn't you say something before now? Bella – why do you think our announcement didn't come as a surprise to my grandparents?'

He's right. It didn't and I saw that for myself – they were thrilled for us both.

'I felt that I didn't belong at Lachlan that day.' It's sad to say, but it's true. That's why I'm nervous about staying there with Maverick over Christmas.

'That line of thought stops now. And while we're being brutally honest, there's something that I need to say.'

What now? 'There is?'

'We're together now and if you don't like this house then it's not a problem, we'll find somewhere you do like.'

My heart constricts. 'Oh, Maverick – I love it here, I really do. But . . .'

'Oh no – there's a but . . .'

'Only in so much as I don't want you to feel that I'm—'

'What? Settling in? Isn't that what our relationship is about now? Because if it isn't, you need to speak up.'

I'm horrified. 'No. I love being here with you. It's a beautiful property.'

'In need of some attention,' he adds, peering at me.

'Yes. But it's not for me to say that, is it?' I point out, supressing a smile.

'It's not that you don't like it then?'

'No – why would you think that?' I reply, scandalised.

'When two people commit to each other, it's not about what's mine and what's yours, is it?'

'No, it's not.'

'Look, we can make whatever changes you want as long as we end up with something that makes it *ours* and not *mine*. Do I look like someone who would care about things like that? I knew this place was lacking something, and now I know that *something* was you. I did have a brainwave about installing a small dome in the garden, though. Like an indoor garden to grow veggies and herbs.'

And that begins a whole other conversation. Isn't life amazing?

Christmas Eve

28.

When the Snow Begins to Fall . . .

It's been snowing on and off all day. We closed the unit at lunchtime, and everyone headed over to The Highland Flower Shop for a little party. Despite the snow, business is brisk and those braving the weather were treated to nibbles and drinks.

Holly and I waved everyone off just after two o'clock. We close at four and the last two hours are quiet, although a few latecomers are still calling in to collect their Christmas orders.

'It's funny how we were all dreading what was to come and yet here we are. The reality is so much better than any of us feared.'

I'm aware that Holly reflects the mood of the entire team, as we stand looking out at the snow. It's being whipped along the pavement into large drifts by the artic wind. It is beautiful, but I feel sorry for the last-minute shoppers as they wearily battle their way back to the car park.

'The new unit is working so well and the shop does look lovely,' I concede. It's rather like walking into a fantasy land with the tall white trees, even though most of the buckets are now empty of flowers.

As we turn to begin the clean-up, we're both in a reflective mood.

'It was good of Nick to offer to drive us all to Lachlan, Holly.'

'Oh, it's nothing. You paid for the log cabin and it's going to make our Christmas. I owe you a lot, we all do. Besides, I said to Nick he should hire something special. As soon as he saw the forecast, he was straight on the phone to Maverick. They decided a luxurious four-wheel drive was called for in case we fancy a trip to Oban over the holiday.'

We grin at each other. 'Boys' toys, eh?'

'I figure there are times when they deserve a little spoiling, don't you?'

'You're right. But I'm worried what the journey is going to be like if the snow gets any worse.'

Behind us, the sound of the door opening and a 'Ho! Ho! Ho! Merry Christmas, Bella and Holly,' makes us instantly turn around. And there stands my wonderful solicitor, looking abashed.

'I assumed you'd be at home with your feet up in front of the fire by now, William,' I comment as he steps inside. He looks down at his shoes, covered in snow. 'Oh, don't worry about the floor – we've been mopping all afternoon.'

'I was supposed to head out an hour ago, but loose ends always take longer to tie up than you think, don't they? You've been busy today. There's not much left. I was rather hoping to grab something a bit special for the wife to apologise for being late.'

William is right, there isn't much left. Holly and I exchange a meaningful glance.

'How about some Christmas roses, William? Hellebores to be correct,' I offer. 'We have one planter left out the back. They can be planted in the garden as they flower every year. They're one of our biggest sellers.'

Holly immediately heads into the office and returns, carrying a large silver planter. It's filled with glorious white flowerheads, their distinctive yellow stamens and lush dark green leaves make it the perfect festive gift.

'Now that is exactly what I was hoping for! Thank you, ladies, for coming to my rescue.'

It's fitting for what turns out to be our last customer of the day. But it leaves me with a problem.

'What on earth am I going to give Fiona now as a little gesture?' I moan as soon as we're alone. Holly shrugs her shoulders. 'I can't turn up empty-handed. Maverick took our gifts over a few days ago to put under the big tree at Lachlan, so I can't even rescue one of those.'

All we have left are a few sprigs of various things that won't amount to much. There are some smaller pot plants that are pretty, but they're not really Christmassy.

'I wonder if she likes snow globes?'

Holly and I both turn our heads to look in the same direction. On top of one of our large display cabinets is a beautiful one I purchased as a display item. It's an old-fashioned snow scene with a country house next to a river, the banks of which are piled high with snow. There is a forest of pine trees behind it and beneath them a snowman peeks out. A lonely fox makes his way towards the river's edge, leaving a tiny trail of paw prints behind him.

'Oh, Bella, that's perfect! I'll get the ladder and you find the box.'

Standing alone in the shop, it suddenly hits me what we've achieved. There hasn't been time to stop and reflect. We did it – this is the future and it's sparkly and bright and wonderful. Aunt Jane was over the moon when I sent her a video of the Christmas Dome. She said that everything happens for a reason, and she thinks Maverick is truly a hero. The floristry business is booming and I can now focus on that. I can't wait for the spring, when I get to fly out to Faro with Maverick by my side to celebrate Aunt Jane and Vic's engagement.

I walk over to one of the trees and look at the photo on the back of the star.

'There you go, Pop. I hope you approve of what we've done. From the store you originally opened that was truly an Aladdin's cave, to the impossibly busy Santa's Grotto Aunt Jane housed at the rear of the old shop with Randall's help, it's been quite a journey. I do miss having everything under one roof, but the dome is truly amazing, isn't it?'

Holly bustles in with the ladder. 'Sorry? I didn't catch what you were saying.'

'I was just talking to myself. It's going to be an awesome Christmas, Holly.'

'I know.' She breaks out into a huge smile. 'I've always thought it would be amazing to stay in a log cabin in the snow. And to be together as a family this Christmas is like the impossible dream for Katie and me!'

And Nick, too. It seems that dreams really can come true.

The journey to Lachlan is a real adventure ride, with more thrills than any of us were expecting. The snow drifts are deep in places, although we've probably only had about eight inches in total. While there aren't that many vehicles on the road, it's difficult going as the visibility isn't good. When the house is finally in view it's a welcome sight.

'The lane forks just before the turning circle, Nick,' Maverick warns. 'There is a road here but you're going to have to take my word for it. It's not much wider than the vehicle, so stay in the middle. Just keep it in low gear and don't stop until you get to the top of the incline. It's not far now.'

It's a white out and, give Nick his due, he doesn't hesitate. He just keeps going. Once the ground levels out we all feel a huge sense of relief.

'It's the first cabin – over there,' Maverick points out. 'You might as well park up alongside.'

The lights are on and the windows glow with a golden hue in the darkness. The smoke rising up from the metal flue is a comforting sign.

Katie's eyes are everywhere. 'Mum, we're staying in the middle of a forest!' she shrieks, excitedly. 'Are there bears?'

It's hard not to chuckle, but Holly immediately responds with a straight face. 'No, but we'll probably see some rabbits and, if we're lucky, maybe even a deer.'

'And you can feed the chickens tomorrow, if you like,' Maverick joins in.

'Why is the house called Lachlan?' Katie asks, wearing her serious expression.

Maverick turns in his seat to look at her. 'It's a boy's name and it means *from the land of lakes*.'

Her face instantly brightens. 'Was that the name of the boy who lived here?'

'Yes, many years ago. Why?'

'Oh,' Katie replies, 'so Santa has been here before. I did wonder how he'd find us.'

Out of the mouths of babes . . . children have a wonderful way of instantly putting a smile on an adult's face, even after a nightmarish journey.

Unbeknown to Katie, Santa has already been. The presents are hidden away on the top shelf of the wardrobe courtesy of Maverick. As we gather our things, Randall comes trudging up the snow-covered bank.

'There you are! Welcome, everyone.'

After doing a quick round of introductions, Randall hands the key to Nick. 'It's all stocked up inside but you're very welcome to take all your meals in the main house. The more the merrier! Drinks are being served at seven and dinner about an hour later as we weren't sure whether you were going to be delayed because of the weather.'

'Oh, that's really kind of you, Randall, but I think this little one just wants to cosy up in front of the fire. It's going to be a quiet evening and early to bed ready for the big day.'

Randall gives Katie a knowing smile, then stoops to talk to her, lowering his voice conspiratorially. 'Santa has a lot of stops to make so it's a good job he drives a sleigh. I doubt the snow will slow him down, so everything is going to be just fine.'

I tune out from the background noise, fascinated by their conversation.

Katie giggles. 'Oh, he's used to it,' she whispers back at him. 'There's snow all year round at the North Pole.'

'Of course! We don't have a big sleigh here, but we do

have a few sledges you can try out tomorrow.' With that, he gives her a wink as he straightens. 'Right, I'll leave Maverick and Bella to help you get settled in.' As he walks away, he calls out over his shoulder, 'Merry Christmas, all!'

Maverick and Nick grab some of the bags from the boot as I follow Holly and Katie inside.

'Ooh, Mum, look at that tree!'

The floor-to-ceiling tree is decorated in silver and white, and large 3D snowflakes hang from the ceiling. With the log-burner roaring, it's toasty and I can see from Holly's face that she's overcome with emotion.

Nick and Maverick step through the door, dumping the suitcases down on the floor. Suddenly, Katie runs up to Nick. She throws her arms around his waist. Holly looks at me in alarm, as Katie bursts into tears.

'What's up, super girl?' Nick asks gently, catching her hands in his as he kneels.

'Santa made this happen, Dad. I said I wanted us all to be together for Christmas.'

Seconds later, we're all wiping a tear – or two – from our eyes.

As Maverick and I take our leave, this is one little family who have everything they need and that's even before Santa's elves place the presents beneath that beautiful tree.

I should have known that Fiona would put us in The Lintie, and I already feel at home in the beautiful room. As we get ready to go downstairs, tonight's dress code is novelty Christmas jumpers. I thought it was a great way to break the ice. I did warn Fiona when she rang me the other day that Holly, Nick and Katie were unlikely to join us. What they need is some time alone together and she understood that. Although, I do think she would have loved to have had a child to fuss over this evening. But I'm sure they'll all be keen to join us tomorrow for the festivities. Randall has all sorts of things planned.

Maverick turns to look at me and I'm so glad I chose the reindeer for him, with its big red pom-pom for a nose. It's hilarious, as it's so not him. I gaze down at my snowman, who looks rather charming with his black hat on a jaunty angle. With black leggings and black ankle boots, I'm feeling cosy and festive.

'Come on, let's get this introduction over and done with, then you can relax.' Maverick can see I'm nervous, even though I'm trying to hide it.

He hurries me out of the door, catching my hand and giving it a reassuring squeeze as we make our way along the corridor.

'It's very quiet,' I whisper.

'Travis and Glenda have the night off. They'll be enjoying a candlelight supper for two in their cottage. It's their first Christmas after moving in and they're going to make it a tradition. Bernie has already prepped the meal for tonight, so it's just the six of us. I suspect my parents are in the west wing, with Grandma and Granddad.'

'Oh . . . right. Thank goodness!' I give a nervous laugh. 'Oh, I didn't mean . . .'

Maverick stops, twirling me around and catching me in his arms. 'Listen, just relax and have fun. I love you and they will too.'

As our lips touch my anxiety melts away. When I'm in Maverick's arms if the roof caved in I'd hardly turn a hair. As long as we're together we'd get through it and that's a comforting thought.

'Let's do this.'

'Bella, this is my father, Douglas.'

As Maverick's father turns around I burst out laughing. He's wearing a hand-knitted jumper that's been very cleverly done. With red and white striped sleeves, the body is a vibrant green elf's tunic. But what's hysterically funny is that hanging down at the front are two stripy little legs finished off with a pair of black elf boots, each with a tiny bell on the end.

'I'm so sorry, Douglas,' I say, immediately trying to regain my composure, 'but that is the best jumper yet!'

He, too, starts laughing, and as our eyes meet, I can see that he's highly amused.

'Santa's number one elf at your service, Bella.' As I hesitate, not sure what to do next he steps forward to give me a hug. 'It's lovely to meet you at last. I haven't seen a smile that big on Maverick's face since he got his first car!'

And just like that the worst bit is over as he reaches out to hug Maverick, giving him a hearty pat on the back. 'That was some journey, I bet. We've all been a bit on edge, wondering whether you'd get stuck on the way. It takes me back to Christmases when I was a boy.'

'Does it feel strange to be back?'

'In a way. And I'd forgotten just how beautiful Scotland is but Lachlan is a very special place indeed.'

Out of the corner of my eye, I spot Olivia, Fiona and Randall hurrying over to us. Olivia is looking cool in her pale-blue jumper with a cute penguin on it and Fiona is sporting a very credible Christmas pudding with a real sprig of holly on the top – ouch! Randall jingles as he walks, the tiny bells on his big and bold Christmas tree a total delight. He calls out, 'I think I'm the winner – watch this,' and suddenly the tree lights up.

'Oh, I don't know . . . Maverick might just have the edge,' I jump in.

As Maverick turns around, the rear end of the reindeer with his stubby little brown tail and antlers peeking up does look funny and we all can't help but chuckle.

'It's time for a drink, let's head into the bar,' Randall encourages, as Olivia moves closer to give me a hug.

'How was the flight?' I ask, as we follow the others.

'A little bumpy and I'm glad we've had a little time to recover. But this is wonderful, Douglas loves the snow.' She indicates for me to walk with her past the bar and into the atrium.

The tree is enormous and it's dripping with silver and gold decorations. It's magnificent, the sort of tree you see on display in a large department store and yet Fiona decorates it herself.

'To be honest with you, Bella, if anything is going to swing this it's the snow. Douglas has fond memories of his winter pursuits, and we go skiing twice a year back in the States. This will bring that little boy out in him again. And as for Lachlan . . . well, who wouldn't want to be a part of making Randall and Fiona's dream come true? I think we're going to pull this off but don't say anything, you know what men are like. We sow the seed and the next thing you know they come up with the exact same idea.'

Her eyes are shining, and I couldn't be happier knowing how the news will be received.

'Are you two in here plotting?' Maverick sidles up to us with a glass in each hand. 'It's always suspicious when people stop talking the moment you enter the room, but I'll forgive you. Anyway, it's time for a champagne cocktail.'

Randall, Douglas and Fiona aren't far behind him.

'We usually have the first one outside.' Fiona gives Randall a pointed look.

'We do. Time to grab our coats. I'll fetch yours, my dear.' He smiles lovingly at his wife. 'Does everyone have a pair of boots by the door?' Randall checks.

I glance at Maverick, and he gives me a salute. 'I'm on it.'

Olivia heads upstairs while Douglas goes to check out the footwear.

'Thank you so much for the time you spent on the log cabin, Fiona. Katie informed us that she'd asked Santa for a family Christmas and we all had tears in our eyes at that point. This is a special one for them – one they will never, ever forget.'

'Ah, it was absolutely my pleasure, Bella. You've made our Christmas; you do know that? Maverick wasn't settling and now none of the things that bothered him before matter.

And having Douglas and Olivia here, well – let's hope it's only the start.'

I can tell from the way she's looking at me that she can guess what Olivia and I were talking about, and as my mouth twitches, her eyes light up.

'There's one thing I . . . while we're alone, I think I should raise the subject. Randall is a man with a conscience, and something tells me that he's probably told you his secret. In confidence, of course.'

The smile leaves my face as quickly as it came, but I say nothing.

'Neither Douglas, nor Maverick, are aware of what happened. I, too, was to blame, but Randall chooses to protect me. He would be wounded if he thought I knew. The way I look at it is that it changes nothing and it's in the past. It was a sad time in our lives as Douglas was the centre of our world. What child isn't? All that matters now is today. And today, Bella, we're all welcoming you into our family.' Fiona leans in to briefly kiss my cheek. 'It's going to be a Christmas that will change all of our lives going forward and that's the best present of all!'

29.

Merry Christmas, Everyone!

Chef Bernie and his family arrive about an hour after we finish clearing the breakfast things. They're staying overnight and, as we help them settle in, Bernie heads straight for the kitchen. Their son and daughter-in-law have a little girl, about a year older than Katie, and the first thing the two girls do is to put on their snow gear and head outside with Randall to build a snowman.

With Maverick, myself and Holly assisting in the kitchen, we have a couple of hours before the other guests start to arrive. Anyone who lives on, or around Loch Awe is prepared for snow and it won't stop any of the neighbours getting here. They simply get the snow chains out and nothing will stand in their way.

Finally, Maverick and I get a chance to tog up and go for a walk.

'It's organised chaos, isn't it?' Maverick reflects, giving me a cheeky grin. 'But it's coming together somehow. In ways I didn't even think were possible.'

'Has your mother said anything?'

'No, but it's obvious she's working on Dad. He has a great opportunity to walk away from his job with a golden handshake.'

'That's a good thing?'

'The project he's been in charge of, which was a developmental one, is now done. The new plane is ready to go into service. He has two options. They'll put him on another project, but it might mean moving to a different location and my mother won't be happy about that. Or leave, and he'll get a handsome bonus. He's fifty-five and it's a big decision to commit to developing something he might not get to see through to completion if he retires at the age of sixty, which was his original plan.'

'Returning to Scotland is a real option?'

'Oh, it's real all right. My mother is excited because she's winning him over.'

'But why does she want to come here, if her family are going to be so far away?'

'Do you know how many executives die from a heart attack? At home he can't relax, he's always working – even when he's not at work. It's like a different world at Lachlan. I still can't get over the fact that my father is actually here and your reaction to his jumper was classic! He loved it. I think he's ready, and if he's going to start over again, this is where he should be. My mother loves him enough to realise that.'

Oh, that's touching.

'Are you having fun?' Maverick checks, his eyes scanning my face as we walk up through the woods to the ridge.

'It was strange doing a video call to my family this morning, but next year Grandma, Aunt Jane and Vic have promised me they'll fly over. They're envious of the snow.'

'That's brilliant news. We'll arrange a big get-together here.'

'We will?'

We've just reached the plateau and I lean against a tree trunk to take a moment to gaze out over the loch.

'It's a magnificent view,' I remark, a little breathlessly. 'Unbelievable.' But when I look at Maverick, he only has eyes for me.

'I love you, Bella, and now everyone knows it. You're a part of this family and you can see how happy it makes them, knowing that we're together.'

I cosy up to Maverick, wrapping my arms around his chunky jacket. 'And in the spring we'll head off to Faro and you can meet the rest of my family. I'll warn you that Grandma is a bit of a party animal, so you might want to brush up on your dance moves.'

And just like that I know that everything will fall very neatly into place.

'Well, what a Christmas this is turning out to be!' Randall says sounding both delighted and humble at the same time, as we all sit around the table watching him.

There are eighteen of us in total and I glance at Katie and her new friend, Della, who are feeling very grown up because Maverick made them their own mocktails.

'As the years roll by one realises that family and friends mean more than anything else. Can I ask you all to raise your glasses to Bernie for an absolutely delicious Christmas dinner; to our wonderful servers – Bella, Holly, my daughter-in-law Olivia, and Bernie's wife, Chrissy – for sorting us all out. To my awesome wife, Fiona, for making sure everything runs smoothly and to Maverick and Douglas for being excellent wine waiters. And to our special guests—' he looks across at Nick, Holly and the two girls sitting together '—for being a part of the festivities. If Lachlan is one thing, it's a place where memories are made. That's quite something and we hope in future to share it with a lot of people in need of a little time away from their everyday lives.'

Randall pauses, clearly emotional, and Maverick jumps up, indicating for him to sit down.

'And here's to Grandma and Granddad for being the ultimate hosts. But I also want to add my own, very special toast. I came here to discover Scotland and what it had to offer. And to spend time with my grandparents. It's been amazing, but little did I know that I'd find the love of my life, Bella.'

There's a hush as all eyes are now on me and I'm touched by the heart-warming response as everyone stands. Rising up out of my chair, I look at Maverick with glassy eyes.

'Wishing everyone a truly wonderful Christmas,' Maverick says, resolutely. 'Whatever the new year brings, we're up to the task because what I've learned since my arrival is that there's always someone willing to lend a helping hand. And there's a snowball fight outside as soon as we're all able to move. That was some dinner, Bernie – you're the man!'

When the toast is over, Maverick makes his way around the table, then grabs my hand and leads me out through into the sitting room.

'You did good there, Maverick. Randall was struggling.'

'I know. I could see that, but he's so happy, Bella.'

We gaze out over the snow-covered banks to the far side of the loch.

'You have to admire your granddad, a man who spent his life building a successful company, only to sell it off and reinvent the dream just to bring his family together.'

With Fiona at his side, Randall knew that together they could still make their seemingly impossible vision come true.

With the glittering disco ball suspended directly above us, Holly, Katie, Della, and I are singing at the tops of our voices as we dance to Wizzard's – 'I Wish It Could Be Christmas Everyday'. Admittedly, I only know the chorus, but who cares? Suddenly, I realise that this is a déjà vu moment. The dream I mentioned to Holly months ago.

At the time it seemed impossible. Neither of us were in a good place and life seemed like an uphill struggle. And now here we are. Nick is sitting at a table across from us talking to Maverick and gazing out over the snowy banks of Loch Awe.

But the biggest surprise of all is the exciting new journey that Maverick and I are about to embark upon. Whatever ups and downs next year might bring, I know beyond a shadow of a doubt that we have what it takes to get through it.

When you surround yourself with people you love, absolutely anything is possible, and together we'll build the future we've always dreamed of having.

Epilogue

From one Christmas to the next it's been an eventful year, but rather like when you form the perfect snowball and launch it up into the air, you want to know what happens to it next. Did it hit its target in a satisfying explosion and then dissipate? Or did it hit the ground and keep on rolling, growing as it gathers speed? It doesn't take long for children and adults alike to work together, using their imaginations to build something very special indeed. And how many snowmen end up with hats, scarves, stick arms, carrot noses and stones for eyes? It's what we do, we are all creators.

As another festive season approaches, I couldn't resist sneaking back to the Scottish Highlands to see how things have developed . . .

The Woodside Garden Centre

The Christmas Dome is looking amazing and when the ride goes live on the first of December, Quinn and Yvonne's son and daughter-in-law will be taking over the running of the Christmas shop.

Working side by side with the charity's volunteers to give visitors a magical Christmas experience, it guarantees a bright new future for the business. Never in their wildest dreams did they expect the response they received when the dome officially opened. And the support hasn't waned throughout their first year.

Their ethos remains the same and they won't be opening

a café or buying in a whole range of items that have no relevance whatsoever to Christmas, or gardening. But to know that the next generation of their family can now join them and be a part of it is rather special. And for that they are very grateful.

Lachlan

It's been six months since Douglas and Olivia took over managing the newly set-up events business, while Randall oversees the building of three more log cabins and the new house up on the ridge.

Maverick runs the website and after badgering his grandmother to take a few photos with the permission of some of their clients, Fiona has found a new hobby. Aside from capturing some of the special moments in between the staged shots taken by the professional photographers, she has also developed an interest in snapping some of the resident wildlife. Including the white-tailed eagle who is still a frequent visitor.

Lachlan will be full to bursting from Christmas Eve to the second of January because Bella's family are all joining them for the first time. Together with a few special friends, including Holly, her mum, Nick and Katie, it's going to be a festive season Fiona could only ever dream about in the past.

And who knows . . . there might even be a few unexpected surprises!

The Highland Flower Shop

The hard work is always in the setting up, but once things were running smoothly and Bella wasn't constantly chasing her tail, it started to pay dividends. Having been the subject of so much upset and speculation over the change of premises, with no option other than to split the business into two, Bella can say in hindsight it was a true turning point.

Within two months of working from the unit, they bagged three new commercial contracts; that meant employing another florist and a part-time admin assistant to help Mrs Mac.

Then it was time for Bella and Maverick to begin transforming his house into their home. That, of course, meant builders and dust and chaos for several months, but in the grand scheme of things not having a functional kitchen for a while was a minor problem.

However, with the festive season almost upon them there's one little surprise that wasn't on Santa's list.

'I've sorted our present for the parents this year,' Bella informs Maverick, much to his delight.

'See, you're so much more organised than I am. You'll have everything wrapped and ready to deliver before I've even hit the shops to get your present.'

'Oh, it's not something that needs wrapping. We're going to give them a grandchild.'

Maverick's jaw drops, as he stares at her in disbelief. 'We are?'

'The doctor confirmed it this morning. I'm eight weeks' pregnant. Are you pleased?'

He swallows hard, gently wrapping his arms around her. 'Pleased? I'm ecstatic! A baby . . . oh . . . wow!'

'Let's keep it just between us for now, is that all right with you? By Christmas I'll be safely past the first trimester, and we'll also have an ultrasound photo to hand them. I know this wasn't quite what we planned but—'

'But it's the best present ever and although I can't pretend that I'm not in shock, it's amazing news. We're going to be parents, Bella . . . I'll be a dad! And it'll mean skipping the engagement party and getting straight onto planning our wedding.' His face lights up like a Christmas tree and Bella knew he wouldn't have it any other way. A surprise is a joy, a gift and this one will keep on giving.

'I know a great place to host a special event,' she adds, and with that their laughter turns into tears of joy.

When they break the news to family and close friends sitting around the table on Christmas Day, it will be the ultimate present.

Some Christmases are truly magical, and this is going to be the first of many, many more.

Acknowledgements

I'd like to give a virtual hug to my editorial director, the awesome Hannah Smith. You are a true inspiration, and this story certainly wouldn't be what it is without you.

And to everyone involved in the lengthy process that turns a manuscript into a finished novel, polishing the words and then showcasing it with an amazing cover. It truly is all about teamwork.

Not forgetting the other incredible driving forces behind the Embla team and Bonnier Books – because our lives *are* built on stories, and each book does matter! It's a thrill to be a part of it.

Grateful thanks also go to my wonderful agent, Sara Keane, for her sterling advice, support and all those long phone calls putting the world to rights. It's been an amazing journey since the day we first met, and your friendship means so much to me.

To my wonderful husband, Lawrence – always there for me and the other half of team Lucy – you truly are my rock!

There are so many family members and long-term friends who understand that my passion to write is all-consuming. They forgive me for the long silences and when we next catch up, it's as if I haven't been absent at all.

Publishing a new book means that there is an even longer list of people to thank for publicising it. The amazing kindness of my lovely author friends, readers and reviewers is truly humbling. You continue to delight, amaze and astound me with your generosity and support.

Without your kindness in spreading the word about my latest release I wouldn't be able to indulge myself in my guilty pleasure – writing.

Wishing everyone peace, love and happiness.

Lucy x

If you loved this wonderful romance from Lucy Coleman,
read on for a sneak peak of her summer sensation
Finding Love in Positano...

Marci James

Prologue

As I stare down at the postcard on the table, the picture is mesmerising. Three small boats are tied to a large wooden stake on an otherwise deserted beach that most people would consider to be a vision of paradise. In the foreground, it's easy to imagine the photographer peering out from behind a clump of vibrant greenery, eager to frame the shot to perfection. Beyond the white sand, the turquoise-blue water is crystal clear and far off on the horizon, the sea appears to melt seamlessly into the sky.

My brother, Guy, slowly turns the card over. The handwriting is instantly recognisable, but I can hardly believe my eyes.

My dearest Marci and Guy

Surprise – I'm in Thailand! Your indomitable godfather is on his travels and sending a long-distance hug. I'm standing here looking at this view right now and life doesn't get any better.

Giving you both a heads-up that an important email will be winging its way to you shortly as I have some exciting news to share.

Hope you and the family are all well.

Sending much love – as always,
Richard

He finishes off with a smiley face drawn in the bottom right-hand corner, but neither of us are smiling. Richard has lived on the Amalfi Coast in southern Italy for the last eighteen years and when I last spoke with him, a mere fortnight ago, there was no mention of him heading off on his travels. What is going on?

May

1.

Drawing the Short Straw

'Un-be-liev-able,' Guy exclaims, exhaling slowly as he continues to stare at his phone. 'Has Richard lost his mind?'

I'm still reading through our beloved godfather's email, thinking much the same thing. Richard Havrington is one of the kindest, most thoughtful men I've ever met, but he's a man who – even he would admit – enjoys a quiet, simple life. Albeit his style is different to most. The words I would use to describe him are flamboyant, fun and grounded – someone who has never believed the grass is greener on the other side of the fence.

'He's married?' I gasp, staring across at Guy, who doesn't seem to have reached that part of the email yet.

'What?' he replies, his finger scrolling down quickly and when he resumes reading again his jaw drops. 'This is sheer madness, Marci. Why is this the first we're hearing about it?'

I shrug my shoulders. 'I have absolutely no idea why Richard decided to keep this a secret from us – it doesn't make any sense.'

With two failed romances behind me, Richard was

always just a phone call away. He was my listening ear and helped me to put things into perspective – even when my heart was broken. And he was the one Guy turned to when he had some pre-wedding nerves last summer, so for Richard to go off and secretly marry someone without even mentioning it, is completely out of character.

Richard was at boarding school with Dad and after university they were both drawn into the world of antiques. They set up a business together in an old warehouse situated at Gloucester Quays. When Richard suddenly announced that he was moving to Italy, it's true to say that his decision came totally out of the blue. But it made sense because for two consecutive winters he'd ended up in hospital with pneumonia. The warmer climate was going to be beneficial for him and it paid off. At the time I was eleven years old, and Guy was about to turn sixteen. Saying goodbye to Richard was tough, he'd been around all of our lives, always present and supportive. As a bachelor, Richard had time for us when our parents were busy and sometimes he'd pick us up from school and treat us to a meal out.

Richard left a hole in our lives when he went, although the irony is that it drew Guy and Dad even closer together.

'I'm not abandoning you, poppet – I promise to come back to see you all at least twice a year,' Richard had stated quite firmly, the day before he flew out to begin his new life. 'Your mum and dad will visit for holidays, and we'll hire a couple of camper vans and meet up somewhere to discover the delights of Italy together.'

And, true to his word, every summer until Dad passed away just six years later, that's what we did. We met up during the summer holidays and for two glorious weeks we travelled around in a little convoy. We toured large areas of Northern Italy together before our lives were suddenly turned upside down.

Losing Dad was devastating for us all, but especially hard on Mum and Guy, who had to shoulder the responsibility of the business while dealing with their grief. And my dream of working at Anvil & Anchor Antiques with Dad never came true, as it was another four years until I gained my degree and joined the team. Naturally, Richard took losing his closest friend very hard, not least because he didn't get to say a final goodbye.

'I know it's a shock, and unexpected, Guy,' I reply, trying to sound composed. 'And I'm surprised he didn't drop any hints when he was here in January. But now I think about it, when I met up with Richard in Rome last year, he was a little preoccupied even back then. One of the contacts I was due to visit was based in Genzano, about twenty-five miles away, and when I mentioned that to Richard, he insisted on driving me. He'd always wanted to visit the town during the flower festival, and he told me it was on his bucket list. There were moments when I felt there was something he wanted to tell me but kept putting it off. Maybe he was already thinking of closing the shop before Angela even appeared in his life.'

'Hmm. And the bucket list? He's only sixty-two,' Guy points out.

'You can have a bucket list no matter what your age, Guy. I have one – whether I'll ever get to tick everything off is another matter entirely.'

'Aren't you a little young for that?' he quizzes me.

That remark makes me smile. Being five years older than me, at the age of thirty-four Guy pretty much still focuses on each day as it comes. Each to their own, as they say!

'He was really excited about visiting Genzano, though, and it was awesome. During the festival, the Main Street is entirely carpeted with flowers. The town is on the edge of a volcanic lake called Lago di Nemi, so the views are stunning. Among the tiny alleyways and cobbled streets, we discovered that wonderful haul of eighteenth-century wooden doors. Do you remember them?'

'I do. We could have sold them several times over, in fact.'

Despite the fond memories, I find myself biting my lip anxiously. Richard would say if his health was failing, wouldn't he? It's hard not to dwell on the years we didn't have with Dad. If he had known how little time he had left, would he have done something totally out of character? Like dragging us all off to Saint Lucia, for the holiday of a lifetime he'd always talked about?

'You think he's going through a bit of a . . . what would you call it? Late-life crisis?' Guy continues.

'It's easy for us to sit here and try to second-guess what's happening, but what if he's finally found the one, after all these years?'

'Fine, if he'd flown his lady love over to meet us all. But he's in Thailand. With his *wife*. And now he's asking one of us to head over to Positano to close his business down and sell off his things. It's bizarre and I refuse to be a party to it. What if this woman is simply after his money?'

'Her name is Angela, Guy, it says so in the email. Perhaps she was on holiday when they met and the attraction between them was instant, who knows?'

I can't help but stick up for Richard and hope that he has simply found happiness. Richard has been my go-to person ever since Dad died. Mum was distraught, but she had to keep the business going and I couldn't bother her with my woes. Then, when she met David Parker, I was glad to see her smiling again, but I was left in limbo feeling on the edge of things. Richard tries, even now, to avoid David on his trips back to the UK and I felt that he thought Mum could do better.

The truth is that I am shocked and a little hurt that Richard hasn't taken me into his confidence. Naturally, I noticed the contact with him has been patchy recently, which isn't entirely unusual when he's busy, but I'm struggling to understand why he didn't talk to me about this. My annual buying trips to Italy are extra special when Richard can make time to join me for a few days, but I guess I'll be going it alone in future.

'Leave it to me. I'll tell Richard straight that I don't intend on doing anything until he calls me, and we can talk it through in greater detail. What do you think?'

Guy shakes his head, frowning. 'Well, he's more likely to listen to you than he is to me. Look – if it does turn out that he's met the love of his life and they want to travel the world together, then good luck to them both. But I'd hate to see him turning his back on the great life he's made for himself, only to end up regretting what appears to me to be a hasty decision.'

'I promise I won't let him dodge my questions. But if he's serious about this, it's a huge favour he's asking.'

Guy puts his phone down on the desk and gets to his feet.

'That's for sure. Richard knows I'll have my reservations, so he's banking on you to sort him out. If you feel it's the right thing to do, Marci, then go for it. Last summer I left you in charge while I disappeared for two months to get married and take a leisurely honeymoon. If you're happy to be pulled into this, then Positano's a wonderful place to spend the summer. I can hold down the fort here. Anyway, I'm in need of a strong coffee – can I get you one?'

I nod, letting out a deflated sigh once Guy is out of earshot.

Oh, Richard, you deserve to find a woman as kind and caring as you are, but I won't relax until I meet her face to face. You told me once that you fell in love at a young age and the woman of your dreams broke your heart. It's taken you forty years to get over it. And now you're throwing caution to the wind. I can only hope Angela's feelings for you are genuine. Guy is right, you'll talk me into doing this for you because what I want more than anything is to know you're no longer alone. Is that hopium? I don't like being on my own, either, but if you can find your soulmate out of the blue, then maybe there's hope for me, too. The problem is we're both hopeless romantics at heart, aren't we?

2.

Happiness is Infectious

'Marci, dear lady. Have you come to rescue me?' Anthony Montgomery is one of my favourite clients. His reputation is infamous, as are the prices he charges his wealthy clients. 'I'm in desperate need!' he declares dramatically.

I fall in alongside him and the two members of staff he was grilling melt into the background, grateful to be rescued.

'Tell me more,' I reply, trying hard to suppress a smile.

'Where do you keep the really *interesting* items?' Anthony demands, the corners of his mouth turning down.

My eyes widen and he looks back at me, shamefaced. 'I know,' he protests, 'I buy them up before they even reach the shop floor. But you must have something I haven't seen yet.'

'Only a few items from my recent trip to France. They're being worked on as we speak. You had the decorative wall panelling, didn't you? And that enormous stone urn?'

'I did. And what an eye you have! But I'm desperate. I can't sign off on my latest project without a few final, finishing touches. The client is big in the art world,' he leans in to whisper conspiratorially.

13

'Well, as it's you, you're welcome to come and take a look around the workshop.'

Anthony's beam is dazzling, the whiteness of his teeth in total contrast to his gorgeous tan. And it's real, as is everything else about him and his glamorous lifestyle. He follows me to the lift, and we head down to the basement. The minute the doors open he takes in a deep breath and groans. 'Oh, the smell of French polish and newly sawn wood. It's heavenly!'

I let him wander, as I stop to chat to two of the guys who are busy sanding layers of paint off an old armoire that I discovered in a dilapidated outbuilding in the Loire Valley.

'Marci!' The urgency in the tone of Anthony's voice makes me turn and walk briskly in his direction. He seems to be arguing with poor old Harry, who has stepped back from his workbench looking somewhat bewildered.

'I'm just gluing this pot back together, Marci. It was on my list for today.'

'Some things were meant to be broken, there's a fragile beauty to imperfection,' Anthony informs him with a level of seriousness that is genuine.

'It seems we have a customer who loves this piece just the way it is, Harry. Can we find a suitable packing case for the main part of the pot and pack the smaller pieces up separately?'

Harry lowers the brush in his hand as a small blob of glue is about to plop off the end of it. 'Of course, Marci.'

'Thanks so much. We'll um . . . leave you in peace, then.'

Anthony links arms with me, his day clearly made.

'You prefer an absolutely stunning French stoneware

confit pot in two pieces?' I enquire, turning to look at him. With the entire neck and one of the handles sitting alongside the pot, I'm at a loss to understand Anthony's excitement. Harry would make the repair look invisible and the pot is a real treasure.

'The gallery I have in mind is full of oversized, colourful canvases. The background dressing should be eye-catching and a broken pot displayed on a pedestal is a statement. Knowing Kelvin, he'll probably end up selling it.'

'I hope so because broken pieces attract a premium,' I banter, jokingly.

'His pockets are deep. What else have you been keeping from me?'

My stomach rumbles hungrily, but who has time to eat when they're in such charming company?

Sitting down at my desk with a hearty bacon, lettuce and tomato sandwich, I start munching before checking my phone – only to discover two missed calls from Richard. Immediately pressing redial, I wait anxiously as the seconds tick by. Just as I fear it's about to go to voicemail, the sound of Richard's voice puts a huge smile on my face, and I turn on the speakerphone.

'You rogue, you! What time is it there?'

'Just after eight in the evening. And I know. I do feel bad, but I'm so darned happy!'

And I can hear that loud and clear. He sounds full of energy. 'Then you're forgiven. We're still in shock, you do know that?' I tease.

'Sometimes life forces you to grab the moment. I'm in

the bar waiting for Angel. She's fussing with her hair, but I told her it's lovely just the way it is.'

Aww. My bottom lip wavers as I sit back in my chair. 'Angel?'

'I never call her Angela. You'll love her, too, Marci. She's a breath of fresh air. I learn something new every single day I'm around her – things that astound me. She's a chiropractor, and my back has never been in such good shape,' he enthuses. 'Angel also practises kinesiology and uses tapping, which is based on the principles of Chinese acupressure. She's practised in holistic centres all around the world.'

'That's incredible, Richard – I can't wait to meet Angel and find out more about her. She's spent a lot of her life travelling then?'

'She has, but now it's time to put down some roots, although we have a growing list of wonderful places we want to experience together.'

So the travels will be ongoing and I'm going to have to look up kinesiology, as I have absolutely no idea what that is.

'I'm assuming at some point before too long you'll be making a trip back to the UK?'

'Not you, too, Marci! I had a bit of a disgruntled text from Guy, but he did send his congratulations. And your mum wrote me a long email. Most of the sentences ended with a question mark, which is precisely why I decided to keep it a secret and tell everyone after the fact. You aren't going to interrogate me, too – are you?'

I sigh, softly. 'That's the price you pay when people love you, I'm afraid. What you forget is that video chats are all well and good, but it's the things you haven't been talking about that worry us.'

Richard chuckles and it feels like he's close by, instead of five thousand plus miles away.

'Duly noted. But there wasn't much to say, it was a whirlwind affair – literally!'

Uh-oh. 'So . . . how long have the two of you known each other?'

There's a pause and Richard clears his throat. 'Three months, one week and four days. And probably nine hours.'

I let out an exasperated 'Oh', unable to disguise a sense of apprehension. 'That's . . . um—'

'—enough time to know it isn't a fleeting thing,' he jumps in. 'I was the perfect gentleman and even though I bought the ring on the day of our one-week anniversary, I didn't ask her until we'd reached the one-month milestone.'

Richard might be a character, but no one would ever describe him as impetuous. One month is a *milestone* in a relationship?

'I'm pleased for you both. At least if I ever meet *the one*, I know I'll be able to count on your support when I run off and get married without telling the family.'

Richard dissolves into a fit of laughter because he knows I'm trying to make a point. 'Touché. Out of you, your mum, my sister and Guy, I knew the only person who would unreservedly forgive me was you, poppet.'

Hmm. Now he's tugging on my heartstrings. He hasn't called me that since I was a pre-teen.

'Us romantics need to stick together, Richard, but—'

'Stop right there. Just be happy for me, Marci, please. Suddenly life is exciting again and I'm at that time in my life when I'm tuning into that inner voice. I don't want to live to regret the things I didn't do, that's all.'

'Inner voice?'

'Angel and I meditate each morning. It's cathartic.'

What's that old saying Gran used to use . . . something about being too late to shut the stable door after the horse has bolted?

'I'm impressed by the new *you*. What exactly do you want me to do?'

'I don't own the shop in Positano, or my accommodation above it which makes life a little easier. However, it's crammed full of stock – you know what I'm like. Collecting has become a bit of a hoarding habit over the years, I'm afraid. There are some fine pieces there, Marci, which I know you'll appreciate, as well as the usual things to catch the eye of tourists.'

I groan inwardly as he continues.

'My dear friend, Luca Romano, is expecting the keys to be handed back by the end of July, so everything must be gone by then. Obviously, I'm travelling light but Angel and I were so tied up organising the grand tour and our exotic beach wedding, that I didn't have time to go through my stuff.'

'Stuff?' I enquire.

'Personal effects. Everything in my office is a bit chaotic, I'm afraid, and will need a bit of a sort before it's all boxed up. Luca will store them for me. The big problem is the stock. I've been reaching out to my contacts to see if anyone is interested in buying it as a job lot but, so far, I haven't had any firm takers.'

I immediately picture Anthony Montgomery's reaction to a whole host of Italian treasures, hand-picked by one of the best dealers I know. He'd think he'd died and gone to antique heaven.

'I'm sure Guy would be delighted to have an influx of new stock if that's an easier option,' I offer. 'I know how excited he is when I return from a buying trip abroad.'

'I was hoping to have it all gone by the time you fly over, so that it was only my personal bits and pieces left for you to deal with.' Richard does sound extremely apologetic now. 'You can blame Angel for being such a tantalising distraction and keeping me otherwise occupied.'

If that means what I think it means, then my godfather is giving me way too much information. I give myself a mental shake to get that thought out of my head.

'I could send Guy photos of everything and get him to appraise it as a job lot, if you like?'

For a moment I think we've lost our connection, then I hear Richard exhale.

'You'd do that for me, just to get me out of a hole? I thought it might be asking a little too much of you both. I'll prod a few people about some of the big-ticket items, while you have a chat with Guy. Oh, a man like me doesn't deserve to have two angels in his life, but I'm blessed. When I emailed, we both know I was only speaking to one of you. My star, my little shining light of happiness and the one person with whom I'd entrust my worldly goods!'

I start to giggle. 'And the only person who is fool enough

19

to help you unpick what has been a wonderful life for you on the Amalfi coast.'

'Luca and his English wife, Celia, also own a local hotel – Il Posto di Luca, home of the extremely popular Ristorante Sul Mare. They've both told me there will always be a room waiting for me if I ever return. But I won't need it. I've waited a long time to find a woman like Angel and, to be frank, I'd given up looking a long time ago – as you know. Ironically, she rather reminds me of you. Strong, intuitive, caring.'

'Ah, so you mean a person who is able to get things done out of sheer determination, and not always in their own best interests?'

'That's something Guy would say, not me – and you know it.'

'Okay. I'm in.'

'In for a delightful summer in Positano! And afterwards you'll thank me because they're going to love having you there. I guarantee it will be fun. Have you ever waited tables?'

'No. Why?'

'Just wondering. Anyway, let me know when you plan to fly out and I'll let Luca, Celia and the family know you're coming. I owe you, poppet – big time! But I wouldn't ask if I didn't think . . . well, this could be your summer of happiness. Regretfully, while I adore talking to my favourite goddaughter, a vision of loveliness is walking towards me and she's threatening to render me speechless. I'll be in touch by email, as we're on the road early tomorrow morning. As for you, it's time to dig out some summery things and put the stuffy suits away on the hangers, Marci – you're in for a treat!'

'Well, what did Richard have to say for himself?' Mum and Guy are staring at me intently.

'He's on a high. Angel has literally given him a new lease of life. In my opinion we should let things settle down and . . . err . . . give him the benefit of the doubt.'

'On what? That this woman isn't after him for his money? Or that she hasn't done this before and he'll end up heartbroken and stranded, with no home to go back to?' Guy's words are harsh and even Mum's eyebrows shoot up into her fringe.

'That's a little unkind, Guy. I know we're all concerned about Richard, but he's nobody's fool,' Mum reminds him, sharply.

'I also feel everything is happening too fast,' I agree. 'But whether he's selling up because of Angel, or this is his chance to take early retirement – the decision has been made.'

'Am I the only one who is concerned about Angela's motives? If there's nothing to hide, then wouldn't Richard have suggested she at least meet us all before their big day? What if he suggested it and she persuaded him otherwise?'

I stare at Guy, my gaze rather unforgiving. 'At the age of twenty-nine, of course it's unlikely I'd run off and tell everyone after the fact. But if I were in my early sixties, then I'd probably say: "Let's do it". In Richard's case, what has he got to lose? It's heart-warming to hear him sounding so happy and we can't stand in judgement of a woman we've never met.'

'His entire world will fall apart if he ends up regretting his decision, Marci. People who listen to their heart over their head either end up ecstatically happy, or in the pits of despair. I don't want that for Richard, in the same way that I don't want that for you.' Mum can't help but vocalise her thoughts about the man she sees as a brother.

It took two goes at serious romance before I realised that I was trying to make something work that was destined to fail. They both let me down and it wasn't because either of them broke my heart, but they made me feel unworthy of love. And that's what hurts.

Richard was always there on the other end of the phone to dispense sympathy and wait patiently as I sobbed my way through handfuls of tissues. Guy would simply give me a hug and then roll his eyes as if he'd seen it coming from day one.

Maybe I should take a leaf out of Richard's play book and start living my life one day at a time. I love my job, I have a lovely house – albeit with a sizeable mortgage on it – and I'm free as a bird. A huge smile breaks out on my face.

'I'm going,' I state, adamantly.

'Where?' Mum asks, puzzled.

'To Positano. Someone has to sort out Richard's things and that someone is *me*!'

About the Author

Lucy Coleman always knew that one day she would write, but first life took her on a wonderful journey of self-discovery for which she is very grateful.

Family life and two very diverse careers later she now spends most days glued to a keyboard, which she refers to as her personal quality time.

'It's only when you know who you are that you truly understand what makes you happy! Writing about love, life, and relationships – set in wonderful locations – makes me leap out of bed every morning!'

About Embla Books

Embla Books is a digital-first publisher of standout commercial adult fiction. Passionate about storytelling, the team at Embla publish books that will make you 'laugh, love, look over your shoulder and lose sleep'. Launched by Bonnier Books UK in 2021, the imprint is named after the first woman from the creation myth in Norse mythology, who was carved by the gods from a tree trunk found on the seashore – an image of the kind of creative work and crafting that writers do, and a symbol of how stories shape our lives.

Find out about some of our other books and stay in touch:

Twitter, Facebook, Instagram: @emblabooks
Newsletter: https://bit.ly/emblanewsletter